"With *Unwound*, James once a   ic
romance. Filled with unforge   d
an all-encompassing love
craving more k
—Tara Sue Me, *New Y*
Seduced by Fire

PRAISE FOR THE NOVELS
OF LORELEI JAMES

"Once again James proves she is a superstar in the genre."
—*Romantic Times*

"Sweet, seductive, and romantic . . . an emotional ride filled with joy, angst, laughs, and a wonderful happily-ever-after."
—*New York Times* bestselling author Jaci Burton

"While James is known for erotic interludes, she never forgets to bolster the story with plenty of emotional power." —*Publishers Weekly*

"As always, Ms. James hits it off the hotness charts."
—Under the Covers

"Sexy, erotic, funny, and engaging" —Smexy Books

"This book is off-the-charts hot. . . . No one writes sexual tension, sexual chemistry, and blazing bedroom scenes like Lorelei J. mes."
—Smut Book Junkie Book Reviews

"Lorelei James knows how to write fun, sexy, and hot stories."
—Joyfully Reviewed

continued . . .

LORELEI JAMES

UNRAVELED

The Mastered Series

 New American Library

New American Library
Published by the Penguin Group
Penguin Group (USA) LLC, 375 Hudson Street,
New York, New York 10014

USA | Canada | UK | Ireland | Australia | New Zealand | India | South Africa | China
penguin.com
A Penguin Random House Company

First published by New American Library,
a division of Penguin Group (USA) LLC

First Printing, March 2015

 REGISTERED TRADEMARK—MARCA REGISTRADA

LIBRARY OF CONGRESS CATALOGING-IN-PUBLICATION DATA:
James, Lorelei.
    Unraveled / Lorelei James.
        p.   cm.—(The mastered series; [3])
    ISBN 978-0-451-47363-9 (softcover)
    1. Martial artists—Fiction.   2. Sexual dominance and submission—Fiction.
3. Man-woman relationships—Fiction.   I. Title.
    PS3610.A4475U57 2015
    813'.6—dc23   2014039721

Printed in the United States of America
10 9 8 7 6 5 4 3 2 1

Set in Bembo
Designed by Spring Hoteling

UNRAVELED

CHAPTER ONE

SHIORI Hirano wanted to beat the fuck out of someone.

And by "someone" she meant that smarmy asswipe Knox Lofgren.

Ob-Knox-ious had been in rare form today, harping on safety protocols until the newly earned black belt class looked ready to commit hara-kiri just so they wouldn't have to listen to their Shihan drone on and on.

And there was another point of contention. Everyone else in Black Arts dojo called Knox "Shihan" since he was the highest-ranking belt after Master Black.

Or he was until *she'd* arrived.

Since Shiori outranked him by one belt level, she called him Godan, one step down in the ranking system—which really got his goat. Then he retaliated by refusing to refer to her by any official title at all, calling her She-Cat or Shitake.

Yes, they were shining examples of leadership.

Her brother, Ronin Black, had left Knox in charge of his martial-arts dojo while he took a ten-week sabbatical to Japan with his wife. While Shiori agreed Ronin deserved the break, she wasn't sure she'd survive working eighty days with Knox.

"Are there any questions before you're dismissed?" Knox asked the class.

Jesus. Loaded question.

And of course the biggest pain-in-the-ass student raised her hand. "Shihan, I'm a little fuzzy on that sit-up guard and sweep. Could you demonstrate?"

The silly chit expected Shihan would beckon her up to demonstrate? And he'd press his big body to hers as he relayed directions in his deep bedroom voice? No. He'd want her to observe and that meant . . .

"Shiori, I need your assistance."

Right-o, Captain Asshat. And I need a gin and tonic. Jumbo-sized. Pronto.

Refusing wasn't an option, so she rolled to her feet and moved to the center of the mat.

"Gather 'round so you can all see this." As soon as the students had formed a circle, he sat and placed his right foot above her left knee.

She went to grab his left leg for the sweep, and he grabbed her white gi top by the lapels and shoved her to the mat, rolling her onto her shoulder and pinning her arm down with his knee on her gi sleeve.

When Knox went into side mount, it took every ounce of restraint not to immediately counter his move.

Little Miss Ten Million Questions asked to see the move one more time. And of course Shihan obliged her.

Finally he dismissed the class. She was about to bail when two hands landed on her shoulders.

So tempting to give in to her instinct and do a sweep and roll and jam her knee into his balls, but she refrained. She deserved a fucking cookie for that.

"Mandatory meeting with ABC instructors in five minutes in the second-floor training room."

"Yippee." She shook off his hands and started walking away.

"Great attitude. I saw some of that in class tonight. Curb it before next class."

"No problem. As long as you curb your tendency to overexplain a simple technique for the benefit of jiggly tits, who'd just love for you to show her every mount technique in your arsenal."

Knox stopped and latched on to her arm. "Jillian? She asked a valid question."

"No, she asked for a demonstration. And I'm pretty sure her nipples pouted when you didn't demonstrate on her. You demonstrated on me again."

"Which is your job."

"No. My job would've been to show the class how stupid that move is in the first place and the best way to counter it."

His eyes cooled. "But you didn't do that . . . in deference to me?"

"Yes, sir."

"There aren't any students around now, She-Cat. So let's take this to the mat."

"That offer is so freakin' hard to refuse, but—"

Knox crowded her against the elevator door. "That wasn't an offer."

Shit. "You're pulling rank on me?"

"Damn straight. You and me. Upstairs. Now." He lowered his head and whispered, "Put your money where your mouth is, Rokudan. Put me in my place."

Shiori balled her hands into fists against his sarcastic use of her sixth-degree black belt rank, Rokudan. What really rankled were the goose bumps flowing down the left side of her body from the rumble of his voice in her ear.

Knox walked off without looking back.

What the hell was wrong with her? She hadn't uttered a peep, hadn't tossed out an insult, hadn't even created silent cutting remarks in her head when he'd made the challenge.

Because Knox affects you in ways you're scared to admit.

When she entered the training room, Deacon looked at her, then at Knox, and said, "Jesus. This again?"

Shiori ignored him.

Knox waited for her on the mat. No hint of smile on his face; just the determined set of his jaw.

"How do you want me?"

That seemed to fluster him for a second before he barked, "Standing sweep."

Knox grabbed on to her and tried to drive her into the floor.

She turned her upper body but kept her feet planted—tricky to execute without ending up with torn ligaments in her knee—and pushed on his center of gravity.

It knocked him back a step, as she'd intended, but his balance recovery was quick. So instead of her dog piling him, he crushed her back to his chest in a bear hug and at the same time he swept her feet out from under her.

They hit the mat hard.

Shiori threw her leg on the outside of his and pushed off with her other foot, which allowed her to control the direction they rolled.

Somehow she'd telegraphed her intent, because Knox countered and shoved her face-first into the mat—after he'd clipped her in the mouth with his elbow.

So he had her pinned down in the most humiliating position—with him lying on top of her, both of her arms trapped.

Then his warm lips were against her ear. "Come on, She-Cat. Put me in my place. Show me how stupid that move was."

"Get the fuck off of me."

"I'm game anytime you wanna teach me another lesson," he murmured again, and then he was gone.

Shiori rolled onto her back. Fuck. Was she losing her touch? She pushed up into a sitting position and wrapped her arms around her calves.

That's when she noticed the blood.

And the crowd that'd gathered around them.

Sophia "Fee" Curacao snatched a towel and doused it in water before she crouched beside Shiori. "You okay?"

Shiori nodded and held the towel to her mouth, where the wound was starting to sting.

Fee stood and glared at Knox. "I cannot believe you drew blood on her the first fucking day you're running the dojo, Shihan."

"It's all right, Fee," Shiori said softly. "I should've been paying better attention."

The sight of blood had changed Knox's taunting mood. "You're damn right you should've been."

Not an apology—not that she deserved one. Annoyed by the guys staring at her and the fucked-up way Knox was studying her mouth, she pushed to her feet. "I'm fine. Let's get this meeting over with."

Knox said, "Not you. Take off. You bleed, you leave."

Shiori rolled her eyes. "That is a shitty rhyme and a shitty rule, so I'm not going anywhere."

"Suit yourself." Knox clapped his hands for attention. "Gather 'round."

Deacon, Ito, Zach, and Jon moved in on Knox's left. Blue, Fee, Terrel, and Gil moved in on his right.

Knox ran through the list of weekly events and changes twice as fast as Ronin would have done, and they were finished with the meeting in ten minutes. New record.

"Anything to add, Shiori?"

"No, sir."

"Then we're done. See you all tomorrow." Knox left immediately. Maybe he had a hot date.

She punched in the number to the car service and requested a pickup. She didn't bother going to the locker room to change since she'd have to soak her gi to get the bloodstains out.

On the way out the front door she realized she had twisted her knee in that scuffle with Knox.

But all in all, a limp and a little blood—not bad for the first day.

THE next morning Shiori was in the conference room on her laptop, answering questions from her account managers at Okada, the family business, when Knox shuffled in.

He hadn't shaved, and she hated that the dark bristle accentuating his angular jaw looked so good on him. He wore wrinkled gi pants and his gi top wasn't closed, so she had a peek at his sculpted chest and muscular abs. She glanced up and caught Deacon staring at her from behind his laptop.

She couldn't help but snap, "You're late, Godan."

"Long night. I had to drive to Golden after class—"

"Not interested in where you go for your booty calls. Deacon and I—"

"Don't you drag me into this, darlin'," Deacon drawled.

Those two stuck together on everything. These next two and a half months might be the most combative of her life—and she'd worked in her grandfather's office, where every day was a battleground.

Knox glared at her as he turned over a coffee cup. "Not a booty call—not that it's any of your damn business if it were—but I had a family thing to deal with."

Deacon said, "Everything all right?"

"Now it is. But I'm fucking tired and need a gallon of coffee to wake up."

He started to pour a cup and Shiori said, "That's not—"

"Jesus, She-Cat. Give me two goddamn minutes before you start in on me."

Fine. Don't say I didn't try to warn you.

Knox took a drink from his cup. A grimace twisted his mouth, and he turned and spewed the liquid into the sink. "What the moth-erfuck is *that* shit?"

"Tea."

"Why? That's a coffeepot, not a teapot." His eyes narrowed. "You did that on purpose."

"I was the first one here, so I made tea. When you're the first one here, you can make coffee." She smiled and sipped her tea.

Knox looked at Deacon for support.

"Don't you drag me into this either. She tried to tell you, but as usual, y'all prefer to snap and snarl at each other instead of listening."

"Are you drinking tea?" Knox demanded.

Deacon grinned at Shiori. "It ain't bad if you dump half a cup of sugar in it."

Knox snagged a Coke out of the fridge. "For the record, I'm buying one of those one-cup coffeemakers so this never happens again."

"Or you could be on time?" Shiori said sweetly.

"I didn't have to sit through this many meetings in the army," Knox complained the next afternoon when they were gathered in the conference room.

"Sorry to inconvenience you when you were so *busy* upstairs playing footsie with Katie, but I don't have the backstory on this situation," Shiori retorted.

"Jealous, She-Cat?" he purred. "'Cause I could talk Katie into letting you play footsie with us sometime."

"Stop bein' an ass, Knox, or she'll put you in charge of answer-ing Ronin's e-mail," Deacon warned.

Not so much with the "I got your back, bro" between these two today.

"This e-mail came in last night." She picked up the printout and read, "'Greetings, Sensei Black. I've recently had a philosophical difference with the leaders of the Cherry Creek Martial Arts Studio and have opted to stop training with them. This leaves me in a bind because the only other dojo I'd consider training in would be ABC, which is now part of Black Arts. I was part of the group of students who stormed into your dojo several years ago when Steve Atwood threw down the fight challenge.'" She glanced up. "What the hell is that about?"

"Steve Atwood is a cocky prick, and our students were beating his students in tournaments. So he showed up here one night with thirty of his highest-ranking students and challenged Ronin to a public fight."

"Of course Ronin accepted," Shiori said.

Knox nodded. "He might've beat him to death if I hadn't stepped in. Anyway, Atwood lost some students"—he grinned—"to us when the parents realized what a fucking tool bag Atwood had become. But as far as I know, we haven't taken on any new students from that martial-arts club since that time."

"That incident is why we have hard-core security before anyone can even enter the dojo," Deacon pointed out. "In hindsight that ended up being a good thing."

"This guy is a third-degree black belt. And he doesn't want to join our program but Blue's." Right after Shiori had come to the United States, Alvares "Blue" Curacao's Brazilian jujitsu dojo, ABC, had become part of Black Arts. "So before we bring this up with Blue and ABC, Black Arts needs to have a united decision."

"Tell him we aren't interested in further discussion," Knox stated.

"No. Set up a meeting. With me," Deacon said. "That way he'll see our updated security and that we don't fuck around. I'm a good judge of sincerity."

Knox snorted. "You? Come on, D. You hate fucking everybody. You are the only instructor who actively tries to get students to drop from your classes."

"Better he sees that than the milk and fucking cookies you've been serving the students in your classes recently."

Anger emanated from Knox, distorting the casual atmosphere like a poisonous cloud. He remained deadly still. Several long moments ticked by before he said, "Your opinion is noted, Yondan. You are excused from this discussion."

Deacon pushed to his feet. He paused at the door and seemed to struggle with whether or not to speak. But he left without saying a word.

And how fucking awesome was it that Knox had learned the "I'm your sensei; my word is law" attitude from Ronin?

When Shiori felt Knox's ire directed at her, as if she'd contradict him, it took her a breath or two to look at him.

"Is that how you'd like me to respond to the e-mail? That we're not interested in him training in our facility in any capacity?" she asked.

"Forward the e-mail to me and I'll respond, but yes, that is my intent."

"Of course."

Shiori slid her laptop closer and started opening screens. Her fingers fumbled on the keys beneath Knox's penetrating stare. "Done."

"Do you disagree with my decision?" he asked coolly.

She met his gaze. "No, Shihan, I don't."

His eyes darkened. "That's the first time you've called me Shihan."

She closed her laptop and stood. "That's the first time you've acted like you deserve the title."

THURSDAY night classes were always crazy. Still, it surprised her to hear, "Shihan needs you in practice room one."

Shiori glanced up at Deacon and moved toward him, standing in the open doorway. "What's going on?"

"I was filling in for Zach in the yellow belt class, and uh, well, now there are a couple of students who are cryin'."

"You made kids cry?"

"The fuck if I know what I did wrong. But you can hear those two girls bawlin'—"

"You made little *girls* cry?"

Deacon looked away. "Just go help Knox."

She passed through the open training areas. The wails assaulted her ears before she reached the room.

Knox had two little girls, age seven or so, up at the front of the class. With the way the building echoed, the girls' cries were actually louder outside the room. She shot a quick glance to the other students, a dozen boys and girls who were watching Shihan with wide eyes.

Shiori set her hand on Knox's shoulder. For the briefest moment she thought he might act instinctively and put her in a wrist lock.

But he cranked his head around and gave her a surprised look. "What are you doing here?"

"Deacon said you needed help. What's going on?"

"Near as I can figure, that one"—Knox pointed to the dark-haired girl sobbing with her forehead on her knees—"attempted a wheel kick and her foot caught *her*"—he gestured to another dark-haired girl sobbing with her forehead on her knees—"in the face. Then girl number two pushed her down and tried to choke her out."

"Are either one hurt?"

He shook his head. "Go back to your class. I've got this handled."

Right. "What set off the waterworks?"

"Deacon put them in time-out for the rest of class and said he'd talk to their parents about banning them from watching MMA TV shows."

Seemed reasonable. MMA was great for showcasing high ability levels for different styles of martial arts, but kids didn't grasp that they shouldn't try those moves until they'd been trained properly. "What are their names?"

"No clue."

"Mind if I try to talk to them?"

"Have at it."

Shiori tapped girl number one on the foot. "Hey. You need to stop crying and get a grip."

Knox snorted. "Great help. And believe it or not, they *are* calmer than they were a few minutes ago."

"Don't you just have the magic touch?" she said sarcastically.

"No, but I do have two little sisters."

He did? Why hadn't she known that?

Knox touched girl number two on the arm. "Can you talk to me, sweetheart?"

Girl number two raised her head. Her sobs had faded into hiccupping sniffles. "Addy is mean. She said she's gonna get her orange belt before me so she doesn't have to be in the same class as me because I suck."

Girl number one looked up. Holy shit. They were identical twins. She retorted, "Abby is just mad because I'm better at jujitsu than she is."

"Are not!" Abby yelled.

"Am too!" Addy yelled back.

"Are not!" Abby yelled louder.

"Am too, and I don't want anyone thinking that you're me, because I *am* better!" Addy shouted.

"Girls," Shiori warned.

A warning that didn't stop the escalating screaming match.

Knox rolled his eyes. Then he sat between the two warring girls. "Enough."

"She started it," Abby said sullenly.

Addy tried to kick her.

Knox put his hand on Addy's leg. "Ms. Hirano, there's another class in room two. Since Addy thinks she's ready to move belt levels, will you please escort her into that class?"

"Right now?"

"Yep. Abby, say goodbye to your sister."

"Come on, Addy," Shiori said.

Addy didn't budge. Abby gasped. "You can't do that! We have to be in the same class."

Shiori shrugged. "No, you don't. My brother and I didn't even go to the same martial-arts school. Plus, the crying and carrying on makes me wonder if you even like taking jujitsu classes."

Another gasp—from Addy this time. "But it's our favorite thing!"

"Then maybe you should act like it. Come on, Addy. Let's get you settled in the other class."

"Please don't put me in a different class," Addy pleaded with Knox.

"I didn't mean what I said," Abby added. "Addy is helping me learn better. Please let her stay."

"You're both sure this is what you want?" Knox asked.

They both nodded.

"Fine. But your actions do have consequences. You will sit out the remainder of class, and if I see any grappling, hitting, or kicking I will have words with your parents."

"We'll be good, Shihan. We promise," Addy said. She mimed zipping her lips, and Abby did the same.

Knox patted them each on the leg and stood. "Pay attention because I may test you after class."

"I'm impressed," Shiori admitted to him grudgingly.

"My sisters yelled and screamed at each other, but the second Mom tried to separate them, they were best buddies again. I thought I'd give it a shot."

"Smart."

"All right," Knox said, standing in front of the class. "Get up. Take off your belts. At the count of ten, we'll have a belt-tying contest." He inclined his head to Shiori. "Ms. Hirano? Will you lead the countdown in Japanese?"

"Ready? *Ichi, ni, san, shi, go, roku, shichi, hachi, kyu, ju!*"

A flurry of belt tying ensued.

"I've always wondered. Did you and Ronin ever take jujitsu classes together?" Knox asked.

"No. He was always way more advanced than me. Our dad didn't feel the same need to push me into it like he did Ronin. Our mother is the one who insisted I train—probably preparing me to spar with my grandfather." She paused. "But once when I was about five I asked Ronin to practice with me."

"What happened?"

"He kicked me so hard—on accident—that he broke two of my ribs. He felt horrible. So horrible that he agreed to play dolls with me every day until I was better." Shiori shot him a sideways glance. "And no, you cannot tell Sensei Black you know that story."

Knox grinned. "No worries. I played dolls with my sisters, too, and I was a helluva lot older than eight."

"Done!" a towheaded boy in the front row yelled.

"Good job, Dylan. Now you get to come up front and pick what we do next." Knox leaned down and whispered in his ear.

His ease with younger kids didn't surprise her, since the man got along with everyone.

Including you?

Yes. They'd forged an unspoken truce yesterday after Knox had knocked Deacon down a peg, proving he could lead.

Now if they could just get through the last day of the week without incident, she might believe—just might—they'd survive the next nine weeks.

IN the locker room Friday night, Fee asked Shiori, "You coming to Diesel with us?"

"Who's us?" Although she hadn't seen Knox since she'd arrived to teach that afternoon, Zach had mentioned Knox was in the Crow's Nest, getting an overview of the classes.

"Black Arts and ABC's finest. It's Friday night and I'm on the prowl."

Shiori pulled the ponytail holder out and shook her hair free. "Had any luck finding prey?"

"Last month I met a bull rider from Brazil. Sweet. Kind of shy until I bought him a few shots. We ended up going back to his hotel and *ay caramba*. He was built, hung like a bull, and knew how to use his hips." She sighed. "I loved that he talked dirty. Made me realize how much I missed hearing my language in those intimate moments." Fee gave her a curious look. "What about you?"

"Japanese men aren't exactly known for dirty talk. So I prefer American guys." Shiori smiled. "Not just the ones who can talk dirty, but the guys who know how to act down and dirty."

"Plenty of those at Diesel. So what'dya say?"

"I'm in. Is Katie coming?"

Fee's eyes narrowed. "What do you have against Katie?"

Besides the fact she's a decade younger, a foot taller, and she's a blond amazon with big tits? "I hate that she literally hangs on the Black Arts instructors when we go out."

"The guys might've invited her," Fee warned. "She's fun and generous in buying drinks. She hangs on the guys because she's a born flirt. It comes to her as naturally as breathing. Best thing to do is ignore it."

"You're jumping to her defense? Last I knew you wanted to bitch-slap her into next week—your words, Fee, not mine. So what changed?"

She smeared on frosted pink lipstick. "She's really trying to make Black and Blue Promotions into a larger entity. She's smarter than anyone gives her credit for—especially my pigheaded brother and yours. Neither Ronin nor Blue gives her ideas any consideration.

I feel for her because I suspect she's been dealing with that attitude her whole life."

"What makes you say that?" Shiori asked.

"I heard a phone call between her and her big-money big daddy. He was a total asshole to her. I saw her crying afterward. It just . . . gave me a different impression of her. She struggles like the rest of us with all the family shit."

Of course Fee played on the one thing that would earn Shiori's sympathy. "Fine. I'll give her another chance."

"That oughta keep her on the straight and narrow, because you scare the crap out of her."

Shiori flashed her teeth. "Smart girl."

Fee shouldered her purse. "Got a few bucks for bus fare?"

"I hate riding the bus. I could call Tom and he'd be here in fifteen minutes."

"No car and driver tonight, moneybags. It'll be good for you to rub elbows with the common folk."

Shiori insulted her in Japanese.

Fee shot back a Portuguese phrase.

Then they both laughed.

"Come on. Booze and boys await us."

The bus ride was tolerable. Diesel was just starting to fill up, but Gil had scored a corner table. Blue sat next to Katie.

Fee said, "What's up, guys?" Then she frowned at Gil. "I thought you were closing down the dojo?"

"Knox said he'd handle it."

"I talked to him, and he said he'd be here right afterward," Katie added.

Of course she'd know Knox's schedule.

Giving her a second chance, remember?

A pitcher of beer and one of margaritas were in the center of the table.

"Pull up a chair and have a drink," Blue urged.

Both Fee and Shiori opted for margaritas.

After the toast and the usual "Thank god it's the weekend" comments, Fee leaned over and whispered, "You've already got one admirer eyeing you."

"Where?"

"At nine o'clock. The guy in the suit at the bar?"

Shiori casually turned her head and looked at the guy. Cute. Lanky. Malleable. He smiled at her. She smiled back.

Just as she started to get up, a pair of hands landed on her shoulders.

Proprietary hands.

CHAPTER TWO

KNOX had been oddly elated to see that Shiori had shown up for a night out with the Black Arts crew. As he approached the table, her gorgeous fall of black hair had swished over her shoulder when she'd turned her head toward the bar.

He'd followed her gaze to see what'd caught her attention and some jackass in a three-piece suit was making eyes at her.

Give it up, buddy. She's not interested.

But then Shiori tilted her head and a crease appeared in her cheek, as if she was smiling at him. As if she was interested in him. Then her ass started to come out of the chair.

Not happening.

Knox pushed down on Shiori's shoulders and put his mouth against her ear. "Going someplace?"

"Yes. Why do you care?"

Her silken tresses teased the side of his face. Her spicy scent filled his nose. She always smelled so damn good. "Because I'm surprised to see you here."

She angled her head slightly to look at him. "Why?"

"You and Fee don't usually hang out with us on Friday nights."

"We work with you guys all week and we need a break from all that testosterone, which is why we go elsewhere."

"Or you don't come out with us because you're afraid we'd cock block you."

"Right." Shiori blinked at him. "You're serious."

"Yep. If we saw the loser guys you planned on hooking up with at that dive bar you two troll in, we'd . . . *encourage* those jack-offs to look elsewhere." His lips brushed her ear and he felt her shiver. "Like the fucker at the bar who was probably texting his wife while he tried to lure you in with a doofy smile. Be happy he's gone."

Shiori leaned back to look at the empty barstool. "Nice going."

"You're welcome."

Next thing he knew she had two fingers squeezing the skin on the inside of his knee. "Don't cock block me again, Knox. You're not my big brother. You don't get to decide who I do and don't fuck."

Jesus. That tiny pinch stung. "You can do better than him. You would've broken him like a twig, She-Cat."

"Maybe that's what I like."

He smiled. "What a coincidence. I like that, too." He stood but left his hands on her.

She pinched him harder.

Why the fuck that made him hard made no sense. He moved away from her and scooted into the booth next to Katie. Not because he had a thing for her, but because it put him directly across from Shiori. He poured himself a beer. "So what'd I miss?"

"Nothing." Katie sat between Knox and Blue. "I thought your MMA guys were coming tonight and cutting loose with you."

"Just Deacon. He's parking his car. Anyone in particular you were hoping to see?" Knox teased.

"Just you, Shihan," she cooed back.

A noise sounded from across the table, and he looked over to see a sneer on Shiori's lips.

Was she annoyed by his harmless flirting with Katie? That was interesting.

Deacon showed up and straddled the chair next to Fee. "S'up, buttercup?"

"Feelin' fly, wise guy."

They did some weird fist-bump handshake thing.

"Are we ordering food?" Deacon asked.

"Not at ten at night. You are a bottomless pit."

He patted his belly. "I'm in training, darlin'. So will you help me burn off calories by—"

"No! You're such a pervert." Fee shoved him.

"You're the pervert. I was asking if you'd two-step with me later."

"I don't know what that is. Like the tango?"

"Lord, I miss Texas sometimes." He filled a mug with beer. "What about you Shi-Shi? You know how to dance?"

"In a club with my friends? Yes. But the moving-around-the-floor-with-a-man kind? Uh. No."

"You don't know how to slow dance?" Knox asked.

Shiori shrugged. "Not really."

"So tell us about this two-timing thing," Fee said.

"Two-step," Deacon corrected.

Knox watched Shiori as she listened to Fee and Deacon. Normally he tried not to stare at her, but it was hard not to, with her exotic looks. Flawless ivory- and rose-colored skin tone. A heart-shaped face with a delicate jawline. Full lips. Topaz-colored eyes, slightly angled in the corners. And that hair—a black sheet that shone like onyx and fell in a straight line down her back.

Yes, Shiori turned heads. He could admit she'd turned his head the moment she'd shown up at Black Arts, sliding into the back row during one of his classes. Laughable really, that she'd believed her beauty, grace, and power would go unnoticed.

After she'd demonstrated that her martial-arts skill level exceeded his, he'd gotten pissy, hating that he'd felt threatened by the bit of a thing. Then he'd worried that he'd lose his stature as Shihan—the highest-ranking belt after Sensei—because Shiori was Ronin's sister. She hadn't pushed to take over his position, but she sure liked lording it over him that she outranked him.

So he used that antagonistic nature between them to mask his fascination with her. Ronin was his friend, his boss, and his mentor. No way could Knox admit he lusted after Ronin's little sister. Even when that sister was a thirty-five-year-old business shark who could buy and sell small countries and kick the shit out of just about anyone.

As he'd gotten to know her over the past few months, he suspected what she showed people of herself was only the surface view—just as her brother did.

"So? What do you think?"

Knox tore his gaze away from her—acting like a creeper much?—and focused on Katie and Blue's conversation.

"I said I'd consider it. *Deus*, woman," Blue complained. "You're like a dog with a bone."

"Because it's a great idea."

"What's a great idea?" Fee asked her.

"Running a pro-bono self-defense clinic on a Saturday at the North Seventh Girls Club."

"That's in a rough part of town," Knox said.

"I know. Which is all the more reason these girls need a self-defense class."

"My guys are putting in extra training hours on Saturday, Katie. I can't spare an instructor," Blue said.

"Ditto for us," Knox said. "I can't pull teachers away from the Saturday students."

Shiori touched Katie's hand when she was busy stirring her drink. "How many instructors would you need?"

"I thought I'd limit the class to fifty. That way four instructors would be enough. It'd just be basics."

"If you set it up, I'll do it," Shiori offered.

"Really? Thank you!"

Knox hid his surprise that Shiori had volunteered.

"I'm in too," Fee said. "Tasha isn't working with the MMA guys, so she could be the third instructor. I know Molly isn't a teacher, but she's passed the class and gone on to take more classes. It'd be good for the girls to hear from a woman who's survived an attack."

"Absolutely fucking not."

Everyone's gaze snapped to Deacon.

"Why not?" Katie demanded.

"Because Molly was traumatized, and she doesn't need to re-live that shit in front of a bunch of people she doesn't know. Leave her out of this."

"If Molly were here, she'd remind you that you're not the boss of her," Shiori said with a sniff.

Katie smirked. "Yeah, what she said. And it won't hurt to ask her, at any rate."

Deacon's gaze winged between Shiori and Katie. "Since when do you two trust-fund babies have Saturdays open to help the less fortunate? Ain't that primo shopping time at Saks?"

Christ, Deacon, do you have any fucking tact?

"Maybe the next time I'm there I'll take you on as a charity case and buy you some goddamn manners," Katie snapped.

Fee put her hand over Deacon's mouth when he started to re-tort. "We all wonder why you don't talk much, and when you do . . . *aye yi*, Yondan. Be nice or I won't do that quick-step thing with you."

The only person paying attention to their interaction was Gil.

Katie and Blue were back in a heated discussion. And Shiori was . . . looking straight at him.

"Still mad at me for chasing off weasel dick from the bar?"

"Maybe."

Knox grinned. "I know what'll make you feel better."

"That's not in the cards for you . . . oh, *ever*, pervert."

"You're the perverted one, since I was talking about dancing." He leaned forward. "Come on. Dance with me."

"Why are you being so insistent about this?"

Because I'd like to know what it's like holding your body against mine when we're not trying to choke each other out. "Because it's a rite of passage that you missed—at least as part of your American heritage. What kind of American would I be if I didn't fill that gap?"

She rolled her eyes—but she didn't say no.

Knox took that as a yes.

Immediately he was on his feet, moving in behind her.

Gil said, "Just a heads-up, Shiori. Dancing is nothing like grappling. But if he grabs your ass, I expect to see a wicked hip throw from you."

Everyone laughed. So Knox didn't take her hand until they were out of heckling range.

Shiori looked at him when they stopped in the middle of the dance floor.

He put her hands on his shoulders and snaked his arms around her waist, pulling their bodies close.

She tried to hold herself stiffly away from him. "I don't know what I'm doing."

"Relax. Move with me. Let your body rest against mine."

"This feels unnatural."

"You're overthinking it. Close your eyes."

She nestled her cheek against his chest and closed the distance between their lower halves.

The slow, bluesy music was the perfect tempo to sway together.

When she sighed and melted into him, he felt the insane urge to press his lips to the top of her head.

"This is nice," she said softly.

"You really haven't ever danced like this?"

"No. I went to an all-girls school. In college when I went out with my friends, we went to clubs where we all danced in a group. We did some dirty dancing as a joke."

"So no drunken groping and sloppy kisses at your friends' wedding dances?"

"Wedding dances aren't a big thing in Japan. Or at least not in my circle of friends."

"Glad I'm your first."

She laughed. "I'll bet you had girls lined up to slow dance with you."

A compliment? He waited for her to tag it with an insult, but she didn't. "Yes, I did. You're looking at the slow-dancing stud of Westwood Hills Junior High."

"And what made you such a hot commodity?"

"I was tall, for one thing. Other boys in my class hadn't hit their growth spurts yet. It was awkward for taller girls to dance with shorter boys. The other appeal of dancing with thirteen-year-old Knox was I figured out girls might *say* they didn't want a boy's hand on their butt, but if you made the move gradually, they didn't notice until you're rubbing circles on their ass and then they realize they like it. So I could cop a feel, but not in a threatening way."

Shiori tilted her head back. "You think I didn't notice your big hand is on my ass?"

He grinned. "Well, you didn't put me in a wrist lock, so I figured it was okay."

While she kept her eyes on his, her hand traveled up his neck to the back of his head. She grabbed a handful of his hair and pulled. Hard.

Sweet baby Moses, his knees nearly buckled.

What the ever-lovin' fuck? How could he like that? Why did he want her to stop and yet . . . at the same time he felt desperate for her to continue.

Knox returned his hand to her lower back.

She released him but kept the lock on his eyes.

"What?"

"Not the reaction I expected from you."

"That's not a reaction I expected to have either," he said without anger or sarcasm.

"You confuse the hell out of me, Knox Lofgren."

"The same could be said for you, Ms. Hirano."

They studied each other, almost as if it were the first time they'd met.

Shiori curled her hand around his neck and stroked the pulse point by the hollow of his throat. "How many songs have we danced to?"

Not enough. "Two. Why?"

"How long do you plan to keep me out here dancing with you?"

Knox slipped his hand up her back and beneath her hair to curl around the side of her face. "Junior-high Knox had worked out a strategy that if he could keep a girl in his arms, moving body to body, by song three she would let her kiss him." His gaze dropped to her mouth. She still had a bump on her lower lip from their angry grappling match on Monday night. He swept his thumb over the mark. "Dammit, Shiori. I'm sorry about making you bleed."

"It's rare for me to say this, but I deserved to get knocked down a peg. But if you really wanted to prove you're sorry . . ."

Their gazes met.

His cock had been behaving. But between the sexy way she'd commanded his attention by pulling his hair and the invitation that she'd welcome his mouth on hers, his cock immediately grew hard and hopeful.

"It's my lucky day, because the third song hasn't even started." Knox tried to keep his gaze secured on hers as he angled his head, debating on a sweet or a fiery kiss, when an arm hooked around his neck, pulling him away from Shiori.

"Quit hoggin' her. My turn to show Shi-Shi how real dancin' is done," Deacon drawled.

One shot to the kidney and Deacon "Con Man" McConnell wouldn't be dancing with anyone, his masculine pride demanded. Who the fuck did Deacon think he was that he could just interrupt a private moment?

Just as Knox was about to follow through with some bodily harm, Deacon wrapped his hand around Knox's neck and gave him a head butt. Under his breath Deacon said, "Sit the fuck down."

He broke Deacon's hold and walked away, trying to keep his temper in check. Instead of going back to the table, he detoured to the bar.

The bartender, a hot twentysomething with bleached hair and a fake tan, aimed a blindingly white smile at him. "What'll it be, handsome? Shot of Jack?"

"I'll take a Coke."

She filled a glass with ice and soda before he got his wallet out. "No charge for designated drivers."

He dropped three bucks on the bar top and headed back to his friends. Only Gil remained at the table. "Where'd everyone go?"

"Katie got a phone call and left. Fee decided Blue had enough to drink so she took his keys and drove home. Deacon . . . I don't know what happened to him."

"He's dancing with Shiori."

"I'm surprised he stuck around as long as he did. He's seriously on edge."

"And he'll be like that until his next fight is over."

Gil picked at the bar napkin beneath his empty beer glass. "He's gonna get his ass beat."

"What makes you say that?"

"Because Deacon doesn't care about winning. He cares about

fighting." Gil glanced up. "Sensei Black is a jujitsu master. He's been a fighter. But he's not an MMA coach. No offense, but neither are you. If Black Arts wants the fighters on their roster to win, you'll have to recruit coaching talent, not more fighters."

The rivalry between Black Arts and ABC had lessened as the two dojos were under the same Black Arts umbrella. And it pained Knox to admit it, but Gil was right. Ronin had added ten new fighters to train at Black Arts. Out of five bouts in the last fight—which was more of an amateur "smoker"—they'd had one winner. ABC had four winners out of five.

"You pissed off at me now?" Gil asked.

"No. I'm frustrated because I know you're right. And I don't know what I can do about it."

"As of this week you're in charge. If there's ever been any time that you can make a change, it'll be in the next two months when Ronin isn't here."

Knox's gaze sharpened. "You're suggesting . . . what exactly?"

"Make the Black Arts MMA program a priority by hiring a high-profile professional trainer. That way maybe Black and Blue Promotions can move out of the smoker category and get into the real fight-promotion business too."

"Did Blue tell you to talk to me? As one second-in-command to another?"

Gil shook his head. "My first loyalty is to Blue and ABC. But I also know ABC would've had to disband if it hadn't been for Ronin's assistance. A stronger Black Arts MMA program only strengthens our position. I'm not looking to sabotage either dojo; I'm only looking to bolster the entire organization."

"Let's say I agree with you. A high-profile trainer doesn't come cheap. I don't have financial discretion at Black Arts, and if I bring someone new on board without Ronin's approval, he'll just shitcan the guy the second he's back in charge."

"You don't have financial discretion, but Shiori does," Gil said slyly. "If you can convince her to back your plan, she'll free up the funds to pay a trainer's salary. And don't discount Hachidan Black's reputation as the real deal. I'll bet you'd be surprised by the number of trainer applicants you'd get just on that alone."

Knox scrubbed his hands over his face. "Fuck, Gil. Why'd you bring this up now?" Then it clicked. He lowered his hands. "You know a trainer who's looking to jump ship."

"Yes. I'm worried once word gets out he's ready to move on, people will start offering him the moon and the stars." Gil leaned forward. "This guy needs a change, and the *right* offer will hook him more than a big offer."

"Stop fucking around and tell me who we're talking about."

Gil paused. "I need your promise it doesn't leave this table. Your solemn promise."

Knox almost snapped off, "I prefer pinkie promises," but he reined it in. "Fine. You've got my word."

"Maddox Byerly."

His jaw dropped. "Are you fucking kidding me?"

"No."

"Why the fuck is he leaving TGL?" TGL—Tieg, Garvey, Linson—based in LA, culled only the best of the best for their MMA roster. They'd trained UFC champs, Bellator champs, Strikeforce champs, but their biggest claim to fame was Judson DeSilva, nine-time world champion. DeSilva had won three world championship titles in each division he fought in—an unheard-of feat. Different divisions had different training regimens because weight and size determined the level of physical activity. And who'd trained DeSilva in all three divisions? Maddox Byerly.

"He's going through a messy divorce. TGL wanted to 'brand' him and then use that as a selling point to franchise TGL." At Knox's blank look, Gil clarified. "Like the Gracie Method in Brazilian jujitsu. TGL called it the Maddox Effect."

"Jesus."

"Maddox hates that corporate mentality. He wants to train individual fighters, not be responsible for a style of fighting."

"How do you know all this?"

Gil's lips tightened. "Because he's married to—soon to be divorced from—my psycho sister, Roxanna. The split has been a long time coming."

"Holy shit, man. He's your brother-in-law?"

"I see the question in your eyes. And yes, Maddox was a long shot to bail ABC out of trouble, but it didn't come to that. He's aware of who Ronin is, even when he's not fully invested in the martial-arts world. So I think the right offer, the chance to relocate and the guarantee he'll be treated like an individual with autonomy and not a commodity would sway him."

"You got any sway with him?"

"Some. I got along better with him than with my sister. I actually told him he was fucking crazy to want to be with her. So he knows it's no bullshit with me."

Knox's eyes narrowed. "So why aren't you aligning Maddox with ABC?"

"Because Blue can't afford him. Ronin Black can. And if Maddox is under the Black Arts umbrella . . ."

"Then chances are good he'll be working with ABC fighters too."

Gil grinned.

"You're a sneaky bastard."

He laughed. "There is a devious mind behind these good looks, amazing physique, and Brazilian charm."

"Snake charmer is more like it," Deacon said, snagging the chair next to Gil. "What's going on?"

Knox had gotten so sucked into the conversation with Gil that he'd forgotten Deacon's dick move. "Where's Shiori?"

"She went home. Her car service picked her up."

"Why the fuck did you—"

Gil stood. "I've had enough drama for one night. See you guys in the morning." Gil's parting shot at Knox was, "Think about what I said."

As soon as Gil was gone, Deacon started in. "I did you a fuckin' favor cutting you off with Shiori when I did. You would've dry humped her right on the damn dance floor in front of everyone. And while that *so what* look in your eyes is charming as hell, keep in mind that other instructors from other martial-arts studios hang out here. After the bullshit Ronin went through with Amery, I can't shake the feeling someone is still gunning for Black Arts. I hope I'm wrong, but in the meantime don't bump and grind on Ronin Black's sister in public where anyone can snap a fucking picture of it, okay?"

"I get what you're saying, but it wasn't like that between us. It was a nice change that we weren't trying to knock each other out."

"Fine. Great. It's a fuckin' relief to all of us who have to work with you two that you've learned how to deal. But don't turn the fact you don't want to kill each other into something more, something it ain't, something it'll never be, dig?"

"Why? Did she say something about me?"

"Christ, Knox. Did you really just ask me that? This ain't third grade." Deacon laced his hands together and placed them on top of his head. "How long's it been since you were at Twisted?"

"Two weeks. Why?"

"Go tomorrow night. Beat the shit out of someone and get fuckin' laid. Then I'll bet Shiori won't look so damn appetizing to you."

Not a bet Knox would take. If he'd been insanely attracted to her even when he wanted to stuff her face into the mat most days, he suspected that attraction wouldn't fade now.

But in Deacon's world everything was cut-and-dried. So Knox told him what he wanted to hear. "You're probably right. Let's get out of here. We've got an early training day tomorrow."

As they walked toward Deacon's car, he said, "What were you and Gil talking about? It looked intense."

He could bounce the idea of hiring Maddox Byerly off Deacon, but he wanted to run it by Shiori first. Get her financial take on it. "His sister is going through a divorce. He just needed someone to talk to."

"Thank god it was you and not me who got roped into that conversation."

"One of these days, Deacon, the idea of talking things out with someone won't send you running toward the nearest strip club for validation that you've got balls."

"Don't bet on it."

CHAPTER THREE

SATURDAY night Shiori walked into the main lounge area of Twisted like she owned the place. The immediate buzz of interest fed her ego, which hadn't been stroked in so long she'd almost forgotten that feeling of power.

The first man to approach her was Merrick McBride, the club's owner. He clasped both of her hands in his and kissed her cheeks. "Mistress B, it's an honor that you've joined us."

"Thank you." She looked around the space—a horseshoe-shaped bar, a large meet-and-greet lounge area with couches, chairs, and floor cushions. The hallways that led to the private playrooms allowed for a separation of casual conversation from serious play.

Master Merrick gave her a slow perusal. For tonight's fun and games, Shiori had donned a platinum wig and a cream-colored lace mask. She'd gone for the traditional Domme look in clothing: a black leather vest with burgundy laces up the front, a pair of hip-hugging burgundy leather pants, and four-inch black platform booties.

She fought the urge to fiddle with the gold band adorning her wrist, which denoted her Domme status at the club. "Do I pass inspection, Master Merrick?"

His hungry gaze met hers. "You are stunning. You'll have subs falling at your feet tonight." He cocked his head. "I'm curious about the mask. When I did your background check, I was told that's always been part of your persona at the club in Tokyo."

"So why would I continue that here in the United States when there's a slim possibility someone will recognize me?" She leaned in. "Besides the fact I'm Ronin Black's sister?"

"Your brother hasn't been here in ages. Which is unfortunate for me, from a business standpoint, because we have some of our biggest crowds when he gives demos."

"I imagine the *bakushi* master is a huge draw to show off his rope skills. He's been through a lot of changes in the past several months, but I'm confident he will return to do demos at some point." Ronin's wife had put off any discussion of Ronin doing bondage demos while he was on medical restrictions due to injuries. But Shiori knew now that he'd been cleared by his doctors, his need to teach would force that issue between them—sooner rather than later. "I assume you mentioned my pending membership to my brother?"

Master Merrick shook his head. "I merely verified you're his sister. It's against the rules to divulge members' names—real or the personas they choose to use."

Shiori touched the mask. "Which is why I wore this. It's become such a part of Mistress B that I felt naked without it."

"It adds another layer of mystery to the exotically beautiful Mistress you already are." He kissed her hand again. "Anytime you decide you want to test your limits on whether you might be a switch, you let me know. I would love to tear that mask away and see the real woman beneath."

Her belly did a slow curl. She touched Master Merrick's face. He was beautiful, the epitome of an all-American guy with his classically handsome looks, athletic body, and easy charm. He definitely had that Master's way about him—where she felt the pull to do what he commanded. "You are a dangerously sexy man, Master

Merrick. You almost make me question my orientation." She smiled. "*Almost.* And I promise if I'm ever in the mood to be topped, you're the first man I'll call."

He laughed. "I'll hold you to that. Now, would you like me to introduce you around?"

"I'll take you up on that later. Right now I'd like to have a glass of wine and get the lay of the land, so to speak."

"Understood." He turned and crooked his finger at a young man poised at the end of the bar. "Tell Greg to pour Mistress B a glass of my private reserve."

"Yes, sir. Right away, sir."

"I rate the private reserve on my first night?"

"I imagine a woman of your stature doesn't drink house wine."

Her stature. There was another reminder on why she'd chosen the mask and become Mistress B. Then no one knew her as a corporate executive and an heiress to billions; they saw her as formidable for an entirely different reason. She flashed Master Merrick a frosty smile. "My stature in the club is Mistress B, and I'm perfectly content drinking house wine. But I do appreciate your gift as a one-time-only welcome gesture."

His eyebrows rose. Then he smiled. "Understood. And I see that you and I will get along very well indeed, Mistress."

After Master Merrick handed her the glass of wine, he took his leave.

Shiori sipped her wine. This definitely wasn't the house special. She looked around and realized she was still getting curious stares. It would be interesting to see who approached her first. When she turned, she realized part of the reason for the attention she'd garnered was the young submissive sitting at her feet. "You may look at me," she said softly.

He tipped his head back and gazed at her with wonder.

Oh, how she'd missed that. "What's your name?"

"Justin, Mistress."

"Well, Justin. Why are you sitting at my feet?"

"Because I want to serve you tonight, Mistress."

She took another long sip of the luscious red wine and considered him. He was young—twenty-two at the most. He had the blond hair, sharply defined cheekbones, and icy blue eyes she associated with a Nordic gene pool. He wore a tiny pair of black athletic shorts and the green bracelet that identified him as a submissive.

"I can strip so you can decide whether my body pleases you," he offered.

"Tell me, Justin. Do you have a preference on whether you submit to a Master or a Mistress?"

"No, Mistress, no preference."

Such a shame. She didn't waste time with men who went both ways. She smoothed her hand over his soft hair. "I appreciate your honesty. You're dismissed."

He lowered his head, and his shoulders slumped. "Thank you, Mistress, for the consideration."

She wandered over to the bar.

The bartender smiled at her and offered his hand. "I'm Greg."

She shook his hand, noticing he didn't wear a bracelet. "Mistress B. I'm new to this club, and I'm not exactly sure what that signifies." She gestured to the black band around his biceps.

"The black bands are worn by security, although that's a loose interpretation of what I do. I float between keeping an eye on the rooms to make sure the rules are being followed, to pouring drinks, to providing certain services to submissives as well as Masters and Mistresses."

"'Certain services' sounds ominous."

He shrugged. "It means sometimes I function as a third player in threesomes. Or mete out discipline. I intervene if a submissive uses their safe word in a scene. Pretty much jack-of-all-trades."

"So is it like an apprentice level? Before you become a Master?"

"No. Black bands are their own station here. Not everyone

aspires to be Dominant. Or submissive. We are the peacekeepers, and we keep the balance in check. We are neutral."

"It's the first I've heard of that kind of role in a club like this."

"Merrick doesn't define the club, except for the privacy policy. So the members run the gamut from hard-core pain sluts, to newly 'out' submissives who aren't sure what aspect of BDSM appeals to them— although that's usually limited to the Friday night membership—to dabblers in the lifestyle, to Dominants and subs just out for a good time, or on the flip side, Dominants and subs looking for a permanent partner. That means the membership fluctuates." He grinned. "Which makes my job interesting."

"I'll bet. So are there any special events going on tonight?"

"A violet wand demo on the main floor. Besides that, just the usual." He sipped from a bottle of water. "What specifically are you looking for tonight, Mistress B?"

"Are you asking because I sent Justin on his merry way?"

"I'm asking because maybe I can help you out."

She smiled at him. "I'm interested only in hetero male subs, if you're curious about me."

He grinned back. "Never hurts to ask."

Shiori finished her wine and slid the empty glass toward him. "Thanks for the info." She adjusted her vest and headed down the hallway to see what awaited her.

KNOX twisted the handle as he swung, sending the flogger to reconnect with the same section of skin as the last three blows. The man made a loud "uff" of pain and his Master stepped in.

"He's done."

"Sir, I can take more," the man in the chains protested.

Knox didn't get involved in the argument. While he had a break, he grabbed the towel, mopped his face, and stepped in front of the fan to cool down. He uncapped a bottle of water and drained the entire thing in four long swallows.

Master Rand motioned to him to help unhook his sub from the chains.

As soon as the guy was freed, he sank to his knees. He wrapped one hand around the back of Knox's calf. "Thank you. That was . . . what I needed."

"Happy to help." He watched as Master Rand hauled his sub to his feet and led him away.

One down; one to go.

He twisted his neck and shoulders, trying to ease the ache in the middle of his back. He'd need a massage after his last scene tonight. Master Angus expected that immediate explosion of pain from the first lash to the last lash. No buildup, just continual bombardment for fifteen minutes. Having a set time frame helped Knox keep his stamina. Wielding a whip for that long took its toll on him as well. Everyone expected a big guy like him to have superior strength and staying power, so that's the image he maintained even if he could barely move the next day. He'd gotten smart and limited himself to three sessions in a night, so his skills were in high demand for those members who craved the type of pain he provided.

Stepping out of the hot box, Knox noticed a crowd had gathered in front of one of the open-use rooms. He meandered that way, thankful his height allowed him to see over everyone's heads.

But he didn't have the greatest view of what held the crowd enthralled, so he got closer.

A platinum-blond Domme in leathers was whipping Dex, a male submissive, with a short-handled whip. The instrument of torture wasn't as interesting as where she was leaving marks. She'd reddened the area around both of his nipples and the skin below his hip bones. She'd stretched him out—a spreader bar between his ankles and his arms equal distance apart above his head. That position gave her access to the front and the back sides of his body.

Dex had been a club member for a few years and hadn't asked

Knox to deliver the pain, but most of Knox's scenes were at the be-hest of submissives' Masters and Mistresses. Since Dex was an unat-tached sub, Knox wondered who the woman was, because she clearly knew what she was doing. Dex's cock, bound with a strap, was fully erect.

Knox watched as she cracked the whip and the tip landed on the inside of Dex's thigh. His entire body jerked and he started to beg her to let him come. But she didn't respond; she just gave him a matching whip kiss on the inside of his other thigh.

Dex hissed—a sound of pain tinged with pleasure.

When the Domme walked behind Dex and delivered two strikes to the backs of his legs, Knox studied her. Her hair might be real, but he doubted it. And then there was the mask that covered her face.

She grabbed Dex by the hair and pulled his head back so she could speak directly into his ear.

He nodded and squirmed when she coiled the whip around his calf with a flick of her wrist and dragged it up. Then she did the same thing on the other side. She reached between his legs and released the cock restraint.

His relief was short-lived when she snapped two hard strikes on his inner thighs and followed through with two more hard strikes on his balls. He immediately started to come, and the Domme used the handle of the whip like a riding crop, connecting with the marks on his inner thighs as he shot his load into the air.

When he slumped against the chains, the crowd thinned.

But Knox remained in place, watching the Domme bring her sub down to earth with whispered words and gentle touches on his chest and back.

And Dex looked at her adoringly. *Dex.* The submissive the Dommes always complained about because he tried to top from below.

When the blond Domme circled Dex and came to stand in front of him, Knox had a niggling sense of familiarity. When she stood on tiptoe to release Dex's arms from the cuffs, her identity hit him with the force of a spinning back fist to the head.

He knew that biteable ass.

He knew she struggled to reach items in the storeroom because she was so short.

When she turned her head, Knox groaned.

He knew those fucking luscious lips too.

In the past eight months he'd fantasized way too many times about taking that sassy mouth in a dozen different ways. And he almost had last night.

Knox watched the rest of the scene unfold. After she freed Dex from his wrist and ankle restraints, she sat him in a chair and draped a blanket around him. She handed him a bottle of water, and when he was too shaky to drink, she helped hold it to his mouth.

This wasn't her first time dealing with a submissive's aftercare.

As if her expertise with a whip wasn't already a sign she was no amateur playing a role.

But fuck him.

Shiori Hirano was a Domme.

A fucking *Domme*.

He shook his head to clear it and watched as Dex dropped to his knees in front of her. He wrapped one arm around her shin and looked up at her beseechingly.

She petted his hair and spoke so softly Knox couldn't hear. But whatever she'd said had pleased Dex, and he stood, clutching the blanket around his naked form before he wandered off.

Leaving the two of them alone.

From the shadows he said, "I like you as a platinum blonde, She-Cat."

She turned around slowly, her gaze zeroing in on him even in the shadows. She said nothing as she sauntered forward, her carriage as purposeful as it was in the dojo, but her hips held an enticing sway he'd never seen before. She kept hold of the whip, flicking it with annoyance like a cat with a twitchy tail.

Too late he realized she'd cornered him completely.

"Well, well, Godan, if this isn't an unexpected treat, running into you at my new club."

His eyes narrowed. "Your new club? You're a member here now?"

"Full-fledged." She ran her whip up the outside of his thigh to his hip. "Identity verified and dues paid."

"How long have you been a Domme?"

"How long have you been a member?" she countered.

"As long as I've known Ronin. Your turn, She—"

She pressed the whip handle against his lips. "Ah-ah. The name is Mistress B. Understand?"

He nodded.

"I've been a Domme for three years. I tried out two other clubs in Denver before this one. Neither worked out for me."

"Does Ronin know?"

"That I'm a Domme? No. So he'd have no reason to expect he'd see me in this club. And it's not like he's been here in months anyway, right? That's information I learned from his missus, not club secrets. When he gets back, we'll sort out the details." She traced the edge of the black band around his biceps. "You're security. A neutral party, according to Greg." Those beautiful golden eyes of hers bored into him. "Why?"

"I started out as a security goon. When Merrick changed the membership rules, he needed more proactive security. We all chose something that interested us. I trained for this type of club work with a Master who specialized in punishment. I'd already been working with Ronin on kinbaku and shibari."

"Are you any good with ropes?"

When he took a breath to explain, he caught a lungful of her exotic scent. Damn her and the intimate web she was weaving around him. He wasn't some green submissive who easily fell under the spell of a Dominant. "Back up, She—Mistress B."

"Am I making you nervous?"

"No. You're making me late for my next scene. So why don't we just agree to avoid each other at the club from here on out?"

She immediately retreated. "Easy enough to find willing men to occupy my time."

Knox should've shut his mouth, but something about this woman just got under his skin. "The male subs won't play with you if all you're doing is beating them and getting them off."

"And you know that . . . how?"

He didn't. But any man worth his balls would want to get her off—why else would he subject himself to pain and humiliation if he didn't get to put his hands and mouth all over her?

"Knox?"

"Maybe if you're really nice someday I'll tell you."

Whap. The whip handle landed across his chest. "Or I could *make* you tell me."

"You think you can bring me to heel?" He laughed. "Gonna hafta grow a bit, kitty-cat." He sidestepped her and started down the hallway.

"You can't stop me from watching your scene."

He turned and grinned. "Not me, but the Master I'm beating prefers privacy."

"Maybe I'll request your services for next weekend."

His humor fled. "I don't beat women. *Ever.* Not even if they get on their knees and beg me. Not even if they piss me the fuck off by insulting me."

"Knox—"

"Drop it, Mistress. Find another toy to play with."

He walked away and didn't look back.

CHAPTER FOUR

THAT night Shiori dreamed that she had Knox strung up.

His gorgeous, big body was spread-eagled in chains, muscular arms straining above his head, his ankles shackled. She'd tortured him with touch, first a feather, then a piece of sandpaper, followed by a Wartenberg wheel, a rubber flogger, and a square of silk. She touched every inch of him, even the bottoms of his feet.

Then she touched him with her hands. Sometimes as soft as raindrops, other times using her nails.

His cock remained erect; his heavy balls were tight in the harness.

She'd had to stand on tiptoe to whisper in his ear. "You said no man would want to play with me if I was just beating him and getting him off. So I'll offer you a choice. I'll give you ten lashes with the cat and then this She-Cat will give your cock ten lashes with my tongue before I jack you off."

"What's my other choice?" he gritted out.

Shiori moved to his other ear. One hand gripped his hair while the other clamped onto his ass cheek. "The other choice is you on your knees with that pouty mouth all over my pussy."

Knox turned his head and his mouth brushed her temple. "I'd rather be on my knees before you, Mistress. Let me serve you."

She'd dropped the chains on his arms so fast he nearly fell forward from the force of it. "I don't know who's more anxious for this—me or you."

He'd raised his head then, and those blue eyes blazed pure sexual fire. "I'll prove that I am as many times as you'll let me."

Cocky. Shiori unhooked his wrist cuffs from the chains and massaged his arms for a moment before she pulled his arms behind his back. She stepped around him to admire her modern-day Viking—from his muscle-bound body, to his handsome face, to the barely leashed power vibrating from him as he fought against himself and his very nature to obey her.

Shiori let her skirt hit the floor and kicked it away as she moved in closer. Her bare pussy throbbed with her arousal—this man made her so hot that the insides of her thighs were soaked. She reached up and grabbed on to the bar holding the chains.

A low growl rumbled from his throat in response to her pussy mere inches away from his mouth. But he wouldn't touch her until she gave him the go-ahead.

"Look at me," she said softly.

His lust-clouded eyes met hers.

"Make me come so hard my knees give out. Then pick me up and do it again." She held her breath as he dipped his head and his tongue shot out, eager to connect with her hot flesh . . .

That's when she woke up. Heart pounding, body tight, thighs quivering, panties wet, mouth dry, and need driving out all rational thought.

She punched her pillow with frustration. When that didn't help, she wrapped her arms around it and screamed into it.

You should've known it was a dream. Where else but in fantasyland would he say let me serve you?

She'd never get back to sleep now.

She threw on some old sweatpants and a T-shirt and headed to the room she'd turned into an art studio. She had a table covered with different types of paint, several easels with pictures at various stages of completion, and small finished canvases lined along the walls. She'd always wanted to paint, but her life had been so hectic before she'd resigned her position at Okada that she'd lacked the time.

Now she had time, but as she studied the paint lines on the closest canvas, she realized that old adage "practice makes perfect" wasn't true for everything because she was a shitty artist. She hadn't improved at all in the last few months. While that bothered her on one level, on another level, she loved the freedom of wasting time.

She cranked up the volume on the MP3 dock and indulged in her other guilty pleasure—Japanese boy bands. So she sang along as loudly as she wanted as she painted pictures of posies and wondered what the hell a therapist would make of her.

ALTHOUGH most of the accounting for Black Arts was done off-site, Shiori still had loose ends to tie up before the week started and she got sidetracked by her own projects.

While she was no longer working full-time in the Okada corporate offices in Tokyo, she hadn't walked away completely. Several of their big food suppliers refused to deal with anyone at Okada besides her—she'd tried to transition them to another account specialist, but they'd threatened to pull their business. The amounts were significant, so she'd sucked it up and stayed on.

No one had asked her how long she planned to stay in the United States. The only reason she was allowed to remain here was because of her work visa. For the first time ever, being on Okada's payroll gave her more freedom instead of less.

After getting everything in order for the accountant, she cut to the training room for cardio. Teaching meant she had to stay in better shape than ever, so she worked out in the weight room four days a week.

She'd just finished a brutal punching combination and was

taking a moment to catch her breath when she heard, "There's a rule against training in the workout room alone."

Her stomach flipped at the sound of his voice, but she ignored Knox and hit the heavy bag three more times. Finished with that, she moved to the next station and added kicks to her strikes against the training dummy. She felt Knox's gaze studying her every move, but she knew he'd find no error in her technique. She didn't let his intense scrutiny rattle her. Now, if Ronin stood behind her, silently critiquing her, she'd make a misstep or ten. When he was in Sensei Black mode, he was intimidating as fuck.

She finished the sequence with a couple of practice sweeps and an uppercut and a jab from the ground. She stayed on the mat, her wrists resting on her knees, and tried to even out her labored breathing.

"Looks like you've been going to Deacon's Muay Thai classes."

"It's free and I'm not teaching during that time, so why not? Every discipline offers different techniques to keep opponents off guard."

Knox knelt down and handed over her water bottle. "Opponents? You plan on joining the underground fighting scene?"

"Maybe." She swigged her water. "Maybe I'll ask Blue to schedule me for the next Black and Blue promotional smoker."

"I'd advise against it."

Her eyes met his. "Why?"

Those piercing blue eyes roamed over her face with such intensity she suppressed a shiver. "Because you don't have anything to prove, Shiori."

WTF? Knox rarely called her by her name. She waited to see what he'd say next.

"You tired?"

"Winded. Why?"

"You held back in class last week with the overwrap to back move. I sensed your frustration that I'd done something wrong, and I appreciate you not calling me out on it in front of the class."

She took another swig of water and realized this was one of the few no-bullshit moments between them. What she said next would determine their future interactions. "I respect you, Knox. You are in charge of the dojo while my brother is gone. And I'm sorry about how the first meeting between us played out months ago, because it set the way we deal with each other. That's not what I wanted."

He grinned—not the arrogant twist of his lips she was used to seeing, but that heart-stopping genuine smile. "Bull. You wanted to make a point with me. You made it. And I deserved to get my face shoved into the mat when I thought I could best you and re-coup my pride."

She smiled back. "Okay. I'll admit there is something very appealing about throwing a big man like you on his ass."

"I'll bet. So can you show me what I'm doing wrong with the overwrap?"

"Sure."

He stood and held out his hand to help her up.

Knox's gigantic hand engulfed hers. For the thousandth time she cursed her small stature, which would always put her at a dis-advantage, regardless of how much martial-arts training she had. "Are you warmed up?"

"I ran four miles on the treadmill."

"Then let's go. Hands and knees."

A strange look crossed his face before he dropped to all fours on the mat.

Shiori positioned herself beside him, one arm curled under his neck, the other banded across his back. "Now, the first instinct is to put the power into your shoulders and use that force to get the body flipped around." She lifted and pushed, but his torso didn't move off the mat, just his arm. "See? I've got no leverage. If you drop your elbow, you can roll me over, flat on the mat. Try it."

Knox shifted his weight, and she had two-hundred-plus pounds of male muscle crushing her. If he'd moved sideways, he could've pressed his legs across her upper body, pinning her head and neck down with the back of his knee, yanking her arm up and locking it to his chest as he put her into an arm bar.

She tapped to get his attention, and he rolled forward. "Jesus, you're a solid man."

"And I wasn't even resting all of my weight on you." His breath fanned over her cheek. "Wouldn't take much to pin you down completely."

"I appreciate your restraint."

He muttered, "You have no idea the amount of restraint I have when it comes to you."

Holy fuckballs.

Was Knox flirting with her? Ignoring the way her pulse leaped at that thought, she resumed her earlier position—one arm curled around his back, the other stretched underneath his chest. When she paused, trying to get her bearings, she became hyperaware of the clean cotton scent of Knox's gi and the underlying salty scent of his skin. She felt the heat and hard muscles of his back against her chest.

"Shiori?"

"Sorry. Just thinking about the best way to explain this."

But you can't explain what you suspect is happening between you and the sexy Shihan.

Shaking off that thought, she said, "This time notice the movement in my hips. When I throw you over, I can lock both of my legs around you. If I keep a tight grip on your neck, I can get you into position for a rear naked choke." Throwing all her weight into her hip, she flipped him, managing to press his arm to the mat beneath her as she maintained her choke hold on his neck.

Knox tapped immediately.

She released him and lay there for a second to catch her breath. "You okay?"

"Grappling with you makes me feel like a flea taking on a dog." He laughed. "Come on, flea. It's my turn."

She rolled to her stomach and pushed up to her hands and knees.

His body caged hers so completely she had a spark of panic and fought her instinct to arch into him and buck her hips.

He murmured, "Ready?"

The Mistress in her rallied with, "It's best not to give a warning—"

And she found herself on top of Knox's body as he tried to choke the life out of her. She tapped his arm.

"That makes so much more sense." Knox patted her shoulder. "Come on. Let's go again."

"Once more. That's it." This time she wouldn't make it easy on him even when the man made it hard to concentrate. His solid body covered hers. His forearm pressed against her breasts. His thick biceps blocked her ear when he wrapped his arm around her neck. Surrounded by hot, hard man, she felt no panic this time. Instead she focused on the shift in his muscles when he telegraphed his intent to move.

Bingo.

At the first half rotation, she curled in, letting his momentum carry them into a full rotation, with her landing on his chest.

But Knox smoothly countered her move, and she ended up pinned beneath him with both of her arms trapped above her head.

He grinned at her. "Gotcha."

"How'd you know?"

"You always try to best me."

"Didn't work this time—did it?"

"No." Knox's face was inches above hers. And the way he looked at her . . . tempted her to buck him off even as she was frozen to the spot.

"Knox. Get off me. You're crushing me."

"No, I'm not. I'm bearing my weight on my arms and legs."

"What are you doing?"

"Thinking." He paused, letting his gaze roam over her face. "Looking." His focus zoomed to her mouth. "Wondering."

"What?"

"If you'll knock me on my ass when I say you're a delicate beauty, but beneath that pretty outer shell is a core of steel. It's an intriguing combination to a man like me."

Her mouth had gone bone-dry, but she managed to croak out, "A man like you?"

"A man who finds beauty in a woman secondary to her strength. You have both in equal measure. So you tempt me beyond anything I've ever experienced."

Shiori didn't—couldn't—move when he released one of her hands so he could trace the edge of her face with his fingers.

"So half of the time I want to rub this beautiful face into the mat."

"And the other half of the time?" she asked, almost breathlessly.

"I want to kiss you." His thumb outlined the shape of her mouth. "Will you let me?"

That's when she knew what he was—even if he didn't yet— and that knowledge sent a secret thrill straight down to her toes. "Yes."

Knox pressed his lip to hers in an innocent kiss before he began to explore her mouth. Licking at the soft, moist flesh on the inside of her lips, nibbling with firm-lipped bites, following the edge of her teeth. Each tease of his tongue encouraged her to open wider and give him more.

Then he kissed her in a full-out blitz of passion. Pouring hunger and heat into the kiss, using bold strokes of his tongue and soft sucks to drive her wild. Even their exchange of hot, panting breath was erotic and fed the furor of need building between them.

And Shiori would've been content to kiss him all day, but she realized Knox's arms were shaking from holding himself up and not crushing her beneath his weight.

As much as she wanted to feel him bearing down on her, she pressed her palms to his cheeks, slowing the kiss down. She whispered, "Give your arms a break," against his lips.

"One more and I promise I'll move."

This kiss was tinged with sweetness and a heady tenderness she hadn't realized he was capable of, but he'd somehow known she'd needed.

He lowered himself onto the floor next to her.

How awkward would this be when they looked at each other again instead of staring at the ceiling tiles?

Then Knox reached for her hand. Just that one simple point of contact relaxed her.

After a bit she said, "What happens now?"

Knox didn't answer right away. "No idea. All of these thoughts keep spinning in my head, reasons why we should just chalk this up to one of those 'seemed like a good idea at the time' things." After a moment he sighed. "Why don't you tell me how you see this playing out?"

"I don't know." She rolled onto her side and faced him. "This isn't a situation where we can just be fuck buddies, because we have to work together."

"And you being what you are, a fuck-buddy arrangement wouldn't work for you anyway."

She'd wondered if he'd bring up Mistress B. "No, it wouldn't. What usually works for you?"

"I'm good with one-offs, one-night stands, whatever they're called. But when sleepovers start to become regular and exclusive, it veers into relationship territory."

"Is that what you're looking for at Twisted?"

"I don't analyze the time I spend there."

"You should."

"Why?"

She took a chance and said, "Because it's not giving you what you need."

Knox propped himself up on an elbow, facing her.

Shiori locked her gaze to his.

"Don't do that, She-Cat."

He'd already put a wall back up between them. "Don't do what?"

"Play the Mistress card. One night at the club and one kiss doesn't make you an expert on me and what you think I need."

"You'd be surprised by what one can learn in a single night. Or with a single kiss." She traced the wide angle of that stubborn jaw. "I dreamed about you last night. It was disturbing in that . . . the scenario was far out of the realm of possibilities for us. Or so I thought. But everything changed with one kiss."

"You talking in riddles again?"

"Perhaps. But only because you are intent on skirting the topic at hand."

His eyebrows squished together. "The question of whether we'll be lovers?"

"No." She didn't know if she could do this, because he wouldn't believe her. She sat up and then stood to gather her things.

"Come on, She-Cat. You've got me all kinds of wound up. Are you sorry I kissed you?"

She zipped her gym bag and turned around. "I'm not sorry you kissed me, because it was as mind-boggling as I'd imagined. But the best thing to do now is to chalk it up to the 'heat of the moment' thing you mentioned earlier and go back to the way things were."

"So you alone get to decide that?"

Shiori stared at him. Posture intimidating, eyes angry, teeth gritted. She wanted to tell him to kneel and she could soothe him, because she knew her touch could do that for him. But he wouldn't see the truth of what he was. He'd argue and bluster. She hitched her strap over her shoulder. "This conversation has deteriorated, as it tends to between us. So it's best if I go. I'll see you in class tomorrow."

Knox stormed toward her, trapped her head in his hands, and kissed the breath right out of her. She didn't manage to gather her

UNRAVELED   { 51 }

wits until he ripped his mouth free from hers. He panted against her ear, "Don't tell me you don't want more of that."

"I do. But you can't give it to me on my terms, Knox." She took a breath and a really big chance. "I'm very good at that one-off, one-night stand thing too. I let men think they've taken the lead when in truth I've directed everything to my liking. I leave them with a smile on their faces, and that's all they remember. But I know differently—I know what I need."

"A lapdog. A man you can crush under your heel," he practically sneered.

Oh, he had it so wrong, and that sliced through her. Even being around the lifestyle, he didn't get it. "I'll ignore that remark because you're lashing out without thought." Shiori got right in his face. "But be assured if you were my submissive talking to me that way? I'd lash out too. With my flogger on your ass." She held her hand up when he opened his mouth. "Before you piss me off further . . . the mask I wear as part of my public persona as Mistress B isn't just a prop; I am that Mistress inside, every day. I can't ignore that part of me. It took me a long time to come to terms with who—and what—I am."

"Goddammit. There is something between us. There has been since the first day you walked into the dojo."

"I agree. I couldn't put my finger on it, chalking it up to us both being headstrong and fighting for Ronin's approval. But the missing piece started to take shape last night, and today it finally clicked into place."

"What missing piece?"

Just say it straight out. You can deal with the blowback. "That you, Knox Lofgren, are a submissive."

He laughed. "You are a riot."

"I'm not kidding." She waited. And watched for the denial.

Anger blazed in his eyes.

Ah. There it was.

"Bullshit," he spat out. "You just tossed out an allegation with nothing to back it up besides hope. And there's no way you can prove it."

"There's something between us because the Mistress in me calls to the submissive in you. You want proof of your unexplored tendency? Fine. You consider yourself a neutral party at Twisted. If you were Dominant, you'd identify yourself as such. No designation after what . . . five years in the club? That tells me you're afraid to admit what you are."

He didn't respond; he just maintained his belligerent posture.

"I have to ask why you stayed until the very end of my scene with the sub. Because you wanted to see how I acted when the crowd left? If I was a warm Domme, or an uncaring one?"

"Wrong. I was waiting to confront you."

Shiori wanted to toy with him. Scrape her fingernail down the V in his gi top to see if he shuddered in pleasure. "I asked about you after our little talk last night. Knox, the man who knows how to bring the pain. I find it interesting that you mainly participate in closed scenes."

"So?"

"So that tells me that you do what the Dominant wants. Which is a submissive trait. And lastly?" She pinned him with her gaze. "You *asked* to kiss me, Knox. You knew there was an intimate dynamic between us that had you asking for permission first."

Those sharp cheekbones bloomed with color.

She retreated. "Those are just my observations. You have every right to call bullshit on it. I imagine you'll be cursing my name the second the door hits me in the ass. I understand how hard it is when self-discovery doesn't come from yourself. But I want us to be able to work together. We'll run into each other at the club too, so it'd be easier if we kept a civil tone to our relationship. Will that be a problem for you?"

He shook his head, but she knew his thoughts were miles away.

She wanted to push, make him talk to her, but she forced herself to walk away. She made it to the door before she heard him call her name.

"Wait. I have a question for you."

Shiori turned to look at him. "All right."

"What were *you* looking for at the club last night?"

"Not a man to crush under my heel. Not a lapdog. Not a slave. Not a whipping boy. I'm looking for a man strong enough to give up control to me when it comes to sex."

"Not a twenty-four-seven Domme-sub relationship?"

She shook her head. "That doesn't appeal to me. I want a man who knows that his complete submission to me means he's under my care. His needs are more important than my own. There's a connection that ensures the highest level of trust. From both sides. And with that comes the hottest sex you can imagine."

"And you can't have that in a normal relationship?"

"I had a so-called normal relationship when I was married. I didn't deny who I was; I didn't *know* who I was. Once I figured that out, I knew why I'd always been unfulfilled."

Knox said nothing.

Shiori took that as her cue to leave. But she really wished he would've asked her to stay.

A submissive.

She thought he was a fucking submissive.

The woman had a screw loose. No doubt about it.

Because of all the ridiculous accusations . . . There wasn't a submissive thing about him.

He snorted. He wasn't a simpering girly man with mommy issues.

She was reaching. She'd seen him in the club as a familiar face, a man who'd watched her scene with a sub, so she'd come to a wrong conclusion and projected that preference—her preference for what she wanted him to be—onto him.

So what if he'd asked permission to kiss her. Wasn't the first time he'd done it in his life. Wouldn't be the last.

Him. A submissive.

Like he'd ever kneel at anyone's feet on command.

Like he'd let anyone put a collar on him and lead him around with a leash.

Like he'd give up control in the bedroom.

He was a fucking man. Men made the first move; men made sure the magic happened between the sheets and the woman was satisfied. God knew he'd never had any complaints.

No. Mistress B was dead wrong on this one.

Knox was a man's man. Period.

To prove it to himself, he beat the fuck out of the punching bag.

Then he went home and watched rugby—a real man's sport.

Then he called Deacon and talked him into hitting the strip club. He paid for two lap dances. That was him, being in control, asserting his dominance. Being a man.

When his head hit the pillow at midnight, he relived the day.

But it wasn't the lap dances and the sports machismo that stuck in his mind.

It was that damn kiss. Because for the briefest moment, he felt the pull of her. Not in his groin, but somewhere deeper inside him.

Knox had no fucking clue what it meant. And he sure as hell wasn't gonna ask her.

THE next afternoon Knox was supervising the new trainees for the MMA program. So far none of these guys impressed him. But they'd paid for the training, so he walked a fine line between false encouragement and the brutal truth. Maybe he was a softer touch than Ronin, but he could still get his point across.

A softer touch doesn't mean you're submissive.

Where the motherfuck had that thought come from?

And of course Shiori picked that moment to stroll in, looking like some fucking queen with the regal way she carried herself.

His admiration of her didn't mean he wanted to bend down and kiss her feet or anything. All the guys who worked for Ronin and Blue thought she was the shit.

She hadn't changed into her gi yet. She wore a sexy suit and heels, entirely in professional businesswoman mode. And he could tell by the way she hung back that she was waiting to talk to him.

He strolled over, keeping his face neutral. "What's up?"

"Can we talk in the office about rescheduling some of the in-structors?"

"Why?"

"I'll tell you in the office." She spun on her high heels and walked off.

Don't run after her. Let her wait. She can't expect you to drop every-thing when she beckons.

Knox stood there with his arms crossed, pretending to watch two trainees swinging and missing inside the ring.

Deacon sidled up to him. "You and Shiori are at it again?"

"Yeah, well, she can't just show up, snap her fingers, and ex-pect me to do her bidding. I got shit of my own to deal with."

"Like how long are you gonna let these wannabes pay tuition when they can't fight their way out of a paper bag?"

"They're paid through the end of the month. Since there's a 'no refunds' policy, it'd be fairest to tell them they're out of the pro-gram when it's time to re-up."

"I'd agree with that. I'd also like to hash it out on why we're wasting our time on these wannabes." He ran his hand over his bald head. "Does Black Arts need the money or something?"

"Doubtful, but I'll ask She-Cat. See if she throws a hissy fit about me questioning the financials." Knox grinned at his own joke.

"Jesus. Can you two just fuck already? That's obviously your problem."

Knox scowled. "I'm not her type."

"Whatever."

Five full minutes later he strolled to the Black Arts offices. Shiori sat at Ronin's desk, pencil and Post-its at hand. "What're you doing?"

"Checking the schedule to see where I can make changes."

Knox moved in behind her, placing one hand on the back of her chair and one on the desk as he loomed over her. "Why do we need changes?"

"Because I have to check out a factory Okada is interested in buying. Since geographically I'm the closest rep, I've been selected to make the pitch."

"Geographically the closest. What does that mean?"

"The factory is in Mexico. The United States is closer than Japan. But since Ronin took the company plane back to Japan, I have to fly commercial."

"Poor baby," he said with zero sympathy. "I thought you quit working for Okada before you came here."

Shiori tipped her head back and looked at him. "I left my position in the company, but I didn't quit entirely. What do you think I've been doing during the hours I'm not in the dojo?"

He blinked at her.

"Oh, so you assume I've been flitting around, shopping, visiting spas, and lunching with all my friends?"

"Or maybe you were practicing your whip technique?" It slipped out.

"It takes practice, as I'm sure you know. But I am required to work for Okada, according to the terms of my visa. Since I'm going out of the country, we need to shift some instructors."

"We'll turn your classes into open exercises and that'll fix it."

She shook her head. "I can see that as a solution if I'd be gone only a day or two. But I'm planning to be gone all week."

His eyes narrowed. "Will this be a regular thing? Because you promised Sensei you'd be fully invested with Black Arts. And now you're taking off the second fucking week Ronin is gone?"

"I don't have a choice."

"Fine. Put Zach in your advanced classes. Chelle can cover your early classes. Then we'll have open exercises in the others."

"That makes it easy. Thanks for your input."

"No problem."

They stared at each other.

"Is there anything else you need to fill me in on before you jet off to Me-hi-co?"

"No. Just that I . . ."

Knox leaned closer. He'd never seen her flustered. It'd be easy to fall back into his dickish behavior, but he couldn't quite do it. "Shitake, you don't have to be embarrassed to admit how much you'll miss me when you're south of the border. Word is I'm a really great guy."

She smiled as he'd hoped she would. "Only in your dreams, Ob-Knox-ious."

"You're all set to go?"

"I leave at eleven p.m. so I can make the morning meetings."

"I don't envy you the red-eye flight. I used to take that one home when I was on leave. I figured I'd rather sleep on the plane than lose time with my family."

"You never talk about your family."

He raised an eyebrow at her. "We can't act civilized to each other long enough to have a conversation about anything."

"That's a fact."

"But when you get back, we need to talk." Shit. That sounded like he wanted to revisit their discussion from yesterday. "About

Black Arts. We need to revamp the MMA program, and we've got a chance to hire the premier MMA trainer."

"Why is he available?"

"He needs a change. I have a rough idea of Black Arts financials. This guy won't be cheap, but hiring him could actually solve half a dozen of our problems with the programs. Problems that Ronin hasn't wanted to face."

"I'm in agreement that changes need to be made. After I get back, bring me the guy's name, his salary needs, his qualifications, and we'll hammer it out."

"Sounds good. Safe travels." He turned and started to leave.

She said, "Knox?" as he reached the door.

"Yeah?"

"Black Arts isn't all we need to talk about."

He couldn't look at her when he said, "I know." Before he said something stupid, he walked out.

CHAPTER FIVE

TWISTED was dead Saturday night.

Knox was in his rotation as bartender. Due to low attendance, he had plenty of time to watch the dozen members who had the lounge area to themselves. Jake and Ginny and were deep in a negotiation. Bill and Joe were facing the fireplace, and the way Joe's head kept bobbing, Bill was enjoying more than a glass of wine. Master Kirk had Patsy wrapped in a blanket after a scene. Leanne sat on the floor by Mistress Annabelle, rubbing her feet. Two new female submissives were chatting in the corner, sending pointed looks to two Doms who looked like they were discussing sports.

Master Merrick slid into a seat at the bar. "Knox."

"What can I get you tonight, sir?"

"Tanqueray and tonic."

After Knox got Merrick's approval on the drink, he rested his elbows on the bar. "Slow night."

"It happens. My bottom line doesn't change if members show up or not. It's nice to have a break once in a while. Which suits you tonight, since bartending isn't your thing."

Knox grinned. "I'm a beer guy, so I'm great at popping tops and pulling drafts."

"With mixed drinks, it's all about taking the time to get the ratios right." Merrick ran his hand through his hair. "I haven't talked to you in a while. How've you been?"

"Good. Busy at the dojo since Ronin is out of the country. I always think he walks around like lord of his domain . . . until I actually have to do his job. Then I remember how much it sucks to be the big boss. How much pressure there is."

"It's not as easy as some assume, being the lord of your own domain," he said dryly. "I swear the majority of my time is spent dealing with privacy and security issues. Doesn't leave free time to enjoy the fruits of my labors."

"I haven't seen you in here much lately."

Merrick poked the ice cubes in his drink with his straw. "The Friday night crew is in need of my presence. Not the staff, but the members who decide to test their limits or try something new. It can be entertaining. I was here last Saturday, just briefly, to meet with a new Domme to the club." He glanced up. "You were here, right?"

He nodded. "I was booked in the back."

"Did you meet Mistress B?" he asked casually.

Knox leaned in. "Yes. And because I work with that woman every goddamn day, I recognized her right away. The mask and the platinum wig didn't fool me. She was as surprised to see me as I was to see her."

"I'll bet. I found it interesting she didn't apply for membership as Ronin's sister. She used her club references in Tokyo. Only after she and I met in person did she tell me who she was." He took a drink. "Will her being here be a problem for you?"

Not in the way you might think, because the damn woman makes me think. Annoyed by that thought, he said, "She and I constantly butt heads at the dojo," a little testily.

"You worried because of her martial-arts skills and being a Domme she'll take punishments too far here at the club?"

Knox frowned at him. "That's the last worry I'd ever have with her. The only person I've ever seen with more control is her brother."

"So is it the idea of seeing her in a sexual situation that's causing your concern?"

He thought back to last week when she'd made Dex come just by commanding it. That'd been hot as hell. But she hadn't demanded reciprocation. What if she had? Could Knox have stood there watching Dex get Mistress B off with his hand or his mouth?

No. And fuck if that feeling of . . . possession didn't annoy him too. As much as he'd like to witness She-Cat losing control and see what she looked like lost in passion, he knew he couldn't stand watching it happen at the hands of another man.

I'd want it to be me *getting her off. Watching her writhe on* my *tongue, my* fingers, *my* cock *as she comes unraveled.*

"Knox?"

He met Merrick's gaze. "I don't know. I talked to her after her scene with Dex. I wasn't surprised to learn that she's a Domme. What I can't wrap my head around are male submissives."

"She tried to explain it to you?"

"Tried and failed."

Merrick studied him in depth.

"What?"

"You've been part of Twisted for five years, Knox. My trust in you is implicit. So I'm going to tell you something that very few people know about me."

When Knox grabbed himself a beer, Merrick laughed.

"You may need that when I tell you I was a submissive for seven years."

Knox choked on his beer. "No shit? But you're so . . . Jesus, Merrick. You know how goddamn formidable you are."

"And there's where your problem originates. You see male submissives as weak, probably as pansy asses with mommy-pleasing issues, the need to be coddled, but I assure you that's a dead-wrong assessment. Dead wrong," he repeated.

"So how'd you meet your . . . ?"

"I met Lizette when I was eighteen. I'd moved to Denver to attend college. She was this beautiful, dynamic woman twenty years older than me, who owned my apartment building and ran her own successful real-estate-development company. She'd come by the apartment complex to check on something and I just happened to be in the manager's office. Somehow we ended up in the courtyard talking for hours. My college education, my family life, the girls I'd dated. Then we discussed business and the difference between setting goals versus having dreams. She firmly believed strong discipline on one side of your life would automatically bolster the other. So she began to train me."

"Did you know what she was?"

Merrick shook his head. "I'd never heard of a woman calling the shots in all aspects of her life being called anything except a cold, calculating, ball-busting bitch." He smiled, but it held a hint of sadness. "Lizette was anything but cold. She was warm, giving, loving, and unashamed of her needs. I was young and so very green. She taught me everything I know about how to please a woman. Which meant I spent a lot of time learning mental and physical discipline at her feet and occasionally tied to her bed. I learned to please her not out of a sense of obligation, but because anticipating her needs gave me a sense of pride and purpose. *No one* knew her like I did. *No one* could give her what I did. When she trusted that I'd given her my all without boundaries or exceptions, she returned that adoration. I'd never felt so . . . complete. I finally felt like a man."

When he paused to take a drink, Knox asked, "So did she expect out of you what I see the Dommes here expecting out of their submissives?"

"Yes. And no. Did I wear a collar? Of sorts. She gave me a

necklace with a tiny charm that had our initials intertwined, and I wore it with the same pride submissives wear their collars. Did I spend time on my knees? Yes. During the first few months with her, she used that as a way for me to focus on her words and her voice. Other times when she demanded I drop to my knees, it was to service her." Merrick glanced up. "Bear in mind all of this happened behind closed doors. She was a damn possessive woman. She hated the idea of anyone seeing me naked but her. So she never would've taken me to a club like this. She never would've strapped on a dildo and fucked me in public for the amusement of others. She used reward with me rather than humiliation. She didn't care if others knew how well disciplined I was; she cared only that *I* showed my impeccable training to her as the ultimate respect for her. When we were together in public, it was trickier. Since she was so much older than me, she introduced me as her assistant." He scowled. "Which rankled my young man's ego big-time. I wanted everyone to know that I was solely hers, but I also understood that her business would suffer if we were out as a couple. We lived together in one of the bigger apartment buildings she owned, but I also had an apartment there—not that I think the ones closest to her were fooled."

Knox swigged his beer. A million questions raced around in his head, but he waited for Merrick to continue.

"I graduated from college and went to work for her company. That year we bought and sold a record number of properties and made huge amounts of money. I had it all. The next year I'd almost had Lizette convinced we could take our relationship public when she . . ." His voice broke, and he took a sip of his drink. "She was diagnosed with breast cancer."

"Jesus fucking Christ, man, I'm sorry."

"Yeah, it wasn't good news. She tried to cut me out of her life. She fired me. She had the locks changed on the apartment. But I refused to accept that. I wouldn't let my Mistress go through everything alone. I made her understand that she didn't need to shelter me because I always had been—and always would be—*her* shelter. Her lame-assed argument was she didn't want me to remember her only as frail and dying. And as I watched her suffer through all the medical treatments, I understood she was stronger than I'd ever fathomed. I realized that *her* being so goddamn formidable didn't make *me* a weak submissive or a weak man. It made me a stronger man than I ever would've been without her.

"Lizette fought the good fight for a year. Even on her deathbed the crazy woman provided proof to her lawyer that we'd lived together for seven years, and that invoked the common-law marriage statute. So she left me everything—her real-estate holdings, money in the bank. I was set for life, but I didn't have the only thing I'd ever wanted, the only person who'd truly ever been mine. She belonged to me as much as I belonged to her." Merrick pushed his empty drink glass toward the edge of the bar. "Can I get a bottle of water, please?"

"Sure thing." Knox walked to the far cooler, needing a second to get a handle on the emotions going haywire inside him. What he'd just heard didn't sound like servitude; it sounded like a normal, albeit tragic, love story. Maybe even better than what was considered normal. He grabbed a bottle from the far back shelf so he could feel the cooling effects of the refrigerated air on his hot face. He stood and walked back, setting the water in front of Merrick, more confused than ever.

"Thanks." Merrick uncapped the bottle and drank. Slowly twisted the top back on. Studied the label for several long moments before he looked up at Knox again. "Why do you think I told you that story, Knox?"

"Checking to see if my tear ducts are working? Or testing the theory that drinkers really do confide in their bartenders?"

"Such a smart-ass." But Merrick smiled. "You said I'm a formidable Dom. That's because I was an equally formidable submissive.

Lizette owned my balls in the bedroom. Outside of that, I could be the biggest dick-swinging macho asshole in the world. And I was."

Knox chuckled.

"After Lizette . . . I was a different man. I knew I'd never be another woman's submissive, so I took what I'd learned from Lizette and became a Dom."

"Not to be morbid, but if she were still alive . . . ?"

"I'd still be at her feet, arguing with her about some stupid shit, because she and I did not see eye to eye on some things. On most things, actually."

That sounded like him and Shiori. The woman could get his dander up with just a derisive look.

"Now I want to get to the real reason you asked me about the male submissive mind."

Knox saw that Merrick had rested his forearms on the bar. And fuck if the man didn't have that "I'm a Dom and you *will* spill your guts to me now" look in his eyes.

Fuck. Fuck, fuck, fuck.

How did he even do this? He glanced down and saw he'd twisted the bar towel into a tight knot.

"Who told you that they believed you are submissive?"

Of course Merrick would just toss that out there. And Knox fought against the need to look around to see if anyone had heard.

"It's really freaked you out that much?"

"Yeah. It's not something I ever considered. It's not like I have secret fantasies of a woman tying me up and doing whatever she wants to me."

"I never did either until Lizette." He paused and tapped his fingers on the bar. "Let me ask you this. Have you ever used a whip or a flogger on a woman?"

He shook his head. "My hard-and-fast rule. I don't beat on women. Period. Not here, not at the dojo, not in any capacity. Ever."

"You're former military."

"Let's skip the 'do I think women belong in combat situations' question because the answer is too damn complicated."

"Fair enough. And your family? Do you have brothers or sisters?"

"Two younger sisters. My mom married when I was sixteen. When I left for the army at eighteen, she'd just given birth to my little sister Vivie. So Vivie is almost eighteen and my other little sister, Zara, is sixteen. What does that have to do with anything?"

"Do they live here?"

"In Golden."

"Do you see them often?"

He smiled, thinking of the latest selfie they'd sent him. "Every couple of weeks. They need me to ride herd on them since they have Mom and their dad, Rick, snowed that they're angels."

"Who told you that they thought you were submissive?"

Knox said, "Shiori," without pause because he'd been thinking of something else. He narrowed his eyes at Merrick. "Smooth, you bastard."

"I didn't get to be a formidable Dom by whips and cuffs alone, Knox."

"Okay. So now that's out in the open, let me ask you the goddamn question that I really don't want an honest fucking answer to."

Merrick laughed. "Hit me."

"Do you think I'm submissive?"

It was excruciating to wait for Merrick's response. "Will an honest fucking answer have you leaping across the bar and kicking my ass with some nasty jujitsu moves?"

"So that's your answer."

He lowered his voice. "Yes, I think you're submissive. But I will qualify that statement. It's not something that was on your radar. It certainly wasn't on mine when I first met Lizette. And like me, I don't think just any Domme can walk up to you and elicit that 'I want to serve you' reaction. There's only one woman who can convince you that she deserves that kind of trust and loyalty from you. Is it a more disturbing thought that you may never find her? Or that maybe you already have?"

Fuck. Fuck, fuck, fuck.

"Are you man enough to overcome your fears that 'real' men aren't submissives?"

"I don't know."

Merrick cocked his head. "Someone asked me once why there weren't more hetero male submissives, not only at Twisted but at other clubs."

"What did you say?"

"That most men weren't strong enough to submit. We're inherently weak creatures; we worry about ego and machismo. I will tell you there is no greater feeling as a man than when you know in your heart that no other man in the world can ever give your woman what you do. And you'd wrap your hands around the neck of the man who even dared to try."

"Master Merrick? I hate to interrupt, but Delilah needs you in the medical room."

"Thanks, Tia, I'll be right there." Merrick gave Knox another look. "My door is open if you need to discuss this further."

"Thanks."

The bar got busy for the next hour. Then everyone cleared out and Knox was back to staring at the clock, wishing for closing time. Wishing he could just drink a couple of beers and stop all the questions pinging around in his head. His world had been turned upside down tonight by Merrick's story, confession, whatever the hell it'd been.

Wrong. His world had been turned upside down the second Shiori Hirano had walked into his life.

"Hey, bartender."

That voice. Not just in his head. He closed his eyes. How was he supposed to think rationally now? He turned around and faced her with a smile. She wore the platinum wig and a light blue mask. "Hey, Mistress B. I wasn't sure if I'd see you tonight."

"I wasn't sure if I'd make it here after being gone all week."

"Was it a successful trip?"

She smiled. "Very."

"What can I get you to drink?"

She cocked her head. "Surprise me."

Was this some sort of test? Knox looked at her and saw that smirk on her lips. "By surprise do you mean . . . ? Am I choosing what you want to drink? Or what I think you'd like?"

"Astute man. How about you make me what you think I'll like."

"One blue-balls special coming up."

She laughed, crumpled up a bar napkin, and tossed it in his face.

Knox remembered Amery had whipped up a concoction called a dirty-girl lemonade. He closed his eyes and latched on to that memory, seeing the bottles lined up on Ronin's bar. Vanilla vodka. Triple sec. Chambord. Sour mix. Lemon-lime soda. He found all the booze and mixed the drink at the end of the bar, away from her curious gaze.

He added two cherries and a slice of lemon to a cocktail sword and dropped it and the straw in the glass. After setting down a cocktail napkin, he put the drink in front of her.

"What is it?"

"Oh, no, Mistress. That's not how this works. You taste it and tell me if I passed your test."

Those golden eyes turned serious. "How'd you know it was a test?"

Knox leaned in. "Because you hope that I've been paying as much attention to you as you've been paying to me."

"You are cocky."

He smiled. "Try it."

When she pursed her lips around the straw, his cock stirred as he imagined those lips at the base of his shaft as she deep throated him. Would she make that same sexy little humming noise as she just did after tasting his drink?

"Wow. Knox. This is very tasty. You did well. What is it?"

"A dirty-girl lemonade."

"Cool name, too. I thought you'd serve me a screaming orgasm."

"Oh, I'd like to serve you that. But not in drink form." What the hell had possessed him to say that? And why was flirting with her becoming as easy as fighting with her?

She bit into a cherry. "Behave or I might have to take you into the naughty room."

"And what would you do to me in the naughty room, Mistress?"

Her gaze slowly moved from his eyes, over his lips and throat, stopping midway down his chest. "I'd take your shirt off."

"And then?"

"And then I'd put my hands all over you. Letting my fingers dig into every muscular groove in your biceps and forearms. Then I'd stand behind you and tell you to flex so I could admire all the dips and grooves in your shoulders and back as well."

His heart had accelerated and his cock was hard, even just from her phantom touching. "After that?"

"I'd want to taste what I'd just touched. So I'd start over and use my mouth."

"I don't see how that'd be punishment, Mistress."

"I planned to be naughty with you in the naughty room, not punish you."

"Uh, can I get a drink down here?" someone asked from the end of the bar.

No. Go the fuck away. I'm busy.

"Knox? You have a customer."

He forced himself to wait on the Dom and his sub. By the time he returned to Mistress B, the moment had been broken.

Or she's broken you. All she had to do to get you eager to follow her like a tail-wagging dog was give you a little dirty talk?

Knox busied himself for the next ten minutes restocking areas that didn't need to be restocked. When he noticed she'd finished her drink, he returned and picked up her empty glass. "Can I get you another?"

"No. I'm good. I'll wander and see who's here."

"You'll be disappointed there aren't any male subs here tonight." He shrugged. "It's been slow."

"You saying I should just go home?"

"I'd never presume to tell a Mistress what to do."

She laughed. "High marks for saying that with a straight face." When he still didn't crack a smile, she sobered. "You're serious."

Was he? Was he playing with this submission thing? Just seeing how far he could push her before he chickened out and backed off? *Or maybe you're not playing.*

"Knox."

Her voice held that razor-sharp edge, and goddamn if he didn't find himself responding. "I don't know what I am besides really fucking confused."

They stared at each other, the heat and unease zinging between them in equal parts.

Then she said, "Come home with me."

His cock was raring to go, but this wasn't a decision that could be made from a half hour of sexy banter. "I'm not ready for that."

She stepped back, and he noticed she wore thigh-high black leather boots and a miniskirt that played peekaboo with the tops of the boots. Fuck. Those were the kind of boots a man dropped to his knees to peel down her legs. With his teeth.

"You're right."

His gaze snapped up to hers. "About?"

"Declining my offer. When you're ready to . . . talk, we'll meet on neutral ground."

"Agreed."

"Good. So thanks for the drink." She turned and walked off toward the private rooms.

Why wasn't she leaving? Hadn't he just told her there weren't male subs hanging around tonight?

But what if that motherfucker Dex was here?

Shit. What if they'd set up a meeting last week for a repeat tonight?

Fuck that.

Knox jumped over the partition and stormed across the room.

"Knox? Where are you going?"

"I gotta check on something."

"No. You are manning the bar tonight. I don't need you in the back rooms."

Knox slowly turned around and faced Merrick.

He said, "Let it go." What he really meant was, *Let her go.*

"Fine." But it wasn't fine. And where the fuck had all this come from all of a sudden? He'd walked in here tonight ready to hook up with a woman. He'd take her to bed, show her a good time, then show her the door. Plenty of women who spent the evening alone at the club were ready for after-hours action. He suspected Chrissy—Christy?—was hanging around up front by the bar to see if he wanted a replay of their mattress mambo from a few months back.

When he calmed down and scoured the bar, she was nowhere to be found.

Probably because she'd seen him with Mistress B and assumed he'd be occupied. Add in the way he'd started to chase after the sexy Domme . . . Yeah. He was fucked for a fuck buddy tonight.

Yet it didn't bother him as much as he'd imagined.

Knox cleaned up the bar area—it closed an hour earlier than

the club—and exited out the main door. He didn't think of Shiori until he got home. Immediately his cock got hard.

He flopped on his bed naked and began to stroke. Imagining her soft little hand moving with surety. Would her tongue tease his nipples? Or would she be rubbing her mouth across his collarbone and up his neck? Blowing in his ear? Whispering dirty words? Grinding her pussy against his leg?

His hand moved faster as he envisioned her here, with him, touching him, directing him, and yes, commanding him.

"Don't come. You come on my command."

But he couldn't hold back. He was too close. He could feel that zing in his tailbone, moving through his groin and then that first tug of release.

"Fuck. Oh fuck, yeah." He kept jacking until he was spent. Breathing hard, he reached for the tissues on the nightstand and cleaned himself up.

Too keyed up to sleep, he got up and ran through a few katas. Then he performed balancing moves that had been hard as hell to perfect for a guy his size, but he'd worked on them for years until he had them down. Now running through the set was a reminder he could do anything he put his mind to.

Which made him wonder if this situation with Shiori was something he needed strength to push through.

Finally after an hour and two bottles of beer, he fell into an exhausted and dreamless sleep.

CHAPTER SIX

ALMOST a week of not working out spurred Shiori to get to the dojo and move her body. She warmed up on the treadmill for half an hour, then switched to weights. During workouts she blocked her mind to everything but maintaining proper form, breathing correctly, and counting her reps.

Except today her head kept replaying last night at Twisted.

Knox flirting with her, but respectfully within the parameters of club etiquette. Knox asking specifics of what she meant as far as the drink order. A small thing perhaps, but he grasped the difference between the options she'd given him. Knox admitting his confusion.

And then Knox leaping over the bar and chasing after her when it appeared she'd gone looking for a playmate.

Of course Knox had no idea she'd seen that.

Of course Knox had no idea how much it'd thrilled her.

She had a small sliver of hope all wasn't lost with him.

As much as she'd dreaded going to Mexico to make a buyout offer, the timing was good. She'd needed a reminder that she still could play a role in furthering the Okada Foods global brand—if she chose to.

Not that her grandfather or her mother were pressuring her.

They opted to call Shiori's time in America a *sabbatical*. Maybe that's all it was. She'd agreed to help out at the dojo while Ronin was under medical restrictions and traveling in Japan. But upon his return, she'd have to make some decisions.

Shiori was so lost in thought that she wasn't paying attention to where she was going and she tripped over the bottom support bar to the weight training machine. She went flying, sending the medicine ball in her hands airborne before she skidded across the mat like a baseball player stealing home. The momentum sent her careening into the rack that held the stretching bands, the jump ropes, and the weight belts. That rack fell over with a loud clunk. Her head smacking into the weight bench leg finally stopped her.

"Ow. Fuck." She squeezed her eyes shut against the explosion of stars behind her lids.

Running footsteps sounded down the hallway and then closer.

"Jesus, Shiori, what the hell happened?"

She pried one eyelid open. "Knox? Is that really you?"

"Who else would it be?"

"I didn't know how hard I hit my head and maybe I blacked out or something."

"And maybe you were dreaming of me again?" he said in an amused tone.

"I didn't know you were in the building."

"I've been on the elliptical for the last thirty minutes. I didn't know you were in here either, so the crash scared the crap out of me." He frowned. "Are you hurt?"

"Is the top of my skull caved in? Because that's what it feels like."

"No." Tentative fingers touched her head. "No blood either."

"That's a relief."

"Let me help you up."

"I've got it." She turned her head and smacked it into the weight bench leg again. "Ow. Fuck."

"Stay. Still."

"Knox—"

"Jesus, don't argue with me for a change. Let me help you." He slid her body down away from the weight bench base. When she reached out to grab on to him, she drew her left hand back with a hiss of pain.

"What did you do to your hand?"

"I don't know." She used his body for support as she stood. Another spike of pain in her head sent her swaying into him. "I'm a little light-headed."

"I've got you. Hang on."

Shiori kept her eyes closed when Knox lifted her into his arms. Damp, warm skin met her cheek. He wasn't wearing a shirt?

"Sorry that I'm sweaty."

"Sorry that I tripped over my own feet."

Her butt met a solid object.

"Feel like opening your eyes yet?"

She fluttered her lashes, letting in a small amount of light. When that didn't send a shard of pain to her eye sockets, she opened both eyes.

Knox was right there in her face, his blue gaze darting from her temple to her mouth. "It's starting to swell. I'll get ice for it in a minute." He picked up her left forearm and bent down to look at her hand. "These are friction burns."

"I slid across the mat." She raised her right hand. "But I don't have them here."

"You must've hit the Velcro strip along that side." He set her hand in her lap. "You twist your ankle or anything? Is that why you fell?" Strong fingers skated down her thigh, over her knee and calf to her ankle. Her skin beaded, begging for a more complete touch. "You've got a scrape here." He circled the area halfway down her shin. Then he gently maneuvered her ankle around and looked at her. "Any pain?"

"No."

"Good." His hand glided back up her leg to the edge of her

athletic shorts. "I'll grab the first aid kit. Don't move." He strolled out the door, and she stifled a groan.

A shirtless Knox was the very definition of temptation. He was so damn big and built like a warrior with those broad shoulders. She could write a dozen haikus about the beauty of how his muscled back tapered into trim hips and a firm, round ass.

Then he waltzed back into the conference room, and his front side was equal to his backside. Ripped arms—biceps, triceps, forearms—almost drew her attention away from the muscled slabs of his chest. He had a hairy chest, but the hair was pale blond and looked as soft as down. Did he showcase a six-pack? No. The man had an eight-pack. Eight little pillows of hard flesh she was dying to put her lips on. His baggy athletic shorts camouflaged his groin and his quadriceps, but she remembered from past peeks that he had those deep V cuts of chiseled muscles.

His eyes narrowed when he realized she was gawking at him. "We're out of ice, so whoever was on office-supply stocking detail dropped the ball."

"I'm fine, Knox, really."

He ripped open a disinfectant pad, clasped her wrist in his hand, and gently rubbed over the surface. It stung, but not terribly. "Did you have fun at the club last night?"

"I had a really great drink."

The corners of his mouth turned up. "Happy you liked it." After he finished with her hand, he opened another wipe and swiped it across the scrape on her shin. "Did you enjoy the back rooms and private rooms?" His voice was tight.

"Knox. Look at me."

He glanced up.

"After you told me you were confused and we needed to talk, I was done for the night. I went home. Alone."

He scooted in closer. Then he pressed a gentle kiss to the bump on her forehead. "I'm glad." And another one, followed by a soft whisper of breath. "So, so glad."

That sweetness might just be her undoing.

"I'm a thirty-six-year-old man, and I don't know what I'm doing here."

"What do you want to do?"

"Kiss you, to start."

Shiori tipped her head back. "So kiss me."

His mouth landed on hers in a hard kiss, no holding back. He unleashed his male heat and hunger, his tongue searching for hers to twine and retreat. He changed the angle of his head and the tenor of the kiss. Turning it into pure seduction.

And she felt his need, his effort to turn this into something he understood.

While he was trying to break down her resistance, she set her hands on his chest and touched him just for the pure joy of it.

Eventually the kiss waned, and he rested his forehead against hers. "So . . . we've got that going for us."

She laughed.

"I don't know what I'm doing here," he said again. "I'd ask you to tell me what I should do, but that's the whole issue—my issue—isn't it?"

"Knox."

"Please." His lips skimmed her temple and her cheek before stopping at her ear. "Tell me what to do."

She closed her eyes, wanting to believe he'd accepted what he was, but how could he when he'd never experienced submission? She brought her hands up to his neck. "Give me one night with you."

He said, "Yes," without hesitation. "As long as it's tonight."

"Why tonight?"

"Because this has been weighing on me for the past week. I've been waiting and wondering if I had the guts to follow through with it. If I don't do it now, I may never find the guts to try it again."

"What are you afraid of?"

He lifted his head, and those hooded blue eyes bored into her. "That you might be right."

Shiori kissed him then. Holding him in place with her right hand around the base of his throat. Exploring his mouth with licks and nips and bites. Absorbing his stillness as she showed him the reward—his reward—in his surrender.

Forcing herself to take a breath, she peppered kisses in a straight line from his mouth, down his chin and neck to the hollow of his throat. "And if I am right?"

"Then I'll be grateful I discovered who I am with you, Mistress."

Hearing the respect in that term, coming from Knox, pushed her to the edge of emotion she'd kept locked away. She murmured in Japanese that he'd humbled her.

"Maybe before I agreed to a night with you, I should've asked how you became a Domme."

Shiori looked up. "I'm not comfortable—"

"Me neither. Let's stretch out in the conference chairs." Without asking permission, he picked her up and carried her to the captain's chair at the head of the table. He sat, settling her on his lap with her head resting between his neck and shoulder. "See? This is much better." He paused. "Or am I supposed to be at your feet?"

"Not until you're ready to be there. So this is fine for now." She squirmed and noticed his hard cock pressing against her. No matter how she moved, she couldn't get comfy.

Knox shifted her body, finding her the perfect spot, and she relaxed into him. "Tell me when you discovered what you are. Before, during, or after your marriage?"

"Does it make sense if I say all three? I'd been unhappy in every relationship I'd ever been in. Then all my friends were getting married and I wanted what they had. I thought maybe a lifelong commitment was the key to fulfillment. So I married Shin Hirano within a month of meeting him, because I'd convinced myself it was a whirlwind love match."

"Was it?"

"No. After we'd been married six months, he told me I bored him in bed and if I didn't figure out a way to change that, he'd start fucking other women."

His body went rigid. "What a fuckhead."

"I had to save face with the marriage because my mother and grandfather were both opposed to it. Sex with Shin wasn't great—something was still missing after we'd exchanged rings—so I agreed to do 'whatever it took' to spice things up. Big surprise he had made some inquiries to swingers clubs."

"How big of him to be proactive," Knox said dryly.

"Yes, wasn't it, though?" She traced his collarbone. "The first club was basically an orgy. The second club had an initiation for new members—you were blindfolded and fucked. You weren't allowed to know who you'd had sex with. I said no way on that. The last one he suggested was a swinger's type club with exhibitionism and voyeurism. I agreed to try that one."

"What happened?"

"He got off watching others have sex. He'd fuck me as fast as possible—we rarely had an audience—so he had the night free to watch other couples. He expected me to give him a hand job when he wanted to get off. Once, he forced me to my knees to blow him. My resentment built because it was all about him, never about me."

"So he didn't drop to his knees and get you off with his mouth?"

"No. Not at the party or at home. After our third visit, another couple asked if we wanted to go to a 'real' sex club. We went, and it was my first foray into kink. Of course, the scenes that interested me didn't interest him. When I voiced my opinion, he decided being submissive would teach me my place."

"Jesus." He pressed his lips to the top of her head.

"I tried being his idea of a submissive, and I hated every second of it. There was no give-and-take. It was all take on his part. Around the same time, I got put in charge of a huge new food line at Okada—a real coup for me. More hours, which, now that I think back, I have no idea how I worked more than I'd already been. I found out that my husband had been going to the sex club without me. So he'd ended up doing what he'd threatened in the beginning—fucking different women."

Another soft kiss brushed her crown.

"I went to the club during the day to . . . I don't know what my intent was . . . but to take out my frustration on someone. Mistress Keiko, the owner, listened to me vent. When I finished, she stared at me for the longest time. She said she'd been watching me because I looked so unhappy at the club. The only time I didn't look miserable was when I watched a Domme in a scene. Then she told me I'd be unhappy as long as I denied my true nature."

Knox murmured, "Sounds familiar."

Shiori elbowed him and he grunted. "But I didn't doubt her. Mistress Keiko asked me to come to the club alone, and she started to mentor me. By then my marriage had fallen completely apart."

"Did your ex know you'd found your . . . niche?"

"No. And even when I knew he was screwing around on me, I didn't cheat on him. I focused on other aspects of being a Mistress—not just sex."

"But isn't a submissive fulfilling your need for sexual satisfaction the most important part of being a Domme?" he pressed.

She shook her head.

"Then what is it? What does your submissive get out of it since you expect full sexual control? Is it just some kind of mind fuck for you?"

Shiori slid her hand up the side of his neck, pushing on his head so she could put her mouth on his ear. "Oh, silly man. A mind fuck leads to a real fuck. I can get you so worked up that you don't need my hand on your cock to get you off." She blew a stream of air in his ear and he shuddered. "I can make you come by my voice alone. Whenever. I. Want."

When Knox tried to pull away, she squeezed his neck in warning and he stilled.

She explored his ear, little flicks of her tongue, sucking air out, sinking her teeth into his lobe. Tremors racked his body, and she could feel him gritting his teeth. "Don't test me, because I promise you I will win."

He inhaled a deep, shuddering breath. "Please finish your story."

"I finally told my mom that I wanted to end the marriage. When she had our attorney contact my husband, he demanded a huge divorce settlement."

"Since you're an heiress."

"Yes. That's when I found out he married me only for the money. And his way of forcing the divorce was to demand swingers clubs. When I didn't balk at that, he pushed me into an even kinkier direction. So he ended up being married to me longer than he'd planned."

"I'm sorry."

"I never considered myself naive, so it was a brutal blow to realize I'd been played. My grandfather agreed to pay the astronomical amount of money for the divorce under one condition. I was so desperate to move on at that point that I agreed to make sure Ronin and Naomi met. After three false starts, I finally made it happen and fucked up my brother's life too." That still ate at her, that her grandfather had manipulated her just as much as her ex-husband had.

"As much as I hated Naomi, you didn't force Ronin to ask her out."

"That's cold comfort now when we discovered what a psycho she is."

"That's on your grandfather more than you, since he's the one who chose her, out of the millions of women in Japan."

She brushed her lips across his jaw. "Quit trying to make me feel better."

"The blame has never solely been yours." He nuzzled her cheek. "Is there more to the story?"

"Not much. We divorced; he left Japan and probably bought a small island with the divorce settlement. Mistress Keiko introduced me in her club as Mistress B, and that's where the wig and mask come in."

Knox adjusted their positions and peered into her eyes. "Any long-term relationships with submissives?"

She looked away.

He touched her cheek to get her to look at him. "Please answer the question."

"You questioning my ability to satisfy submissives?"

"Not at all. Part of me wants to know if tonight I'm just another one in a long line of many."

Her eyes searched his. "Would it be a deal killer if I said yes?"

"It would make me sad that so many have failed to give you what you need, Mistress."

Too smooth an answer to be genuine. Or was it? "I ended up in a Dominant-submissive relationship for a year. It wasn't exclusive for either of us."

"How can a relationship not be exclusive?" he demanded. "Then it's not a relationship but just a regular hookup." He caught himself and backtracked. "Shit. Sorry. That's none of my business—"

Shiori placed her fingers over his lips. "I want you to trust me, Knox. So I'm going to trust you with something I've never told anyone. It's always felt like a dirty secret. The guy—my submissive— liked pain. He needed it. That's not something most people understand. He couldn't tell his wife he needed pain regularly, because she wouldn't have understood. Anyway, I gave him the pain he craved."

"What did you get in return?" he asked softly.

"I learned to use every whip, flogger, paddle, and cane he brought me." She smiled sadly. "He started my Hello Kitty whip collection."

"Did giving him pain get you off?"

She shook her head.

"Did he ever get you off afterward?"

"He had a code of honor. Plus he was married."

"Who was he to you?"

"My bodyguard." She'd had to cut all ties with Jenko after he'd returned to Japan. They'd both known the relationship wasn't healthy.

Knox tapped her ass. "I've got a cramp; I need to move."

She stood and walked toward the door, lost in thought.

He spun her around. "Sex has to be part of this, Shiori. Otherwise—"

"It is. Or it will be." *Tell him you've never been attracted to a man like you are with him. Tell him the idea of leashing him, the big alpha dog, to your will, gets you hot. Tell him you can give him what he's always been looking for.* "Come to me tonight."

"Will I get to fuck you?"

"Pushy, aren't you?"

He lifted her hand to his mouth and kissed her knuckles. "Yes. So I'm warning you I'll probably be a terrible submissive."

Shiori grinned. "I have ways of dealing with that."

"I'll bet you do."

"Show up at seven. The guy at the front desk will let you up."

CHAPTER SEVEN

KNOX entered the lobby of Shiori's apartment high-rise and headed to the security desk. "I'm Knox Lofgren to see Shiori Hirano. She's expecting me."

The armed security guard held out his hand. "Two forms of ID please."

He opened his wallet and passed over his driver's license and his military ID.

The guard scanned them both and passed them back. "Follow me." At the bank of elevators, the guard swiped a keycard to get the doors to open. He stepped inside, used his keycard again, and inserted a small key next to the highest number on the panel. "That will take you up to the penthouse level. If you hit any other floor number, the elevator will stop and bring you back down to the main level."

"Understood. Thank you."

"Have a good evening, sir." He stepped out, the doors closed, and the elevator started going up.

What was with the Black siblings and their need for such extreme measures with security? And their need to live on the top floor? Oh, right. Being Okada heirs gave them a dose of paranoia, thanks to their grandfather's billions. Access to trust funds meant they didn't have to compromise and live in a shitty fixer-upper. Ever.

But that wasn't entirely fair. Ronin had lived modestly for many years. Knox doubted Shiori had lived modestly a day in her adult life.

For the hundredth time, he asked himself what he was doing. Did he really want to become a rich woman's sexual plaything? Have her calling the shots? She said she wasn't into humiliation, but what if her idea of humiliation and his were vastly different?

A voice of reason intervened. *This is Shiori. You like her. You respect her. You promised her you'd try it one night. If it doesn't work, you can go back to the way things were.*

The elevator doors opened into an entryway. Off to the left was an elaborately carved wooden door. When he reached the door, he saw she'd taped a note:

> *Welcome, Knox—inside please strip down to your underwear. Wait for me in the living room. I've placed two candles in the large window, stand between them in military rest position, looking out at the city view.*

No signature. Had that been intentional? She wasn't Mistress B to him, and yet signing her name didn't seem formal enough.

He closed his eyes and inhaled, then let out his breath on a slow exhale before he opened the door. Once inside her lair—not cool that was the first word that'd popped into his head—he took stock of the entryway. Not the gilded crown molding and marble he'd expected, but it still screamed money.

Quit gawking; start stripping.

Knox yanked the long-sleeved Henley over his head and folded it, putting it on the bench. Next he ditched his socks and shoes. Last he removed his jeans and folded those too. The habits he'd picked up from his years in the army were hard to shake.

Speaking of shaking. Jesus. He hadn't been this nervous the first time he'd jumped out of an airplane.

The wood floors were warm beneath his bare feet as he left the foyer and entered the main living area. He allowed a quick glance at the large space with a minimal amount of furniture before his gaze zoomed in on the candles flickering in the window.

Wow. What a view. It was too dark to see the Rockies in the distance, but the lights of Denver spread out as far as the eye could see. He took another quick look off to his left. More windows. Another bunch of furniture in front of a fireplace.

Then Knox faced forward and got into position: feet apart, shoulders back, hands clasped behind him. Normally his head would be up, but he suspected she'd want him looking at the ground.

He tried to calm his mind using the Zen tactics Ronin had taught him, but the thoughts bouncing around in his brain refused to be contained.

What are you doing here, almost naked and waiting for a woman to toy with you? No wonder you call her She-Cat. She's the predator and you're the prey.

How long would she make him wait?

Focus on breathing.

That helped.

She approached him from the side, so he saw her in his peripheral vision. He didn't look at her, but the instant her hand caressed his biceps, his heart started to race.

Shiori continued to touch him. From his wrist to the ball of his shoulder; then her fingertips trailed across his back. She detoured up the back of his neck, pushing her hand through his hair to the top of his scalp and then back down to sweep along the curve of his shoulder and caressing his other arm.

Those simple, exploring touches brought his dick to full attention.

Her arms circled his waist and she pressed her face into his spine below his shoulder blades. "Quite a sight you are in my living room, Knox. All these acres of muscles to pet and squeeze and tease. I'm a lucky woman tonight."

He closed his eyes, pleased by her praise.

She scraped her fingernails down the backs of his arms and gooseflesh broke out. Then she threaded her fingers through his. "Come on." She tugged on him and led him past the second living area.

Knox couldn't keep his eyes off Shiori's ass, displayed in a tiny pair of skintight spandex shorts. Would she let him touch her tonight?

She turned the corner, leading him into a bedroom. Candles gave the room a soft glow and filled it with the aroma of flowers and herbs. The bedding had been stripped.

She flattened her palms on his chest and caught his eyes. "You all right? You haven't said anything."

"I didn't know if I was supposed to speak."

Her hands moved up to frame his face. "You can speak at will, as long as it's respectful or unless I specifically say no talking. Understand?"

"Yes, ma'am."

"Kiss me hello, Knox."

He knocked her hands free when he reached down and slipped his fingers beneath her jaw. He kissed her very, very softly at first. Letting the shape of her lips form to his as he gently glided side to side. Each pass she parted her lips a little more, so when he felt her breath, he pushed his tongue into her mouth. As he tasted her fully, he clamped his other hand on her butt and pulled her against his lower body.

Shiori's fingertips dug into his abs as she created distance between their bodies, reminding him she was in control.

Knox couldn't get enough of her mouth. He poured every ounce of passion he felt for her into the kiss; then he eased off, playfully nibbling on her upper and lower lip, sucking on her tongue. Between sweet, slow kisses, he murmured, "I could kiss you all damn night."

She laughed softly and that ended the kiss. "But I do have other plans for us." She stepped back and ran her finger along the elastic band of his boxer briefs, outlining the tip of his cock, which had escaped the confines of his underwear. When he glanced down to watch her touching him, she said, "Look at me."

His eyes met hers.

"How's your orgasm control?"

Jesus. "Meaning can I last a long time when I'm fucking? Yes."

"Good to know," she murmured. "But I'm talking about when I've got you facedown on the bed and I'm touching you all over. With my hands. With my body. With my mouth. Can you control yourself?" She swept the pad of her thumb across the ridge of his cock head. Over and over.

Everything in him tightened, and he felt like a teenager getting his first hand job. "I, ah, don't know as I've never been in that situation where I have to hold back."

"I appreciate your honesty. But I think I'd better put a cock ring on you." She kept stroking him. "Ever worn one before?"

"No."

"No, what?"

"No, ma'am."

Shiori stepped back. "Take off your underwear and return to rest position while I grab your cock ring."

He shoved his briefs down and folded them in half before draping them on the end of the bed. This time when she sauntered back, he didn't bother keeping his gaze lowered.

"This is a silicone cock ring." She held his dick with both hands and rolled the black ring down his shaft. Then she rubbed her face in the patch of chest hair between his pecs and sighed. "I love the way you smell. I love chest hair. There's just something so primal and male about it."

Knox stared down at the top of her head, completely off balance. She said nothing about his cock. And yeah, he was a guy, so he knew his dick was bigger than average and he'd never gotten a complaint on how he used it.

After another nuzzle and a kiss, Shiori retreated and looked at him.

For the first time tonight he felt the power in her. It flowed over him and blew his fucking mind. He had the overwhelming desire to do anything she asked . . . But on the heels of that came his skepticism.

"Tonight is about us getting to know each other outside of the roles we're familiar with. So when I ask you a question, I want an honest answer. Now I want you on the mattress in a spread-eagle pose, not painfully stretched out, but comfortable."

"Yes, ma'am." He eyed the bottle on the nightstand warily—lube?—before he did her bidding.

Shiori straddled his hips and sat on his butt. "I didn't literally mean facedown. Turn your head to the side so you don't suffocate or get a pain in your neck."

He turned to the left.

She placed one hand at the base of his neck and the other played with his hair. In the last few months he'd kept it longer than a military buzz cut. When she started to scratch his scalp, he couldn't help but expel a soft sigh.

"You like getting head . . . massages. So noted."

"Is that what you're doing? Giving me a massage? Shouldn't it be the other way around?"

"I'm touching you, Knox. Learning what you like. What drives you wild."

"I could just tell you."

"And deny myself the pleasure of touching every inch of this hot, hard body of yours? This is about my pleasure, and it pleases me very much to pet, stroke, and taste"—she dragged her hot little tongue across the nape of his neck—"whatever part of you I please."

"You're gonna torture me, aren't you?"

"Mmm-hmm. I bet I'll find spots on your skin that even you didn't know would make you buck and moan."

He doubted that.

And in the next two minutes she totally proved him wrong.

Shiori began kissing the back of his neck and along his shoulders. His skin tingled and tightened, and he couldn't deny it felt great. He expected she'd move her mouth down his spine and kiss other sections of his back. But no. She kept kissing and sucking and biting on the same area without pause. Oh, she'd let the ends of her hair tease his skin, but then she'd be back at it until he started to rock his pelvis into the mattress. Goddamn, he was gonna come just from her kissing his back.

She leaned back and latched on to both butt cheeks, digging her fingers in deep so it surpassed pleasure straight into pain. "Stop dry humping the mattress."

"Fuck. Ow."

More pressure on his ass. "What did you say?"

Knox went still and said, "Yes, ma'am."

She released the death claws and resumed the erotic torture. Licking down his sides. Then she tucked her knees by his ribs and gyrated her hips, rubbing her pussy against his back while that wicked mouth started in on his arms.

Jesus. Who knew the muscles in his biceps and triceps could quiver more from the teasing touch of her wet mouth than when he bench-pressed two hundred pounds?

By the time she'd exhausted every inch of the rear side of his body, including using her teeth and tongue on the bottom curve of his butt cheeks—how the fuck hadn't he known *that* was one of his hot spots?—his heart rate was in overdrive and his mouth was dry as dust. A sheen of sweat coated his body, and his cock was so hard it fucking ached.

She murmured, "Roll over."

Knox wouldn't survive her full exploration of the front side of his body. Good thing he wore the damn cock ring. Especially when she put her ass in line with his dick and bumped the tip every time she rolled back.

"Uh. I thought you were asking me questions."

"I changed my mind. I don't give a damn about your sexual past when you're responding to my touch so beautifully." She blew in his ear. "A cliché for sure, but your body is my wonderland."

He groaned when she started in again. His pleasure receptors were on overload. A haze of bliss flowed through him, and he didn't bother to hold back anything.

"There's what I wanted from you," she whispered as she stroked the tops of his quads. Then her mouth was on his, feeding him dizzying kisses.

Shiori tucked herself into his side and touched his cock for the first time since she'd put the ring on it. She petted his balls and removed the cock ring. "You come when I say, Knox. Not before."

He nodded and fought the urge to buck his hips into her hand.

She teased his nipple with the tip of her tongue before she nursed on it.

Motherfucker. That nearly sent him into orbit.

Suckling strongly, she scraped her fingernail up the length of his shaft.

"You're killing me."

"You can take a little more." Shiori blew on his damp nipple and then bent down and blew a stream of air over the wet tip of his cock.

His legs twitched, and he clenched his ass cheeks together.

"Look at me."

He lifted his head and met her gaze.

She said, "Come now," and dragged her finger up his shaft. When she started to suck his nipple, he had a vague sense that she was sucking on the head of his cock—two hot mouths sucking on him at once.

That's when he started to come. Hot, intense spurts of pure sensation. His cock rested against his belly as he shot his load, each pull of her mouth on his nipple sending another tug to his balls.

When the last shot released, he flopped back to the mattress and squeezed his eyes shut.

Holy fuck.

She'd made him come on command.

That'd never happened to him before.

When Shiori touched his face, he jumped.

He peeled his eyes open and looked at her. "Sorry."

"It's okay." She caressed his cheek. "You did very well."

He didn't know what to say. *Thanks for the erotic torture?*

"Your eyes got a little dreamy. What were you thinking?"

That I could get used to feeling like this. But that seemed too . . . honest, so he backtracked. "Are you giving me equal time to touch you?"

"If I say no, what will you do?"

Knox pushed a chunk of her hair over her shoulder. "Yell. Curse. Throw shit." He smiled. "Kidding. I'd be disappointed because I've been dying to get my hands all over your beautiful body."

She kissed his abused nipple. "I want your hands on me. But there are parameters. No touching my pussy unless I specifically tell you to. And that means with your hands, your mouth, or your cock."

He grinned. "Good thing you clarified that."

She pushed into a sitting position. "Clean yourself up. There's a bathroom in the hallway."

As he washed himself off, he had time to think. Tonight hadn't gone at all like he'd expected. He hadn't equated Dommes with a loving touch—except for after they beat the shit out of their subs.

They hadn't talked about pain play; hell, they hadn't really talked about anything besides trying this out once and seeing where it went.

"Knox? Did you fall in?" Shiori yelled from the bedroom.

He dried his hands and returned to her. "Sorry. Got a little lost in thought."

"What were you thinking about?"

"You." He wrapped his hand around her ankle and playfully tugged. "Are you still wearing clothes because you want me to take them off you?"

"What if I asked you to work around them?"

"I'd ask if that was an order or a suggestion. Because I really want to see you in nothing but skin, ma'am."

Shiori grabbed the bottom band of her sports bra and pulled it over her head.

Knox was so focused on those fucking perfect tits that he almost missed her hiking up her hips and ditching her spandex shorts. He groaned when she rolled over and he got his first glimpse of her bare ass.

She sent him a saucy look over her shoulder. "Now, why don't you show me what those big hands can do."

Oh, he planned to use more than his hands. And just because she hadn't talked while she drove him wild didn't mean he'd do the same.

He rested on his haunches over her thighs. She hadn't spread out yet; he'd move her as he wanted. He brushed the hair from her cheek and spread that black silk out across the mattress. "Why'd you cut your hair?" When she'd arrived in Denver, the ends of her hair had reached the curve of her ass.

"I wanted a change."

He kept stroking the black tresses, starting at the top of her scalp. "When you first came to class and you had that deadly double braid, I fantasized about wrapping my hands around it and holding you in place while I tasted your sassy mouth."

"I would've thrown you on your ass if you'd tried it, even when I secretly might've liked it."

"We've been circling each other for a while." Knox traced the outside of her ear with his lips. Then he placed a soft, lingering kiss in the hollow below her lobe. He nuzzled the nape of her neck, and she couldn't hide the shiver. Her reactions gave him a road map of how she liked to be touched.

He used his teeth.

He used his tongue.

He used the long, sensual scrape of his callused fingers.

By the time he reached that bitable ass, he worshipped those taut round globes, all the while basking in the sweet scent of her wet pussy drifting from between her legs. "Goddamn, I love your ass."

"I can tell."

He massaged her thighs and her calves. Before he turned her over, he layered his naked, aroused body to hers, pressing his groin into the bottom curve of her ass. "I want to take you like this sometime. Me moving on you, in you, as hard and fast or as long and sweet as you want. Using my mouth on your shoulders and the back of your neck, seeing if I could make you come just from that."

Shiori wiggled her butt and canted her hips. "Off."

"Why? Am I tempting you?"

"No. You're squishing me."

Such a little liar. But he said, "Yes, ma'am." Before he asked her to turn over, he ran his hands over every delicious inch of her one more time. Then he patted her hip. "Other side, please."

Before she could spout off a reminder of her rules, he fastened his mouth to hers and kissed her. And kept on kissing her until some of the tension left her body.

He should've gradually moved from her mouth down her neck, but he made a beeline straight for her tits. He straddled her body so he could get both hands on that firm, soft flesh. "Look at you. These are perfect. Absolutely fucking perfect." Dipping his head, he tickled the tip with a small flick of his tongue. As soon as the skin puckered, he latched on and drew strongly.

Her back arched and her hands fisted in his hair.

Yeah. That's what he wanted. An unpracticed reaction out of her.

He kneaded her other breast and switched sides, licking and sucking. Pushing her breasts together put her nipples so close that he could almost get them both in his mouth at the same time.

Once she'd quit writhing, he slid his hands down the sides of her body, palming her rib cage and letting his thumbs drag down the indent in her torso. Her core muscles were tight, even in rest. He paused when the base of his hands rested on her hips. Shiori was compact here too, but as he'd been on the receiving end of her hip throws, he knew size was deceiving.

His thumbs stroked the section below her belly button, and her skin rippled. He focused his attention on that area, teasing with his lips and breath. Letting his chin slide over the rise of her mound. Hoping she'd give him the signal to bury his mouth between her thighs.

She tugged on his hair.

"Mmm?"

"You seemed to've gotten stuck in one spot."

"I like this spot." He looked up at her, across the plane of her body. "But do I have permission to move down to what'll likely be my favorite spot?"

"No. But I would like you to massage my feet."

Knox banked his disappointment. He pushed back and sat on his heels. When he circled his fingers around her ankle, she flinched. Interesting reaction. He set her heel on his thigh and pressed his thumb into the middle of her foot, pushing in circles from the ball, down her arch, to the start of her heel and back up.

She sighed. "You've done this before."

"No, ma'am."

"So you're just a natural, hitting all the good spots?"

He worked his thumb between her toes. "No. But I've seen guys with a foot fetish working it, and I took notes."

"Very good notes."

She'd left her legs parted, allowing him an unimpeded view of the pink tissues that glistened with her arousal.

"Stop that," she warned.

Knox forced his gaze away from that tempting slice of heaven. "What?"

"You keep looking at my pussy and licking your lips."

"You'd rather I was licking your pussy?"

She pointed. "Back to the foot massage."

Before he switched feet, he angled his head and started kissing her ankle. The divot beside her ankle bone, then the ankle bone itself and the curve above it.

Shiori's leg twitched so violently that she almost kicked him in the face.

He kept worshipping her delicate ankle, damn pleased with himself that he'd found one of *her* hidden hot spots.

"Knox. Stop."

After placing several soft kisses on the top of her foot, he switched feet. And began again. Like before, she damn near levitated off the bed when he focused on her ankle.

This time she didn't stop him. Instead, while he nuzzled and teased, her hand crept between her thighs. She ran her middle finger up and down her slit, getting it wet before she started rubbing on her clit. Slowly at first and then faster.

Her other arm was thrown above her head; her body was a graceful arch as she pleasured herself. She moved her finger side to side and then tapped the nub several times in rapid succession before she returned to rubbing.

It was one of the sexiest things he'd seen. Watching her get herself off was almost as good as getting her off himself.

Almost.

Shiori's legs went rigid. Her finger moved faster, and she let out a soft gasp as she started to come.

Knox watched her greedily, this beautiful woman giving him

a secret peek of her self-pleasure. When her hand fell away, he lowered her foot to the bed, awaiting further instructions.

"Come here."

He levered himself over her and nuzzled her neck, breathing in the scent of her damp skin, feeling her heartbeat beneath his lips. "Thank you for that, Mistress."

She made a hum of acknowledgment. Then she gently pushed on his shoulders. "Get dressed and I'll meet you in the living room."

Her dismissal stung, but it wasn't unexpected.

Knox slipped on his boxer briefs and returned to where he'd left his clothes. After getting dressed, he prowled around the gigantic space, which felt more like a mausoleum than a home.

Maybe she preferred austere surroundings, but from what he could tell, there wasn't a personal item anywhere. Nothing revealed insight into the person who lived in this glass-walled penthouse besides wealth.

There was so much more to Shiori than that.

She appeared in her robe, her hair in a messy knot on top of her head. She held out her hand and led him to the lounging area. She sat in the high-backed leather chair and indicated he should sit at her feet.

He had a momentary flash of resentment that they couldn't just sit together on the damn couch, so he kept his gaze aimed at the carpet.

"We should've talked more about each of our expectations and limits before we became intimate. As the Domme, that's on me."

Knox raised his head. "Please don't say you have regrets."

She touched his face and let her hand drift to his neck. "No regrets."

"Then what?"

"I asked you to give me one night. You have. I'm grateful for your trust, Knox. I know it's not easy for you. I don't know if this night convinced you of anything."

Was she cutting him loose? "It convinced me that I need more than one damn night to figure this out."

Those golden eyes seemed to measure every inch of him. "You're sure?"

He turned his head and kissed the inside of her wrist. "Yes, ma'am."

"I'm happy to hear that. Still, I think it'd be best if we waited a couple of days to try this again. I need to allow you enough time to think everything through."

While he understood she was doing this to protect him, it annoyed him. She didn't know what was best for him.

Isn't that what a Domme does? Arguing will just prove that you aren't ready for her to make decisions for you.

So he swallowed his protest and said, "That makes sense."

Shiori bent forward and kissed him. "I'll walk you out."

At the elevator, Knox gathered her into his arms. "See you tomorrow."

SHIORI didn't show up at Black Arts until around ten the next morning. She didn't really need to be there. It was a holiday, and banks, schools, and most businesses were closed. She'd convinced herself she needed to check Ronin's penthouse, just to make sure everything was okay. But the truth was she wanted to see Knox.

The office and the conference room were empty. As she headed down the hallway, she heard the familiar sounds of body parts striking plastic practice gear. She paused just inside the door to the training room. Deacon and Ito were grappling. Knox served as Ivan's punching bag in the ring while Fisher supervised, yelling out instructions.

She hated to admit it, but their MMA program shouldn't even be listed in the same brochure as the Black Arts jujitsu program. Yes, it was still in the early building stage, but Deacon and Ivan were the only decent fighters. The rest of the guys who paid to train here were wasting their time and money, as well as tying up the instructors so they didn't have enough time to work with Deacon and Ivan.

Knox took a blow to the chin and she winced. Sometimes she felt bad he was the only guy Ivan's size and had no choice but to partner up with him. Knox moved very, very well for such a big guy. He wasn't clumsy or lumbering—either on or off the mat. And it seemed like Ivan had become lighter on his feet after watching Knox move.

She'd tried not to obsess on Knox's visit to her apartment last night and what it meant. She'd sensed his resentment a few times, and she hadn't been sure if she should be impressed by him masking it, or upset that he hadn't been honest with her about how he felt. Since it'd been their first time together and it was new territory for both of them, she'd cut them some slack.

And there was her problem. Should she tell Knox that she'd never been in a long-term relationship with a submissive? That being a one-man Domme would be as new to her as being submissive was to him? Or would that admission foster a lack of confidence and trust?

In her club in Tokyo she had three different men she played with, mostly because she hadn't found one man who gave her everything she needed. Out of those three subs, she'd had sex with only one. Oh, she'd let the other three pleasure her, but sometimes all she wanted was a man to pet her. If she needed to get off, she owned a collection of vibrators. But that body-to-body, skin-to-skin contact couldn't be duplicated. Hard touches, tender caresses, a lazy sweep of a rough-skinned hand, a warm mouth sliding across every inch of her flesh . . . That's what she craved, because that's what she'd always been denied.

Now, after being naked with Knox and having his hands and mouth all over her, she knew sex with him would be explosive. His natural, submissive instincts with her would push her to the pinnacle of pleasure, so she had to make sure she retained control at all times.

The sound of footsteps reached her, and she turned to see who else had shown up today.

Fee.

"I knew you'd be here," Fee said.

"Why?"

"Because this place feels like home." She seemed surprised by her own admission. "Anyway, if you're not busy, can you come upstairs and we'll go over what we're teaching at the self-defense class on Saturday?"

"Sure. Do I need to change?"

Fee's gaze flicked over Shiori's bronze blouse tucked into widelegged brown and cream plaid trousers and her nude heels. "No. You look fantastic, as usual. Too bad it's wasted on these guys." She jerked her head toward the training room. "Katie just wants to double-check to make sure we don't go over the allotted time."

"All right. Let's go."

An hour later, they'd fine-tuned every detail. Katie had planned everything almost down to the minute, which was over-kill, but better to be fully prepared.

They rode the elevator down to the second floor and had stopped beside the exit to the front door to discuss lunch plans for after the self-defense class when Knox stuck his head out the door.

"Shiori, I need to talk to you . . . if you're done discussing Denver's best tequila bars."

Fee muttered, "Jerkoff."

Katie smiled brightly at Knox. "She's all yours, Shihan. We're outta here. Everything on the third floor is shut down."

Shiori waited until they'd left before she faced Knox. "You bellowed?"

"Get in here."

She wondered what his problem was and hated that his cranky attitude would likely rub off on her.

Inside the office she saw Knox standing by the window with his back to her. "Shut the door."

"If this is about us doing the self-defense class, I'll remind you that both you and Blue passed on it." She walked to her desk and set the printout from Katie next to the report on recent equipment breakage.

"That's not why I called you in here."

"Then why?"

Hands landed on her shoulders and she jumped. God. He was as stealthy as Ronin.

"Why? Because I can't get you—or what happened last night—out of my damn mind."

She smiled, although he couldn't see it.

"Then, just when I'd blocked thoughts of your naked body and what I'd really love to do to you the next time you ordered me to my knees, I saw you standing in the doorway to the training room."

"Oh?"

"And Ivan took advantage of my distraction and punched me in the face."

She snickered. "Poor baby. Need me to get some ice for that?"

"No. I need you to kiss it and make it better." Knox turned her around and loomed over her.

"If someone walks in, Knox, they'll think—"

"No one else is here."

She set her hands on his pecs. "Isn't that fortunate."

"You tell me. Can I kiss you or not?"

It made her almost giddy that he'd asked. "Yes, you may kiss me."

He clutched her hips and said, "Jump up." As soon as she was sitting on her desk, he lowered his mouth to hers. The kiss started out sweet and slow, but it quickly built up steam.

As much as she loved the way he kissed—with his whole body—if they didn't stop, he'd be banging her on the desk. She turned her head away, breaking the seal of their mouths.

Knox nuzzled her temple. "So I've thought about what you said last night."

"And?"

"And I'd like to explore more with you."

The way Knox kept touching her was wonderfully distracting. She grabbed his wayward hand, holding it between hers. "If we're going forward with this, we need to be on the same page."

"You are such a rule follower, She-Cat," he murmured against her neck.

He lazily flicked his tongue over the pulse beating at the base of her throat. She had no doubt this man could make her body sing, but he needed a reminder that she got to pick the song. Shiori reached up and wrapped her hands around his throat.

Knox immediately backed off. But he didn't drop his gaze. He didn't speak either, which earned him points.

"I'm serious, Knox."

"I know you are." He closed his eyes. "Last night was . . . not what I expected. What if it was a onetime fluke?" Those gorgeous blue eyes opened and were clouded with concern. "What if I can't do this?"

"Be submissive?"

He nodded.

Oh sweet, sexy man, I'll wipe away all of that doubt if you'll let me. She slid her hands over his strong, masculine jaw and framed his face. "I think you're more afraid that you *can* do this."

He said nothing. Just stared at her.

She let her hands fall away. "Here's what I propose. Let's each make a detailed list of what we want from this"—*relationship* seemed too intimate a word and *contract* sounded too businesslike, so she settled on—"arrangement. Also what we don't want and the concerns about how it'll affect our working together."

Knox groaned. "You're giving me *homework*? There's no doubt you're a Domme, because that is pure punishment."

She laughed. "Luckily, I grade on a curve. But this is important, so don't skimp on specifics."

"Fine. When did you want to exchange notes?"

"We could meet for dinner Friday night. There's a great
restaurant—"

"No. We're not discussing this where we could be overheard.
And knowing us, I'm betting our negotiations will get a little heated."

"True."

He clasped her hand and kissed her knuckles. His affection
delighted her because it came so naturally to him. "Since we're
closed to classes due to the holiday, how about if you come to my
house tonight and I'll cook for you."

Shiori didn't hide her surprise. "You cook?"

"Not healthy gourmet stuff like your brother, but I know my
way around the kitchen." Knox kissed the inside of her wrist.
"When was the last time someone cooked for you?"

"Every night, because I'm a lousy chef."

He bit the base of her thumb. "Smart-ass. I meant when have
you had a home-cooked meal, prepared by someone who wants to
feed you but isn't getting paid to do so?"

Never. Not a lover anyway. Ronin and Amery had invited her
over a few times, and she'd loved that. In Japan she and her friends
went out to eat—dinner parties at private residences were rare. "All
right. You've convinced me. But no—"

"Funny business. I get it. No Barry White playing in the background, no candlelight, no sexy finger foods to feed each other. I
won't even change my sheets in hopes that I'll get you between
them."

"Very accommodating. But who's Barry White?"

Knox laughed. "Never mind. What time should I pick you up?"

"Give me your address and my car service will drop me off."

"I don't mind coming to get you, Shiori."

"I know. But it's just better this way."

He didn't look convinced, but he didn't argue.

"What should I bring?"

"Just yourself. I'll text you the address. Show up around six." Knox kissed the back of her hand and retreated. "Now I'm leaving you to lock up since I have to hit the grocery store."

CHAPTER EIGHT

KNOX had everything ready ten minutes before six.

He wasn't nervous, just impatient. He wanted to know what Shiori's expectations were if they agreed to continue this . . . whatever *this* was.

This is you agreeing to get on your knees, show your throat, and give her your balls.

Fuck. He smacked his hand into the counter, wishing that voice of doubt would just shut the fuck up, because he had no goddamn idea where the voice was coming from. He'd always been secure in his masculinity and his sexuality—how other people lived their lives and how they made their choices was no reflection on him. That was part of what'd appealed to him about Twisted. Embracing the *different strokes for different folks* philosophy.

And Shiori's assessment that he hadn't chosen a side bothered him only because she'd pointed out something he hadn't acknowledged. He never played with other men sexually because that wasn't his thing. But he had no problem using his skills with instruments of pain on other men. His one hard-and-fast rule at Twisted was he didn't beat on women. Period. So he'd been the third player in different scenarios. Doms punishing and rewarding their male subs.

Dommes punishing and rewarding their male subs. Doms who needed to connect with pain but didn't trust another Dom to be discreet. Male submissives who sought to test their pain thresholds before playing with a Dom or a Domme. Male submissives who needed a break from playing with a Dom or a Domme—craving the pain and skipping the mind fuck that went along with it.

So the ironic part of him being the whip master? He wasn't a big fan of pain. He'd had the instruments he used on members used on him, just so he experienced what he administered. Pain didn't arouse him. Neither did inflicting pain. He looked on it as a service he provided to the club and the members.

The benefit of wielding the whip and the flogger were the women who saw him as powerful. He'd never had to work hard for pussy. That suited him, because the expectations between club members didn't go beyond sex. It'd never bothered him to be with a woman one weekend and then see her with someone else the following weekend. Unlike Ronin, Knox had utilized the sex part of the sex club more than the kink aspect.

He had to wonder if kink ran in the Black family. Shiori hadn't indicated if she'd studied shibari and kinbaku, but he wouldn't be surprised if she had, since she'd followed in Ronin's footsteps and had become involved in martial arts.

All this speculation was driving him nuts. He cracked open a beer and checked the time just as the doorbell rang.

Finally.

Knox didn't rush to answer the door like he wanted to. When he opened the door, his gaze rested on her face briefly before movement in the street caught his attention. He glanced up to see the car service driver leaning against the right rear passenger door with his arms crossed. Like he was deciding whether he should leave Shiori here or remain parked at the curb. Without taking his eyes off the man, he kissed Shiori's forehead. Then he said, "Send your driver away or I will."

"What?"

"Your driver is eyeballing me like I'm shit on your shoe and he'd love to scrape me off."

"Not everything is a pissing contest, Knox."

"Tell that to him."

She sighed and turned around, waving him off. Then she faced Knox. "Happy now?"

"Very happy that you're here, She-Cat." He pressed his lips to hers, proving it with a very thorough kiss. When he pulled back her eyes held a warning, but her lips curved into a smile.

"Taking liberties off the bat, Ob-Knox-ious?"

"Yep. Come in." He stepped aside. "Let me help you with your coat."

Shiori turned, and he tugged the black trench down her arms. Beneath it she wore a light brown sweater, jeans, and riding boots.

"You look great, but I'll admit I'd hoped to see a corset and a short leather skirt under this trench coat." He placed a kiss on the back of her neck. "Or better yet, nothing at all."

"Behave." She faced him. That's when he noticed she held a small wrapped package.

"What's that?"

"A thank-you for inviting me into your home." She handed it to him. "Just a little token. No big deal."

Knox unwrapped the plain paper and crumpled it in his fist. Inside the small frame was a watercolor painting, very Asian in style, of boats moored at a dock. The serenity of the scene was astounding. "Whoa. This is terrific. Where did you get it?"

"It's just something I had around."

"Thank you." He propped it up on the mantel. "I'll give you a quick house tour, and then we can eat. Leave your boots on because we'll be going outside."

"I was surprised you live in a house and not in a condo or an apartment."

"After living in government-assisted housing projects growing up and then spending twelve years in the service, I was more than ready for my own place." He gestured to the living room. "I knocked out a wall to open up the space."

"You did the remodel yourself?"

"A lot of it. I'm a hands-on guy."

She ran her fingers up his arm. "I know that. I like that about you."

Sweet Jesus. These little glimpses into her were killing him. So when her hand dropped away, he didn't let her off that easily. He slipped his fingers through hers. She didn't protest when he towed her behind him as they headed to the kitchen. "I cook, but I didn't need all the fancy appliances that go into most houses these days."

"I like this breakfast bar and eat-in kitchen," she said.

"I got rid of the formal dining room, and it opened up the space between here and the living room." They cut down the wide hallway. "This is a three-bedroom house, but because I'm a single guy who doesn't give a rip about decorating, I won't show you the two rooms filled with crap."

She laughed.

Knox opened the last door. "Here's my bedroom."

Shiori let go of his hand and stepped into the room. Then she looked over her shoulder. "You and my brother must shop for beds in the same place, because this bed is as huge as his."

He shrugged. "I'm a big guy. A king-sized bed is fine, but having a custom-made bed built for a king is even better."

"Was this room this size originally?"

"Nope. There was a rear porch that was pretty useless, so I expanded into that space. That allowed me to put in a master bathroom." He gestured to the door to the right of the bed. "Take a look."

Her laughter echoed off the tile walls. "Totally a guy's bathroom, Knox. I love it."

He moved in behind her. The walk-in shower was big enough so he could stretch his arms out and not touch the walls. He'd had a teak bench put in so he could sit and enjoy the sauna option he'd added. His mother had joked he had more water jets in his shower than a carwash. But he hated freezing his ass off, and with so many adjustable showerheads, water hit every part of his body.

"So plain white tiles, huh?" she asked.

"It was cheaper. I put the money into the plumbing fixtures."

"It's nice." She faced him and smiled. "But no place to take bubble baths?"

He snorted. "Do I look like a bubble-bath guy? I'll show you the backyard."

They backtracked to the kitchen and exited out a side door. He led her up the set of wooden steps to the deck he'd built the first year he'd lived in the house.

"You have a lot of yard space."

"That's the main reason I bought this place. You can't find lots like this in metro Denver anymore."

"There's room for expansion after you get married and have a couple of kids. It'd be easy to add on bedrooms, a family room, and a mudroom for the dog. Back by the trees would be a perfect place for a swing set and those jungle-gym forts."

He stilled. She'd voiced his thoughts perfectly.

Then she remembered herself. "Enough with the show-and-tell, Godan. Feed me."

"With pleasure, Mistress B."

She whacked him on the ass.

Inside the house, he said, "Have a seat at the breakfast bar and I'll serve you."

"That could be taken a couple of different ways."

Knox leaned across the counter and let her see the heat in his eyes. "You say the word and I'll offer whatever services you desire."

"Let's satisfy our appetite for food first," she murmured.

He pulled the roast out of the slow cooker and set it on a plate, happy that the meat separated easily with just his fork. He scooped the potatoes, carrots, and onions into a bowl, then filled the gravy boat with the meat juices. "Help yourself. What would you like to drink?"

"Any flavor of soda is fine."

After pouring her a Coke, he took the rolls out of the warmer and dumped them in a basket. When he glanced up, she hadn't touched anything.

"What's wrong? You don't like pot roast?"

A sheepish smile appeared. "I don't know since I've never had it."

Knox forked meat onto her plate. Then potatoes and carrots. He smashed the vegetables down and poured the clear, flavorful juices over everything on the plate. "There. And you use the dinner rolls to sop up any extra bits."

Shiori took a tentative bite and then closed her eyes. "God. That is so good."

"Thanks. My mom's recipe." He loaded up his plate. That they didn't talk during the meal didn't feel awkward. Especially since she ate two plates of food.

She set her napkin down. "I'm done."

"So no room for dessert?"

"Maybe later. Right now I'll waddle to the couch and hope I don't fall asleep during our talk."

"While I'm hoping we don't yell at each other, I don't want you nodding off on me either."

She touched his cheek. "I won't."

"Good. Go on. I'll put the food away."

"You need help?"

"Nah. I'll just dump it all back in the crock and shove it in the fridge."

When Knox walked into the living room, he noticed Shiori

had taken her boots off. She had her hands in her back pockets as she stared out the bay window.

In that moment she didn't look like a Domme; she looked small and fragile and maybe a little lost. Sometimes it was hard for him to see past her various personas—the high-powered business executive, the billionaire heiress, the martial-arts master—to the woman beneath.

He moved in behind her. "Do I need to ask before I put my arms around you?"

She looked over her shoulder and said, "Never."

Knox enfolded her in his arms. He had to bend down to rest his chin on the top of her head. She held such power in a small package.

After a bit she kissed his biceps and wriggled free. "You ready to go over your homework?"

He chuckled. "I'll warn you, I've always been a C-minus student."

She sat in the corner of the couch and pulled her knees to her chest.

Her protective posture annoyed him. This conversation would be easier if she sat on his lap and he could touch her. He mirrored her pose on the other end, but he stretched out his long legs so they encroached on her space.

Already testing her boundaries?

"Let's go over the problem areas. First, we work together. You're in charge at the dojo. I'll respect that. When we're alone together outside the dojo, you'll defer to me."

"In all things? You dictate where we eat, what we do, what movies we watch?"

Shiori frowned. "Okay. Back up. I'm talking about sexual submission. So we won't be doing any of the normal-couple things like if we were starting to date."

Knox said, "Then I'm not interested."

That startled her. "I'm confused."

"Yes, ma'am, you are. I've never been in this type of relationship, and I don't know your rules, but I do know mine. I like you. I want to spend time with you. Outside of the dojo and outside of Twisted. That means we do couple things together. We watch TV, we share meals, we get to know each other. I'm willing to let you direct our intimate relationship, but the key word there is *relationship*. I'm not interested in you calling me to show up at your penthouse when you're feeling horny and need a man to service you. There are places that cater to that type of need. Or you can just hold off and get what you need from one of the male submissives at Twisted."

Her eyes flashed. "How are we supposed to have a relationship? We can't let anyone at the dojo know we're involved."

"Why not?"

"I have no idea how Ronin will react, and he should hear about it from us, not thirdhand gossip from Katie."

"It's none of his or anyone else's business."

"Wrong. Black Arts *is* his business. He made us assure him that we wouldn't kill each other while he's away. His worries wouldn't be any less if he knew we were involved. So we'd have to keep it strictly between us."

"Basically, we'll be sneaking around," he stated.

She cocked her head. "You're trying to rile me on purpose?"

Fuck. This was not how tonight was supposed to go. He leaned his head back and stared at the ceiling for ten counts before he looked at her again. "Fine. If we're keeping this on the down low, then that means no signs we're together at Twisted either."

"You can't make that determination."

"Yes, I can. If I can't claim you in public, then you can't claim me either."

Shiori set her chin on her knees and considered him. "Is this your manipulative way of being my submissive without having to learn what it means to be a submissive?"

Knox shook his head. "I am learning; keep that in mind. Is

public approval of club members important to you as a Domme? Do you need it to prove your dominance over me?"

No response, but he knew he'd touched a nerve.

"You can teach me to be what you want and need in ways public humiliation never will. Any type of humiliation in any setting is my hard limit."

"I'd never do that to you," she said softly.

"Promise?"

"I promise."

"Be warned—if it ever happens, I will walk away."

Annoyance briefly flashed in her eyes. "I get it."

"Good." He refocused the conversation. "Have you ever had a submissive of your own before?"

"I had one guy in Tokyo whom I used more than others. But no, I've never brought a sub to my place to play." She smiled. "Or had a sub cook me dinner. So this is all new to me."

"We can figure this out, ma'am."

"Call me Nushi."

He lifted an eyebrow. "What's that mean?"

"Master, lover—it's the simplest Japanese word for it."

"Nushi," he murmured. "I like it. It's more personal."

"I hope so, because you'll be saying it a lot."

There was his cocky woman.

Shiori studied him. "Your hard limit is public humiliation. Any others?"

"No other players. Specifically, no one else in bed with us and no play with others at Twisted."

"Define play. Because you dish out pain at the club upon request, and that is play for those members."

Knox shook his head. "Not if you don't become aroused by it."

"I disagree. But here's where I'm willing to compromise. I'll be in the room with you when you're doing another Master's or Mistress's bidding."

That could actually be really hot, having her eyes on him as he worked a submissive over. "Deal."

"But . . ." She gave him a cagey smile. "You don't get to lie about our relationship. If asked why I'm observing, I get to answer that it's your Domme's prerogative."

Knox knew part of her wanted to lay public claim to him. But he had the right to demand the same thing. "Agreed. But for every Master or Mistress that you tell I'm your sub, I get to take you out on a real date. Where I pick you up and pay for the night out." He lightly bit the tips of her fingers before kissing them.

"You are awfully damn demanding, sub, but I'll agree. As for when we get to the stage where we're having sex, we'll use condoms?"

"Fine. Can we get tested so down the line we don't have to use them?"

"Then what would we do for birth control?"

His eyes narrowed. "You're not on the pill?"

"No. And it's not something I'm interested in going on."

That sucked.

"What about restraints?" she asked.

"Cuffs, straps, ropes? I'm good with that."

"Sex toys?"

He thought of the cock ring. That hadn't been bad. "Fine. No stupid-looking fetish wear for me or breath play."

Her nose wrinkled. "I'm not into that either. When we're together, I'll expect you shirtless and wearing a pair of athletic shorts until I tell you to remove them."

Here came the demands. "Yes, Nushi."

She touched his hair. "When I snap my fingers, I'll want you on your knees. Immediately."

His response was more a grumble than agreement.

"Disrespect and defiance will result in punishment at my discretion, but will not include any type of public humiliation. I'm willing to negotiate on some things, but when I say done, we're done."

"Understood."

"When it's just us, like this, alone? You are mine, Knox. To do with as I please. You're not convinced you're submissive, so I may push you a bit." She paused, gauging his reaction. "Is there anything else we need to address?"

"No, ma'am."

"Ah, but there is one thing. I'm here on a work visa. It's unlikely I'll get sent back to Japan before Ronin returns, but it is a possibility. So I should make you aware this won't ever be a permanent situation."

His gut clenched at the idea she could just . . . leave. Was he prepared to let her go?

You don't have a choice.

He tucked a strand of hair behind her ear. "Then try not to fall for me, Nushi. It'd be tough to beat my ass for breaking your heart when you're in Tokyo."

She laughed—just as he'd hoped. "I was going to offer you the same suggestion, *namaiki.*"

"Is that a new pet name for me or something?"

Another laugh. Then her hand gripped the hair at the back of his head and she pulled. "Stand and take off your shirt."

Apparently negotiations were over.

Knox stood and removed his shirt, slowly undoing the buttons as he tried to shift gears from playful to subservient. He let the shirt flutter to the floor.

Shiori snapped her fingers.

He lowered to his knees. She hadn't said he had to keep his head down, but he did so anyway.

"Very nice." She scooted to the edge of the couch and ran her hands across his shoulders and her palms flat to his pecs. "I have a thing for your chest. It's so broad and muscular."

Was he supposed to say something?

"What would you do if I stripped off my pants and spread my legs wide so you could see every inch of my pussy?"

"I'd do nothing until you told me to do something, Nushi."

"Oh, you are a fast learner, my sweet. So I'll tell you what I'm going to do. After I ditch my pants, I'll lean back on this comfy couch and see how well you use that mouth."

His cock went hard. He fought the urge to lick his lips. He heard fabric rustling; then her pants hit him in the face.

She pressed her bare toes against his groin. "You like this oral exam I'm giving you, don't you?"

"Yes, ma'am."

"Come here and show me what you've got."

Knox bit back a growl when he saw her pussy, smooth everywhere except for a small patch of hair on the curve of her mound. So pink and hot and wet. Then he had his hands on the insides of her thighs, opening her up so he could get at every glistening inch. A hard tug on his hair caused him to look up.

"I don't want to come fast. Tease me. Make me beg."

He'd make her beg all right. And then he'd make her scream. He gave her a feral grin. "You gonna let me bury my face in your pussy now?"

In answer, she released her grip on his head.

Rather than diving in, he decided to take her demand to the extreme. He acquainted himself with the insides of her thighs. First, featherlight brushes of his lips. Then soft sucking kisses. He wished he hadn't shaved so she could feel the burn of his bristle on her tender flesh.

When Knox finally forged in closer, he closed his eyes and breathed in her musk. Nothing on earth compared to that intimate scent.

Except for that first taste.

He swirled his tongue inside her pussy, letting her juices flow into his mouth. Each time he went back for another taste, he buried his tongue farther inside her until each breath he took was full of her scent. All he could taste was her. All he could hear were her soft gasps.

He explored her folds, licking and nibbling on her hot flesh. From the way her hips jumped, he knew she liked it when he painted her slit in long, wet strokes. Next time he'd do that with his thumb as he used his teeth on her clit. He hadn't touched that hot button yet, although he couldn't hold off much longer. He wanted to kiss it and tease it, make it swell. Feel it quiver beneath his lips.

So he flicked just the very tip of his tongue across that sweet spot and returned to fucking her with it. A nuzzle here, a lick there, and whoops—another short pass of his tongue between her pussy lips to mix things up. He planted kisses across the denuded skin of her mound, letting his nose tease her lower belly as he dragged his mouth back and forth across that tempting patch of hair.

Shiori had started to bump her hips into his face, practically chasing his mouth to get him to put it where she most needed it.

Ask me. Beg me. Because, baby, I can do this all goddamn night.

After another round of lick, suck, bite, when he then blew on her hot and wet tissues, she finally gave in.

"Enough. Stop teasing."

Knox lifted his mouth enough to say, "Beg me," and then tickled her clit with his lips.

"Make me come."

Not the begging he'd wanted, but her command was pretty damn hot. He said, "Yes, ma'am," and latched on to that pouting little pearl, lightly tonguing it until the first hard pulse against his mouth. Then he sucked in time to the rhythm of her body.

She expelled a loud gasp that was as good as a scream.

Teasing her had the desired effect; her orgasm seemed to last awhile, and he stayed with her to the last slow pulse, wanting to gift her every bit of pleasure he could.

He pressed his mouth to her even after she went limp against the back of the couch. Even when his jeans were trying to cut his dick in half.

Then her fingers were stroking his hair. "Okay. You can back off now."

"But I don't want to."

She sighed.

"So does that sigh mean I passed?"

"With high marks."

Knox pushed back onto his knees, dying to tear off his jeans and fuck her any way she told him to.

But when Shiori bent to retrieve her pants—interesting that she'd gone commando—his hopes deflated even as his cock stayed hard and proud.

After she put her pants back on, she took her phone out and poked at the buttons. Then she perched on the edge of the couch and smoothed his hair back, gently mapping his face before she leaned in and kissed him.

Her kiss was equal parts gratitude and control. When she broke free, Knox stubbornly kept his eyes closed.

"Look at me."

Warning himself not to glare, or look fucking pitiful, he peeled his eyes open halfway.

"I know you're hard and uncomfortable and are probably cursing me for it. But since I'm not going to do anything about it, you can't either." She waited, probably expecting him to explode with outrage, but he knew it'd be a waste of breath.

"You don't get to touch yourself or get off until I say. So no washing your cock and balls in the shower and the next thing you know, you're jacking off when you didn't mean to. Ditto using wet dreams as an excuse of why you came when I told you not to.

"I'm not doing this to torture you, Knox. I'm making this demand for two reasons. First for you to learn you have no control. Accept it. Accept that you won't always like it. The second reason is orgasm denial builds stamina. If you can get off whenever you want, then it's harder for you to get off when *I* want. Understand?"

He blinked at her.

"Have something to say?"

"No, ma'am."

"Don't pout."

He bit off, "I. Don't. Pout."

She pressed her lips to his. "Kiss me."

But Knox's mouth was closed down as tight as Fort Knox.

Yep. Definitely pouting. She laughed. "Kiss me like you mean it, Knox. Kiss me and touch me as if I'd given you the green light and you were carrying me off to bed."

That broke his frustration. He brought her on top of him and rolled down to the floor. One hand in her hair held her head in place so he could eat at her mouth the same way he'd eaten at her pussy, the other hand pressing down on her lower back, so he could rock his dick against her pubic bone.

Shiori's hands were trapped between them, and she just dug her nails into his chest and held on.

Finally the frustration eased and he released her.

"That's what I want from you," she whispered against his throat. "An honest reaction." She rolled to her feet and offered a hand to help him up.

Knox laughed. "I'm not falling for that. You might just throw me on my ass for fun, and wouldn't that be the perfect capper to my night?"

"Any regrets?"

He scrubbed his hands down his face and looked out the window rather than at her. A Lincoln Town Car pulled up to the curb. "Doesn't matter. Your ride is here. And for the record, Mistress, I fucking hate that you won't at least let me take you home."

She slipped her coat on without his assistance. "I'll consider it for next time, okay?"

"Thank you."

"I'll see you tomorrow. Good night." She bowed to him before she fled.

Bowed.

As he watched her drive away, he realized whatever justification he'd made about this situation felt hollow.

CHAPTER NINE

SHIORI, Fee, Katie, Tasha, and Molly met at the North Seventh Girls Club Saturday morning. Molly, being her usual sweetheart self, brought doughnuts for everyone—including the girls in the class.

Katie served as the MC, introducing everyone, and did a great job of explaining the differences between traditional jujitsu and Brazilian jujitsu. Then she emphasized how long each of the black belt instructors had been training and what tournaments they'd placed in. It surprised Shiori that Katie had that info on her because she'd never given Black Arts a full bio. So the woman was resourceful; she'd grant her that.

Then she introduced Molly. Molly's story of her attack, her recovery, and her enrollment in self-defense training kept the girls riveted, especially the part where Molly swore knowing she could defend herself had made her a stronger, more confident person in all aspects of her life.

Shiori and Fee demonstrated the simplest self-defense techniques on Tasha and Molly while Katie explained each step. The girls, ranging in age from eight to fourteen, were partnered up by size, and then the real work began. Although Shiori supposed that fits of giggles were better than crying fits.

Katie kept an eye on the entire class and alerted the instructors when she could see who hadn't been helped at all or who needed extra help. Plus she offered lots of praise in a genuine manner that boosted the students' confidence and made them work harder.

Time flew by. Before they ended the class, the girls begged Shiori and Fee to do a grappling demonstration. It didn't take much to convince them because they liked to mix it up.

Neither woman held back. And maybe some of the hip throws and takedowns were over-the-top, but the audience loved it. By the time they finished the match, they were both sweating, breathing hard, disheveled, and happy for the challenge.

Katie declared the match a tie. While Shiori and Fee were evenly matched in skill in some areas, in others Shiori had a clear advantage. The last time they'd faced each other in an MMA fight, Shiori had won. But she knew Fee wanted a rematch. Maybe that would be a way to increase ticket sales for the next Black and Blue Promotions event. She'd bring it up with Katie first. From what Shiori had seen, both Blue and Ronin were dismissive of Katie's abilities in the promotion business. That didn't make sense to her. Why would they keep her on staff if she wasn't contributing in a positive way? Sure she was a knockout as a ring girl. Amery had mentioned that Katie had a six-month probation period, but that'd passed. Yet Blue and Ronin still hadn't allowed her to do the job she'd been hired for. It seemed the only person who listened to her ideas was Knox. No wonder she hung around him whenever possible.

Ronin had asked her to keep an eye on Black and Blue Promotions, so maybe it was time to dig deeper into the business plan for the next year.

"What do you think, Shi?" Fee asked.

"Sorry. I was thinking about something else. What did you say?"

"I said those guys were so smarmy about us going shopping; I say we shop our asses off. Then let's have a girls' day and night. Dinner, drinks, dancing . . . Who knows where it'll lead?" Katie said.

Tasha spoke first. "As much fun as that sounds, I have to work tonight. But you guys have a blast." After a round of goodbyes, she got in her car and sped off.

"What about you, Molly?"

Molly pulled the elastic band down, releasing her ponytail. Then she fluffed up her dark brown hair. "Well—"

"God, I hate you. Both you and Fee. You've been moving around and sweating for four hours and your hair looks that amazing immediately afterward?" Katie's gaze winged to Fee. "Go ahead and do the hair flip and primp thing so I can lament the hideousness of my overprocessed stick-straight hair and bask in the gloriousness of yours."

"Yes!" Molly did a fist pump. "Katie envies *me* for something! I'm writing that in my diary."

"Me too," Fee said. Then she added, "Or I'll write it on my girls-of-the-ring calendar with Katie's hotness as Miss September."

Katie flipped her off. "The calendar was for charity, *Fifi*."

"Fuck. I hate that nickname. Fee is so much better than the drawn-out *So-fee-ah* that my mother saddled me with. But *Fifi* is the name of a damn dog. I want to kick him in the face whenever he says it."

Shiori frowned. "I've never heard Blue call you that before."

"Blue calls me *brat* or *Sophia*. Gil is the one who teases me with that."

"Anyway, the two perfect-hair chicks can't complain about a bad hair day keeping them from shopping and carousing. What about you, Shi? Ready to do some damage to your credit limit?"

"Let's do it."

"Saks first? Then the boutiques downtown?"

"Perfect."

Molly and Fee were whispering to each other.

"Share with the class, ladies," Katie chided.

"Okay, here's the thing." Molly looked at Fee again. "Where

you two shop is way out of mine and Fee's budgets. *Way* out. But it'll be fun to see how the one percenters live. So we'll come along, as long as you both understand we'll be window-shopping."

"Yeah, and this isn't a hint for you to take pity on us and buy us shit." Fee grinned. "And I really wanna see how much Katie spends on shoes."

Shiori had never considered it might be uncomfortable for Molly and Fee. Her entire life she'd had the luxury of buying whatever she wanted. Price didn't matter, and she'd never had to stick to a budget. Their way of living was as foreign to her as hers was to them. But she was glad they had been honest about their hesitations. She nudged Katie with her shoulder. "You heard them. Shoe shopping first."

BY the time they sat down for dinner at Denver's hot new western-styled Mexican food cantina, they were ready for a pitcher of margaritas.

"So how often do you shop like that?" Fee asked, helping herself to chips and salsa after the waitress took their orders.

Katie shrugged. "Not as often as I used to. Now I understand the term shopping *spree* because that's how I do it."

"What about you, Shi?"

"In Japan I used to shop with my mom. I miss that. I miss her." Ever since she'd walked away from the career path she'd been on at the family company, she and her mom had drifted apart. But part of that was their physical distance.

"You seemed familiar with the stores here," Katie pointed out.

"I am. I mostly shop when I'm bored. When I first got here, before I was teaching at Black Arts and I had a plane at my disposal, I'd fly to Vegas or Chicago to shop."

Molly's hand holding her margarita stopped in midair and she gasped, "For real?"

"For real."

"That's so crazy to me. I'm saving up to take a vacation in Daytona. And you can just jet off whenever you feel like it."

"I have to admit I didn't realize it was so far to fly—for a foreigner it's hard to grasp the size of America. Flying off to shop wasn't something I did regularly in Japan. My job with Okada was seventy hours a week, so Saturday was the only day I had off. It was tempting to sleep, but I forced myself to have a life. So in my younger years, in order for me to have time to go to parties or events or the clubs, I hired a personal shopper so I didn't spend my one free day shopping and I always had the hottest clothes." The way they were looking at her after she finished speaking, she wondered if she'd said too much.

No, you didn't tell them shopping had been your refuge during your marriage. That no matter how chic or well adorned you were, it didn't hold your husband's interest for long.

"I never had to work for the money I got from my family," Katie offered. "My dad didn't think I had the drive or the brains to be part of any of his businesses. I fell into that mind-set for a while—if he thinks I'm a fuckup, why shouldn't I just be one?" She paused. "I got over that attitude after some bad choices. But I still live off the family trust fund, because what I'm making at Black and Blue Promotions definitely won't keep me in designer shoes."

They all laughed, and Shiori's tension lessened.

"So is having that kind of money almost like it's not real money?" Molly asked. "Because if I would've bought those cute boots that were five hundred bucks, I'd have to cut back on something in my budget to make up the difference."

Fee snorted. "I'd have to tell my brother, hey, I can't pay my portion of the mortgage this month, but look at these awesome new shoes! He'd bury me in them."

Another round of laughter. The conversation lightened up. Then the food arrived—good thing because they'd downed the pitcher of margaritas.

While Fee and Molly were discussing roller derby, Shiori brought up Black and Blue Promotions.

After some casual back-and-forth, Shiori said, "I'd like to see your proposals for promotion."

"All of them?"

"Yes. Even if there are ones that Ronin and Blue discounted, I'm still interested in them. And I'd like to take a peek at the remaining schedule for this year."

"Absolutely." Katie bit her lip and leaned forward. "But I suggest we do this after hours, when Blue is gone. He's constantly looking over my shoulder. He doesn't have any faith in me or trust that I can actually do this job and do it well."

Or maybe there was another reason Blue monitored Katie so closely.

"Hey, no telling secrets," Fee said, butting into their conversation. "And no work talk."

"We're not talking about work. We're arguing over what flavor of margarita we should order next," Katie retorted. "Blood orange? Or blueberry?"

"Yuck. Neither. This mango kind is good."

"I vote mango too," Molly said.

"Mango it is." Katie gestured with the pitcher to the waitress for another round. "So where are we going tonight?"

"Not Diesel," Fee and Shiori said in unison and laughed.

"Agreed," Molly said.

"Do we wanna dance? Or just drink? Or watch hot guys dance together at a gay club while we drink?" Katie asked.

At the mention of a club, Shiori found herself wondering if Knox was going to Twisted tonight. The past four days had been so crazy she and Knox had seen each other in the dojo and that was it. They hadn't been left alone for even two minutes.

"Speaking of hot guys . . . who is the hottest guy at Black Arts and ABC?" Katie asked. "Molly, you first."

"Ronin Black."

Katie said, "Fee?"

"Ditto on Ronin."

"That makes it unanimous because he's my choice too—Sensei Black is the reigning smoking hottie."

"It's not unanimous because I didn't get to vote and *eww*, not voting for my brother," Shiori said.

"So who do you think is the hottest?" Fee asked.

Knox. Without a doubt he was the hottest, sexiest, most exasperating man she'd ever known. But it wasn't like she could tell them that. She smirked at Fee. "Blue."

"Blue, as in my brother, Blue? Oh no. Not going there. So let's start over—besides the owners of the dojos, who's in the running?"

"Deacon," Molly tossed out. "Even when he's an ass."

"Maybe that makes him even more attractive," Katie said.

"He does have that 'I'm a heartbreaking jackass' vibe that makes you want to dig deep and see if there's a sweet center inside his hard outer shell," Molly mused.

Fee said, "I'm picking Gil because he is so pretty to look at . . . until he opens his mouth."

Shiori nodded. "Same with Knox."

Everyone looked expectantly at Katie.

"I pick Ivan. He's hot, fierce, driven, and knows when to keep quiet. Always a plus." Katie held up her phone and started texting someone.

The margaritas arrived, and they wasted no time in filling up their glasses. Katie kept texting until Fee said, "What the hell, K? Quit sexting and drink with us."

"I'm texting with Ivan." She grinned. "He's working security at his dad's club, and he invited us to a party in the VIP section."

"Sweet! Wait, which club?" Molly asked.

"Fresh."

"Isn't that some kind of fetish/fantasy/role-playing club?"

"Yes, but it'll fun because we'll all be dressed up!"

"Screw that, Katie. I'm not going to a club where I have to wear a costume."

Katie looked at petulant Fee. "Suck it up, *Sophia*, and take one for the team. Dressing up doesn't mean we have to wear a skanky French maid's getup and carry a feather duster. It just means we can dress slutty and take in all the Fresh craziness from the VIP section."

"You're acting like you've never sat in a VIP section before," Fee said.

"I've never been in the one at *Fresh*," Katie retorted.

"I'm not sure I can go because I don't have anything to wear." Molly looked to Shiori for support. "Right?"

Rather than admit she had a closet full of sex-club outfits, Shiori said, "Clothes aren't as important as the right attitude."

"You want to go to this place?" Molly asked.

"Why not? You were all talking earlier about needing to get laid. Here's your chance."

Katie looked happy enough to burst. "Then it's settled. And so no one chickens out, we'll get ready at my house. I have three huge closets full of clothes—something shameful and slutty for everyone. Let's go."

KATIE'S house was a mini-mansion in a gated community. She told them that she rented the property for next to nothing from her brother, who'd bought it at a foreclosure sale. Why Katie felt the need to explain her housing and financial situation surprised Shiori. Then again, the way Americans were so open about personal issues baffled her.

After another round of margaritas, the parade of clothes began. Katie hadn't exaggerated her clothing selection, and she laughingly admitted to being a compulsive shopper and a hoarder. Since she'd struggled with her weight her entire life—another personal fact she just blithely tossed out there—she had outfits ranging in four different sizes because she never got rid of anything. And Katie considered it a sign from the fashion gods that their shoe sizes were within half an inch of one another. Then she showed them another custom closet that had more shoes than Saks.

Molly selected a pair of leopard-print skinny jeans and a black leather halter top that accentuated the breasts she took such great pains to hide.

But since conservative Molly had thrown caution to the wind, so did Fee. She chose a pair of electric-blue capris and paired it with a silk top hand-painted with vibrantly hued flowers. With butterfly sleeves and a high-necked collar, the shirt looked demure in the front, but it essentially had no back.

Katie called her ensemble "fet life meets whorehouse"— skintight red leather pants and a red-and-black-striped bustier with black lace edging.

Shiori's look was old-school glam—a black and gold sequined miniskirt and a gold lamé tank top with a black blouse. She switched out her Fendi bag with her party purse, which was a small black pouch that held her ID, credit card, and phone. The chain circled her waist looking like a piece of jewelry and the pouch rested at her hip.

"Man, I want one of those," Molly said. "Where'd you get it? Wait—don't tell me. Japan."

"Lucky for you, I know where to get more." Her phone buzzed. She scrolled to the text message. "The car is here, Katie. What's the gate code to get in?"

"Nine four nine seven."

She texted that and slipped her phone into her pouch.

"Let's hit it, ladies."

Shiori grabbed her shopping bags and gym bag. She would leave them in the limo until it returned to take her home.

Next they all piled into the limo. Everyone voiced disappointment there wasn't a bar, but Shiori figured they'd had enough to drink for a while.

A very tipsy Molly leaned her head on Shiori's shoulder. "This is so much fun. We should do this every weekend."

"I don't know if my liver could take it," Fee joked.

"So what's the plan at the club?" Katie asked. "Are we ditching the 'if we arrive together, we leave together' rule?"

"Absolutely. If I get a chance to get me some . . . suckers, I'm gone," Fee said. "Although I don't think I'll find a guy who trips my trigger at a fetish club."

"Oh, I don't know. What if you see a guy who has an obsession with Thor? If he's built like that and dresses like that—"

"Then chances are he's gay," Shiori and Molly finished together on a laugh.

That started the whole gay, not-gay conversation, followed by what made a man sexy.

"Swagger," Molly said. "If he owns his sexuality, then you know he'd own you in bed."

Shiori bit her lip against saying, *But what if I want to own him?*

"I think fierceness is hot," Fee said. "He wants you, he'll have you, and then he'll do everything he can to protect you."

Now, that description fit Knox perfectly.

"What about you, Katie?" Molly asked. "You haven't given us your usual laundry list of what's sexy."

"Tenderness," she said softly. "A man who isn't afraid to show you gentleness and sweetness as well as passion."

Okay. She certainly hadn't expected that from Katie. And she agreed with her, even when that quality was as rare as black pearls. But . . . she had witnessed that sweetness in Knox.

"Your turn, Shi. What's your definition of sexy?"

"A man who's not threatened by me calling the shots in the bedroom."

They burst into laughter. Which forced her to play it off as a joke.

"Seriously. What's sexy in a man?" Katie demanded.

"Since you laughed at my other one, I'm going with chest hair and a big cock."

The limo stopped just as she finished speaking.

Perfect timing.

"We're here!" Katie was so excited she flung open the door and hopped out.

Shiori left instructions with the driver before she joined her friends in line.

Katie had already draped herself over Ivan's back and was whispering something in his ear that made him grin.

When they approached Katie and Ivan, Katie announced, "This little soiree is in honor of Ivan's birthday!"

"Really? Happy birthday!" Molly said.

"Thanks." He handed them each a lanyard. "Drinks on the house. Table is set up in the VIP section."

"When are you done working so you can party with us?" Katie asked.

"Soon."

"I'm holding you to that." Katie kissed him square on the mouth. "Does this club have a spanking station? Because I'm thinking you need a few whacks on the butt, birthday boy. But you won't need one to grow on; since I'm sure you're big in all the right places."

Shiori looked over at Fee and Molly, who wore the same WTF? looks.

Ivan took it in stride. "Have fun, ladies, and I'll be in when I can."

As they entered, Fee and Molly announced they wanted to look around, so they split off.

Katie saw the balloon at the VIP table and laughed. "I wonder whose idea that was." She peered at the writing on the tape. "It's in Russian. It'd be hilarious if Ivan's badass father set up a birthday party in a fetish club for his son."

The cocktail waitress took their orders once they were seated. Shiori was done drinking for the night, so she'd make this drink last.

"Why do I get the feeling this type of club isn't as shocking to you as it is to Fee and Molly?" Katie asked.

"I've been to places like this in Tokyo and Germany. And I'll point that question right back at you."

"I dabbled in Goth culture," Katie admitted. "We were always looking for weird and edgy, so we ended up at some pretty strange places."

"I can't picture you in Goth makeup and wearing all-black clothes."

She smiled. "That's eventually what pulled me out of it. I wanted to wear pink and be happy once in a while."

Fee and Molly joined them.

"What kinky things did you see that you wanted to try?" Katie asked them.

"There's more stuff I'd *never* try than anything that looked appealing," Fee said. "I mean I don't find it disgusting, but I just don't get it either."

"For instance?" Shiori asked.

"Well, there *is* a spanking station. And I can't figure out if those people want to be spanked because they weren't spanked as a kid, or if they were spanked and they loved it so much they want to keep experiencing it."

"None of the guys you've been with has ever smacked your ass during sex or when you're messing around?" Katie asked Fee.

Fee shook her head. "I'd probably react instinctively and dislocate his arm." She looked at Molly. "What about you, Miss Corn-Fed Nebraska?"

"Have I ever gotten a full-blown ass paddling before sex? No. But besides my random bad-boy hookups here and there, the guys I've dated have been tame. Would I try it? Yep. I've read some really hot spanking stories." She volleyed the question back to Katie. "What about you?"

"This older guy I had a brief fling with liked spanking me. But he was a great dirty talker too, so I'm not sure which made me hotter."

Then they all three looked at Shiori.

"What?"

"You're being quiet, so you're holding back. Spill it," Molly demanded.

Shiori fiddled with the straw in her drink. "I'll tell you if you promise not to laugh."

"Omigod, you've got a spanking fetish," Katie exclaimed.

"Not a fetish. I'm just really good at it."

"*How* are you good at it?" Fee asked.

How honest could she be? She definitely couldn't lie and say getting whopped on the ass with a board was part of jujitsu conditioning, because Fee would call bullshit on that. But she couldn't admit she was a Domme either. She settled for a semi-true story. "My ex and I went to some of the kink clubs in Tokyo. There was a spanking station and he wanted to spank me, so I said yes—as long as I got to spank him too. So he leveled five really wimpy whacks with a paddle. It did nothing for me. When my turn rolled around, I put a lot of muscle into it. He threw a hissy fit for me taking it too far, hurting and embarrassing him. Then he took off and left me at this club."

"What a jackass."

"But another guy asked if I'd spank him hard like that. So I did. I ended up with a line of people who wanted me to redden their asses, which took the sting out of my dickhead husband bailing on me."

Three sets of eyes scrutinized her.

Then Katie leaned closer for a fist bump. "You are the motherfucking shit. But you know I'm gonna hafta ask you to prove it."

Fee and Molly nodded agreement.

"What? How am I supposed to do that?"

Katie smirked. "You leave that part to me. You warm up your spanking arm. Because some lucky bastard is getting his ass smacked by you tonight."

CHAPTER TEN

"I don't wanna go to some stupid fetish club," Deacon complained. "Why can't we just stay here and drink?"

"Suck it up. Ivan asked us, and it'll be a good chance to get to know him better. We need solid footing with the fighters before Maddox shows up," Knox told him.

"And rips everything to fucking shreds. You think Maddox gives a fuck if we bond? No. It makes his job easier if we don't get along." Deacon smirked. "Don't be surprised if he holds you and Shiori up as an example of how mutual animosity can work."

"Fuck off." Their hostility had been supplanted by sexual heat. Not that anyone had noticed the difference.

Maybe because there isn't a difference.

They'd grappled as usual. Bickered, although not as much. In the past four days Shiori touched him at random times. Just a soft brush of her hand on his neck or shoulder. If he needed to tell her something he spoke directly in her ear, knowing how it affected her.

But they hadn't been alone together since the night at his place. He'd half hoped they'd spend tonight together, but he hadn't heard from her all day. Being a new sub, he wasn't sure on protocol; if he could call her first or if he was supposed to wait for her summons.

*You sure this is what you want? Waiting on her to decide if she'll deign
to see you?*

"Knox?"

He glanced up to see Deacon scowling at him. "What?"

"Who else we waiting on?"

"Blue and Fisher."

Deacon raised his eyebrows. "Fisher? He never goes out with
us." He paused. "Ah, hell, does he have some kind of fetish I don't
wanna know about?"

"No clue. I just know he and Ivan have gotten tight."

Blue and Fisher walked into Diesel together. Blue, as usual,
wore a dour look that warned people not to cross him. Or even
speak to him. Fisher, on the other hand, was smiling for a change.
He'd joined Black Arts as a boxing trainer for the MMA program
and had enrolled in classes two years ago, mostly to learn defensive
moves in the ring. While boxers did okay in MMA matches, there
was a reason it was called mixed martial arts and not mixed boxing
styles.

"Fisher, my man. You're gracing us with your presence tonight?"

Fisher and Deacon did some hand-slapping, fist-bumping,
half-man-hug thing. "I've been working most Saturdays, and by
the time I knock off at dark, I'm too damn tired to do anything.
But since I just pushed paperwork today, I thought what the hell.
I'll see if I can find a chick who has a fetish for my cock tonight."

Knox laughed. "I've never been to this club, but I've heard it's
more an amateur 'see and be seen' wearing weird clothes than a
place to explore real fetishes."

"I went one other time with Ivan, and there are some kinky
things going on."

"Like what?" Fisher asked.

"Now, why would I spoil the surprise, eh?" Blue said.

"Who's driving?" Deacon asked.

"I'll drive if you don't mind sitting on construction plans and tools in my truck."

Blue took shotgun. Knox and Deacon climbed in the back of the truck's cab. Deacon and Fisher talked about Fisher's construction business. Blue chimed in. Knox stared out the window and checked his phone to see if Shiori had messaged him.

Talk about pussy whipped. And you don't even know if her pussy is worth it.

After they pulled onto the freeway, Deacon poked him on the arm. "What?"

"You've been off all week. Did you go to Twisted like I told you?"

"Yeah."

"You get out of your rut?"

Knox withheld a grin. "Like you wouldn't imagine."

"You wishing you'd gone there tonight instead?"

"Nah." Even if Shiori were there, they'd have to pretend to be coworkers. It sucked they couldn't be out anywhere. "What about you, D? What fetish you hoping to see?"

"Not a fetish guy. I don't care what the outside wrapping looks like. I wanna see tits and ass."

The club was in a sketchy part of Denver. The upside was plenty of free parking. The place looked packed, from what Knox could see as they walked up the sidewalk.

Ivan checked IDs at the door. A beefy ex-football player gave clubgoers the evil eye as they passed through the door. Ivan grinned when he noticed them approaching.

"Looking snappy in that suit," Deacon drawled. Another round of MMA hand jive and man hugs followed.

"Thanks for coming. My father gave me his VIP table tonight." He handed out laminated cards. "Flash this at the guard by the balcony."

"Which table we looking for?"

Ivan groaned. "It's the one with the birthday balloon taped to it."

"Your dad is making you work on your birthday?" Fisher asked.

"Funny man, my father. Tells me birthdays are just another day, and celebrations are for girls. But he taped a fucking *balloon* on the table, and I think there might be cake later."

"As long as there's a naked chick jumping out of said cake."

Knox looked at Deacon. "What is wrong with you?"

"What? It's a fetish club. That ain't outta the realm of possibilities. I could develop a fetish for licking frosting off pound cake, if you know what I mean."

Ivan said, "I've gotta do one thing before I can join you guys."

Music blasted inside the warehouse. A multilevel dance floor started in the center of the room. Four bars were spread out, one on each side. A lighted staircase led to the second floor. He looked around as they made their way into the main room. Lots of leather. Lots of chains. Lots of piercings and tats on the partiers. So far he hadn't seen anyone on a leash like at Twisted.

Blue pointed to the staircase. "Fetish clothing and demonstrations are up here."

"Where's the VIP section?" Fisher asked.

"Upstairs, on the other end. If we walk through the fetish area, we'll hit it."

Fisher, Blue, and Knox started toward the stairs. Deacon hung back.

"You staying down here on the dance floor to get your groove thang on?"

"Jesus. You're an old fucker. Who even says 'groove thang' anymore? I thought I saw someone I know. I'll catch up with you guys."

At the top of the stairs were warning signs that the demonstrations were given by trained professionals and no one should attempt to duplicate the scenes without guidance from an experienced professional.

Yeah, like that'd keep people like these, who live on the fringe, from experimenting.

Booths that sold fetish items were lined against the wall. A long display table had cuffs and spiked collars, jewelry, but no nipple clamps. His first thought was that he'd love to see Shiori wearing those, a golden chain between her tits weighted with jewels.

Fisher tapped him on the arm. "Check that out."

In the next booth was a display of latex and rubber clothes. They carried more colors than just the standard black. A woman in a catsuit was demonstrating how to put on a latex mask that only had one small mouth opening. The second she put it over her face, Knox had to look away. Just thinking about being so covered up and only able to suck air through a tiny hole made his lungs seize up. At Twisted he'd always declined to monitor the rooms where breath play was involved. He heard that rasping wheeze for breath and found himself clawing at his own throat.

He wandered to the next booth, which had rows of floggers, whips, paddles.

"Anything you'd like to try out?" asked a young woman who looked far too adolescent to be shilling punishment items.

"Just looking."

Then Knox saw her exchange an eye roll with the scruffy punk beside her that plainly said, "This guy is old."

His pride surfaced. "You know, why don't you hand me that nine-inch single tail."

She looked confused. "All of our whips are longer than nine inches—"

"The handle size is nine inches." He leaned over and pulled it off the pegboard. Then he ran his hand down the whip, trying to find the balance. "I'd like this more if the handle weren't braided. Chances are high in a long session I'd end up with blisters." He flashed his teeth. "And if wanted pain, I'd be on the receiving end of the whip instead of the giving end." He replaced it on the board and moved on, unable to hide his smirk.

"Great bluff," Fisher said. "I almost believed you were some kind of S and M guy."

Jesus. He'd forgotten that Blue and Fisher weren't aware of that part of his life.

The last two booths on this side didn't interest him—foot-fetish stuff and role-playing costumes. He turned to ask Blue and Fisher if they were ready to hit the VIP section, when he saw a flash of black.

Weird. That looked the way Shiori's hair moved when she was doing katas with her hair down. Then he saw it again.

He cut through the crowd until he could see what was going on.

Goddammit. It *was* her. She had some guy bent over a spank-ing bench and was whacking his ass with a long paddle. The guy had pulled his jeans down, keeping his butt covered in plaid boxers.

He heard the chant, "Ten more, ten more," and saw Katie, Molly, and Fee as the instigators surrounding her. They were laughing and hanging on one another like they were really drunk.

His focus zoomed back to Shiori. What the fuck was she doing?

After two really hard blows, Knox stepped in and snagged her forearm mid-strike. "Enough. You're done."

"Why'd you stop?" As soon as the guy on the spanking bench looked up at her with worshipful eyes, Knox lost it. No one got to look at his Mistress like that except him. *No one.*

Before Shiori bent down to talk to the guy, Knox was crouch-ing next to him, obstructing her from his line of sight. "Look at me," he demanded.

The guy's pleasure-glazed eyes tried to find focus. "What?"

"Pull your pants up and get the fuck out of here."

"But . . . she—"

"Is too fucking good for you. And if you look at her like that again, I will beat the fuck out of you."

His pulse had shot through the roof, and he could feel his anger heating his skin.

"Sorry, man. We were just playing around."

"Not with her. *Never* with her. Got it?"

He nodded and pushed to his feet, yanking up his pants as he scurried away.

Knox counted to ten before he stood. Then he faced down the woman who'd probably beat the fuck out of him for what he'd just done.

Shiori was studying him coolly. "What are you doing here?"

The woman defined beautiful, but she wouldn't appreciate the compliment now. "Ivan invited us." He might as well just face this head-on. He crowded her, blocking her from her friends' view and out of their earshot. "What the hell were you doing whaling on that guy?"

"The people selling this shit"—she shook the paddle in Knox's face—"don't even know how to use it. So I said I'd show them."

"Did you pick him or did he volunteer?"

"He volunteered. And you don't get to be pissy about this."

"The fuck I don't. You aren't his Mistress; you're *mine*. And I already told you I don't goddamn share what's mine."

Shiori blinked. "I didn't know you'd be here."

"That doesn't make it all right."

Then Katie wormed her way between them. "Can you guys cut the arguing for one night? We're here having some fun, doing some kinky stuff. And, Knox, I don't think anyone cares that Shiori is an instructor at Black Arts, if you're worried how that looks."

Katie could go right on thinking that was his issue. "She represents us wherever she goes."

"So she spanked a hipster in public—most people would've let her go on beating him longer. It was all in good fun. No harm, no foul. No one got hurt, right?"

Knox kept his gaze affixed to Shiori's.

"Truce for tonight?" Katie pleaded. "Let's drink and celebrate Ivan's birthday."

"How long have you four been celebrating?" Knox asked.

"All damn day." Katie nudged him. "You need to catch up."

Katie was a fun drunk, but a determined one, and he knew better than to outwardly circumvent her. "Lead the way."

They followed single file behind her. Everyone had filled in around the table marked with the single balloon. Molly sat between Fisher and Deacon. Blue and Fee were laughing in the corner. Katie plopped right on Ivan's lap. Two chairs were left, and Knox pulled out one for Shiori automatically. She sat with a murmured, "Thanks."

"Ivan needs to do a birthday shot," Katie said. "So what do you want, birthday boy?"

Ivan whispered something that sent Katie into a fit of giggles. "Such a dirty mind. You definitely should get spanked for that." She squinted at Shiori. "You oughta dish out Ivan's birthday spankings since you were so good with that paddle."

"Yeah, how did you manage to hit that guy on the butt in the same spot every time?" Molly asked.

"Yeah, and that was *after* you'd been drinking," Fee said.

Deacon quirked an eyebrow at Knox.

Knox manufactured a blank look.

Shiori shrugged. "Accuracy is accuracy whether in martial arts or other activities."

"I hear ya." Molly nudged Fisher. "My accuracy has improved since Fisher has taken me on."

"What do you mean 'taken you on'?" Deacon asked in a combative tone.

"I'm giving Molly private boxing lessons," Fisher said.

"Whose idea was that?"

"Mine," Molly said. "So back off."

"The hell I will." Deacon leaned back and glared at Fisher. "Since when is it all right to poach another instructor's student?"

"What? Whoa. I didn't know—"

"That's because there's nothing to know," Molly told Fisher. "I'm in his kickboxing classes. That's it. If I want to hire you for private lessons, that's my business."

"Is it, Shihan?" Deacon demanded.

Knox looked at all the players and held up his hands. "I'm out of this one."

The birthday shots arrived.

Forcing himself to be jovial, he knocked back the vodka. But it seemed he was the only one projecting a happy face.

Blue was flat-out growling in the corner, watching Katie's exuberance over Ivan's birthday. Whenever Katie looked at Blue, she made a lewd comment. But Blue refused to take the bait.

Fisher and Fee were taking advantage of the open bar. So far they'd downed Titty Twister shots, Blow Job shots, and were flirting as they waited for the next round.

Katie's good humor disappeared when the cocktail waitress struck up a conversation with Blue—and Blue couldn't tear his eyes away from the woman's gigantic breasts.

Molly and Deacon went from ignoring each other to getting right in each other's faces as they whispered and argued.

And Shiori wouldn't even look at him.

Enough.

Knox stood to make his escape. "I'm gonna walk around for a few minutes."

As expected, no one noticed his departure.

But a minute later, after he'd nearly cleared the hallway, a hand slipped through his. He glanced down at Shiori.

"Nice try, leaving me there with the horny, drunk, and bickering bunch."

He laughed.

Shiori moved in until they were chest-to-chest. "I love your laugh. That's the first time I've heard it this week."

"Is that your way of saying you missed me?"

"Yes."

"So prove it."

Immediately, she pulled him into an alcove. Then her hands were on his neck and she brought his mouth to hers and proceeded to kiss him until his lungs were filled with her scent and her taste filled his mouth.

The kiss didn't slow. It just kept getting hotter.

He forced himself to put the brakes on. "Damn, woman. What you do to me with just a kiss."

"Need to make an adjustment in your jeans before we go back?" she said with a cocky smirk.

"Yeah." He swept her hair over her shoulder. "What if I said I didn't want to go back?"

"They wouldn't miss us."

"Then let's go look around."

"We have to pretend we're not enjoying walking around together," she warned him.

"I'll send you dirty looks once in a while."

"As long as you're secretly thinking dirty thoughts."

"So dirty I'm afraid my eyes will turn brown."

She laughed. "Come on."

Off the main floor was another room with more shops. These booths had demonstrations. The vendor selling candles was doing a wax-play demo. Same with the violet wand vendor. A small crowd had gathered in the back, so they moved in that direction to see what was going on.

Rope play.

An African-American woman with huge tits was sitting in a

chair while a man tried to get his ropes untangled—which should've been dealt with before the demo. The man kept up a running dialogue. When people got bored and started to leave, the rope model pulled on her hoodie and left too.

Knox was about to move on when the guy said, "Do I have any volunteers?"

"For what?" Knox asked.

"To be tied up." His gaze rolled over Knox. "You interested?"

"No. But I am interested in doing the tying."

"That's not possible. I'm a trained professional. This is not as easy as it looks."

"I didn't say it was."

A challenging look settled on his face. "You know what, hotshot? Put your money where your smart mouth is."

"I will, thanks. Do you have Japanese hemp rope?"

"No. You get to use these." He kicked the pile of ropes toward Knox. "Knock yourself out."

"I need a volunteer." He pretended to scan the crowd. Then he crooked his finger at Shiori. "You look like the type of woman who likes to tie men up in knots."

She rolled her eyes.

"Let's turn the tables on that. Come on up here, darlin'."

Shiori affected a look of concern. "I don't know. Is it safe?"

A hefty woman in a bustier nudged her. "Honey, if you won't do it, I will. I'd love to have him putting his big hands all over me."

As Shiori strode forward, she mouthed, "No nudity."

Knox faced her toward the audience and whispered, "No one but me gets to see those perfect tits." He checked the rope. Wasn't the best, but it'd do for this quick demo.

Quick? You'll have her tied up. Under your control. Why wouldn't you drag this out as long as possible?

Great idea.

"Take off your blouse, please."

Shiori undid the buttons and pulled the fabric free from her skirt. She handed her shirt to Knox and he draped it over his neck.

The camisole tank she wore was shiny and the folds rippled like water. He smoothed his hand down her spine. "Can you clasp your elbows behind you?"

"Like this?"

"Yes. Loosen your shoulders." He dragged his fingertips down the backs of her arms, knowing how sensitive that area was. The creases of her elbows received a gentle stroke before he scraped his nails across the insides of her forearms.

Knox purposely kept the rope bundle at Shiori's feet. As he fed more rope into the design, she'd feel the rough jute teasing her bare leg.

As he wrapped her wrists, his fingers brushed the slice of skin between the waistband of her skirt and her top. So warm and soft. He let his breath flow across her neck as he found the perfect angle to finish this part of the binding. Then he crossed his rope and stood in front of her.

Shiori had closed her eyes. Her lips were parted; outwardly everything about her screamed stillness.

But Knox knew better. He felt her coiled energy, tension thrumming through her. And that filled him with a rush of power.

He stretched the rope between her breasts and didn't pretend he wasn't feeling her up. He had to check the tension from her lower belly up and over her chest to her shoulder. When he started that process on the other side, he rubbed the backs of his knuckles over her nipple, happy she hadn't worn a bra so he could feel how she reacted to his touch.

This rope session had declared war on his cock, making it so fucking hard he ached. It didn't help that his jeans pinched his balls even when he wasn't bent forward. But his discomfort was worth it seeing hers. She'd given herself over to him—a very un-Domme-like move for her.

Another knot allowed a caress of her sweet, hard nipple. He heard her swift intake of breath.

He'd finished the chest harness but didn't want to lose the moment, so he skated his palms up the outside of her arms to her shoulders. With his back to the small audience, he could speak softly and only she could hear.

"You are beautiful. And if it were just us with rope play, I'd kiss you as I untied the ropes."

"Where would you kiss me?"

"Everywhere you allowed it."

She smiled.

He stood behind her and said, "Behold the simple chest harness," to the crowd.

A smattering of applause.

"How long did it take you to learn to work rope like that?" one guy asked.

"I'm lucky enough to work with a kinbaku and shibari rope master. But this harness is a beginner's level design."

As Knox answered more questions, he started untying her. The spectators drifted away and he quickened his pace. "Any numbness?"

"A little in my arms."

He vigorously rubbed them to get the circulation going.

"You're good at this, Shihan."

"I learned from the best."

That's when he realized her entire body vibrated. Dammit, she'd started to come down from rope subspace. As he helped her put her shirt back on, he said, "I don't have a blanket to wrap around you."

She opened her eyes halfway, and the lust he saw shining in those golden depths caused a growl of need to escape. "Then I guess you'll just have to wrap me in your arms."

The last of the rope hit the floor.

Knox had his hands on her hips as he propelled her through the crowd. He spied a side exit and then pushed through the door.

They'd ended up in an alley access, out of the elements and in a dark recess away from curious eyes.

The sexual beast inside Knox roared, desperate for that connection of bodies. His mouth attacked hers, tongues warring and breath coming hard and fast as they fed the fire between them.

Clamping his hands on her ass, he hoisted Shiori against the brick wall. The insides of her thighs pressed against the outsides of his hips, and a sharp stab of pain came from her stilettos jabbing into him.

Fuck. He didn't care if her shoes gouged out chunks of his flesh. He finally had her where he needed her: writhing against him, her pussy hot enough and wet enough to leave a mark on the front of his jeans.

She slipped her hands beneath his shirt to get at his chest. Her fingers clutched his pecs with enough pressure she'd leave marks as she scraped her thumbnails across his nipples.

As frenzied as he was to fuck her, to finally know the wet heat of her body surrounding his shaft, to hear the sounds she made as she came around his cock, he knew she'd decide when that happened.

So he squeezed her butt cheeks, and each time he pressed, his fingers inched closer to her core.

"Knox," she breathed against his lips. "I need . . ."

"Tell me and I'll give it to you." His mouth was on her throat, drinking in the sweet and salty taste of her skin.

"Oh god. I could come just from your mouth sucking on my neck right there."

"Then come for me, Nushi."

Shiori canted her hips, grinding her mound into his hard length, letting her head fall to the side, giving him full access to her neck.

He stayed still, letting her move on him as he used his teeth and the soft suction of his mouth to drive her to the edge.

Her fingers dug into his chest and her legs tightened in that second before the orgasm hit. Her soft noises of pleasure filled his head and taunted the beast inside him that demanded the same satisfaction.

All for her. You'll get your turn.

She scraped her fingertips down to his abdomen and lazily stroked him. "That was a good warm-up."

He nuzzled her collarbone, wishing he could hoist her higher to get to her tits.

"Do you think you can make me come again?"

"If you let me use my cock."

"What will you do if I make you get me off but won't let you come?"

Knox gritted his teeth against the protesting pulse in his cock and balls. "Whatever Nushi wants. Use my body to please yours."

"Knox. Look at me."

He opened his eyes but wasn't able to hide his need or his frustration.

She brought her hands up and framed his face. "Undo your pants."

He fumbled with the button and zipper. Once undone, his jeans fell to his feet.

"Briefs too."

One tug and his bare ass was exposed for all to see.

Shiori rubbed her thumb along the inside of his bottom lip. "Do you want to make love to me?"

Say yes.

But an anguished, "No," escaped.

"No?" she repeated.

Then Knox was nose to nose with her. "No. I want to fuck you so hard you'll still feel me inside you next week."

Keeping her eyes locked on his, she sucked his lower lip into her mouth and bit down with enough force he flinched. She flicked her tongue over the spot and said, "Then do it."

A snarl left his throat, and he reached between them to yank her panties aside. His fingers came away wet. As much as he wanted to bring his fingers to his mouth and suck off every bit of her sweet juices, that hot, wet cunt was his for the taking.

Knox shifted his stance and his cock head connected with her opening. He rocked into her with such power he ended up on his toes.

"Oh, fuck, you're big," she said with a groan.

He put his mouth on her ear. "You'll get used to it." Then he plowed into her repeatedly, her pussy a hot, wet haven.

He released a groan every time he bottomed out inside her, feeling the wet kiss of her inner muscles contracting around his shaft. He buried his mouth in her throat, trying to taste her, touch her, fuck her, mark her—all at the same time.

"I want your hands above me on the wall, Knox."

He started to raise his head to protest, but she said, "Now."

The sharpness in her tone had him obeying immediately. And this angle didn't give him as much leverage since he had a different balance point. He had to move slower.

The fingers in his hair tightened, and Shiori pulled his head back to get at his mouth.

Her lips captured his in a hot kiss that shot straight to the inferno stage.

With his cock urging him to kick up the pace, Knox discovered he could snap his hips at the last second and drive into her hard.

She broke the kiss to whisper, "Yes. Like that. Just like that."

With Shiori's mouth on his, her grip on his hair, the slow, hard fucking he was giving her, he started to feel that buzz in his balls.

Not yet. Jesus.

"Knox," she said between kisses. "Slide side to side."

He gyrated his pelvis as he stroked in and out.

"Don't stop. Don't go faster."

His arms began to shake, and he bent his head to flick the sweet spot on her neck with his tongue. That tease elicited a gasp, and she held his head there with an iron grip.

The fog of lust had dissipated into a sensual haze where his sole focus was on the precise way he fucked her. A slow grinding glide, a hard thrust. His world boiled down to the hot clasp of her pussy around his shaft, her hand fisting his hair and his mouth at her throat.

"Yes. Now."

Knox pulled her skin between his teeth and sucked, sending her entire body into spasms.

By the time her tremors subsided, sweat dripped down his back and dampened his chest.

Shiori's palms smoothed over his cheeks, and she tipped his head back to look at him. "You did well."

"It was all for you."

"Now it's your turn." She brushed her lips across his. "Ask me."

"Please, Nushi, let me come."

"Come for me now."

He slammed into her one last time, and immediately one of the most powerful orgasms of his life roared through him. As the pulses slowed and stopped, he realized why everything had felt so damn good from the start, why his sensitivity was heightened. It had nothing to do with a Domme–sub encounter; it was because they'd forgotten a condom.

Shit.

When he tried to pull out, Shiori's heels dug into the backs of his legs. "Stay still."

"Dammit, Shiori, we forgot a condom."

She froze.

Knox looked at her. "I'm sorry. I know it's not an excuse—"

"It's okay. It's more my fault than yours because I'm supposed to be looking out for you."

He rested his forehead to hers. "How about we just say we both fucked up?"

"Okay." She ran her hands over his head. "Kind of a buzz-kill."

"Yeah. But it was goddamn great before that."

"I thought so too." She pressed her lips to his. "This is not a big deal. I can take one of those 'oops' pills in the morning and we'll be covered."

"You're sure?"

"Positive."

"Does that mean you're not interested in coming home with me tonight?"

"Are you asking me?"

"Yes." Knox let his lips trail down her temple and cheek. He nuzzled her ear. "I'd like you in my bed all night. This offer does include breakfast in the morning and a workout partner."

"Do you have condoms?"

His heart rate spiked. "A brand-new box. I had them for the other night, but it turned out we didn't need them."

She laughed. "Maybe we'll need them tonight."

"Is that a yes?"

"Yes."

"Thank you." Knox pulled out and set Shiori on her feet. As they righted their clothes, he remembered he'd ridden to the club with Fisher. The thought of going back in and trying to act normal caused his stomach to knot.

"What's wrong?"

"I didn't drive."

She shrugged. "I can call for a ride from my car service."

"We'll take a cab."

"And that's different from a car service . . . how? Besides, cabs smell bad and they're more dangerous."

The difference was he'd be paying for the cab. Not having the billionaire heiress squiring him around. "We're taking a cab."

A hand slapped on his chest and he looked at her.

"Eyes on the ground."

Shit. He dropped his gaze.

"This is not a time for your pride. This is about convenience and economy. I pay a monthly fee to have a car available to me twenty-four-seven. It's a waste of your money to get a cab. So you can just suck it up and enjoy the ride. Understand?"

"Yes, ma'am."

She pulled out her cell phone. "And while you're enjoying the ride, try to come up with a suitable apology for butting into a situation I had under control."

"You mean the guy you were spanking?"

"Yes. And did he really deserve the threat of what you'd do to him if he ever looked at me again?"

Knox balled his hands into fists. "With all due respect, ma'am, that low-life fucker didn't deserve your attention. He certainly didn't appreciate it, and I didn't appreciate the way he looked at you."

"So you took it upon yourself to defend me?"

"No. I wanted to make it clear to you that you don't need to find an unworthy whipping boy when you've got me. I was jealous of the attention you paid to him. And I was pissed he was looking at you with the same adoration I would've been had you given me the chance." That part was hard to admit.

Her gaze softened. "I like having you as my champion, Knox."

He relaxed.

"But this incident will require some discipline."

Fuck. Nothing in her eyes was soft now.

But why did the idea of being at her mercy make his dick rock hard again?

CHAPTER ELEVEN

SHIORI wasn't surprised by the sullen look on Knox's face.

She probably should've waited to tell Knox about his impending punishment. But then again, letting him think about what he'd done and how she intended to correct that behavior might be easier on both of them since this was the first time he'd screwed up.

In the scheme of things, it wasn't even that bad. And she'd gotten a secret thrill when Knox told the guy he wasn't worthy of her. Knox's jealousy surprised her.

It shouldn't have. He's the type of man who, once he stakes his claim, he'll do anything to protect and defend it.

And yet again Shiori was glad they wouldn't be playing at Twisted. Because Knox would spend his time snapping and snarling at any sub who even looked at her, and she'd be forced to keep him leashed. Which would be a pity because the man was magnificent when defending her honor. She'd never experienced anything like it before.

Silence had settled between them as the car service drove them to Knox's house. He held her hand, but he'd directed his attention out the window. She ran her fingers through his hair. Such a fighter. Such a leader. Such an amazing lover.

Knox leaned into her touch, letting his head fall back against the headrest and closing his eyes. "Why are you staring at me, Nushi?"

"Because you are so very nice to look at."

"Am I just a toy to you?" he asked softly. "Take me out and play with me when it suits you, and the rest of the time I'm shelved someplace where I can be admired but not touched?"

She'd never credited him with so much insight. "Have I made you feel that way?"

"Not yet. But I do worry that it's in my future."

She rose up and tugged his earlobe between her teeth. "It's not in your future tonight."

He turned his head, and their faces were so close their noses almost touched. Those blue eyes were dark with determination. "I want to renegotiate the time we spend together."

"Now?"

"At some point tonight."

"All right. We can discuss it."

The car stopped. And of course Knox leaped out to help her out before the driver had a chance to.

Once they were inside the house, he led her to the kitchen. He hoisted her onto the breakfast bar, the highest counter, which gave her the height advantage.

"I didn't mean to embarrass you."

"That's not an apology."

His nostrils flared. "I don't know if I can apologize, because if I had it to do over again, I'd do the same damn thing. If that increases my punishment, so be it."

"Such a stubborn man." She framed his face in her hands. "I don't expect I'll have to discipline you often. But when I do, the punishment will fit the crime. So since you switched into the Dominant role, I have to remind you you're not a switch. I want you to go into your backyard and cut a switch from a tree and bring it to me."

"Yes, ma'am."

Then he was gone out the side door.

Shiori closed her eyes and played through the scene in her head.

Knox returned sooner than she expected. He handed her a thin branch. By the green color, she knew it was all new growth. Lightweight. Lots of give.

"Good."

He said nothing as he kept his head bowed.

"Go into the living room and strip. Then wait for me."

After he was out of sight, she slid off the counter and tested the give of the switch. The top section was so thin it almost had the feel of a stiff whip.

Okay. She could do this. She *had* to do this. For him. For them.

When Shiori reached the living room and saw Knox was standing in rest position, she snapped her fingers.

No response.

She moved in behind him. "For future reference, when I say wait for me, that means on your knees."

He lowered to the floor.

She dragged the tip of the switch across his shoulder blades. Down his spine. Drew a zigzag pattern on his back and tapped his butt cheeks. "Now I want you to brace your hands against the wall by the front door but remain on your knees."

"Mistress?"

"Yes?"

"Do you want me to crawl over there?"

"Knox. Look at me."

When he turned his head, she saw two spots of color had darkened his cheeks. He'd schooled any anger, but that telltale muscle in his jaw ticced.

She set her hand on his shoulder. "I told you no humiliation. I meant it. Of course you can walk."

He pressed his lips into her knuckles. Then he rolled to his feet and walked to the wall.

Once he'd dropped into position, she moved beside him. "Ten marks from the switch."

Knox said nothing.

"You will count them out." She landed the first blow high on his back.

He flinched and said, "One."

She bent closer to see how the mark looked. Red, but not too much. She could go a little harder.

So she did.

She laid four marks across the broadest part of his back. Then she gave the last six on his ass. And with those marks, she put more power into it because that part of the anatomy could take it.

Afterward she ran her hands all over the marks, feeling the heat and the sweat on his skin. Last she placed a kiss at the base of his neck. "You did beautifully."

He grunted.

"Need me to help you up?"

"No. I've got it." Once he was upright he said, "Do I need to ask permission to use the bathroom?"

So he was still a little surly. Understandable. But not acceptable. "No. You don't have to ask. But watch the attitude," she warned, "or I'll come up with a more creative punishment than a switch for that sassy mouth."

"I apologize."

"Slip on your shorts. Take a moment. I'll be waiting for you in the bedroom."

Shiori presented the Domme carriage and attitude, but inside her stomach churned. Although she and Knox had had sex tonight, this was also the first time she'd used discipline. He wasn't into pain, so there'd been no pleasure in it for either of them.

But it'd been necessary.

Hadn't it?

What if he said this was one and done? They'd fucked, and maybe their lust for each other would cool. Would it be easy for him to say he wasn't interested in Dominant-and-submissive games?

It wasn't paranoia on her part. From the start Knox hadn't been convinced he had submissive tendencies. Now, knowing that she could be deliberate in her punishments . . . he'd likely backtrack.

How could she convince him to stay the course? That they'd figure this out together?

She spun back around and was startled to see Knox leaning against the doorjamb, watching her pace.

His eyes weren't blank or cold, but wary. He'd dressed as she'd indicated, athletic shorts only, so maybe he wasn't about to get defiant. And because she needed to know if he was all in, she decided to test him. She snapped her fingers.

Surprise? Resignation? Both emotions appeared to cross his face. His steps were measured as he moved forward and dropped to his knees.

Her heart rolled over, and some of her worries faded into the background. She touched the top of his head and he rested his face against her thigh.

"Forgive me, Nushi."

"We're done with that, and we can move on."

"I know. But I . . . broke one of your rules yesterday."

Her eyes narrowed at him. "Which rule?"

"The only one you gave me."

"About not touching yourself?"

"Yes, ma'am. I gave in to temptation and jacked off last night."

"Explain."

"I observed you from the Crow's Nest as you taught the brown belt class. You were so fluid and dynamic in your movements, so exacting, and demanded the same from your students. My thoughts drifted back to Monday night. Getting to put my mouth on you and feeling how hard you came. I got so lost in remembering how you taste that I stuck my hand in my pants without really thinking and whacked off."

"Was it satisfying?"

"As I was coming? Yes. Afterward? No. The guilt ate at me, and I'd decided to lie to you when you asked."

Shiori counted to twenty before she responded. "You don't think that I can detect a lie?"

"I've no doubt you can."

"What changed your mind about telling me?"

"Your discipline. As much as I disliked it, I understood why you did it. And I realized if I did lie to you about my round of self-love, I'd be doing both of us a disservice. I'm supposed to be exploring this side of myself, and if I'm lying, that's holding back. I don't want to hold back."

Not entirely what she wanted to hear, but it was a start. "I appreciate your honesty. I'm not happy that you blatantly broke the rule, but you were thinking about me, which is different from if you'd been watching porn."

"You are far sexier with your gi on than most women are naked."

Shiori curled her hand beneath his jaw and tipped his head back to gaze into his eyes. "Hoping flattery will soften me up?"

"No, ma'am. It is the gospel truth."

"What was the sexiest thing about fucking me tonight, Knox?"

Sexual heat flared in his eyes. "That the urgency between us had built to the point we went at it in an alley with most of our clothes on and we forgot a fucking condom. That never happens with me. I've never craved a woman like I do you." He groaned and briefly closed his eyes. "I'm sitting here on my knees, my ass stinging, knowing I've got more punishment in store, and my dick is getting hard just imagining being with you again."

"Once you get going with the honesty, it's hard for you to stop," she murmured.

"I'm a talker. Drives Ronin and Deacon crazy, but a lot of stupid shit can be fixed or changed by a simple conversation."

"I'm happy you're a talker. I don't want to have to try to guess what you're feeling." She glanced down at his crotch. "Although sometimes physical reactions speak volumes."

He grinned.

"What am I going to do with you?" she murmured, mostly to herself.

"Are you asking for suggestions?"

She cocked her head. "If I were? What would you suggest?"

"You let me take you to bed."

"And then?"

"We either fall asleep twined together, or we stay awake a little longer."

"Meaning we could watch TV or something?" she teased.

"If you want." But it was apparent that wasn't what he wanted. *Since when does what a sub wants factor in?*

Always.

"Tell you what. I'm going to indulge in a hot shower in your stadium-sized bathroom. While I'm in there, get ready for bed. I'll need a T-shirt to sleep in. And I'd like a cup of tea before I go to sleep." She paused. "Do you have tea?"

"No, ma'am. Would you like me to go to the store and get some?"

She scraped her fingernail along his collarbone. "They wouldn't sell to you because I'd insist you go like this. But in the future I'd suggest you stock up on chamomile tea."

"Of course. Whatever you want."

"Stay in this position until I'm in the bathroom. Then you can make preparations for bed."

"Yes, Mistress."

Once inside the bathroom, she pinned her hair up. After she'd stripped and climbed in the huge shower, she wished she'd asked for instructions on how to turn it on since there were five different handles. She messed around until blessed hot water hit her.

Normally she didn't shower at night, but she needed a moment to find her balance. Because Knox was certainly doing his best to keep her off balance. He'd gone from possessive and unapologetic to contrite, then to teasing. She'd never met a man like him who wasn't afraid to show all the facets of himself.

She dried off and returned to the bedroom.

Knox lay in the middle of the big bed, the white sheets a perfect foil for his golden skin. He pushed up on his elbows when she approached. "How was your shower?"

"Excellent. But I think I might've pulled something in my back when I used that spanking board."

"Would you like a massage?"

"Yes." Shiori dropped the towel and stretched out facedown on the bed.

Knox straddled her butt, being careful not to sit on her. When he dug his thumbs into her neck, she moaned. He was gentle but thorough.

"You're quiet," she remarked when he started down her spine.

"I'm trying to relax you."

"It's working. I feel like I could just nod off."

"Go ahead."

"You have great hands."

Then he stopped massaging, and he swept his fingers across her shoulders and arms. His palms drifted down the middle of her back. When he reached her hips, his thumbs moved in a slow arc over the dimples above her butt. Then he did it again. Twice more.

And in that moment his tender caresses were more potent than his mouth on her nipples and his fingers on her sex.

She tapped his thigh and he moved, allowing her to roll over.

He touched her face. "What?"

"Grab a condom."

Knox's eyes darkened with desire. "You're not teasing me?"

"No."

He grabbed a condom and watched her watching him as he slowly rolled it on.

"Can I just say that I really love that you have a big cock."

He balanced on his knees at the end of the bed. "So you weren't being complimentary before when you called me a big dick?"

Shiori smirked. "No. Although that one time last month when you were demonstrating choke holds on me and had me tucked against you? You had a hard-on."

Knox crawled toward her. "You noticed that."

"Hard not to. But I was more afraid that you were turned on by the idea of choking me out than that you were hot for me."

He chuckled. "No comment."

She was surprised and pleased that he'd stopped to await further instructions.

But his focus was between her legs.

"See something you like?"

"Christ, Mistress, you have the prettiest cunt I've ever seen."

She reached down and lazily stroked a finger up and down her slit, watching him clench his jaw and his fists, fighting against his need to touch her and taste her. "How wet do you think I can make myself by doing this?"

Knox growled. "I can make you a lot wetter, a lot faster."

There was his male ego. "Prove it. With just your mouth on my pretty cunt. Let's see how fast you can make me come this time."

He scooted in closer and bent at the waist. It was sexy as hell the way he paused above her tender flesh and just breathed her in before he lowered his mouth.

She loved that first contact of wet heat. Then the exploration of a soft tongue down her slit and back up to her clit. The gentle probing. The tease of his breath. The gentle sucking of her pussy lips and the sweep of his tongue down to her hole and jamming that wicked, wiggling tongue so deep inside her pussy she felt the bite of his teeth.

Then he used his flicking tongue to outline the flesh of her pussy between her inner folds, following the edge up to the top, where that ridge of skin covered her clit.

She wanted to remind him this was supposed to be a fast orgasm, and he appeared to be taking his sweet time, when he firmed his lips and pushed the skin up and suctioned his mouth around that hidden nub.

Normally she preferred indirect contact with her clit at first, but this . . . this concentrated, relentless sucking made her hips arch off the bed. And it was so fucking hot when he held her hips down, forcing her to take his sensual assault and showing her a bit of his defiance; she'd told him he couldn't use his hands on her pussy, but she hadn't said he couldn't use them at all.

He never wavered in his constant suction.

Her nipples tightened, and the zing of sensation started in her tailbone and shot straight to her core. That was the only warning before the orgasm blasted through her.

Knox sucked hard on that pulsing pearl, whipping the tip of his tongue back and forth with such precision the spasms seemed never ending.

So when the pulsating stopped, she actually whimpered.

Knox chuckled against her sensitive tissues, and the vibration made her breath catch. He lifted his head and kissed a path up between her hip bones.

She looked down at him as he ran those talented lips across her lower belly, his eyes dancing with pride and heat.

"So, Mistress, was that fast enough for you?"

"You certainly love a challenge," she murmured, reaching down to run her fingers over his hair.

"When it comes to you? Yes."

Shiori had the biggest challenge yet for him. It'd be interesting to see how he handled it. "Lie on your back."

Knox pushed up and rolled over; the motion made the bed shake.

She straddled his groin and balanced herself with her hands on his pecs. "Hold your cock."

His big hand slipped between their bodies and he aligned the tip with her opening.

"Stay still."

Knox's entire body went rigid as she pushed his shaft inside her slowly until her clit pressed against the root of his cock.

"You feel good in me."

"Yes, ma'am."

"I'm going to fuck you, Knox. I'll ride you hard and fast until I come again."

"Anything you want." His seemed about to say something else, but he closed his mouth.

"Talk to me."

"Can I touch you while you're riding me?"

She leaned down and kissed him. "As much as you want. Anywhere you want."

"Thank god."

As soon as she pushed upright, Knox sat up too.

He kissed her neck while his right hand slid up her back. He ran the tips of his fingers up and down her spine from the dimples above her ass to the nape of her neck. His right hand cupped her breast, alternating between kneading the flesh and teasing her nipple with a combination of sweeping caresses and hard pinches.

Shiori rested her forearms on his shoulders as she propelled herself up and down on his thick, hard shaft. Squeezing her cunt muscles around the base, she started grinding her clit against his pubic hair on every glide back up.

Knox constantly moved his hands. Tormenting her breasts. Squeezing her ass. Dragging those wonderfully rough fingertips up and down her thighs. All the while his mouth focused on her neck, and her ears, and her shoulders. Sucking kisses. Biting kisses. Soft nibbles. The man worshipped her body with every caress, every kiss, every stuttered breath. And yet he gave her total control. He didn't rock his hips or thrust up into her. He let her fuck him. That surrender made this connection all the more powerful.

And she fucked him hard, using the strength in her thigh muscles to lift and lower her body. A light sheen of sweat coated her skin from the exertion. But as much as she rolled her pelvis and clenched around his cock, it didn't get her any closer to orgasm.

He sensed her frustration. He brought his hands up, curling them around her face and forcing her attention to him. "Let me get you there."

"We're not changing positions," she warned.

He rubbed his lips over hers. "I'd never presume, Mistress. But if you lean back and grab on to my thighs, I'll have more room to touch you how you need it."

Shiori smashed her mouth to his, kissing him crazily, loving the tender way he held on to her face even as she bit and sucked at his mouth.

Then she leaned back, clamping her hand just above his knees. Her hair swung free, drifting over the tops of his thighs. She kept her pelvis aligned with his so her movement didn't cause his cock to pop out.

Knox's mouth followed the arch of her neck, down past her collarbone to her left breast. He sank his teeth into her nipple before he sucked away the sting with suctioning pulls. His right hand traveled down the side of her body to her hip and then slid over to her core. Her clit spasmed once as he began to stroke.

She whispered, "Faster," and groaned when he achieved the perfect amount of friction.

The orgasm that seemed so elusive now teased her with being so close.

"I need . . ."

"What? Tell me and I'll give it to you."

"Push your hips up when I push down."

The first time he did it, she moaned. The second time he did it, she felt that goose-bump-inducing tingle. The third time she remained still while he fucked up into her hard.

That sent her tumbling over the edge. All the good parts of her body throbbed; the nipple he sucked on, her clit that he stroked, her pussy clenching around his cock. A gray haze filled her vision, and she lost herself to her release.

A tickling on her ear brought her back to reality. She groaned as Knox tugged on her earlobe.

"You are beyond sexy. Seeing you come . . . I could've come just from watching you."

Shiori wrapped her hands around the back of his neck, pressing her thumbs beneath his jaw as she tilted his head and kissed him. A sweet coming down from an orgasm kiss. Then she rested her forehead to his. "You are everything I've ever wanted in a submissive but I've never had. Thank you. So it's hard for me to tell you that you don't get to come."

"Fuck."

"I appreciated your honesty in telling me you rubbed one out this week. But I specifically told you not to. Coming by your hand means you blew the chance to come inside me."

She felt him grit his teeth. Felt him clench his ass cheeks together. Felt his breathing change.

But he didn't utter a single word of protest.

After several long moments, he sighed and buried his face in her throat. "I'm sorry."

"I know you are." She smoothed her hand down the back of his

UNRAVELED { 167 }

neck. "Now you're done with discipline or punishment or whatever we choose to call it."

"So are you leaving now?"

"I want to stay with you all night, Knox."

She felt him smile against her throat. "Good."

Shiori pecked him on the mouth and separated their bodies.
"Ditch the condom and come to bed." She narrowed her eyes at
him. "Straight back here, and your dick better be that hard when you
return."

He rolled off the bed and gave her a regret-filled once-over.
"Trust me, Mistress, it'll still be hard. I learned my lesson."

She smiled. "See? You're already making progress the first night."

CHAPTER TWELVE

SHIORI woke up alone, naked. The sunlight streaming through the blinds indicated she'd slept later than usual. She rolled onto Knox's side of the bed and wrapped her arms around his pillow.

It'd been ages since she'd spent the night with a guy. Being so vulnerable in sleep beside a stranger had always scared her. After her divorce she'd gone a little wild, trying to reconcile the Domme side of herself with societal expectations. Hadn't taken much time to figure out as long as a guy was getting laid, he didn't care who was in charge. So her hookups had been brief.

The aroma of bacon cooking wafted to her, and her stomach grumbled. Just as she started to get up, Knox walked into the room.

God, he was a drool-worthy sight first thing in the morning. He'd tamed his hair, but blond scruff spread from his jaw down his neck. He was bare-chested, and a pair of navy plaid flannel pants hung low on his hips.

And his smile when he saw she was awake seemed brighter than the sunshine. "Morning, gorgeous."

"Morning yourself. Something smells good."

"Nothing fancy, so don't get your hopes up."

"Anything is good since I usually eat sugar-coated cereal."

"Ronin would have a fit."

She smiled. "So, was your offer for breakfast in bed?"

His hungry gaze roamed over her naked body. "Only if you're my breakfast this morning."

Her stomach did that slow, lazy roll, and she knew Knox feasting on her would be the perfect way to start the day. She stretched her arms above her head. "I'm all yours."

Knox crawled across the bottom of the bed. Once he reached the middle, he pushed to his knees and placed his palms on the insides of her thighs, spreading her wide-open. "Am I waiting on your signal?"

"No. You can—" The rest was lost when his mouth engulfed her pussy. She was quickly lost in a flurry of wonderful sensations. His softly stroking tongue. Firm-lipped bites. Sucking kisses, one after another. He spread her to reveal her tender tissues and fastened his mouth there, making her arch off the mattress. He didn't talk; he just built her up lick by lick, stroke by stroke, a teasing flick of his tongue.

When Knox inserted two fingers into her pussy and rubbed her inner wall while he lapped at her clit, she went off like a rocket.

She gasped and bucked against his mouth until the last spasm faded. She slumped into the mattress with a groaning sigh.

Meanwhile his talented mouth peppered the insides of her thighs and across her mound with kisses.

After her brain went back online, she pushed up onto her elbows.

Their eyes met, and he gave her clit one last suck before he lifted his head and grinned. "Breakfast of champions."

"Come here, crazy man."

Knox crawled up her body and hung over her on all fours. "Yes, ma'am?"

Shiori wreathed her arms around his neck and brought his

mouth down for a lazy kiss, loving the way she could smell her musk on his face and taste herself on his lips and tongue. After the kiss changed into tender smooches, she said, "How's your ass today?"

"Not bad."

"Did you rub one out this morning when you got up with morning wood?"

He pulled back and stared into her eyes. "I assumed when you wouldn't let me come last night that I couldn't take care of myself until you gave me the go-ahead."

"You're right. And because I reward good behavior, you can fuck me in any position and you can come when you want."

"Thank you, Nushi," he murmured against her lips. Then his mouth spread into a wide smile. "On your belly. I want you from behind."

She turned over and spread out, loving the decadent feeling of nakedness and the cool cotton sheet on her passion-warmed skin. Turning her head, she saw Knox reach for a condom and heard the sound of ripping plastic.

Warm lips trailed down her spine, and strong hands dug into her hips. "One of these days I'm gonna map every muscle in your back with my mouth. You're so strong, and that is so fucking sexy."

Chill bumps danced across her skin.

Knox hiked her hips up and aligned his cock, pushing into her on a slow glide. Then he stopped.

"Something wrong?"

"Everything is right when I'm inside you. I just wanted to watch your body swallowing my cock."

She bore down on him when he was buried fully.

"Keep doing that and I won't last long."

"Come when you want, remember?"

He pressed his chest into her back. "Which only means I'll wait until you come again." He nibbled on her ear. "That's guaranteed to set me off." He lifted up, and his thrusts intensified.

She snaked her hand between her thighs and rubbed her swollen clit. She probably couldn't come again so soon, but the fantastic way he was fucking her had definitely gotten her juices flowing.

Knox's hand started moving across her back, making long draws with his fingers like he was dragging them down a chalkboard.

Oh yeah, that was good.

"You like that," he murmured.

The more he touched her, the more her body responded. Then his hot breath fanned her shoulder. "Tell me what will get you there."

"Keep your hands on me."

As soon as Knox returned to the hard, sweeping press of his fingers, that tingling sensation started in her tailbone.

Shiori wasn't even touching her clit when she started to come. Her pussy clamped down on his cock and the pulsing rush happened deep inside her, sending another wash of vibrations through her.

"Jesus. Yes." Knox kept the same rhythm as he reached that point. She felt his cock jerking within her as his balls emptied.

He let out another grunt and started to slow the pumping of his hips. Before he stopped moving entirely, he pressed his chest into her back and dragged an openmouthed kiss from behind her ear to the ball of her shoulder. "You are amazing. Thank you." He pulled out and flipped her onto her back, taking a moment to kiss her thoroughly before he went to ditch the condom.

Now Shiori was too hyped up to go back to sleep. When Knox appeared by the side of the bed, he'd already slipped his lounge pants back on.

He held out his hand. "I'll finish cooking you breakfast."

"I'm not doing the walk of shame even in your kitchen by putting my club clothes back on. Do you have anything I could wear?"

Knox rummaged in the closet. He handed her a long-sleeved white shirt.

"This?"

He shrugged. "I wanna see you in one of my shirts, knowing you've got nothing on beneath it."

She shoved her arms into the sleeves. "Speaking of shirts? Only button-up or snap shirts when you're with me. I hate having to fight to get my hands on your chest."

"Yes, ma'am."

The tail of Knox's shirt brushed her knees. There seemed to be six inches of material left over in the sleeves. She stopped in front of him. "I look ridiculous."

"You look ridiculously sexy." He rolled the cuffs up past her elbows. "There. Now you look perfect." He kissed the top of her head. "Don't know what the hell happened to your panties."

"Do you have shorts with a drawstring? I don't want to leave cooter marks all over your kitchen."

He laughed. He opened the top drawer in his dresser and fished around until he found a pair of boxers. "Best I can do."

"That'll work." She slipped them on and followed him into the kitchen.

"I wasn't sure if you wanted eggs. Or I can make pancakes or French toast."

"Eggs would be great. Scrambled, please."

"Coming right up." Knox curled his hands around her waist and said, "Jump up," and hoisted her onto the counter.

Shiori swiped a piece of bacon off the rack and watched Knox crack four eggs and whip them with milk. Then he threw a pat of butter in the pan. When it sizzled, he poured in the egg mixture and dropped two pieces of bread in the toaster.

"I'd ask if there's anything I could do to help, but I'd probably electrocute us or burn the place down."

"No worries. I've got this handled."

"I like watching you cook."

Knox looked up, surprise on his face. "Really? Why?"

She shrugged. "I've never really had a man cook for me before."

Fearing she'd said too much, she added, "And because I can see the muscles in your biceps flexing as you're whipping eggs. It's sexy."

Then he was in her face. "Right now I wish I were a five-star chef so I could wow you with some fancy dish."

"I'm glad you're making me plain scrambled eggs while I sit on the counter next to you and steal all your bacon." She grinned and crunched another piece.

"I'm keeping track. Those two pieces are coming out of your bacon allotment."

"Or I could just command you to give me your bacon," she said sweetly.

Knox laughed. "She-Cat. I'm submissive in the bedroom only. Out here? I'll take you to the mat over bacon, baby."

He buttered the toast, dished up their plates, and divvied up the bacon. Then he insisted on feeding her. Which was sweet and funny and intoxicating and just so . . . Knox.

Afterward, he cleaned up.

Shiori was ogling his ass, wondering how long he'd last in a game of blow-job torture, when he spun around and leveled that stare at her. "What?"

"You do realize you made a devious chuckle that had my balls shriveling with fear?"

"I wasn't aware of that."

"The hell you weren't." He stepped between her knees and tugged her to the edge of the counter. "Will it startle you into di-aling your car service when I say I want to hang out with you like a normal couple today?" He smoothed her hair down with his hands. "Watch a movie or TV or go for a drive."

Four loud raps sounded, followed by the squeak of the door opening and a feminine voice yelling, "Knox? I saw your truck outside, so I know you're home."

He swore and headed to intercept his houseguest. "Vivie. What the hell? Since when do you just walk into someone's house?"

"Fair game when the homeowner was stupid enough to leave the front door unlocked," she retorted. "And why are you half naked?"

Jealousy gnawed at her even when she couldn't see Knox's visitor. Too bad she couldn't drop to the floor and slink into the bedroom.

"Vivie, you're a shithead," another female voice said. "I told you to wait until he answered the door before you barged in here."

"Shut it, Zara. He's speechless because he's so happy to see us, huh, bro?"

Bro?

"Does Mom know you two drove into the city?"

"Yes. We learned our lesson last time."

Knox snorted.

"Omigod. Who is that?"

And . . . she'd been spotted. Shiori hopped down from the counter and did up the two buttons on the shirt before she turned around.

Knox took her hand and pulled her forward. "These are my two little sisters. Vivie"—he pointed to the tall blond girl—"and Zara." He pointed to the other tall blond girl.

They really were a family of Vikings.

Vivie offered her hand. "Nice to meet you . . . ?"

"Shiori Hirano. Knox and I work together." Why had she qualified it?

"I knew it!" Zara said with a smug smile. "You're the one who knocked Knox on his butt the first time you met because you outrank him."

She looked at Knox, shocked that he'd told his sisters that story. "Yes, technically I outrank him, but he's still considered the highest belt level besides Sensei at Black Arts."

"I can't believe someone so little threw down a guy your size, bro."

"Me either. Don't let her size fool ya. She's packing mean."

"So are you guys dating?" Zara asked, her gaze winging between Knox's bare chest and Shiori wearing only Knox's shirt.

"Yes," Knox answered without hesitation, "Shiori and I are involved, but we're keeping it on the down low since we work together."

"Wait a second." Vivie's brow was furrowed. "You're Ronin Black's sister?"

"Yes. But don't hold that against me."

"Ronin is like—"

"The hottest guy we've ever met in person," Zara finished. "He's just so—"

"Perfect," Vivie finished.

"Well, I think *your* brother is the hottest guy I've ever met," she said.

Knox kissed the top of her head.

"He's not bad, I guess, for an old guy," Zara teased.

"Thanks for the vote of confidence," Knox said dryly. "And Ronin is three years older than me, so there."

"None of that PDA crap when we're at the mall today, okay?" Vivie said.

"Mall?" Knox repeated.

"Why do you think we're in Denver?" Vivie poked him in the chest. "We talked about this, remember? My senior social? I need a dress?"

"Yeah, but it's not until next month, so why are you shopping now?"

Shiori exchanged a "men are clueless" look with Vivie and Zara.

"How'd I get roped into this again?" Knox asked.

"Because you won't let her buy a dress that's skanky," Zara said, "while I'd probably encourage her to dress slutty." She looked at Shiori. "We balance each other out."

"What's the age difference between you two?" Shiori asked.

"A year and a half. Vivie's a senior this year and I'm a junior."

"Technically, Knox is old enough to be our dad," Vivie said.

"You're jumping on the 'Knox is old' bandwagon too, Viv?"

"But we love you." Vivie kissed his cheek. "Got any food? I'm starved."

"Me too," Zara said.

"You two are always starved." He sighed. "I can cook you eggs or grilled cheese."

"Grilled cheese," they said in unison.

It was fascinating to see Knox in the big-brother role. He had an easy rapport with the teenagers, and yet she knew if his mother sent him shopping with them, he wasn't a pushover. And it made her heart melt a little seeing his nurturing side.

Shiori had a pang of jealousy that her relationship with her brother hadn't been like that. Wanting to leave them to their family time, she tried to sneak out.

But Knox caught her around the waist halfway down the hall. "Where you going?"

"I need to get dressed and call the car service for a ride."

"Why?"

"Because your sisters are here."

He looked confused. "So?"

"So they want to spend time with you, not me."

"They want to spend time at the mall. I want to spend time with you, so you're coming with us."

"I only have my walk-of-shame clothes here, remember?"

"I don't know what your deal is. You looked fantastic last night, nowhere near slutty. What you wore is fine even in the light of day. Better than fine. Come with us."

"All right." Her eyes searched his. "And if we run into anyone we know?"

His eyes cooled. "I don't like this sneaking-around shit. Part of me gets why we have to, but a larger part of me wants to say fuck it." He traced the deep V of the shirt. "We're together. People can deal with that." His unspoken, *You can deal with it too,* hung between them.

"Would you be so willing to tell people you're my submissive?"

"Apples and oranges, kitten." He gave her a lingering kiss and returned to the kitchen.

Shiori made herself as presentable as she could.

Knox walked in, threw on jeans, a button-down shirt, and ran his hand through his hair. Ready and looking delectable in less than two minutes.

"Why are you scowling at me?"

"Never mind. By the way, I used your toothbrush."

"No worries. But you might wanna think about keeping some of your stuff over here."

Why that annoyed her—she had no idea. "Maybe you should consider keeping some of your stuff at my place."

He smiled. "Whatever works. You ready to go?"

"Where are we going?"

"Cherry Creek Mall."

SHOPPING with Knox's sisters yanked her out of her sour mood. She'd not spent any time with teenagers since she was a teen, and she didn't remember her friends being so funny. Probably because they were trying so hard to be cool.

Vivie and Zara didn't care about being cool, and she had to credit their upbringing for making them want to be true to themselves since Knox was the same way.

The dressing-room door opened and Vivie sashayed out in dress number ten.

"Dear god," Zara said, "that is hideous. Are those . . . *mushrooms* in the floral pattern? Because from here they look like dozens of dicks of all sizes."

"Dammit, Zara, can't you keep your voice down?"

She looked at Knox. "That *was* my quiet voice."

"Shiori? What do you think?"

She shook her head. "Too high fashion."

"Not to mention the slit goes up so high I can see your underwear," Knox added.

Vivie stormed back toward the dressing room. "At this rate I'll never find a dress."

The saleslady returned with four more dresses and whisked the discarded ones away.

Five full minutes passed before Zara got up and pounded on the door. "Hurry up."

"I can't reach the zipper on this one because it's so low."

"I'm saying strike one for that dress without even seeing it," Knox muttered.

Zara stepped inside to help her.

A lot of squealing ensued.

Then Zara opened the door. "Ta–da! This is one of those dresses you make an entrance in."

Vivie strolled out in a pale blue satin and tulle dress. The style was modest in the front: cap sleeves, shirred satin panel on the bodice, a nipped–in waist, and a full skirt.

"Isn't this dress to die for?" Zara exclaimed.

"Yes, you look stunning, Vivie," Shiori said.

"It's weird because I've never thought about it before, but this dress makes me feel like a princess." She twirled and giggled.

Knox smiled softly. "You look awesome, brat."

Vivie stuck her tongue out.

"But I've gotta be the voice of reason and ask to see the price tag."

"But it's perfect!"

"It's not the only dress in the world. And Mom and Rick don't have an unlimited budget to spend on one dress, sweetie. You know that."

She fussed and adjusted the dress in the big mirror. "Okay, I looked at the price tag and it's way more than I can spend. Even the babysitting money I have saved up can't make up the difference."

Shiori started to open her mouth to say she'd cover the difference because Vivie deserved that dress. But she felt Knox's gaze burning into her as a warning.

Zara held her hand down to Vivie and said, "Low five."

"No doubt." She sighed and spun in the dress one more time. "Now I'm done shopping. Maybe I'll sell my blood for extra cash." She smirked at Knox in the mirror. "Or my body."

"That'll earn you five bucks," Zara said.

Vivie smacked her. "Fine. I'll put it back on the hanger. But I need to wallow in ice cream."

"And French fries," Zara added.

Knox sighed. "Ditch the dress and we'll go to the food court."

CHAPTER THIRTEEN

AFTER they'd been in the food court twenty minutes, Shiori said, "Where are the restrooms?"

"Back behind the taco place," Vivie said.

"Thanks. Excuse me."

Knox couldn't help but watch Shiori walk away. As his eyes tracked her calves to those fuck-me shoes she wore, he wondered how they'd line up if he fucked her against a wall.

Zara snapped her fingers in front of his face.

He looked at her. "What?"

"You've got it bad for her. But watching you mentally stripping her in front of us is sorta gross, so can you tone it down?"

"I'll try."

"So Mom will be super-stoked you've got a girlfriend."

His gaze moved to Vivie, who was dipping her French fries in her chocolate shake. "We're keeping this quiet, remember?"

"Even from Mom? That's bullshit. She worries about you, and this would make her so happy."

"Why would Mom worry about me?"

"Because you're thirty-six and you've never been married."

"That's not that unusual," Knox said, trying not to get defensive. "I was engaged once."

"That doesn't count. You were, like, what? Twenty?"

"I think it's fine if you don't want to get tied down," Zara said.

"Thank you, Zara."

"But don't you want to find your soul mate? And let everyone share in your love and happiness by having a big wedding?" Vivie said with a dreamy sigh.

"I think the princess gown infected you with the happily-ever-after virus."

Zara snickered.

But Vivie wouldn't let it go. "You don't wanna have babies?"

"Not especially."

"What?" Zara and Vivie exclaimed simultaneously. Then Vivie demanded, "Why not?"

"Babies are loud and smelly and demanding. They suck every ounce of fun and free time from your life. So no, I don't see myself strapping on a diaper bag anytime soon." He grinned. "Besides, I'm old, remember? Wouldn't want people mistaking my kid for my grandkid."

Shiori returned. "What did I miss?"

"Nothing," Knox said sharply, mostly to his sisters so they'd keep their opinions about brides and babies to themselves.

"We should probably get going," Vivie said. "Dad is cooking supper tonight."

Knox pointed to their snacks. "Better not tell him you already ate."

"Don't worry. We'll be hungry by the time we get home," Zara said with a grin.

In the mall parking lot, he slipped Vivie twenty bucks for gas and watched his sisters drive away.

Shiori wrapped her arms around him. "They're great."

"They keep my life interesting." He gazed into her face. "What do you want to do now?"

"Is go home and sleep an option?"

He shook his head.

"What do you want to do?"

"Curl up with you on the couch and watch a movie."

"And if I fall asleep?"

"I'd let you sleep." He pushed a piece of hair behind her ear. "I don't care as long as I get to be with you." And just so she didn't think he was clingy, he added, "But if you have other plans, that's fine."

"I'd planned on working out at the dojo today."

"Me too." He grinned. "But I'm sure you can come up with a way to get us both hot, sweating, and breathing hard—without a treadmill."

Shiori fisted her hand in his shirt and dragged his mouth to hers.

Her kiss damn near had him dropping to his knees in the parking lot.

She released his mouth, nipping his bottom lip before she backed off. "I'll watch a movie with you, but Mistress rules apply. And we have to load up on junk food, because I require Junior Mints and black licorice with my popcorn."

"Whatever it takes to make you happy, ma'am."

"And I get to pick the movie."

Knox shook his head. "No can do. My TV, my movie."

"No horror."

"Agreed."

"No movies with car chases and explosions."

"Now you're just wrecking my fun, She-Cat. But we ain't watching a chick flick, either."

"As if I like that kind of mushy stuff."

He brushed his lips across hers. "Such a little liar you are. I'll bet you've seen just about every romantic comedy released in the last ten years."

She wrinkled her nose. "Just because I saw them once doesn't mean I need to watch them again and again."

He laughed. "Gotcha."

"How about sci-fi?"

"Not a big fan."

"No martial arts," they said at the same time.

"It might be fun. Every time the stunt double does some impossible maneuver, whoever spots it first can make the other one remove an article of clothing."

Shiori poked him in the chest. "Then you'll be naked pretty damn fast since you'll only be wearing athletic shorts."

"True. We're running out of choices. I'm not an art-house-film guy."

She nodded. "Movies based on real history are usually boring."

"Agreed. So that leaves us with animated or my old standby for movies."

"We are not watching porn."

"Don't need to watch porn when I've got you in my bed," he growled.

"What movie?"

"*Pale Rider.*"

"Is that a . . . ?"

"Western," he supplied, "starring none other than the man himself, Clint Eastwood."

"I've never seen any of his films."

"Then it's past time for you to behold the glory."

"All right." She smiled at him—the devious smile that didn't bode well. "But next time I get to pick."

"Nothing with subtitles," he warned.

Shiori tugged on his hand. "Snacks await."

When they reached the checkout at CVS, Shiori pulled out her credit card and he had to muscle her aside to keep her from paying.

Back at his house, she changed into the casual clothes she'd picked up at the mall. He liked the slim fit of the designer sweatpants, but why any woman wanted to advertise Juicy on her ass escaped him. He stripped down to his boxer briefs since all his workout clothes were dirty.

They'd settled in with bowls of popcorn, sodas, and candy, ready to watch Clint wreak havoc, when his phone rang. He quickly glanced at the caller ID, then wondered why Merrick would be calling him on a Sunday.

"Hello?"

"Knox. It's Merrick. I hope you're having a good weekend. We missed you last night."

"I wasn't supposed to be there, was I?"

Shiori looked at him, and he mouthed, *Merrick*.

"No. I'm calling to ask if you'll be around next weekend."

"I hadn't planned that far ahead. Why?"

"Master Mike has requested an hour of your time."

"You need to know now?"

"Yes. Those private rooms fill up fast."

Knox opened his mouth to say yes—until he remembered Shiori's demand to be present during the scenes he participated in. "Hang on a second." He hit mute and faced her.

"What?"

He explained the situation and felt resentful when she demanded to talk to Merrick. Jesus. He hated how this felt like Shiori was his mommy.

You willingly signed on for this.

Reluctantly, he handed the phone over.

Shiori unmuted the call. "Merrick. It's Mistress B. I'm fine, thank you." She sent Knox a hot look. "So far he's done very well."

Why did her praise take the sting out of needing her permission to do what he'd been doing at the club for years?

Because you are submissive. Try to accept it and quit fucking whining.

"As far as Master Mike? Are he and his sub good with me observing? Yes, I'd appreciate it if you'd get confirmation on that. And from now on? As long as Knox is with me, he won't be doing solo scenes with couples." She laughed softly. "Very fit to be tied. But he agreed to the terms." She paused. "No. We're not to that stage. Thank you. Let Knox know what Master Mike decides." She groaned. "Your Japanese sucks. Stick to English, Master Merrick. Goodbye." She ended the call and handed his phone back. "Does Merrick always ask your permission about scenes?"

"I told you I have a say in whose scenes I help out with."

"That makes me happy." Then Shiori set both of their popcorn bowls aside and straddled him.

Instant erection.

"But you know what makes me really happy?"

"What?"

"That you deferred the situation to me." She swept her thumb across his bottom lip. "If I punish you when you've broken a rule, then I should reward you when you uphold one."

"Okay. What's my reward?"

"You can either have my mouth on your nipples while I jack you off. Or your mouth on *my* nipples while I jack you off. Choose."

"I want my mouth on you."

That catlike smile curled her lips. "Excellent choice." She stood and whipped off her shirt. "Ditch the underwear."

Knox had them on the floor in no time.

She perched her ass on his thighs and circled her hand around the base. "You want lube?"

"Just your hand."

"Can you reach me?"

He tipped his head down and sucked on her nipple.

"Guess that answers that," she murmured.

She hadn't indicated he couldn't use his hands, so he cupped her tits and drew circles beneath one nipple as he sucked on the other one.

"Let's test your stamina."

Fuck.

Knox suspected *test his stamina* was code for cock and ball torture.

Shiori stroked him so fast he wondered if he'd have friction burns on his shaft. Right when his balls were about to spew, she made her fingers into a cock ring and stopped him from coming. How she'd known the exact moment boggled his mind.

Not that he was thinking clearly. His chest heaved, his jaw was tight, and he had to drop his face from her view or she'd see his frustration.

Next she took his mouth in a sweet kiss he'd almost believe was somewhat apologetic if he hadn't feared this *reward* was a double-edged sword.

When she returned to sitting beside him and said, "Start the movie," he wanted to ask, *What the fuck? What about that hand job?*

Fifteen minutes later, after his cock had gone soft and he'd become invested in the movie, Shiori trailed her fingers down his chest to his groin and toyed with his flaccid cock. Which didn't stay flaccid for long when she expertly started to work him over with those magic fucking fingers.

At least she hadn't gotten him close to orgasm that time before she stopped.

He couldn't even focus on the movie because she'd set her hand on the inside of his leg and he'd think, *Here she goes again*. But she'd just gently stroke his skin, not caring that his cock rallied for her attention at the slightest sign she might touch him.

They didn't speak beyond Shiori asking him to put his arm around her. At least he had that as a distraction, drawing circles on the ball of her shoulder or twining a section of her hair around his fingers.

The next time she slipped her fingers between his legs, she just played with his balls. Rolling them, tugging on them, squeezing them, teasing them with a featherlight touch. Yeah, his dick had gotten hard. Mess with the berries and the twig wants in on the action. But again she left him hanging.

The fourth go-around was exactly like the first.

At that point it took every ounce of his control not to just walk to the bathroom and take care of matters himself. The whipping with the switch hadn't been that bad. A few hard swats on his ass would be worth it if he could alleviate this ache.

The fifth time she touched him, he let his head fall back against the cushion in total defeat.

Then her lips were on his ear. "This time I'll let you pick if you want to come or not."

"And if I choose to come, what happens then?"

"Neither of us will have the satisfaction of knowing how long you could've lasted."

Of course she was challenging him. "I won't come."

"Good man. Watch my hand jacking you. See how hot it looks."

He lifted his head and peeled his eyes open. His cock was an angry red, the head nearly purple. And her hand looked delicate wrapped around his girth.

She pumped his meat in her tight fist faster and faster. Again her soft lips brushed his ear, sending goose bumps down the left side of his body. "You tell me when to stop. But don't flinch, my beautiful sub. Let me get you right to the very edge, where you're balancing on one foot and windmilling your arms to keep from plunging over . . . and then pull back."

Christ. He held out until that moment right before his balls lifted and he said hoarsely, "Stop. Just stop."

Once again her fingers became a cock ring.

Maybe he had a sense of accomplishment when she murmured, "I'm impressed."

Knox tried to level his breathing. And while he did that, he tried to get his cock to stand down.

She patted his leg and resumed crunching popcorn as if she weren't turning him inside out.

"It makes me wet," she said nonchalantly, "seeing you with such iron control, knowing you're doing it for me because I asked."

He growled at her admission and grabbed a handful of hair at the back of her head to get at her mouth. Taking the kiss, the contact he needed. Besides, what worse punishment could she give him?

Shiori allowed the kiss, but when she lightly bit down on his tongue, he backed off.

The next time her hand crept between his legs, he didn't bother to try to keep his body from reacting to her touch.

"How are you liking your reward?"

"This doesn't exactly feel like a reward, Mistress."

"It will." She blew in his ear, and he felt it all the way in his balls. "Relax and let all your tension go."

"I'm trying."

She smacked his leg. "Loosen up."

Knox inhaled a deep breath and focused on the tension leaving his body the same time as the air in his lungs.

That's when a strange sense of peace flowed through him. He felt her hand working him and the tightness in his balls. He wanted that rush of release, ached for it, but he trusted her to get him there.

"That's what I wanted, Knox."

He might've offered her a dreamy smile.

"Come for me, lover. Come now."

The orgasm was like an out-of-body experience. He'd never come so hard, for so long. Wave after wave rolled through him, tossing him about a sea of pleasure so intense for a split second he wondered if he were dreaming. His seed was scorching hot on his skin. His balls just kept shooting out stream after stream. He shuddered. He yelled, but no sound came out.

When she finally stopped pumping his shaft, he curled his hand over hers and said, "Just a little more. Please."

As he helped her bring him down, she whispered, "You were magnificent."

He grunted, and she caught the sound in her mouth. Shiori kissed him with tenderness and care. Running her free hand over his face and neck and chest, letting him know this wasn't a fantasy; it was real.

Knox didn't know how much time passed before he opened his eyes. But the first thing he saw was her beautiful face.

He had the overwhelming urge to drop to his knees. But it warred with his overwhelming urge to run. To get far away from this woman and the absolute surrender she demanded. It scared the fuck out of him, anyone having that kind of power over him.

"Don't." She kissed him again.

"Don't what?"

"Ruin this for yourself by thinking too hard."

So you want me to be your mindless sex slave? That I'll do anything to feel like that again and again?

"You were magnificent," she repeated. "Strong, sexy. So hot, giving your will to me, that when you started to come, I did too."

He lifted his arm, wanting to touch her face, but he realized his hand was sticky. So was his belly. So was his cock. Time to clean up, take a step back, let his big head take back control. Hopefully his legs wouldn't fail him when he stood.

She put her hand on his arm. "Where are you going?"

"To wash up. I'll be right back."

Her fierce eyes locked to his. "I didn't say you could move."

"Shiori—"

"Mistress," she snapped. "Are you even aware your body is shaking?"

Knox glanced down and saw his knee bouncing. "Shit."

"Stay fucking put. And yes, that's a goddamn order."

She left the couch and walked to the kitchen. Water ran. Then she returned with a handful of paper towels.

When she began to clean him up, his cheeks burned with embarrassment, and he snatched the wet paper towels from her. "Stop. I'll do it."

"You are the most stubborn man."

He cleaned his right hand with his left. Then he took another paper towel and wiped his belly. "Isn't cleaning jizz off your sub beneath you, Mistress?"

Lightning fast she wrapped her hand beneath his jaw and jerked his face up. "Taking care of you is my responsibility, Knox. That includes commanding you to get turned on, getting you off, cleaning you up, and making sure you don't do something stupid in the aftermath."

"Like pissing off my Mistress because I don't know how the fuck I'm supposed to act after . . . whatever that was?"

"Yes."

"I'm sorry."

She dropped her hand but remained right there in his face. "I know. How is it that whipping your butt with a switch didn't freak you out but an orgasm that sent you straight into subspace . . . did?"

Fuck. "I don't know."

She stood. Then she reached for her bra and shirt and put them on.

When Shiori started cleaning up the popcorn bowls, the candy boxes, and the paper towels, he didn't protest because he'd probably catch hell for it.

After she disappeared into the kitchen again, he closed his eyes.

When he woke up, his house was completely dark. A blanket covered him, but he was naked beneath it. As soon as he pushed upright from his prone position on the couch, he knew Shiori had gone. The only thing he didn't know was what had chased her away without a goodbye.

CHAPTER FOURTEEN

SATURDAY night Shiori showed up at Twisted an hour before the scene with Master Mike and his submissive was scheduled and sat at the bar. She hadn't been in since the night Knox had played bartender, so she didn't know anyone besides Merrick, Greg, Knox, and Dex.

Speak of the devil . . . She glanced down and saw Dex on his knees beside her chair. "Dex. What lovely form."

"I aim to please, Mistress."

"What can I do for you?"

"If you haven't picked a sub to receive your attentions this evening, I'll humbly offer myself."

She reached for her Coke and sipped. "In what capacity are you offering yourself?"

"In any capacity that you choose."

"That's very vague, and dangerous, Dex. What if I demanded needle play?"

He swallowed hard. "I'd . . . consider it with you."

Bullshit. "And what about fire play?"

A shiver worked through him. "I've never tried it."

"But you'd be willing to feel the burn . . . for me?"

"Yes, Mistress B."

Shiori put the toe of her shoe on his sternum. "You need to learn limits, Dex. You're not getting what you need by offering everything just so a Dominant will play with you."

He didn't look up.

"So let's try this again. And be honest. Respect your boundaries or no one else will. I'm interested in needle play."

His mouth opened. Then closed. "Sorry, Mistress B, but I'm scared of needles."

"Good boy, Dex. Now, how about fire play?"

Another shudder. "No. No fire. Ever." He started to hyperventilate.

She dropped her foot from his chest and leaned over to place her hand on his head. "Breathe, Dex. You're all right."

He nodded.

She kept petting his hair.

After a bit he rested his face against her shin and sighed.

"Is there something I can assist you with, Mistress B?" Knox said coldly behind her.

Dex's head snapped up. He glared at Knox. "We don't need security, so back off."

Knox grabbed him by the arm and hauled him up. "Remember who you're talking to. Learn your place. And I guarantee you it is not at her feet. Are we clear?"

He jerked out of Knox's hold. "I go when Mistress B tells me to go."

Both men looked at her.

How could she be mad at Knox for defending his territory? He'd told her he wouldn't stand for any other submissive putting his hands on her and Dex had been touching her. She'd touched him first, but Dex knew the rules. But Dex didn't know she and Knox were together, so who was in the wrong here?

"Dex, I hope I helped you tonight. You're excused."

"Thank you, Mistress B. If there's ever anything I can do for you—"

"There isn't," Knox snarled. "Get gone before I toss you out."

Dex stormed away.

Shiori gave Knox her back, trying to control her amusement and the rapid beating of her heart from Knox's display of possession. It sent a thrill through her that Knox watched out for her even when she wasn't expecting it.

This is Knox you're talking about. He's the chest-beating, don't-touch-my-woman kind of man. You should've expected even more than that.

Knox didn't touch her, but he scooted in close enough behind her that his breath fanned her hair and she could practically feel the tension vibrating from him.

He said, "Are you mad, Mistress?"

She slowly turned around.

He didn't move a muscle, so her knees bumped into his hard thighs. He stayed in rest position. His chest was heaving, his neck and jaw muscles were tight, color dotted his cheekbones, and his eyes were icy.

"I don't know if *mad* is accurate. If we were out as a Domme and sub, then your reaction to Dex at my feet would be acceptable. Since you're not wearing my collar, yet I know who you are to me and who I am to you, I don't know what to do—if anything at all. Dex did take a liberty, but it was more as an impulsive thank-you than him trying to get me to play with him."

"I misread the situation, then?"

"Yes. But like I said, it's difficult to be angry with you when you were only doing what you thought was best for me."

His eyes softened. "I'm all about ensuring your needs are met and any threat is dealt with quickly."

"Thank you. But I'm fine."

"Mighty fine." His burning-hot gaze started at the tips of her lavender Louboutins and moved up her bare legs, past the dark purple sequined miniskirt, and the black silk sleeveless wrap shirt, to the delicate gold-colored sequin mask. "You're beyond compare tonight."

"I look forward to the session."

Knox picked up her hand and kissed the inside of her wrist. "Me also. See you down there."

Shiori didn't spin back around until after that fantastic ass was gone from view. When she faced the bar, Merrick stood right in front of her. "Master Merrick."

"Mistress B. You're assisting Knox this evening?"

"I hear he's excellent with a whip. I wanted to see for myself."

"Just don't ask him to demonstrate on you, because he won't."

"I know."

"I assumed you did." His smile turned guarded. "Interesting display earlier."

"A misunderstanding easily remedied."

"Have you brought Knox to heel yet?"

Her gaze narrowed. "Excuse me?"

Merrick waved her off. "Knox spoke to me. Being called out as submissive caused more questions than denial about being a submissive."

"He still questions it. We're working on it. In private. He's not ready for public acknowledgment." She stirred the ice cubes in her glass. "I don't know if he ever will be."

"I can't say as I blame him."

"Can you explain that?"

"Most men are subservient to women—they just won't admit it. Most men do whatever it takes to make their wives or partners happy in the hopes it'll get them laid more often. Women have the sacred pussy. They are in control."

"Nice philosophy."

He shrugged. "It's true. Knox is a former soldier. He's a martial-arts instructor. He is the kind of man the term *alpha male* was invented for. He may kiss your feet in private, but chances are slim he will in public. Why? Because it's personal, it makes him vulnerable, and he'd have to deal with judgmental assholes thinking he's weak for doing . . . exactly what other men are doing. But they don't call it submissive behavior—those men call it caring for and protecting their women."

"You've thought a lot about this."

"I have to. Knowing what makes people tick means I can tailor my club to certain tastes."

Shiori leaned in. "Bullshit. You were speaking from the point of view of a man who was worried about being judged, which means you understand the male submissive mind-set because you were one."

Merrick smirked. "We all have our secrets, Mistress B, and as long as Knox serves you well in private, does it really matter what the rest of us think?"

"No. But if private relationships were meant to stay behind closed doors, then you'd be out of business."

"You're absolutely right. Put a leash and a collar on that man and remind him who's the boss."

She laughed.

"Knox is incredibly possessive of you. And that has nothing to do with him being submissive but because he's a man in an intimate relationship with you. I imagine he's exactly the same way in public; he'd verbally and bodily threaten anyone who touches you because he holds you as precious. But here at Twisted? His possessiveness will be attributed to him being submissive since you're a Domme. So be careful in your attentions to males he'll deem a threat, okay? Because you will effectively out a man who's not ready for it—and may never be."

"I hadn't thought of it that way. Thank you."

"It's what I'm here for." He headed down to the other end of the bar to help a customer.

Shiori left the bar area, letting her gaze wander to the various goings-on. But she didn't see anything; her thoughts were on her conversation with Merrick.

As soon as she saw Knox leaning against the back wall monitoring a threesome, her focus shifted.

A woman was tied to a wide sawhorse on her belly, hands bound behind her with rope. If Shiori remembered right, that sawhorse had a vibrator attached to the back end. So while one guy had his cock shoved in her mouth, his partner was ramming his cock into the woman's ass. The woman with all her orifices filled clutched a bandana. If she dropped it, the scene ended. But she appeared to be enjoying herself too much to stop.

Shiori didn't bother Knox since he was working. Instead she took stock of the crowd. One guy was openly masturbating. Several other couples were grinding against each other. But one young brunette with tits the size of beach balls, and probably just as plastic, was watching Knox. The scene would catch her attention, and then she'd be back gazing at him with an I've-got-this-in-the-bag smirk.

Jealousy stabbed her in the gut like a hot poker. Had Knox fucked that chick? How long ago?

Doesn't matter. He's with you now.

That's when he scanned the crowd and saw her. He aimed a happy grin at her, and she gloated at being the sole focus of his attention.

Suck it, boob job. He didn't smile at you like that. Just me.

She wanted to do more than just smile back; maybe she should blow him a kiss. But Merrick's warning had stuck with her, so she just returned his grin.

As soon as the scene ended—with come shots on the woman's face and ass, just like in bad porn—Knox meandered over.

"Hey. You ready for this?"

"For what? I'm just sitting in on your session."

He shook his head. "I asked Master Mike if he wanted a twofer, and because he's such a perverted guy, I had to explain it wasn't me servicing both him and sub Mike, but two whips for double the pleasure, double the pain."

"What'd he say?"

"That it'd be a great surprise for sub Mike."

"Dueling whips. That's something I've never done."

Knox raised his hand, as if to touch her face, but dropped it back to his side. "Me neither."

"Hi, Knox."

The brunette who'd been eye-fucking him got so close she almost stepped between them.

"Hey, Angel."

Shiori's gaze sharpened. Why the fuck was he calling her *angel*?

"So are you still on duty?" she asked.

"For the rest of the night."

She stuck out her lower lip in a pout that missed the mark of being sexy. "Too bad. It's been a while for us. I'll be around if you get off early." She batted her lashes. "Or if you wanna get off. Come find me."

Knox didn't say anything. Then he looked at Shiori. "What?"

"Angel?"

"I doubt that's really her name, Mistress B."

So it wasn't a term of endearment—lucky for him. Shiori closed the distance between them and set her hand on his chest. "Your taste in women has improved."

He laughed. "Bored and horny in a sex club doesn't always make for the best choices."

"Poor thing. You've probably ruined her for all other men."

"You do realize I'm a sure thing tonight and you don't have to pile on the flattery to get into my pants?"

She rubbed her thumb across his nipple. "Maybe she was a sign that I should be flattering you more. Because you are worth it."

His eyes glittered with pleasure. "You're killing me here."

"You should know—"

"Knox. Punctual as usual," a deep voice said behind her. "And who is this lovely?"

Shiori turned around. A good-looking guy in his mid-fifties with salt-and-pepper hair held hands with a younger man who had such ethereal beauty that her mouth fell open.

"Yes, my pet gets that a lot. Don't you, sweetheart?"

"Yes, sir."

"I'm Mistress B. You must be Master Mike."

"I'd heard about the exotic beauty who'd joined our happy little Twisted family, but the reports didn't do you justice." Master Mike kissed her hand.

"Thank you."

"So, Mike, I've got a treat in store for you tonight." Master Mike wrapped his hand around sub Mike's jaw and lifted his face up. "Mistress B has whip skills. Both she and Knox will get you where you need to be, all right?"

Sub Mike immediately dropped to his knees. "Thank you, sir."

"You can thank me appropriately later. For now, let's get you naked and strapped down." Master Mike looked at Knox. "I'll open the door once we're ready."

After the Mikes went into the room, Shiori said, "Is this normal?"

Knox nodded. "Master Mike undresses his sub and chooses how he'll be bound for this. Then I come in, do my thing, and leave."

"Do they tip you?"

"Funny."

"So what happens if I get really horny? Where do we go if I need you to fuck me?"

He blinked as if he didn't believe her. "If you're serious, I can reserve a private room."

"Better do it just to be safe." She paused, thinking back to the conversation with Merrick. "Unless you'd rather not be seen spending time in a private room with a Domme."

"We're already associated tonight. Most everyone knows I do more than one session a night. I'll be right back." He disappeared around a corner.

Out of curiosity, she followed him. They walked into another corridor with private rooms. She walked past the first two doors that read *occupied*, but there was no way to peek inside.

Right when she and Knox returned to the first hallway, Master Mike opened the door. "Ready."

Shiori entered the room first. Sub Mike dangled from chains in the ceiling, and his ankles were cuffed to hooks in the floor. He wore a blindfold.

"His rule is no blood play. My rule is *I* call a halt to the session. I'd tell you where his hot spots are, Mistress B, but I rather enjoy seeing you discovering them on your own. So I'll ask you to begin."

She bowed to Master Mike, almost without thought. After she chose a short single tail from the choices his Master had laid out, her heels clicked on the cement flooring as she circled the sub.

It was tempting to tease him, to build the anticipation, but she snapped the first blow on his nipple.

Sub Mike arched and gasped.

Nipples were good.

She stopped behind him. The way he was positioned, with his ass sticking out . . . The next strike landed on his anus.

He released a low, sexy groan.

The base of his armpit.

The inside of his thigh.

The back of his thigh where his leg curved into his ass.

The last area of his body she picked was a no-brainer. The whip tip connected with his balls.

Shiori met Knox's gaze. He inclined his head and chose a

cat-'o-nine-tails and a flogger. Then he proceeded to whip the hell out of sub Mike's ass.

And that's how it started. She'd finesse the marks, leaving them on sub Mike's hot spots. Then Knox would apply a lot of pain all at once.

It was a sensual tease between her and Knox. Circling sub Mike and each other. Trying to see who could elicit the loudest cry.

Shiori wished Knox had taken off his sleeveless T-shirt so she could watch the muscles in his back ripple when he swung. She wanted to see the sweat dampening his shirt glistening on his skin.

Air teased the backs of her legs, and she realized Knox had snapped the flogger at her but had purposely missed.

She retaliated, cracking the whip and connecting with the baggy part of his jeans on the outside of his thigh. She smiled at his lifted brow.

They worked sub Mike until Master Mike said to stop.

Master Mike tipped his sub's head back and saw that he'd reached that dreamy-eyed look of subspace. He looked over his shoulder and smiled at Knox and Shiori. "You two are a helluva team. Thank you. This is exactly what he needed."

"Happy to help." Knox put the cat and the flogger on the table. "Anything else you need, Master Mike?"

"No. We're good."

"Very good," sub Mike said.

Knox followed Shiori out of the room. He slumped against the wall outside the door. "Look. I don't want to be a buzz-kill, but—"

"I know 'providing your services' doesn't turn you on."

"Did it turn you on?"

"Watching you was hot. But I get hot watching you move in class, so I'm a bit of a whore where you're concerned."

He smiled. "Works for me."

"I want to try something with you."

Knox waited.

Shiori slid her hands over his chest, loving how the damp material of his shirt clung to his musculature. She took her time touching him, especially at his neck and shoulders where the muscles were tight with tension. "I'm taking you to my masseuse next week to get some of these kinks worked out—and there will be no arguing."

"Yes, Mistress. But I hope she doesn't work all the kinks out. I'm kinda fond of kink."

Her eyes met his, and she smiled at the devilish twinkle she saw there. "Me too. And especially kink with you." With her hand on the back of his neck, she pulled his mouth down to hers. The kiss sparked her need to make something else out of this night. Something good. "Come into my lair, my sweet," she murmured against his lips, "and we'll have us some kinky fun."

Knox eased back to look into her eyes. "Okay. Seems I'm a bit of a whore for you too."

"Go into the room and get ready for me. Mistress rules. I'll be right there."

He walked down the hallway.

Shiori tracked down the closest security guy and asked where she'd find the items she needed. He directed her to the empty pleasure den—a room she'd never been in. She briefly explored the space and wished she could bring Knox in there, but the room had a large viewing window that couldn't be closed off.

She shoved the things she'd found in a satin pillowcase she'd liberated from the bed and returned to the private room. She pulled in a deep, calming breath before she walked inside.

Knox sat with his back to the door. He'd taken off all his clothing except for his boxer briefs. Her rush of excitement stemmed from the sight of his nearly nude body, not just his submissive position. Still. She had to wonder if this was the first time he'd been in that position in the club.

After setting the sack of toys close by, she placed her hand on the back of his neck. "Takes my breath away to see you waiting like this for me. Thank you."

He didn't respond.

"Stand and face me, please."

Knox rolled to his feet and turned toward her.

"We haven't established a safe word. Would you prefer a word besides the universal club word *red*?"

"No, Mistress. But I have to ask why we need a safe word at all."

"So you have a choice in what I plan to ask you to do."

His eyes darkened.

"Pick up the bag beside you. Take everything out and line up the items on the bench."

He kept his back to her as he took out each item.

Shiori stood beside him and examined the offerings. A set of nipple clamps. A vibrator with remote control. Fur-lined hand-cuffs. A flogger comprised of buttery-soft leather pieces and strands of fluffy feathers. A blindfold. A paddle lined with rabbit fur.

When she touched his arm, he flinched. "Sorry. Just seeing this stuff makes me jumpy."

"Why? I'm not going to use it on you . . . You're going to use it on me."

Knox's head whipped around. "Excuse me?"

"We're mixing it up tonight. So of all the items on the bench, you get to pick one to use on me, and I get to pick one for you to use on me." She kissed his biceps. "I'll even let you go first."

He didn't hesitate in his choice. He picked the nipple clamps.

She smiled and walked to the other side of the bench, deliberately picking up every item although she'd made her choice earlier. She curled her hand around the feather flogger and lifted it. "This one."

"Mistress. You know that I don't——"

"Knox. This is not a real flogger. Look at it."

That stubborn chin jutted out. "This is why we're using safe words. Because you knew I'd refuse."

"I'm not so sure you are refusing. And I think if you truly want to keep your Mistress happy, you'll see this is an instrument of pleasure. Not pain."

"Say I use it on you. And next time you bring in your bag of tricks, will you include a regular flogger? Will you keep pushing past my boundaries and comfort zone just to see how far I'll go in the name of obedience?" he said with a hint of anger and panic.

She curled her hands around his face and pulled him down until they were eye to eye. "No. I'd never do that. Never. And this isn't about obedience or pushing boundaries. This is about how hot it made me seeing your skills with a whip. I don't want pain. And when I look at the feather flogger? All I can see is that you would know how to use it in such a way that you'd drive me out of my mind with pleasure. Does it feel like soft breath? Does it feel like I have dozens of sets of hands teasing my skin? Does it feel like your hair tickling me? You can use it on me any way you want, Knox."

He studied her for so long that when his lips parted to speak, she feared she'd hear the word *red*.

"I'll do it if that's truly what you want, Nushi."

Relieved, she pressed her mouth to his for a kiss and then dropped her hands. "It is."

"At what point do I stop?"

"When I beg you to fuck me."

His gorgeous smile appeared. "Okay. One other thing."

"Name it."

"I want to restrain you. That way I can access both sides of your body. Anytime you want me to release you, just tell me."

The idea of being chained up had always been one of her sticking points as a submissive. It'd never been an issue as a Domme. But she had to show Knox she trusted him as much as he trusted her. If he was willing to let her push him past his comfort zone, then she'd let him push her past hers too. "All right. But only as long as you don't get the idea you're in charge, sub. I'm allowing this because it pleases me to do so."

"Thank you, Mistress."

Shiori circled her arms around his waist and buried her face in his neck. "Get the restraints ready while I get undressed."

She purposely gave him her back as she ditched her clothes. When she walked to the part of the room where the chains dangled from the ceiling, Knox quit fiddling with a wrist cuff and drank her body in with very thirsty eyes.

"As always, the sight of you naked makes it hard for me to think of anything else."

She slid her heels into the marks on the floor and closed her eyes when Knox snapped on the ankle cuffs. His footsteps made a soft *shush-shush* across the cement when he moved to stand in front of her.

He kissed the insides of her wrists before he placed the cuffs on. Then he cranked the pulley system, lifting her arms into a T formation and locking it there.

Panic set in. Why had she agreed to this? In this vulnerable position, he could do anything he wanted to her and she'd be helpless to stop him.

Knox's strong arms circled her. The heat from his body and the gentleness in his embrace calmed her.

Shiori turned her head and breathed him in. Then she trailed her lips down the cord straining in his neck, letting the taste of him on her lips and tongue stir her desire and extinguish her fear. He'd sensed her mood shift, and without a word, he'd given her exactly what she'd needed. After several long moments, she whispered, "Thank you."

In response he placed a tender kiss below her ear.

She missed his solid presence after his arms fell away. She concentrated on keeping her shit together. Counting during each inhale and exhale.

So his wet mouth sucking on her right nipple tore a soft groan from her. She felt the tip tightening into a rigid point; then a sharp pinch followed.

Her eyes flew open and she gasped.

A smug smile danced on Knox's lips. "Forgot about the nipple clamps, didn't you?"

Yes, dammit. "No."

"Oh, then no need to go slow for this one." His warm lips briefly teased her left nipple. As soon as it puckered, he snapped the clamp on.

Fuck. Ow.

"I like how that looks on you," he murmured, rubbing his thumb beneath the section of skin where the clamps bit down.

Shiori opened her eyes and watched his face as he touched her.

"Too tight?"

"No. I'm okay."

He dipped his head and dropped a kiss on the sensitive sweep of flesh between her neck and shoulder. Then he picked up the flogger and ran it back and forth across her breasts.

Holy shit. That felt good.

Knox moved behind her and seemed to hesitate. Just as she was ready to command him, that first lash landed between her shoulder blades.

It wasn't a hard blow, it didn't hurt, but it wasn't what she'd had in mind either.

His breath teased the nape of her neck. "Like that?"

She angled her head and rubbed her face against his. "No."

He stiffened.

"It didn't hurt, but it's not what I expected either."

"What do you want?"

"Tease me with it. Drag it across my skin. Just because you're using that doesn't mean you can't use your hands and your mouth. Drive me crazy, Knox." Her teeth found his earlobe and she tugged on it. "Make me arch my back. Make me writhe and rattle these chains. Show me you know exactly how to please me."

A beat passed. Then he sank his teeth into the section of her neck that made her knees weak and pressed his hot, bare chest to her naked back. His deep, gravelly voice teased her ear. "You are so fucking hot. But, baby . . . remember you asked for this."

When Knox stepped back, she almost whimpered at the loss of contact of his body against hers. But then he started using the flogger. Sweeping it across her upper back and arms. A slow drag and then a quick flick that felt like the pressure of fingertips on her shoulders. A ghostly caress over her ass cheeks and down the insides of her thighs.

Just on the first pass he'd turned her entire body into a mass of gooseflesh. Her heart raced, sending the blood pumping faster though her body, making her nipples throb.

Then the flogger disappeared, replaced by Knox's big hands. His fingers traced the delineated muscles of her biceps and triceps. The underside of her arms. His callused finger teased the valley between each of her fingers and around the cuffs on her wrists. The chains shook when he grabbed on to them above where she was restrained. He fit his damp chest against her back and pressed his groin into her ass, rocking into her so she could feel his hard cock through the fabric of his underwear.

Heat spread throughout her core. She moaned and let her head fall forward.

Knox took that as his invitation to attack her neck. Torturing her with tiny nips and sucking kisses. Doing that pause thing that caused her to tremble. His hot breath floated across her nape as he built her anticipation of where his mouth would land next.

His hands slowly slid down the chains, then over her arms, then followed the curves of her body from beneath her armpits all the way to her calves.

When the feathers and leather drifted over her skin again, she jumped.

This time the tease lasted longer. The repetitive nature of his strokes brought awareness to every nerve ending on the back side of her body.

His warm, wet tongue licked up her spine, starting at the top of her butt crack and ending with a sharp nip of teeth at her hairline.

Shiori gasped. And trembled. And found it hard to catch her breath when she had no idea what he planned to do to her next.

Knox's voice, sweetly seductive this time, reverberated across her scalp. "Please keep your eyes closed, Mistress, while I switch positions."

He slid the braided end of the flogger handle between her legs, dragging the nubby leather from her clit to the pucker of her ass. Back and forth, building that need for release in her until she shook like a junkie in need of a fix. And then he sent her soaring, rubbing furiously on her clit as she came undone.

Before she fully regained control of her brain cells, rivers of softness floated from her collarbones to the skin between her hip bones. Another quick flick of his wrist and the leather straps sharpened the impression of impatient fingers digging into her flesh.

Earlier, in the stillness of the room, she had heard the sounds of their rapid breathing, the clank of her chains, and the whisper of his footsteps. But now all Shiori heard was the white noise in her brain as Knox overloaded her entire being with myriad sensations.

Again she jerked in the restraints when he pressed his skin to hers. The nipple clamps dug into his chest and he spread his hands across her back, forcing their upper bodies closer together.

His hard stomach muscles flexed against her belly when he nestled his cock against her mound. "Tell me when you've had enough, Nushi."

"Never," she whispered. "I'll never get enough of feeling your hands on me."

Keeping her eyes closed, she blindly sought his mouth for a

kiss. A hot, openmouthed, frantic kiss that ramped up her desire. She shifted her head, wanting a deeper kiss. A harder kiss.

Knox growled and ravaged her mouth with such hunger that if she could've rubbed her legs together, she would've come.

This was what she wanted. This was what she'd been missing her entire adult life. This unspoken connection with a man.

And without her having to direct him about what she wanted, Knox used his hands and his mouth on the front side of her body. Lips and teeth and callused fingers mapping every square inch of quivering flesh.

When she sensed he'd dropped to his knees, she fought the urge to look and see what he planned to do to her next.

He swirled the flogger around her ankle and her knees buckled. But that didn't deter him. He just used his knowledge about one of the most sensitive spots on her body to his advantage, and to hers.

She didn't know how much more of this she could take.

Before she could ask him to release her restraints, Knox's big hands clamped around her hips. Then he settled his mouth on her pussy. No teasing licks. He just circled his lips around her clit and sucked until she shattered.

Then he snapped open the cuffs on her ankles. His body brushed hers as he stood and she moaned.

"It's all right," he murmured. He snaked an arm around her back, holding her close as he undid the arm restraints. "I need to get you out of these before you bruise this beautiful skin." After he released her left arm, he pressed kisses around her wrist. "I'm not overstepping my bounds, Mistress. It's my responsibility to see to your needs. You needed this."

Shiori let him hold her up as he fiddled with the last cuff.

But before he did, he trailed his lips up the side of her neck. "You were right to push me. I've never wanted to please anyone as much as I want to please you."

Reaching up, she pressed her cool palm to the back of his neck. "You pleased me beyond what I expected, Knox. Putting me in restraints was a great idea."

She felt him smile against her throat.

Click and then her arm was freed.

Knox didn't move. He kept her upright until she found her balance.

When she slid her hand up his chest, she paused for a moment to feel his heartbeat. Wildly erratic. Then she stepped back.

Knox's face was flushed. His eyes were dark with lust. His cock poked out of the top of his underwear. She sensed his impatience, so it meant the world to her that he waited and gave her the lead.

Shiori took his hand and placed it over the nipple clamp on her right breast. "Remove them. One at a time."

He slipped his hand beneath the bottom curve of her breast and freed her nipple with his other hand.

Sharp, stinging pain flooded her breast, and his hot mouth was right there, sucking away the hurt until she sighed with relief. Then he switched sides, and while he tongued her nipple and eased the sting, his thumb swept across her other nipple, keeping it sensitive. When he pulled away, she noticed his smirk.

"I like how the clamps made your nipples such a rosy red."

"Maybe I'll use them on you sometime." She snapped the waistband on his boxer briefs. "Take these off and sit on the bench."

No protest, but he did sweep everything off the bench and onto the floor.

She grabbed a condom from the bowl by the door and returned to the bench to hand it to him. "Put this on and lie back." As soon as he'd complied, she straddled him. "Hold on to me or drop your hands to the floor. And you don't come until I say."

She loved that he picked the option where he touched her. Those big, skilled hands settled on her hips like they belonged there.

"Lift your head and watch as I take you in." Wrapping her

fingers around the base of his cock, she aimed the head at her opening. She lowered onto him as slowly as her shaking legs allowed.
"Feel how wet I am? You did that to me." One at a time she brought
her legs onto the bench, squeezing his hips between her knees. She
pressed her palms on his pecs and leaned forward. "I want to kiss
you." Her gaze fell to his mouth. "But I want to fuck you hard."

He groaned a soft, "Yes."

When she started to move on him, she expected he'd thrust his
pelvis up. But he didn't. His hands tightened on her hips.

Since he'd tortured her—even at her own request—she opted
to return the favor. His ears were one of his hot spots, so she licked
and sucked and breathed heavily into both of them before she focused her attention on his neck. His skin tasted of musk and salt.

She ran her tongue along his collarbones and tried to bury her
face in his chest hair, but the angle was wrong.

No matter how fast she bounced on him, he didn't start pumping his hips. Yet she could tell by the way his eyes were squeezed
shut and his jaw clenched that it was taking everything he had to
hold back.

Slowing down gave him a breather and allowed her to grind
the way she needed to. She rocked against him, driving herself toward the edge, pushing harder when her midsection tightened.
Finding that sweet spot, she started to come for the third time. It
wasn't as intense, but she loved having his cock filling her as her
cunt muscles spasmed around that hardness.

When Shiori blinked away the white fog and looked down,
Knox said, "You're so beautiful and fierce when you come."

She kissed his lips like she could suck the words into her soul.
Before she released that tempting mouth completely, she whispered, "Come whenever you're ready."

"Thank you, Mistress."

They stared into each other's eyes as she rode him. When he
arched his neck and turned his head away, she didn't falter in her

rhythm. Their bodies were slick with sweat as they moved together, and Knox came with a hoarse cry.

He looked pretty fierce himself.

Shiori stretched out on him completely, nestling her face into his neck and sighing deeply.

His hands left her hips and trailed up and down her back, creating those delicious goose bumps.

They remained like that until the sweat on their bodies started to cool after one last kiss to his neck; then she rolled up and let him slip from her body. She stood and gathered up her clothes.

For some reason Knox didn't get up. He remained sprawled on the bench, staring at the ceiling. He didn't even acknowledge her when she picked up the toys he'd swept to the floor.

Finally she said, "Knox? Are you okay?"

"Yeah. Just wrung out."

But that wasn't it. Something else was going on with him. "Are you sure?"

"Jesus, Shiori, let it go. I'm fine."

Since they'd finished this scene or whatever it was, she ignored his use of her name. But she knew if she stayed in here with him a moment longer, they'd end up in a fight. So much for them continuing the fun and games for the rest of the weekend.

Every time it felt like she'd made progress with him, something had him pulling back.

Feigning confidence she didn't feel, she swung the pillowcase over her shoulder. Without looking back she said, "Clean up the room before you take off," and walked out, leaving him to his regret, because she suspected that was what he was feeling.

AFTER leaving the club, Shiori went home.

She poured herself three fingers of scotch. Rather than sitting in the stark living room with the incredible city view, she headed straight to her bedroom. She stripped and flopped on the chaise lounge. The plush sheepskin covering felt absolutely decadent on her bare skin. This was the only piece of furniture she'd bought—the penthouse had come furnished—and she loved every freakin' inch of it.

The smooth, smoky scotch did nothing to soothe her jangled nerves. She didn't know where to begin dissecting what had gone wrong tonight.

Maybe you don't need to.

No. She had to figure out where she'd made her missteps with Knox—because it was obvious she'd stumbled.

He'd submitted in every way she'd asked him to. Kneeling. Asking her permission. Waiting for her signals. Last weekend when she'd taken two hours building his lust and his stamina before she'd rewarded him with a hand job, after he'd come, he looked at her like she was everything.

That's what she needed from him. His understanding and acceptance that taking him to his own blissful headspace was her joy, maybe even more so than his.

But he hadn't allowed her to reach that part of him tonight. How could she convince him to let go every time?

Maybe it wasn't Knox's issue but hers. She'd never had to break down a sub before. So how did she go about breaking down Knox's walls without breaking him?

Frustrated with her lack of insight, Shiori grabbed her phone and checked the time. It was just before noon in Tokyo. She scrolled through her contacts and selected the name.

The phone rang almost a dozen times before it was picked up. "This had better be an emergency," the gravelly voice warned.

"It is. I promise."

"Shiori-san! Is that really you?"

She smiled. "Yes, Mistress Keiko, it's really me."

"While I am happy to hear from you, I would prefer a call later in the afternoon."

"I'll be sleeping by then." Shiori sipped her scotch, savoring the delicious spread of warmth down her throat. "I'll get straight to the point so you can return to your beauty sleep."

"Ha." Fabric rustled in the background. Mistress Keiko spoke to someone in a soft and sweet tone. "Sorry for that. Now that I'm up, I'm sending Muja to make my tea."

"Muja lasted more than a month? I'm surprised."

"Muja is my only submissive these days," she chided gently. "If you'd been here even once in the last year, you'd know that."

"It's not like I'm avoiding you. I'm still in the United States."

"Permanently?"

"No." That sounded more definitive than she'd intended.

"So what can I help you with?"

That was all the prompting Shiori needed. The situation with Knox poured out of her.

Mistress Keiko remained quiet for quite a while after Shiori finished talking. Then she sighed. "You know what I'm going to say."

She braced herself.

"You need to cut him loose."

Her stomach flipped. Her heart ached. An automatic denial sprang to her lips. "Give me a really good reason why you think that's my only option."

"Because even if he truly accepts what he is, you can't keep him without harming him."

"So I should set him free before he withers and dies in my captivity?"

"Your *temporary* captivity," she corrected. "Proceed with caution, Shiori-san. From what you've told me, I suspect he'll be submissive to only one woman—the first woman who breaks down his walls. Say that woman is you. You're there now, but you don't intend to stay. What happens to him then?"

"I don't know."

"Yes, you do," she said sharply. "Be honest with me, but most of all, be honest with yourself."

"I leave him here with an awareness of what he is and no Mistress to guide him or give him what he needs," she recited with a bitter edge.

"Exactly. So you put the crack in his walls. Let some other Mistress knock them down the rest of the way and put him back together as she sees fit."

A spike of jealousy caused her to snap. "So I just say, 'Thank you for giving me your trust, but I'm done playing with you now' and walk away?"

"Yes. Do it as soon as possible before you lose any more control of the situation." Mistress Keiko sighed. "Your job as a Dominant is to set the parameters to suit yourself, not to suit your submissive."

Bullshit. Maybe at first she believed in Keiko's philosophy; be a rigid Mistress, act all-powerful and all-knowing at all times. But now Shiori realized she didn't have to follow anyone's rules but her own. "Thanks for the reminder, Mistress."

"You're just saying that to placate me," Keiko complained. "You are stubborn and you will do whatever you want regardless of the advice I pass on."

Shiori laughed. "True."

"Then why did you call me?"

"You're my mentor, and I wanted to make sure I was on the right path."

"I *was* your mentor, and you've gone off the path completely. But I can't fault you for that." She paused. "Trust your instincts and he will too. Good luck." She hung up.

A sense of melancholy washed over her. Then her thoughts rolled back to her conversation with Merrick and how he viewed her. After Mistress Keiko had cut her loose, as Mistress B she'd found freedom and confidence in herself, even if she did nothing more than strut around proclaiming her status as a Domme.

That jarred her.

Had she only been playing a part and that's why she'd always heeded her mentor's advice and rules?

No. She was a Domme. She hadn't needed her own rules because she'd never ventured outside the club scene—which had its own rules. Now she had the submissive she'd been searching for. From the very start Knox had given her everything of himself, everything she'd asked for.

What had she given him of herself in return besides orgasms?

Nothing.

So much for your claim that you'd put his needs above your own.

Had she even considered his needs?

She remembered last week he'd mentioned changing the parameters of the time they spent together. Why hadn't she made time to talk to him about it?

Because she'd been too concerned with maintaining her distance. Keeping a solid line between Shiori, his second-in-command, and Mistress B, his Domme.

If she wanted this to work, things had to change—she had to change.

She just hoped she hadn't come to this realization too late.

CHAPTER FIFTEEN

MONDAY afternoon before evening classes started, Knox called a meeting with all the MMA instructors. He could've just kept it to Black Arts instructors, but he invited Blue and his crew from ABC because chances were good the two programs would meld into one in the next year.

"The Black Arts MMA program needs a kick in the ass. And the faults with the program don't lie solely with the instructors, but with our organization as a whole. For the past few months we've been letting Joe Blow off the street take part in MMA training as long as he can pay the training fees. On the business side, that's not a bad move. Steady income keeps you all employed, and the students who want to excel will. Or so we thought. But what I'm seeing is our trainers giving equal instructions to the guys who'll never go anywhere outside of the occasional smoker as they give to the guys who have serious potential.

"This is Sensei Black's dojo. Even when I'm temporarily in charge, I'd never take action to change how he runs things. But I do feel that the MMA program is in its infancy here, and since Sensei hasn't been as involved in it, changes need to be made so it will have the reputation that Black Arts does. An incredible opportunity has

presented itself to us." Knox looked at Ito, Fisher, and Deacon. "I
will put your teaching skills up against anyone's. So we're looking
to enhance what we've already got, not demolish it."

He took a breath and looked at Shiori. She tapped her wrist,
telling him to get on with it.

"Maddox Byerly is looking to move from LA and find a new
challenge."

"Whoa." Fisher held up his hand. "*The* Maddox Byerly?"

"Yes. Shiori and I had a video conference call with him last
week. We gave him our offer and time to think it over. He got back
to us today." Knox grinned. "He accepted! He'll be moving to
Denver in the next month."

Everyone in the room started high-fiving one another. After
they settled down, Knox said, "We've gotta keep this quiet until
Maddox makes the announcement. At this point I'm not sure when
he'll tell people he's revitalizing our program, or what."

"Revitalizing?" Deacon said. "Hell, he'll reinvent it."

"The other thing is since Ronin is out of pocket, he's not aware
of this development."

Shiori leaned forward. "We've signed nondisclosure agree-
ments, so we can't address specifics, but between us here in this
room, I personally guaranteed Maddox's salary for a year. If Sensei
doesn't want to re-up Maddox's contract after that, it's his business.
I just didn't want to see an opportunity wasted. I knew if we didn't
make the best offer we could afford, Maddox would go elsewhere."

Half a million dollars. Knox still couldn't wrap his head around
having that kind of money in the bank, not to mention lending it
without hesitation. Shiori's phone call to her bank to move some
money around lasted ten minutes. Within an hour they had the funds
to make the offer.

"What's the catch?" Deacon said.

"Maddox is starting the MMA program from scratch. He'll
hold auditions for fighters. After a one-on-one conversation with

candidates, he'll make his selections. It'll be structured the same way—fighters paying us a training fee."

Ito raised his hand. As the senior member of the dojo training staff, at least age-wise, Ito's opinion held a lot of weight. "What are the chances he'll want to hire his own training staff?"

"I don't know. But we spent our entire budget on his salary, so there's very limited budget for additional instructors," Shiori said. "We e-mailed him bios from you three." She turned and addressed Blue, Gil, Fee, and Terrel. "As well as all of yours since we'll have crossover. I'd suggest, too, that your best fighters audition for him."

"I'd ask if ABC would be expected to kick in for Maddox's salary, but it sounds like Ronin isn't kicking in either," Blue said.

More laughter.

"And none of this would be possible if it weren't for Gil," Knox pointed out. "He's the one with the personal family connection to Maddox, and he alerted us to the opportunity. So thanks, Gil."

He inclined his head.

Fee raised her hand. "Is Maddox interested in a women's fighting program?"

"I don't know."

She harrumphed and exchanged a look with Shiori.

Okay, what was that about? "Any other questions?" He paused and looked around the room. "Then we're done."

The room emptied, leaving him alone with Shiori.

"That went well."

"They're not the ones I'm worried about. It's Ronin." He drummed his fingers on the table. "I wish he'd call in so I could talk to him."

"We did the right thing." She placed her hand over his. "Do you want to come over tonight?"

He pulled away from her. The lines between their public and personal relationships were getting harder to maintain. For him anyway. And he wasn't in the mood for servitude. Yeah, Shiori would get pissed if she knew he'd called it that. "No, thanks. I'll be ready for a beer and ten minutes in my steam shower when this day ends."

"What is going on with you?"

I like you and want you to be my girlfriend as well as my Mistress. And I feel like a total whiny fucking pussy telling you that because you refuse to consider it.

Two raps sounded on the door and Blue poked his head in. "Got a minute?"

"Sure. Come in." After Blue sat across from him, Knox said, "What's up?"

"I didn't want to bring this up in the meeting, but I think we'll need to cancel the upcoming fight, smoker, whatever we're calling it."

"Why?"

"Low advance-ticket sales for one. We've changed the lineup twice. And if we cancel ten days out, we only lose the ticket sales plus a ten-percent penalty for the venue. And now knowing that Maddox Byerly will be in the mix for future events, it's better if we cut our losses."

"Who've you talked to about this?"

"Katie. She's been trying to drum up interest, but nothing is working. We're set to do a poster and flyer campaign starting next week, but that's just more money flying out the door."

Knox sighed and rubbed his eyes. "The guys have been working toward this, putting in extra hours . . ."

"And it hasn't helped them a damn bit, because they all still look like thugs on the playground."

"What the fuck, Blue?"

"It's true. You've got two good fighters. Deacon and Ivan. It'd be best for you to cut your losses with the other trainees and not put them on an amateur card at all. They don't need false hopes." Blue leaned forward. "And do you really want to parade any of those guys past Maddox Byerly?"

Fuck. He hadn't thought of that. "Deacon told me to let them go too."

"Smart man." His gaze moved between Shiori and Knox. "You okay with the fight card getting canceled?"

"What about delaying it?" Shiori suggested. "Pare the roster down to eight bouts. Have all of Black and Blue's fighters on the card. Up the game. Get a big rival of Black Arts involved. ABC's too. It's worth a shot."

Blue studied her. "Great idea. I imagine your problem-solving skills are missed at Okada."

"I was the one stuck dealing with the poorly solved problems after the fact. So I'm happy to be here helping before problems become, well . . . problems."

"Would you have time to meet with Katie in the next couple days?"

"I'll check my schedule."

"Cool. Thanks." He stood. "Great news about Maddox. I'm glad you were able to step in because I sure couldn't afford him."

Knox got up after Blue left. "I'm heading down to catch Molly before Deacon's class starts. I'll tell her to contact Katie about event scheduling changes before she starts any promotion."

"Knox."

There was the Mistress voice. And dammit if it hadn't made him stop. "What?"

"What is going on with you?"

"I'm just stressed."

"Bullshit. Look at me."

He turned and glared at her. "Don't. Remember where we are. Something came up, so I'm turning over the advanced black belt class to you tonight."

"Shihan—"

"Later. I've got shit to do."

HIS shit to do included grabbing a six-pack and parking his ass on his back deck. He'd dragged out his fly-fishing gear, even when he hadn't hit a stream in more than two years. Something about trying to perfect a series of line-snapping casts quieted his mind.

Yet the thoughts kept churning.

So far in three weeks running Black Arts in Ronin's absence he'd managed to:

Piss off Zach and Jon by refusing to put them in the rotation to test for their next belt level.

Agree to totally dismantle the MMA program.

Hire a training coach whose first-year salary was more than the value of Knox's house.

Fuck Ronin's sister.

Maybe Ronin would fire his ass. Then what would he do? Not only would he lose his job, but he'd lose his friends. His identity.

Knox wasn't one of those guys who wanted to own his own business. He'd always been content being second-in-command. Being told what to do and getting it done.

And yet you're so surprised you're submissive?

He tried to shut up his brain with another beer.

After a while he did lose track of time. He decided he'd take a real vacation this summer. Pack his fishing gear, find a stream and . . . Then again, vacationing alone seemed pathetic.

Man, he was riding high on a pity-parade float today.

His cell buzzed in his pocket and he ignored it. About a minute after it stopped buzzing, it started in again. He pulled it out and checked the screen.

Shiori.

She'd called twice. As he sat there with his phone in his hand she called again. So he answered. "Hello."

"Knox? Are you at home?"

"Yeah, why?"

"I've been knocking on your door for five minutes."

She was here? "Come around the side of the house and through the gate. I'm on the back deck."

"Oh. Okay."

The hinge creaked, and he watched for her to appear out of the darkness. The second she did, his mood shifted. "What are you doing here?"

"I was just in the neighborhood and thought I'd drop in."

"You were out cruising the Denver suburbs?"

"Looking for a good time. So I hope I came to the right place."

Knox tugged her against him and wrapped her in his arms. He didn't say anything, just held on to her. They'd been wary around each other all day after the way things ended on Saturday night.

Shiori tickled his armpits to force him to release her.

"What was that for?"

"Because I want a kiss." She tipped her head back, closed her eyes, and puckered her lips.

Their bodies were still close—but not close enough—so he pressed his left arm into the small of her back. "Is that right?"

She cracked open one eye. "Yeah. And it'd better be a good kiss, too."

Knox pulled out all the stops as he leaned in to press his lips to hers. Teasing and controlling, mixing heat with sweetness, and then reconnecting with that consuming passion. When he broke the seal of their lips, Shiori actually chased his mouth for more.

"That kiss was good?"

"I don't know. Maybe you'd better kiss me like that again so I can be doubly sure."

"Greedy."

"When it comes to you."

This was what was killing him. Getting to know all sides of

this complex woman and liking every single one. And wanting to spend as much time as possible with her. But she didn't appear to feel the same way.

"So what were you doing out here in the dark?"

"Dinking around. Having a beer. You want one?"

"No. But I like the way it tastes on you."

"I've had two. That's my limit." He brushed her hair off her shoulder. "Do you wanna go inside?"

She shook her head. "I'm good staying out here with you."

Knox took her hand and led her up to his lounge chair. He plopped down and pulled her onto his lap, enfolding her in his arms with her head resting beside his neck.

Shiori shifted to gaze into his face. "Were you upset with me today?"

"I don't know if *upset* is the right word." He twisted a section of her hair around his finger.

"Then what?"

He kept twisting and releasing that hank of hair. "I got an *Omigod! Omigod! Omigod!* shrieking phone call from Vivie today. Seems she received a package from me, a package that contained the dress she tried on last weekend. Ring any bells?"

She blinked innocently. "Vaguely. Fill in the blanks for me."

Knox pulled her hair. "Nice try. Explain yourself, She-Cat."

"That dress looked perfect on her. So you, being the thoughtful big brother, bought it for her."

"But I didn't buy it for her." He realized the instant they started talking about money, a mask dropped over her face.

"Yes, you did. You get to be her hero, Knox. I'll bet she forgets who her date was for this event, but she'll never forget the dress."

"Hero." He snorted. "That's stretching it."

"Not from where I was standing. Vivie and Zara worship you." She traced circles on his chest. "You being there for them whenever they need you means more to them than a party dress. And I'll admit

I'm jealous of them because I wonder what it would've been like to have a brother like that."

"So the distance between you and Ronin . . . ?"

"Isn't a recent development. He left for the martial-arts academy when I was fifteen. He promised to keep in touch, but I didn't see him for four years. And that was only to tell us he was moving to the United States. So in a way, buying that dress for her was filling in an empty space from my teen years."

"That was incredibly generous of you. But that's who you are. Buying a dress for a girl. Buying a trainer for your brother, who hasn't always been there for you."

"It was a loan. If Ronin gets on board with Maddox, I will expect repayment." She bit her lip. "So that was part of your problem earlier at the dojo. After you'd heard from her, you thought I was trying to buy her affection."

"The thought had crossed my mind. Until I realized if that had been the case, you would've taken credit for it." He kissed her. "So thank you."

This time she held him in place when he tried to pull away. "Knox. I can feel your restlessness. Will you let me take care of you tonight?"

"Isn't that against the Domme code or something?" he joked.

"Completely. I'll probably get kicked out of the 'I don't give a shit about my sub's well-being because it's all about me' Domme club. Oh, right. I don't belong to that club anyway, so we're good."

"There's that smart mouth. I've missed it since we've become civil to each other."

"Then I'll try to insult you at least once a day." She pressed her palms to his cheeks. "Go into your bedroom, strip, and lay facedown on the bed."

"Shiori—"

"No games. I just want to touch you." She hopped off his lap and held out her hand. "Lead the way."

It was late, and the two beers had made him tired. He shed his clothes and pulled back the covers on his bed before he stretched out.

Then she was there, straddling his butt, leaning forward to rub her naked breasts on his back. She whispered, "Hard or soft?"

"What? My cock? Getting harder by the second."

She playfully sank her teeth into the nape of his neck. "No, your massage. Do you prefer hard or soft?"

"Hard."

When Shiori dug her fingers into his shoulder muscles, he let out a hiss of pleasure. He made that sound frequently as she worked him over. Reaching those deep tissues by pressing with her thumbs. Using her fists in a circular motion and digging her knuckles in.

Giving himself over to her—a sneaky way for her to prove her dominance—Knox felt himself sinking deeper into the state of bliss.

"Turn over so I can do your front."

She massaged his hands. His forearms. His biceps and triceps. His nipples hardened when she massaged his pecs. When those caressing fingers stopped at his sternum, he forced his eyes open.

Shiori brushed the back of her hand down his face. "Keep your eyes closed. No matter what."

"Okay." He stared at her, struck by the softness in her tonight. It was a side of her that he never would have believed a month ago.

"Starting now."

He let his eyelids flutter closed. And his body, which had been relaxed almost to the point of sleep, perked back to attention when her silky hair trailed down his belly.

His cock went erect as the moist breath from her soft laughter blew over the tip.

Knox clutched the sheets beside his hips instead of grabbing her head.

In true Shiori fashion, she teased him with licks and hand action. Stroking his balls. Letting her hair drift up the insides of his legs.

The teasing ended abruptly, and she sucked him into her mouth, past her lips, over her teeth.

So wet, so hot, so fucking perfect.

When she began to bob her head, he drifted into an altered state. The hot, wet suction felt amazing. Tiny swipes of her tongue in the magic spot beneath the head of his cock. Then long strokes as she pulled back and pushed his shaft back in deep.

She started with sexy humming noises that drove him to the edge. With all those sensations together . . . this would be an embarrassingly short blow job.

Shit. He couldn't come until she allowed it.

"Stop. Please." He panted. "I can't hold off."

"Yes, you can. Two more minutes. Count the seconds off in your head."

Definitely was the fastest he'd ever counted to one hundred twenty. But it'd worked.

She let his shaft slip from her mouth. "Good."

Her hand worked his cock, slippery with her saliva. Then she bent her head, and holy fuck his balls were in her mouth as she rubbed her thumb over the strip of skin behind his sac and his anus.

The sensations were so intense Knox couldn't control the shaking in his legs.

But he kept his eyes closed.

His balls were wet and tight when she pulled away. He thought she'd finish him with a hand job, but she said, "Come now," and all that delicious heat enveloped his dick again.

Four sucking glides and he was done. He groaned with relief when that first spurt shot out and she swallowed it down. He pulled the damn sheets off the bed when she caught the rhythm of his release and sucked in tandem with every spasm.

Add in the way her nails scored the insides of his thighs brought even more sensation. It was the mother lode of blow jobs.

At some point his consciousness might've left his head and spun around the room because he lost any sense of reality.

This? This was a true fucking Zen moment.

Her soft body moved up to lie next to him. Smooth lips brushed his. "Now you can open your eyes."

He lifted his lashes a little at a time, so he could drink in her beautiful face slowly from her stubborn chin, over her full mouth, her nose, to those golden eyes. "Thank you."

"My pleasure."

Knox twisted a section of her hair into a spiral, watching as it uncurled and straightened. "Not that I'm not happy to see you, but why are you really here?"

"Because I missed you."

"We saw each other on Saturday night," he pointed out. That'd easily been one of the hottest nights of his life. But it had gotten weird. After he'd come so hard he worried he'd ruptured brain cells, it seemed she hadn't cared about his inner struggle because she'd basically left him with his dick hanging out. "Then I didn't hear from you or see you until today."

Shiori tucked herself along the left side of his body and positioned his left hand on her lower back—a subtle reminder that she needed his touch. "My departure Saturday night was rude. I'm sorry."

"Why did you leave like that?"

"Because I wanted to invite you to spend the night with me. Then we could have had a repeat of last Sunday."

Knox lifted his head to look down at her. "And that would've been bad . . . why?"

"It wouldn't have been bad. It would've been great. But I don't know how this kind of thing works, okay? Every other sub I've been with, we parted ways at the club. Last week, when we ended up at your house, it was an easy transition. Saturday night after the scene, you acted like you didn't want anything to do with me."

"You could've just commanded me to come home with you."

Her eyes were so serious. "I know. But I didn't want to fuck this up, and I ended up doing it anyhow. Last weekend wasn't us only being Domme and sub, or coworkers. We were—"

"New lovers getting to know each other outside of bed."

"Exactly!"

He kissed her forehead. For someone so smart, sometimes she overanalyzed things too much. "Shiori. There's a word for that. It's called a relationship."

She sighed. "I suck at this."

"You suck very, very well, so don't ever apologize," he murmured against the top of her head.

She pinched his side.

He pinched her ass.

They didn't speak for several long beats as they each gathered their thoughts.

"I did some thinking, which is why you didn't hear from me," she said. "I also did some painting, but that was way less productive than the thinking."

"Painting? Like painting the walls?"

"No. Like painting pictures. But I'd be hard-pressed to call my paint smears art."

"Wait a sec. Did you paint that picture you brought me the first night you came over?"

"Yes."

"I love it. I put it front and center on my mantel."

She smiled against his chest. "I'm glad."

"Keep going with the other part. The thinking part."

She propped her chin on his chest and looked up at him. "Ironically, what I decided is exactly the opposite of what I originally told you."

This caginess drove him crazy. "Get to the point."

"I don't want to hide that we're romantically involved. Not from the people we work with or anyone else."

Knox couldn't stop his big grin. "Seriously?"

"Yes. I know how to be your Domme, but the rest of it outside that . . ."

Knowing how much pride she had, he understood how hard that'd been for her to admit. "I'll make you a deal. Since you are the big, bad Domme for sexy times, I'll take the lead on the relationship side. If what we do together as a couple is in the gray area of who calls the shots, we'll discuss it, okay?"

"Okay."

He kissed her, and soon soft and sweet turned into hard and hungry. He wanted to eat at her pussy the same way he ate at her mouth. "Stay with me tonight."

"I can't. But ask me tomorrow."

"And every day after that. I like having you naked in my bed, kitten." He let his breath tease her ear. "Be forewarned; I'm staking my claim on you tomorrow at Black Arts."

"How do you plan on doing that?"

"Well, I have this fantasy of bending you over my desk and fucking you until you scream, *Yes, Shihan*, over and over."

"You'd have to get my permission to do that, remember?"

"Huh-uh." Knox nuzzled her neck. "The dojo is *my* domain, remember? I'm in charge."

She sighed. "Nailed on a technicality."

"Literally." He laughed. "But I promise I'll only nail you when we're alone. No one gets to see any naked bits of you, Mistress. They all belong to me now."

"Same goes," she murmured.

"And since you outed yourself as my Mistress to Master Merrick, that means I get to take you out on a real date this week too."

"You are enjoying the hell out of this."

"Yes, ma'am."

CHAPTER SIXTEEN

TUESDAY morning Ivan walked into the conference room and caught them kissing.

His face turned the color of borscht and he left without uttering a word.

"Won't be long now," Shiori said.

"Three minutes, tops."

Sure enough, Deacon stormed in. His gaze went from Shiori, sitting on the conference table, to Knox, standing between her knees, to Shiori's hand on Knox's chest, to Knox's hands on Shiori's ass. "I told Ivan he'd probably misread the situation. Either that or I'd misheard him—figuring he'd meant you two were *killing* each other, not kissing each other."

Knox brushed his lips across hers. "Ivan's eyes did not deceive him. We got a little carried away. Probably something you should get used to seeing."

"You've gotta be fucking kidding me. You two are together?"

"Yep."

"How long have you been secretly playing grab ass?"

Shiori tugged the lapels of Knox's gi top. "A couple of weeks."

"That's it. I'm making a call."

Deacon made it to the door when Knox said, "Wait. Who are you calling?"

"My priest. Seeing the two of you sucking face is a sign the end of the world is near, and I've got a lot of shit to confess."

After Deacon slammed the door behind him, Shiori said, "That went well."

Knox laughed.

Later that afternoon, when Shiori was changing in the women's locker room, Fee ambushed her. "You're bending the bedframe with that knockout Knox and you didn't tell me?" She hit the metal locker with her fist. "I thought we were friends."

"We are."

"Sisters share shit like this, Shiori."

"Say that five times fast," she muttered.

"What?"

"Nothing. Look, we didn't tell anyone. We weren't sure it would last beyond—"

"One good, hard fuck?" Fee said.

"Yes. What if we fizzled instead of sizzled in bed? Not something we wanted everyone we work with to know about."

"I'm assuming the sizzle factor won out."

Shiori slumped against her locker. "It's so fucking hot between us sometimes I think we should wear fire-retardant clothing."

Fee held her hand up for a fist bump. "Damn, girlfriend. You've bagged Knox. I'm jealous."

"Thanks . . . I think."

She laughed. "Now you can wear that well-fucked look with pride, my friend. After sneaking around, you've earned it."

Shiori returned to the office and found Knox alone, staring out the window. She didn't hesitate to move behind him and wrap her arms around his waist. "What's up, Shihan?"

"My man cred."

"What?"

"Evidently my man cred is at an all-time high because I'm boning Black Arts's beautiful badass."

She groaned. "Who called me that? Wait. I don't want to know."

"If they would've kept talking, you'd know exactly who said it by their black eye or busted lip."

Knox didn't sound amused. She wormed her way in front of him, creating space for herself. She slid her hands up his chest and looked into his eyes. "Are you mad?"

"I tried to be cool when they broke you down body part by body part. But you're so much more to me than a fantastic ass, killer arms, and a wet-dream mouth." He rested his forehead to hers. "I know guys say stupid shit about women and I used to chime in. But it's different when it's my woman."

"We'll be old news by Wednesday. For what it's worth, I'm happy we're out." She touched her lips to his. Once. Twice. "Because now we can do this anytime we want."

"You're right. And if we need privacy, the door to the storage room does lock."

After the first couple of days, the catcalls and *bow chicka wow* sounds tapered off.

Deacon still complained about their PDA, regardless of whether he found them holding hands, grappling, or even sneaking hot looks at each other across the dojo, but he was the only one.

She and Knox started spending every other night together, alternating between his house and her penthouse.

The sweet, crazy man even took her on a date. A fancy date where he brought her flowers, picked her up wearing a suit and tie, and piled on the compliments about how stunning she looked in the slinky cocktail dress she'd worn. The restaurant he'd chosen had a bohemian vibe from the food to the decor. She couldn't stop staring at him throughout the meal—especially considering how the glow of candlelight sharpened the angles of his face, making him almost beautiful. After eating they'd strolled around downtown

Denver and stopped into a jazz bar for a nightcap; then he'd taken her back to her place, where he'd leveled her with a mind-blowing kiss at her door before he said good night.

Knox proved he could be a perfect gentleman.

The more quirky, sexy, funny things she discovered about Knox, the more she wanted to uncover.

No surprise they were total opposites. He did everything himself from working on his house, to changing the oil in his truck, to washing his clothes. Whereas she dropped her clothes off at the dry cleaner, she never fixed a meal, and she didn't own a vacuum. Knox liked the outdoors. Fishing, camping, target shooting, and hiking were his idea of a good time. She was happier inside, where she wouldn't get sunburned or bitten by bugs and had access to the Internet and takeout menus. As a jock, if Knox wasn't playing sports, he was watching them: MMA, football, basketball, rugby, and hockey. Shiori considered shopping a sport. She exercised only so she didn't have to monitor every bite she ate.

But somehow the manly man and the girly girl worked so far. They really worked when it came to sex. She loved the glazed look in Knox's blue eyes when she switched into Domme mode. She loved how quickly they segued from lovers snuggled on the couch to Knox awaiting her command. She loved that he anticipated her needs, and he took pride in fulfilling them. She loved that they pushed each other's boundaries; his role in the bedroom and hers outside of it.

Yet Shiori wasn't thrilled with Knox's latest attempt to increase her independence. Her argument that her dependence on others to do things for her had created jobs made him laugh.

"Kitten, you're pretty even when you're surly, but lose the pout and let's get moving."

"You can't make me."

More laughter. "Yes, I can."

"How?"

He shot her a smoldering look. "You know how."

"By withholding sex?"

"Got it on the first try."

Shit. "So? Sex is overrated."

"Says my Mistress who fucked me twice yesterday." His voice deepened. "You riding me in the shower first thing yesterday morning ringing a bell? Or how about you riding my face last night?"

"Is that a complaint?"

Knox aimed his hungry stare at her mouth. "Never."

She leaned closer and nuzzled his cheek. "If you take me home, I'll suck your cock until the top of your head blows off."

"Nice try. But no. You'd keep me hanging on the edge for hours just so we didn't have to come back and do this. So suck it up or there'll be no sucking of anything between either of us."

"That's it," she huffed. "I'm using my safe word."

His mouth brushed her ear. "You don't have a safe word. *I* have a safe word, remember?"

"Knox." That sounded whiny. "Why are you pushing me on this?"

"Because you're thirty-five years old and it's time you learned to drive."

She pointed to his big truck that was like twenty-seven feet off the ground and had tires the size of a bulldozer. "I'd rather not crash and burn a monster truck."

"Stop saying that. This is a standard-sized pickup."

"It can't be."

"It is."

"Compared to what? Tractors? Have you seen the size of cars in Japan?"

"Nope. And we're not in Japan; we're in America, where our public-transit system in the Wild West isn't up to Japanese bullet-train standards."

"Not the same thing."

"Quit being a pain in the ass and get in."

"I don't like your tone."

Knox got right in her face. "You won't like my hand smacking your ass either if you don't get it moving."

"Acting a little cheeky today, sub."

"I'm not your sub right now, remember? So quit stalling, whining, and bitching, and pull up your big-girl panties and get in the damn truck."

"Fine. I assume you have a ladder?"

He muttered something. Then he pointed to the thin piece of silver chrome below the door. "That's the running board. Use it to get in."

Shiori opened the door and launched herself into the driver's seat. First thing she moved the seat closer to the steering wheel. If Knox's knees were hunched against the dashboard, it was his own fault for being so tall.

Knox climbed in the passenger side. More muttering. Then, "Move the seat back. You don't need to be directly under the steering wheel to drive."

She eased the seat back.

"Now. You have two pedals at your feet. But you're only going to use one foot. Gas is on your right. The brake is in the middle. Now look on your dashboard and see the letters *P, R, N, D, L*?"

"I see them."

"What do they stand for?"

"Pretty Reckless New Driver, Lookout?"

He didn't crack a smile.

She sighed. "Park, reverse, neutral, drive . . . no idea what the L is for."

"Low. You can drop it into a lower gear if the weather is bad or if you're driving down a steep grade. Now turn the key and start 'er up."

"It seems too soon. Shouldn't we go over the safety features of this vehicle?"

He shook his head. "Turn the key and press on the gas at the same time."

"I have to do two things at once?" she practically shrieked.

"Shiori," he snapped. "Stop freaking out. If sixteen-year-old kids can do this, so can you."

She turned the key and slammed her foot down on the gas pedal. The engine roared.

"Good. Now put your foot on the brake and move the gearshift into drive."

"So then we'll be moving."

"Hopefully."

"Where are we going?"

"Around and around in this empty parking lot until you feel comfortable behind the wheel."

Jesus. They'd be here for two months if that held true. She pulled the gearshift down until the red needle was on the D. "Now what?"

"Now take your foot off the brake. The truck is in gear and it will move, but not much until you apply the gas. So when you step on the gas, do it gradually, not all at once."

Okay. Here goes.

She fought the temptation to close her eyes. She put her foot on the gas like Knox said, and the truck lurched forward. She took her foot off and slammed on the brake. Then she tried it again. This time it went smoother. She tried a little more gas and it didn't lurch.

"Doing great. Now, try not to drive down the middle but stay to the right."

"There's so much to remember."

"When you get to the end of this row, turn right and go up the other side. And you might get a better feel for driving if you went faster than ten."

Was he snickering? She didn't dare take her eyes off the road to glare at him or take her hands off the wheel to flip him off.

She putted down four rows, gradually increasing her speed. By the time she'd reached the end of the last parking row, she'd ramped the speed up to twenty-five. When she saw the curb and the cement block base for the streetlamp in her path, she panicked. She cranked the wheel hard and the truck almost spun in a circle.

Knox yelled, "Brake! Brake!"

She jammed on the brake with both feet and they lurched forward. Good thing they wore seat belts.

"Jesus Christ, Shiori. What the hell were you doing? You trying to roll my damn truck and give me a heart attack? You can't take a corner at twenty-five!"

"You kept telling me to speed up!"

"Not when you're turning a corner. That's when you slow down!"

She moved the gearshift into park. Then she turned the ignition off, unbuckled her seat belt, and bailed out of the truck. Wrapping her arms around herself, she started walking.

Tears fell, which pissed her off.

Knox ran past her and planted himself in front of her.

She just stepped around him and kept walking.

Then he blocked her path again. "Shiori. Can you please stop?"

She stopped.

He framed her face in his hands and tipped her head back. "Why are you crying?"

"You yelled at me."

"I've yelled at you a thousand times before."

"But not like this. You scared me." She sniffled. "I don't want to learn how to drive! Not knowing how to drive a car doesn't make me a lazy, stupid reject. I hate that everyone makes me feel that way."

"Do I make you feel that way?"

"Sometimes."

That surprised him.

"I've done the financial analysis on owning a car versus hiring a car service. When you add gas and insurance and depreciation and maintenance, I'm actually ahead at the end of the year by not driving. Not to mention the work I get accomplished when I'm being driven."

"Hey. Come here." Knox crushed her to his chest. "I'm sorry if anything I've ever said makes you feel like a reject. You're far from it." He kissed her forehead. "You know how I feel about you, Nushi. You're the most amazing woman I've ever met."

That caused the tears to fall a little harder. Knox worshipped her—every day in every way, without her having to demand it or beg for it. That was so new, so precious. She was so afraid of losing it, afraid of losing him.

"I was a dick to push you on this."

"Why did you push me?"

"Because you're stinking rich and can buy any fast car you want. How cool would it be to be able to drive them?"

"That's your reason?"

"No, I'm kidding. I just hate that you have strange men driving you all over town and you won't turn that job over to me."

"You're busy running the dojo. You don't have time to be my chauffeur."

"It's my right to take care of you," he argued. "And if you won't let me do that, at least let me teach you to take care of yourself."

She placed her hand over his heart. "Thank you for thinking of me and looking out for me."

"It's not jealousy about Tom the chauffeur playing fetch and carry for you."

But she knew that was a large part of it. Any man who did anything for her made Knox feel like he was slacking. Wanting her to rely on him for everything was unrealistic. And what happened if she leaned on him—only him? At some point he'd get resentful. She'd been through it before. "Knox. This *is* me taking care of myself."

He stared at her, the muscle in his jaw flexing as he struggled with how to respond.

"How about if we start small with the driving thing? Every time we drive past that indoor go-kart track you tell me how much you'd love to take me there."

His eyes lit up. "You'd go today? Right now?"

"If you take me out for sushi afterward. Oh, and frozen yogurt." She walked her fingers up his chest. "Of course that'll have to be to go, because I plan to use your body as my dessert plate."

No surprise Knox burned rubber taking her there.

ANOTHER boring Thursday.

She'd done payroll.

She'd done promotional research.

She'd done the dishes in the break room.

Her gaze zoomed to Knox. There was one thing she hadn't done today.

Shiori pushed her chair back and stood. "Pick a fight with me."

Knox looked up from his desk. "Excuse me?"

"You heard me. Say something cutting like you used to."

"Why?"

"Because I always secretly got a thrill out of verbally sparring with you." Sauntering across the room, she said, "Insult me."

"Is this some kinda test?"

"No." She reached his desk and spun his chair around, pressing her hands into the armrests. "Say, 'Jesus, She-Cat, why didn't you just do the log-in reports in crayon since it looks like a second-grader did them?'"

"Funny."

"Or how about . . . Ms. Hirano, your attitude sucks balls today."

Knox raised an eyebrow. "Maybe because you had my balls in your mouth last night?"

"No, you never said sexual things to me before."

"At least not to your face."

She smiled. "See? Stuff like that."

"Kitten, I don't know what you're after here. Is this a Domme game?"

"No. It's a you and me game. While I love the fact we're getting along so well, I miss that back-and-forth we used to have."

"What do you want to do about it?"

"How about if we start this over?" Shiori straightened up. "Play along."

"Yes, ma'am."

"When I walk in, act like it's the first time you've seen me today."

Knox still seemed confused, so she hoped he picked up on what she wanted.

To make the scene authentic, she shouldered her purse and slipped out the door, closing it behind her. She wandered down the hallway, careful not to get too close to the training room.

After five minutes had passed, she opened the door and meandered in, slamming it shut behind her.

"Wow, you're here before the crack of noon today, She-Cat?" Knox said with total sarcasm. "That's two days in a row. Are you hoping that'll put you in the running for Employee of the Month?"

"Bite me, Ob-Knox-ious." She tossed her purse on her desk.

"I'll pass since I doubt you've had a rabies shot recently." He smirked.

"I've gotta give you props for not giving up. Even when your jokes always suck ass, gosh darn it, you keep on trying to convince me you're funny."

Knox flashed his teeth. "Maybe it's a cultural thing, Shitake. American humor escapes you."

"Of course that's it." She smacked herself in the forehead. "It's a language barrier."

"Glad you're coming to terms with your limitations."

Why the fuck was this getting her hot? Her heart raced. Her belly had butterflies. Her face felt warm.

"How about if we cut the crap? I looked at your so-called log-in reports," Knox said snidely.

"And?"

"And why are they in Japanese?"

"Because Japanese is my first language?" she replied.

"How in the hell am *I* supposed to read them?"

She crossed her arms over her chest. "That's the thing, Knox. Those reports aren't for you. Which I've told you umpteen times, not that you ever pull your head out of your ass long enough to listen to me."

The hard muscle in his jaw flexed. "You finished them in another language so I couldn't double-check your data? Real mature, She-Cat."

"I don't need you going over those reports like a teacher checking my homework."

"How do I know you're not trying to hide something?"

"Are you fucking serious right now? What could I possibly be hiding?"

He shrugged. "Maybe you're having parties in Ronin's penthouse since you're the only one with access to it."

"Parties?" she repeated. "You really think I'd jeopardize my brother's privacy as well as his trust in me?"

"Like I said, I don't know. That's why I need to read those reports. You could be having rooftop keggers up there every Saturday night for all I know."

She stalked over and slammed her hands on his desk. "Am I even supposed to know what that means? What the fuck is a kegger?"

Knox's gaze had turned molten. He was just as turned on by this as she was. "Keggers. Wild parties with kegs of beer where the goal is to get drunk, lose articles of clothing, and see how stupid you can act."

"That sounds right up your alley, Ob-Knox-ious. Is that why Ronin didn't leave *you* a key to the penthouse?" she asked sweetly.

"Yeah, well, he had to give *you* some kind of token since he left *me* in charge of the dojo."

"You are such a dickhead."

"Yeah? Baby, you've taken *bitch* to a whole new level."

Shiori leaned closer. "I wish we were on the mat right now, Godan, because I'd pound that smug fucking face of yours into the ground."

Knox's big hands circled her wrists and he got nose to nose with her. "You have that backward, kitty-cat. I think you'd like me pounding your hot little body into my mattress—not the training mat. And I'd be more than happy to oblige you, but I'd probably have to gag you first."

"You'd have to pin me first," she shot back. "And we both know who's got the better skills when it comes to takedowns."

"Don't tempt me to prove you wrong."

They were so close they shared the same air. Fire danced in his eyes, and she could smell the heat of his skin. The embers that'd been smoldering between them ignited.

"Knox."

He didn't answer; he just brushed his mouth across hers. Once. Twice. "Is this what you missed, kitten?" he murmured against the corner of her mouth.

"Yes."

"Me too." He angled his head and ran his nose from her temple down below her ear. "What are we gonna do about it? Because right about at this point in the conversation is where you'd walk away."

"If I walk away this time, will you follow me?"

"Without a doubt."

She nuzzled his cheek, breathing in the scent of aftershave and arousal seeping from his skin. "Do you have a condom?"

"Since fucking you is now a reality and not a daydream?" He planted a hot kiss below her ear. "Baby, I shoved a whole box in my bottom drawer."

"Hoping I'd fuck you in the dojo, Shihan?"

"Always." His lips followed the shell of her ear. "Since we *are* in the dojo, which is my domain, Mistress rules don't apply. So get your ass in the supply closet and wait for me."

Here was a test. Technically, Knox was right; he called the shots at Black Arts. But since this was about sex, it should be her show.

Isn't it your show? You made him act a scene out with you. This is the result. You letting him have control and making sure he knows it's only because you allowed it adheres to the Domme-sub rules you've established and isn't him pushing boundaries.

When Knox whispered, "Play along," her internal debate ended.

Shiori sought his mouth and kissed him hard. Reminding him who had the power and she'd exercise it whenever it suited her. Then she pulled away and crossed the room to the small supply closet in the corner without looking back.

CHAPTER SEVENTEEN

KNOX rubbed his hand over his mouth as he watched her walking away.

That ass. Jesus. It called to him like the gravitational pull of the moon.

The second the supply-closet door closed, he yanked open the bottom drawer and ripped off a single condom package.

He forced himself to wait another minute before he chased after her, which gave him a chance to plan how this encounter would play out. He understood the leap of faith she'd taken, offering him the chance to take charge—he sure as fuck didn't want to blow it.

Shiori's role-playing game had gotten him all kinds of worked up. It reminded him of the months they'd gone back and forth nearly every day. And he was man enough to admit it'd gotten him hot then too.

The minute was up.

As Knox crossed the room, he wished his shoes made more noise on the wooden floor so she could hear him coming for her. The hinges squeaked on the door when he opened it slowly. He closed it behind him and locked it, then took a moment to study her, building her anticipation.

Shiori stood in front of the window. With the way she'd angled her head, the sun shone on her ebony hair, and a section reflected as fiery red. When he started toward her, he saw her hands tighten on the ledge.

Two floor-to-ceiling shelving units flanked the room on both sides. Since this was an old building, the ceilings were high, as were the windows. He'd always thought using this as a supply closet was a waste of good space—until now.

Knox moved in, pressing his body to hers. He reached beneath her arms to begin unbuttoning her blouse and rubbed his lips against the back of her neck. Her scent teased him—warm skin with the hint of spice. After he'd managed the buttons, he stripped off her blouse and her bra.

He groaned at feeling her soft, bare skin beneath his hands. "I love touching you."

"I love the way you touch me," she admitted. "And I need you to take your shirt off so we're skin to skin."

"Anything for you," he said into her hair. He made quick work of ditching his shirt and pressed his bare chest to her naked back.

A small hiss escaped her.

She'd worn pants today. His hands followed the contour of her upper torso, down her sides to her hips. He traced his finger along her waistband, just to feel her quiver from his touch. Then he un-hooked the clasp on the inside of her pants and pulled down the zipper, all the while letting his mouth drag openmouthed kisses across her shoulders.

As soon as her pants were loose, he pushed the soft fabric down her hips and over the curve of her ass until they pooled around her ankles. "Step out of them and kick off the shoes."

Even when Shiori shifted sideways, he kept his hands and his

mouth on her, not only in a show of control, but as a constant reminder he couldn't get enough of her.

Knox put his lips at the base of her neck, following the ridges
of her spine with his tongue all the way down until he had to drop
to his knees. Now her mouthwatering ass was right in his face.

Nice.

He hooked his fingers into the sides of her black panties and
pulled them down, eliminating the last barrier between them.

When she kicked her underwear aside, he tapped on the insides
of her calves as a signal to widen her stance.

Then he teased those dimples above her ass with his lips until
the fine hairs stood on end and she tried to rub her thighs together.
It was very tempting to give her a good, hard smack on the ass to
make her stay still, but he wasn't sure how far he could push her. So
he opted to distract her, pressing against her lower back and changing the angle of her hips.

Her breathing had become erratic, and he glanced up to see her
breath fogging the window.

He allowed himself a small grin before he zeroed in on his next
target. Moving his hands down the outside of her butt, he placed
his thumbs just inside the crack of her ass so he could pull her
cheeks apart. Then he dragged his tongue down the split, lifting
her slightly so he could reach that pink pucker.

Shiori cried out, "Oh god," at the first wet lash of his tongue.

He swirled his tongue around the outside of the tight rosette,
lapping at it until the muscle loosened. Then he jammed his tongue
inside.

Another loud gasp echoed to him and he felt her legs start to
shake.

His cock pulsed. He'd gotten so lost in the chance to touch and
taste Shiori however he wanted that he'd forgotten his body's
needs.

That's your submissive nature. Making sure your Mistress is satisfied before you are.

And for once, his male ego didn't argue. It just urged him to get on with it.

After one last long lick where he got his first taste of the juices flowing from her pussy, he pushed to his feet. Somehow he managed to get his pants down and the condom on one-handed because he kept a hand on her at all times. When they'd first become physical, she'd demanded some part of him be touching her all the time. And now he needed that connection as much as she did.

Knox planted a kiss on her shoulder. There was a ledge above the heater that might be rough on her knees, but it put her at the perfect height. Keeping hold of her hips, he said, "Knees on the ledge and then I want your hands on the window."

As soon as she'd gotten into position, he rocked his pelvis to her ass. He held his cock in his left hand and spread his right hand between her hip bones, adjusting the angle and allowing his middle finger to connect with her clit.

And another swift intake of breath as he stroked her there.

He pushed inside her pussy slowly. Once he'd filled her with his cock, he said, "Hard and fast."

Her "Yes" came out with a whimper.

Knox pulled out and impaled her. Again. And again. The sound of skin slapping against skin and Shiori's soft grunt each time he bottomed out inside her echoed in the small space.

Now the window had a wider patch of steam from their combined heavy breathing. Her back was slick with sweat, as was his chest, making them stick together.

He rubbed on her clit gently, knowing she didn't like aggressive touches at the start. But the harder and longer he pounded into her, the wetter she got, and he could increase the speed of his strokes.

When Shiori's body went stiff beneath him, he grabbed a handful of her hair and pulled her head aside to get at her neck. At the touch of his lips to her damp skin, goose bumps erupted and she moaned.

"I love fucking you. I love everything about how we are together. The sounds, the scents, the tastes, the feeling of your body moving against mine."

"Knox . . ."

"Do you like the way I fuck you, Nushi?"

"Yes."

He sucked the tender skin below her ear. "I want to take that sweet little asshole of yours like this someday. Getting it good and stretched out with my tongue before I ram my cock in hard." He nuzzled the back of her neck. "Tell me you'll let me do anything to you that makes you scream when you come."

"Anything." She panted. "Anything I tell you to do."

"Tell me what will make you come now."

"I'm so close. Faster on my clit. And your mouth—"

"I know where you want my mouth," he growled. Then he pulled harder on her hair, forcing her to give him access to the spot she was protecting. He latched on to it with his teeth and sucked hard, flicking her clit and managing to keep the slamming rhythm of his cock.

He knew the instant she started to come; one hand left the window and got a death grip on his hair. Her cunt muscles contracted around his dick, and her clit spasmed beneath his stroking finger.

"Fuck, yes, oh yes." Shiori didn't scream, but she gasped and moaned through every pulsing throb until he heard her voice turning hoarse.

After the storm of pleasure ebbed, she curled her hand around the back of his neck and pressed the side of her face into his. "You . . . that . . ." She sighed. "Yeah, I love the way you fuck."

He wondered if she'd noticed the grinding of his teeth and how he'd slowed his thrusts to keep himself in check.

Shiori angled her face to capture his lips. After teasing him with almost kisses and an exchange of breaths, she said, "Thank you for this." Another lick on the inside of his bottom lip because the woman knew how crazy that made him. "You rocked me."

"My pleasure. Mistress, can I come?"

"Yes." She returned her hand to the window, knowing he'd finish this with sheer force.

Knox curled both hands into her hips, anchoring her to receive these last few pile-driving thrusts. He watched himself plunging into her until that moment when his balls lifted and his orgasm jetted through him in pulsating waves.

It felt so fucking good to be sated and soft within her hot walls that he kept pumping even after that last blast.

Shiori didn't stop him. Didn't say, "Enough. Pull out." She just let him come down from his orgasmic high gradually. She got him. Every single time she knew what he needed and found a way to give it to him.

No wonder he worshipped her.

Immediately after Knox eased out, he helped her down from the ledge. He turned her around and kissed her for a good, long time, knowing that's what she wanted. Bodies and mouths touching, not to establish her dominance, but to strengthen their bond.

Once he was certain she had regained her sense of balance, he dropped to his knees, despite the awkwardness of having his pants around his ankles. He didn't ask for permission since she'd given him the appearance of his being in charge. He lowered his mouth to her pussy, using his thumbs to get at the sweet pearl already returning to hiding within her pink folds. He sucked gently but relentlessly until she came against his mouth. He drank her orgasm down, swallowing her juices like fine wine.

She petted his hair afterward. "Being with you is like nothing I've ever experienced, Knox."

"I'm striving to make a good impression."

"You've succeeded. Thank you. Now we need to get dressed."

Even dressing separately wasn't uncomfortable, which proved to him how easy it was being with her. Shiori didn't play mind games. She didn't try to trick him or trip him up so she could punish him. She simply . . . enjoyed him, in whatever manner she chose.

And it was a real boost to his ego that he could make her mindless, that he could make her come so hard she couldn't breathe or speak. That she'd chosen him to be part of all that with her.

"What are you thinking about so hard, over there?" she asked.

Knox buttoned his shirt, watching as she did the same. "That you're right. We need to have more fights."

She laughed.

"Seriously, is it all right if I look for activities we can do together that keep the competitive nature alive between us?"

Her eyes softened. "I'd love that."

"Cool." He opened the door to let her leave first.

Right as they walked out of the supply closet, Deacon walked into the office.

Deacon looked from Shiori to Knox and then to the closet. "Were you two fucking around in the supply closet?" He paused and held up his hand. "Never mind. I don't want to know."

"Did you need something?" Knox asked.

"A couple of the guys you cut from the MMA program would like to speak with you."

"Did they show up with flowers and chocolates to thank me personally for cutting them?"

"I wish they'd come in through the dojo and not up to the business offices. That way they would've gone through the metal detector."

Shit. "That bad?"

"Spewing shit like any other dumb fucker who thinks looking tough and acting tough translates to toughness in the ring." Deacon cracked his knuckles. "They're punks."

Knox ran his hand over the top of his head. "All right. Let's go." He looked at Shiori. "Translate those reports into English."

She smirked. "Sure thing, boss. Don't you want me to help explain a few things to the punks?"

"Nope. We'll handle it."

For a moment it seemed like she'd argue, but she slipped behind her desk.

Knox and Deacon walked side by side down the hallway. "Who showed up?"

"Radley and Lotte."

"Of course it's those two. They don't know when to shut their fucking mouths." Knox dropped his voice. "Where the fuck did they get their egos? Jesus. It's not like they did anything of note to earn them."

"No clue. They're pathetic little wannabes. Ronin wouldn't let me work with them full force or they wouldn't have lasted as long as they did."

When they entered the training room, Blue gave a subtle nod and slipped out the side door.

Both guys had taken on belligerent postures like punk-ass gangbanger rejects. They also looked high. Great. "What are you doing here?"

"It's bullshit that you think you can just cut us from the MMA program with no warning," Lotte said.

"Yeah, you tell him, bro," Radley piped in.

"Black Arts is a private dojo, and we have the right to revoke training privileges at any time." Knox's gaze swung between them. "Is that all you needed me to clear up?"

Lotte sneered. "You don't have the fucking authority to kick us out."

"I'm in charge of the dojo while Sensei Black trains out of the country. What I say goes. You're both done. I know you packed up your gear and were refunded the balance of your fees, so I don't get why you're here."

"You act like you're hot shit, but you don't know shit. You're the joke in the MMA program." Lotte threw back his shoulders. "You have no skills to offer. You just wander around the training room like a big, stupid ape."

Even these bottom-feeders see how worthless you are to the program.

His ego picked a helluva time to push that crisis to the forefront of his thoughts.

"Yeah," Radley added. "When Sensei Black gets back and hears that you cut his two most promising fighters, he's gonna be pissed."

Knox flashed his teeth. "Black Arts's two most promising fighters are still on the roster, and it ain't you two. Won't *ever* be you two. You sucked the day you walked in. Your so-called skills became more laughable the longer you tried to pretend you were badass motherfuckers. Am I right, Deacon?"

"One hundred percent right as usual, Shihan."

"Do you suck his dick too?" Lotte and Radley high-fived.

"I hear the comedy club in Writer Square is hiring . . . bus-boys," Deacon drawled. "You jokers oughta fit right in. Now, get the fuck outta here."

Lotte and Radley looked at each other.

"Here's where you say, 'Make us leave,' giving us the chance to kick your scrawny asses down the stairs. Or you do the smart thing and shut your mouths and get out." Deacon stepped away from the door, giving them a clear path.

"We'll leave, but this won't be the last you'll see of us," Lotte warned.

"Yeah, you'd better start locking your door during the day," Radley said smugly. "You never know who could show up. Homeless guys are always looking for a place to hide out during the day. Maybe we'll tell the hobos at the Sixteenth Street Mall about this place."

"Was that a threat?" Knox asked.

"Call it whatever you want. A warning." Lotte grinned nastily. "A premonition."

"That's supposed to intimidate me into putting you back in the program?"

Lotte shrugged.

Knox started toward them. "Tell you what. If one of you bests me? I'll let you train." He crossed his arms over his chest. "So which one of you is it gonna be?"

"Me," Lotte and Radley said simultaneously.

"There can be only one," Deacon said, deadpan.

Holy fuck. Knox was about to burst out laughing at Deacon's *Highlander* reference. This whole thing had headed into farce territory.

"I can punch a fuck of a lot harder than you," Radley said to Lotte.

"That's the only fuckin' thing you can do," Lotte shot back. "My takedown skills are way better than yours."

Radley snorted. "Because you took a year of tae kwon do at the Y? Give me a fuckin' break."

Where the hell had Ronin dug up these dumb fuckers?

"Make a goddamn decision," Knox snapped.

Lotte stepped forward. "Me."

A quick spike of adrenaline juiced him as he closed the distance between him and that cocky little punk. Lotte started to speak, but Knox swept his feet out from under him.

Lotte landed on his ass.

Then Knox flipped him onto his belly, pulling his right arm crossways to his opposite hip and trapping his left arm beneath the front of his body. He pressed his boot on the side of Lotte's face. He didn't bother to lean down or to whisper. "I've got you pinned down, bro, and I'm using only one of my arms and one of my legs. Guess *worthless* applies more to you than it does to me."

"Let me go."

"I will. Then you'll take your little friend and get the fuck out of this building and never show your faces here again." Knox pulled on Lotte's arm until he whimpered. "The training room is under surveillance, so if a single homeless person shows up here? The tape goes to the cops. Got it?"

Lotte nodded.

"Answer the fucking question out loud so I know you understand."

"Yes."

"Yes, what?"

"Yes, sir."

He released Lotte.

Radley didn't wait for his bro. He hightailed it out the door. Lotte slunk out like a scalded cat, and Deacon followed them to make sure they got gone.

Knox scrubbed his hands over his face. He didn't need that shit today. When he looked up, Shiori leaned in the doorframe.

"Impressive, Shihan."

"All in a day's work."

"I love watching you deliver the smackdown. No one expects a guy your size to move that fast. In fact, it really turns me on." She sauntered forward with that heated look in her eye.

Instant boner.

Shiori stood on tiptoe to whisper in his ear. "I finished those reports."

"Okay." Goddammit, he loved that little bite of pain when she dug her fingers into his abdomen.

"I left them in the supply closet."

"Why?"

"It's time you had a lesson in Japanese. Oral is the best way to learn, don't you think?"

He groaned. "My brain just totally went offline and I can't think at all."

"Luckily, as your Mistress, it's my job to think for you. Get your ass in the supply closet."

"Yes, ma'am."

CHAPTER EIGHTEEN

KNOX followed through with his idea of keeping a friendly athletic competition going between them, since their grappling practices had deteriorated into a game of grab ass.

He'd rented out the rock-climbing wall and obstacle course at a local gym that catered to the outdoor set. Something about Knox's pleased grin had Shiori worried.

"Is there a reason you're beaming sunshine from those pearly whites, Ob-Knox-ious?"

"Could be I'm thinking about watching your ass as you're moving up the rock wall. Or it could be I'm thinking about kicking your ass, timewise, when we climb the rock wall, She-Cat."

Shiori adjusted her shoes. "So confident."

"I am."

"Willing to make a wager?"

"Depends. What are you offering?"

"If you win, I'll let you top me tonight. But if I win, I get to break out the strap-on I bought for you."

He smoothed back a piece of hair that'd escaped her ponytail. "While I'm humbled by your offer, Mistress, I have no desire to change that dynamic between us, even for one night."

Her jaw almost hit the floor. "You're serious."

"Yes. I've realized that when I'm with you . . . I'm who and what I'm supposed to be. I want to make you happy that you took a chance on me."

This was the moment she'd waited for. And now that it was here . . . she had no idea what to say. Or do. "It was a no-brainer. I mean look at you. You're this hot-bodied Viking. Even if I couldn't bring you to heel, I'd have a great time trying to convince you *submissive* doesn't mean *subservient*." She smirked. "At least not all the time."

"You're being flip about this. Which I know you well enough to know means the conversation makes you nervous. Why?"

Because every day I'm falling for you a little more and I'm imagining all sorts of ridiculous romantic scenarios where you are mine, just mine, for good.

"Shiori?"

"Because this isn't a conversation I want to have here." She poked him in the chest. "Stop trying to get in my head and put me off my game. Not happening. The bet stands. Take it or leave it."

"Leave it, but I'll take you. Anytime, anyplace." He kissed her with sweet heat that blew her concentration to hell.

They walked hand in hand to the cavernous room with four different wall configurations.

The hipster guide named Errol ran over the safety rules before he turned them loose.

Knox bowed to her with a smile and kissed her knuckles. "Mistress first."

Shiori eyed the wall, trying to discern a fast rise pattern. In the end, she just went for it. She scaled the first wall freehand and made it to the top in less than three minutes.

Knox high-fived her. "Great form." He put his mouth on her ear. "And I'm not just talking about that delectable ass, kitten."

"Stop distracting me or I'll yell out filthy suggestions during *your* turn and see how well you can climb with a hard-on."

"Hmm. You know, a third leg might come in handy."

She whopped him on the arm.

The second wall required a harness. Finding both her balance and the right footholds proved difficult. She finished without falling—major feat—around the ten-minute mark.

Not a great time. But she reminded herself that being small and agile was an advantage in this contest.

Knox swung his arms and did a couple of frog jumps to loosen his muscles. She stared at his crotch, wondering if he wore a cup. Wondering if there was any way he could grip the rocks so she could climb him and ride him.

"Eyes off my junk," he warned.

Then he started up the wall, moving across it like a spider. He reached the top in less than two minutes.

Dammit. Evidently long legs and long arms trumped small and agile.

She high-fived him. "Looking good."

"Thanks." He took a long pull from his water bottle.

"I love the way your butt muscles flex and bunch. I'd definitely tap that ass."

Knox spit water across the floor at her comment.

On the second rock wall, Knox ran into a little trouble, but he still beat her time by a minute and a half. Which, when she looked at the performance wall where the climb times were divided into performance levels, she could see that Knox hit expert level on both climbs.

Sneaky fucker.

She stayed close as he removed the safety rigging and helmet.

"Something on your mind, She-Cat?"

"Was this a trick? You're some kind of rock-climbing stud?"

"No. But I'm happy you think my technique—my winning technique—makes me a stud."

"We still have the obstacle course left, so don't think you have this competition in the bag." When he didn't respond, she said, "But you have to admit you've got some experience with rock climbing."

"We did rappelling exercises in combat training—which is going down a wall as fast as possible. But all that focused on was a stealth exit."

"Is there anything you haven't done?"

"Lots of things. What I did get to do Uncle Sam paid for. It's not like I could afford to go heli-skiing or surf the big breakers in Hawaii."

Shiori flopped down beside him and swigged from her water bottle. "I can afford to do those adventures, but I never have."

"No interest?"

"No time. Between my job and my martial-arts training, if I had an extra hour, I shadowed Mistress Keiko."

"When I see all you've accomplished in your thirty-five years? You make me feel like a slacker."

She gave him a peck on the mouth. "You're far from that, Shihan. But fair warning: I'm gonna rock this motherfucking obstacle course."

"I've no doubt of that." He tugged on her ponytail. "But you'll have to bring your A game to beat me. Because we did run lots of obstacle courses in the army."

Shit. She was doomed. Maybe if she did a little trash-talking she could throw him off his game. She shrugged. "Don't count on it. You're older now. Your muscle memory isn't as quick. Your knees are weaker. You looked a little out of breath on the climbing wall, so your stamina might not be as good as it used to be."

"Only time my knees are weak is when I'm around you." He dragged his finger down the line of her jaw. "Same for that breathless feeling." Then he curled his hand around the back of her neck and swept his thumb across the pulse pounding in her throat. "And, kitten, because of you, my stamina is way better than it's ever been."

Note to self: You suck at trash-talking.

But Knox? Holy fuck, the man could make her wet with just words.

She had to refocus. "So it'll be fun to see if your body can back up your ego."

Knox laughed. "Lead the way."

The obstacle course had two different levels. Easy and moderate. It also had a different scoring system for men and women, since the course was geared toward men.

The instructor gave a basic rundown and indicated he'd be scoring them.

Shiori was a little disappointed there wasn't the crack of a starter's pistol to get her going.

The first obstacle was a series of tires—putting a foot through each hole. Easy enough.

The next challenge was a warped balance beam four feet off the ground, which bowed in spots and wobbled as she crossed it. Again, the beam seemed easy, but she knew men had a harder time with it.

In the third run, she had to dodge life-sized chunks of swinging foam that resembled boulders. They swung in random patterns. Shiori headed straight through the middle, leaning back to avoid one and ducking down to avoid another. The last boulder dropped straight down and narrowly missed her leg. But then she was free.

Obstacle number four was the rope climb over an eight-foot wall.

Don't overthink it.

She rushed toward it, grabbing on to the rope and planting her feet halfway up the wall. She had upper-body strength, but nothing like Knox's. Gritting her teeth, she inched up the wall at a snail's pace.

The rope is your tool.

She remembered seeing one of those Japanese game shows on TV, with wacky physical challenges, where a woman used the wall as a springboard and bounced her way to the top. Shiori tried that. Three bounces as she moved her hands up the rope. Three more bounces and she was over the wall. It took her only two bounces to scale down the other side of the wall.

She bent at the waist and caught her breath as she noticed the next obstacle. Steel monkey bars, then a set of rings, then another set of monkey bars.

One right after another.

Yeah. This course was totally geared toward men.

But she wasn't giving up.

She jumped up, grabbed the first bar with both hands and started to swing. Her arms weren't long enough that she could skip more than one steel bar.

By the time she reached the rings, her arms ached. But again, she built up a swinging momentum and was able to skip every other ring. The true test now would be making it to the end of the monkey bars.

Her hands were sweaty, and her arms shook. She threw herself onto the first bar. That's when she knew she couldn't swing anymore. Muscle fatigue and damp hands were a bad combination.

Come on. Back to basics. How did you do this when you were a kid and had zero upper-body strength?

One bar at a time.

She had to reach out with one hand, as if she were doing a pull-up, then bring her other hand beside it. Eight bars. The process was slow, but she made it.

The last course loomed ahead. She'd have to crawl through a long steel tube and then leap across a water trap into a sandbox.

Excitement hit her like a shot of adrenaline.

She was small enough that she wouldn't have to crawl through the tube on her belly. If she hunched her shoulders and crouched down, she could duckwalk through it. That could shave seconds off her time.

And it worked amazingly well. High on her cleverness, she sprinted toward the water trap and launched herself over it, landing on her hands and knees in the sandbox.

Done. She'd done it.

Then Knox was there, lifting her to her feet, swinging her around in a circle, peppering her face with kisses, telling her how proud he was of her and that she deserved to win after her awesome display of athletic ingenuity.

She loved how Knox got so swept up in everything. He never held anything back.

After parking her on a bench with a bottle of water, he crouched in front of her. "You sure you're all right? No shame in barfing. Most people do."

"I'm all right. Can you give me a few minutes to catch my breath before you run the course? Because I want to watch."

"Of course."

He kept staring at her. Finally she said, "I swear I'm not feeling sick."

"That's not why I'm looking at you."

"Then why?"

"You'll think it's stupid."

"Only if you don't tell me."

His eyes roamed her face. "You scare me."

Not what she'd expected. "Why?"

"I've wanted to try this place for three years, but no one would ever agree to come with me. Then you didn't even hesitate when I suggested it. You're everything I wanted in a woman—more, actually, because you've opened up part of me that I'd never acknowledged." Knox looked at a spot over her shoulder. "So now you're in my life, but I know it's not permanent. And that sucks."

Shiori jumped to her feet and wrapped her arms around his

waist, pressing her face against his chest. A thousand words bounced around in her brain, but she couldn't find the right ones, so she said nothing.

Knox ran his hands down her arms and stepped back. When she looked up at him, his smile was cocky, and no humor danced in his eyes. "See you at the finish line." He turned and jogged away.

How had that happened? They'd been having a great day. What brought on his abrupt shift in mood?

This was a reminder why she played in a club situation. The expectations there were all short-term. Like Knox, she'd become cynical that she'd ever find not only what she wanted but what she needed.

But brooding about it wouldn't solve anything. Although she knew she'd be breaking this down piece by piece later.

Shiori saw a flash of red and realized Knox had started the course. So she moved to a better vantage point.

Oddly enough, the tires gave Knox trouble. His long legs were a disadvantage for this portion.

Next he moved to the balance beam. And again he struggled, nearly falling off at the midway point. He righted himself and finished by using huge strides to get himself to the end of the beam.

She studied his face. Such concentration. It was a little jarring to recognize he wore that same look when they were naked and he was trying to make her come.

The swinging boulder obstacle proved no challenge for him at all. He dodged, ducked, and spun and ran to the rope climb.

He didn't need time to catch his breath. At his height, his first jump put him midway up the rope. Then he shinnied up the thing like a damn monkey. He stood on top of the wall and used the rope as a guide to slide to the ground.

Son of a bitch. Why hadn't she thought of that? She'd bounced down like she had on the other side.

But when Knox faced the monkey bars, she wondered if he had rope burns on his palms.

If he had them, it sure hadn't affected him. With his long arms, he made it across the breadth of the steel structure, utilizing only the middle bar before reaching the end. He did the exact same maneuver with the rings. He took a second to breathe before he tackled the final set of monkey bars. Then he swung to the ground.

Shiori moved along the outside of the course and saw Knox drop to all fours at the entrance to the steel tube. With those broad shoulders, it'd be a tight fit. From the moment his feet disappeared she counted one-one-thousand, two-one-thousand, three-one-thousand, four-one-thousand, five-one-thousand. By the time she hit six, Knox scrambled out of the tunnel.

Immediately he sprinted and soared over the water trap and nearly cleared the sand trap too.

She raced over and threw herself at him. "I wish I would've taped that on my phone. It was picture perfect, baby!"

He laughed and set her down. "Need to breathe. Give. Me. A. Sec."

"Oh, sure. Right."

When he bent over with his hands on his knees, she stuck close by, rubbing his back.

Knox slowly straightened up and hauled her into his arms, although he warned softly, "Don't do that."

"Don't do what?"

"Be so goddamn sweet and gentle with me, Shiori. It'll just make it twice as hard."

Confused, her eyes searched his. "Make what twice as hard?"

He rested his forehead to hers. "When you go back to Japan. I can lie to myself about the Domme-sub aspect of this, chalking it up as a sexual experiment. I can compartmentalize our fights at Black Arts as coworker disagreements. But this? Having fun, sexy banter and then your sweet, caring touches? That I can't explain away because I like you too damn much. And I'll miss you like fucking crazy when you're gone. I'd wonder what I should've done to make you stay."

Floored by his confession, she had to take a few moments to force herself to breathe. How long had he felt that way? Shiori tilted her head back, needing to look into his eyes, but they were interrupted.

"Holy cow, man. You annihilated the fastest course time!" Errol said with genuine awe.

"Really?"

"By, like, fifty seconds. Dude. You should totally try out for *American Ninja Warrior*. They have open auditions all over the country. You'd be a shoo-in."

"Thank you for the vote of confidence."

Shiori handed Knox a bottle of water.

"Anyway, as the new course holder, you should have your picture on our wall of fame."

"That's not necessary. We're just here having a good time."

Errol's lip lifted as he started his rebuke.

Shiori put her hand on his arm. "He's a very private man in a highly sensitive occupation. Putting his picture up would violate about twenty rules in his contract." She lowered her voice. "Don't you think if I could tape him in all his hot-bodied glory I would have?"

"Uh. Yeah. Probably."

"But I didn't. So see? I'm making a sacrifice for him too."

Errol dropped the cool act and stared at Knox as if he were Superman, Batman, and Spider-Man all rolled into one. "Sure, I wouldn't want to get you in trouble when you're just blowing off some steam, man."

"No problem."

"After you get your stuff gathered up, you can exit out the side door."

They'd brought only one gym bag to share, and after switching out their shoes, Knox shouldered the bag and they headed out.

Shiori snagged his hand and towed him to the front of the building.

"Kitten, my truck is the other direction."

"I know. But I want a picture of my record-holding *American Ninja Warrior* in front of the building."

"Jesus. Seriously? Why?"

"So we have a record of this."

"Shiori—"

She shut him up with a kiss. Then, in a more commanding tone, she said, "Not a request. Go stand over there."

"Yes, ma'am."

When he positioned himself in front of the sign, wearing sunglasses, his sweaty shirt molded to his amazing chest, his athletic shorts showcasing his strong, muscular legs, she took a moment to feel the possession that this man was hers. She could touch, kiss, lick every part of him, anytime she wanted.

But for how much longer?

She had to lower her phone for a second as Knox's words hit her in the gut. *I'll miss you like fucking crazy when you're gone. I'd wonder what I should've done to make you stay.*

"Are we done?" he said loudly.

"No, hang on. I had something in my eye." She snapped two pictures and then said, "Smile in this one, Shihan."

His smile . . . God. She was beginning to think she'd do anything for that smile. She tucked her phone away and waited for him to come to her.

As usual, he kissed her and had to have his hand on her someplace, which she loved.

"Where to?" he asked.

"You hungry?"

"I could eat."

"Find us a steakhouse and I'll buy you a piece of meat worthy of a record-holding champion."

"Sounds good. Only you're not buying."

They had this argument all the time. He figured as the man it was his job to pay. She figured as his Mistress, it was her job to pay.

"We'll arm wrestle for the check."

Shiori flexed her biceps. "Watch out because I've been lifting weights."

In one fluid motion, Knox picked her up and rolled her entire body against his chest like he was doing curls.

He grinned, looking mighty pleased with himself. "Gonna hafta grow a bit, kitty-cat."

"Show-off."

CHAPTER NINETEEN

COME to me, please.

The text had been sent at ten p.m. There was no follow-up to the message.

Knox hadn't hesitated to act on it, and he saw no reason to analyze his reaction. No need to respond because she knew he'd show up. She was every bit as obsessed with him as he was with her.

So he got in his truck and drove.

Half an hour after receiving the text, Knox arrived at Shiori's penthouse.

In the entryway, he shucked off his boots and jeans, then tossed his jacket on the bench, followed by his button-down shirt. His boxer briefs would have to do, as he'd forgotten a pair of athletic shorts.

He tracked down a glass vase in the kitchen for the flowers he'd brought her—a dozen cream roses with pink-tipped petals that'd reminded him of her skin. He set them on the coffee table in the living room because she'd never see them in the kitchen.

The candles weren't in the usual spot in the window. And he hadn't seen a note anywhere. He cut through the open library to the hallway that led to her bedroom.

She'd left candles burning in her bedroom, and he paused for a minute to notice it made the enormous space cozier. Then he saw that the door to the bathroom was ajar. He knocked twice. "Mistress?"

"Come in."

As Knox entered the bathroom, a sweet perfume drifted to him—possibly from the candles she'd scattered in here too. Or maybe from the bubble bath. Peaks of foamy white rose out of the waters in the soaking tub. And amid those bubbles sat his beautiful Mistress, her hair piled on top of her head, a hint of pink on her cheeks.

"You look like you're in heaven," Knox said, noticing she held a wineglass.

Shiori's assessing gaze rolled over his chest with such intimate possession he felt it as powerfully as an actual caress.

"I'm in heaven now," she said huskily.

"What would you like me to do?"

"Drop the boxers and get in the tub with me. But first . . ." She handed him her wineglass. "Would you mind refilling this? The wine is in the bucket on the counter."

"It'd be my pleasure." Another wineglass waited beside the bucket, and he filled them both. He handed hers back and slid off his underwear before throwing his leg over the edge of the tub.

"You should know I like my bathwater hot."

"Hot-tub hot?"

"Not quite. More the temp of the onsen in Japan."

"Onsen. Those are hot-water mineral springs, right?"

"Right."

She watched him as he eased his feet in, then his calves, and submerged himself completely. He leaned back and grabbed his wine. "Very nice."

"Glad you approve."

"So can I ask you something without offending you?"

"Interesting way to phrase it, but go ahead."

"You don't seem like the bubbles-up-to-your-chin, soaking-in-floral-scented water, sipping-wine-and-reading-a-book kind of woman."

Her lips curled into a smile. "I'm not. I prefer a hot shower to start the day. Sometimes a longer shower to end it. But every once in a while, I like to indulge. And if I had to guess, taking baths isn't your thing either."

"To be honest, I've never soaked in a tub with a woman. Never mind doing so amid bubbles and candlelight, sipping wine—so you popped my romantic bubble-bath cherry."

She laughed softly.

"I missed you." She'd been gone three days—a phone call on her way to the airport had been his only warning.

Shiori looked at him and swirled the liquid in her glass. "Sorry for bailing on you at the last minute. I want to say it won't happen again, but it probably will."

"Did you have a good trip?"

"Productive. Maggie, who runs the Seattle office, is always two steps ahead, which is a nice change from being two steps behind."

Knox took a tentative sip of wine. Normally he wasn't a fan of rotten grape juice, but this stuff wasn't half bad. "Is your mother your contact person at Okada?"

"Yes and no. After I resigned my position, they promoted my assistant, which was a smart move. She keeps me up to speed on the contracts I still handle. My mother . . . She's the one who sent me to Mexico to negotiate that deal. She's the one who sent me to Canada to negotiate this last one. My grandfather is essentially retired. Makes me wonder what he's doing with all his time." She sighed. "I doubt he's shaping bonsai trees."

Being this close to her and not touching her had him reaching beneath the water to circle his fingers around her ankle.

"I missed you too. Which is why I sent the text."

"I'm glad you did."

"At one point this morning, when I looked across the Seattle office and heard everyone speaking Japanese, I swore I was in our Kyoto office."

"Do you miss Japan?"

"Yes, I do. More than I thought I would."

Was it too much to hope for that what they'd become to each other would make a difference in whether she stayed?

Yes—this was just another aspect of their relationship where he had no control.

Knox set his wineglass on the back edge of the tub and floated toward her. Putting his palms on her knees, he said, "Can I kiss you, Mistress?"

"Yes." She set her glass aside, wreathing her arms around his neck when they were face-to-face. Shiori's eyes were a darker gold tonight.

He slanted his mouth over hers, keeping the kiss lazy, all soft lips and twining tongues. Their bodies weren't plastered together, just barely touching, and he had a dizzying need for more of her. "Can we switch this up so I'm holding you?"

"Maybe I wanted to hold you?" she countered.

"That works for me."

"Sit on the step in front of me."

She spread her legs, and he started to drop down onto the step. But it was deeper than it appeared, and Knox felt the water close over his head.

He surfaced, sputtering.

"Guess that wasn't a great idea."

He spun around and faced her. "Sit on my side. The seat is bigger."

Shiori floated over to him, pressing her back to his chest and straddling his thighs. "Before we get too comfy, we need more hot water."

Knox reached over and cranked the handle.

"Must be nice to have such long arms."

He rubbed his lips across the top of her ear. "All the more to wrap around you, kitten."

She sighed. "I think I might like your sweet talk even better than your dirty talk."

"I can give you a dose of that too, Mistress."

Shiori closed her eyes and angled her head, allowing him full access to her throat and ear. "Yes, please."

"I love your neck." He let his breath flow over the damp skin. "Long. Graceful. Begging for a man's mouth right here." He slid his lips up and down and back to her ear. "So responsive."

"Nice. But that's still being sweet. Give me dirty."

"Oh, Little Miss in Control, I can do dirty. See, I fantasize about grabbing ahold of your hair like this"—he latched on to the mass on top of her head—"and bending you over the nearest surface. No sweet and soft words. I push your skirt up, rip your panties aside because I'm too fucking impatient to wait. I finger you, opening you up so I can plunge in deep on that first hard stroke. My mouth at your neck, my hand pulling your hair, my cock stretching your pussy."

"Keep going."

"But I still have one hand free. So do I stroke your clit? Do I snake my hand under your shirt and pinch your nipples? Do I slip my hand between your thighs and tease your asshole?" She shivered. "There it is. That's what you want, dirty girl. Using your pussy juices as lube, I'd start swirling around it with just the tip of my finger, coaxing that pucker to open up. Once I breach the tight ring of muscle, I'd add another finger so you can feel me at both places inside you. Fucking your cunt so hard your hips will have bruises. Jamming my fingers in your ass, wishing it were my cock. You're moaning and aching, telling me to fuck you any way I want. And, oh baby, do I want in this ass in the worst kind of way."

She squirmed on his lap.

"I pull out of your wet pussy and poke that pucker until it yields. I push my cock into your ass slowly. Distracting you with my mouth on your skin. My hot breath in your ear. Can you feel your ass throbbing it's so full of me? When I ease out, I leave just the fat head of my cock inside that spasming hole, keeping it open . . . so you'll feel that sharp edge of pain and pleasure when I unleash myself on you. Riding your ass like I own it. Plunging harder, trying to get deeper with each frantic thrust. Then you toy with me. Test my stamina. You clench those anal muscles around my pistoning cock. Milking my release as soon as my seed explodes from my balls. I can't stop fucking you, because my come makes that tight heat so slippery. I keep slamming into you until I come again."

Shiori hadn't said anything.

"You okay?"

Then she spun around and fused her mouth to his, guiding his hands to her ass. Rubbing her slit up and down his dick. The cooling water and the increasing friction, soft woman and hot mouth—everything felt so damn good.

As they rocked together, water sloshed over the edge of the tub. The fast pace of their breaths echoed off the walls.

Knox swept his thumb over that rosette, and it quivered at his touch. Shifting his hand, he drew circles with his middle finger and slipped the tip in, pushing past the resistance. The tight walls clamped down around his finger when he fucked it in and out. From this angle he could brush the opening to her pussy, and he shoved his thumb into her cunt.

She broke the kiss with a gasp and started to come, humping his cock while her anal passage spasmed around his finger, his thumb lodged in her spasming pussy.

As she came, he whispered, "Such a naughty, sweet girl, liking ass play, wishing it were my cock in your ass instead of this finger." He carefully removed his hand, and she smashed her mouth to his, kissing him in an out-of-control manner that wasn't like her at all. While she had plenty of passion, she maintained a short leash on it.

"Take me to bed, Knox."

He stood and she wrapped her legs around his waist. Bubbles plopped on the floor, sliding down their slick bodies as he stepped out of the tub. He snagged a towel and wiped off her back and her legs as he carried her into the bedroom.

As soon as he set her down, he finished toweling her dry. Then he dried himself.

Shiori had scooted to the middle of the bed.

When Knox paused by the side, she raised an eyebrow. "Problem?"

"Permission to join you, Mistress?"

"Of course." She pulled him on top of her. "Let's get back to where we were."

He planted his mouth on hers and felt her hands mapping every ridge and valley in his chest. When her hands moved to his hips, he followed the arch of her neck down to the hollow of her throat. Then he dropped even lower to latch on to her left nipple.

She arched into him and her hands grabbed his ass. She squeezed and caressed his butt cheeks and her fingers edged closer to the crack of his ass.

He glanced up when she pulled the lowest part of his cheeks apart.

Her lids were heavy, and she'd sunk her teeth into her lower lip. Then she smiled. "I bought something for you."

Knox had a tiny flare of panic. "Should I be worried or excited?"

"I'm hoping both."

"You want me to stop what I'm doing right now so you can give me this present?"

"Yes." She squeezed his ass again. "Roll on your back, close your eyes, and spread your legs. Remain still no matter what I do to you."

Sometimes when they were naked together he forgot they were Domme and submissive. They were just lovers with need and passion driving them. But when Shiori used the Domme voice and issued directions, he drifted into the headspace where he was hers to do with as she pleased. The freedom in surrender blew his mind and had created a bond between them that went beyond just physical.

The bed jiggled and she moved in between his legs. Her smooth skin rubbed against his. She kissed his neck and his chest, taking time to play with and suck on his nipples. Her southerly path continued over his belly. Then she pushed his legs up, one at a time, so his feet were flat on the mattress.

Her breath tormented his cock. He waited for the tight grip of her hand, but the soft warmth of her mouth closed over the tip.

That felt so fucking good, yet he didn't jerk or grab on to her head; he remained still.

Shiori didn't offer him praise, because she expected him to follow her orders. His pride in himself was secondary to her silent approval.

She slid her mouth up and down his shaft at a steady pace, and her fingers fondled his balls.

Fuck, he loved that. Loved everything about blow jobs. Just when he relaxed, intending to enjoy the hell out of it, her fingers swept over his asshole. Knox automatically clenched.

She pulled her mouth off his dick and said, "Don't do that. Relax."

He had a better go of loosening up when her mouth did that deep glide down his cock . . . until she smeared something slippery across his asshole.

Then she started tonguing the rim of his cock head with sassy little flicks of her tongue, and his legs twitched in anticipation.

The next time Shiori took his shaft into her throat, something prodded his hole.

She repeated the cock head tease. Then wet heat suctioned

around his shaft. About halfway down his length, the pressure increased on his rectum and whatever she'd pressed against his ass slid
inside.

Knox automatically clenched around the foreign object lodged
in his butt.

But this time when Shiori's mouth popped off his dick, it stayed
off and she slowly kissed her way up his belly.

Don't ask.

He *had* to ask.

When he opened his mouth, Shiori was right there, sinking her
teeth into his bottom lip and then thrusting her tongue into his
mouth. After several brain-melting kisses, she whispered, "Condom."

"There's the magic word." He opened his eyes, sat up, and
reached on the nightstand for a plastic packet she'd thoughtfully
placed there.

Shiori rose up onto her knees and looked over her shoulder at
him. "We haven't tried this position yet, but your cock is long
enough it shouldn't be a problem."

After Knox suited up, he scooted in behind her, his knees
bracketing hers, his chest plastered to her back. Pressing kisses on
the ball of her shoulder, he waited for her direction. Because she'd
tell him exactly what she needed, he could concentrate on tasting
her, touching her.

Reaching between them, she circled her fingers around the base
of his shaft, aligning the head with her opening. "Push in slowly
and stop."

He groaned as her hot cunt swallowed his cock. The slowness
of the motion increased the pressure of the—plug?—anal beads?—
in his ass, and wow. Okay. That extra sensation didn't suck.

Shiori rested her cheek against his. "Since you gave me an anal
play-by-play in the tub, I'm returning the favor. Keep this big cock
of yours moving slowly so the plug presses in the right place."

"I feel it."

She dug her fingers into his neck. "Have you ever worn a butt plug?"

"No, ma'am."

"Drive up hard with your hips when you bottom out."

Knox snapped his pelvis, causing the plug to hit him . . . sweet baby Jesus. Right. Fucking. There.

"Yes, like that." Shiori used her teeth on his jaw. "You like fucking me?"

"Mistress, you naked in my arms is the best part of any day."

"Such a sweet mouth." Another scrape of her teeth, this time right below his jawline. "You've let me fuck you and it's been hot. But I don't have the right appendage to fuck you how I want."

Knox forced himself to focus on her words and not how amazing her pussy felt squeezing his cock and how every time she bore down on him, he clenched against the butt plug too. "How do you want to fuck me, Nushi? With your fingers? With a vibrator? With a strap-on?"

"Can't you see me swaggering around with a big cock hanging between my legs?"

"I like it when my cock is between your legs," he murmured in her hair.

"I do too. But before I bend you over, I'd want to feel the cock that would be fucking you, fucking me." She nuzzled his cheek. "Do you want to hear what I'd do first?"

"God, yes."

"I'd be sitting at the edge of the bed with you at my feet. I'd hand the silicone cock to you, telling you to work it inside me. You'd get that hungry, jealous look in your eyes because I'm getting so wet."

"Do I get you off with it?"

"No. Before I come, I take the dick away from you and slip it into the harness." She turned her head, letting her breath whisper across his ear, and he shivered. "That rigid silicone is coated in my juices, and I rub the tip across your lips, giving you a taste. And knowing you, a little taste isn't enough. So I start to push my cock between your lips."

Knox stilled. Sucking cock wasn't something he wanted to try.

Shiori sensed his unease and rubbed her cheek against his. "It's not a man's cock. It's *my* cock. You're sucking my come from it—that's all you need to think about. You can smell how wet I am. You can see it. I stroke you like this"—her fingers brushed up and down his jawline—"to get you to open up wider. Then I push over your soft lips and hard teeth, over your tongue until I'm past your gag reflex. Think of how good it feels when your cock is so deep in my throat that you feel me swallow."

He groaned at the sexy, vivid image she painted.

"I'm tempted to fuck your face. Seeing your eyes on mine as I'm thrusting in and out of your mouth. But the need to feel you bucking beneath me as I'm fucking your virgin ass is stronger. I let my hands roam all over your chest. My fingers rifling the soft down between your pecs. My thumbs brushing your nipples." She bit his earlobe. "You stopped fucking me."

"Sorry, Mistress. I was distracted by your word porn." Knox began the slow pump of his hips again. This naughty play-by-play was making her hot—her pussy was sopping wet.

"Then I'd want you on your hands and knees. Your ass in the air. And I'd take my time lubing you up, because it's about pleasure, not pain." Shiori stroked the back of his neck with her fingertips. "It's not about humiliation. It's about you trusting me to give you something you've never had, something that will make you feel good. A new experience for both of us that erases any doubts about what we are together."

His mouth found her ear. "Something that proves I'm yours."

"Yes."

Another shudder worked through him. Even as he filled her with his cock, in another part of his mind, he was on his hands and knees, waiting for her to slide that strap-on into a part of him that'd never been breached. Feeling her hair tickling his back as she moved in and out of his body. Feeling her soft kisses on his spine. Feeling the press of her fingers into his hips as she held him steady and fucked him.

"Is this scenario making you hard?"

He clenched his ass around the plug, and the movement zinged to the tip of his cock as he rammed into her, proving how goddamn hard she'd made him.

Her sexy laugh vibrated against his throat. "This word porn will make you harder yet. Because when I slide into your tight ass, I'll slip a warm gel tube down your cock and jack you off with it, so it feels like I'm fucking you with my cock and my pussy at the same time." Her tongue teased the razor stubble on his jaw. "Doesn't that sound like fun?"

"Yes, ma'am."

"Drive me over the edge, Knox. I'm so close."

He pushed his middle finger down her slit, getting his fingertip wet, and returned to rub the tender flesh of her clit until her belly, her thighs, her arms, and her lips quivered. That slow pace forced him to focus on every stroke. Every thrust.

Shiori sank her teeth into the side of his neck as she started to come. And fuck if that didn't about do him in, her harsh cries muffled against his skin as her pussy clasped his cock in soft ripples.

His ass tingled and burned. His balls were drawn up and ready to blow. And yet he kept up the same rhythm as she returned to herself with a drawn-out sigh.

Then her voice flooded his ear. "Come now."

Her voice had become his trigger, just like she'd warned him. He plunged in fast and hard with one, two, three, four strokes, and then *kaboom*!

Knox came so hard, his vision turned hazy. Ass, cock, balls tightened and released so violently, with such molten heat, that he couldn't keep himself upright. In his state of bliss, he felt himself spinning, falling, and then he realized`he really was falling forward, and he managed to catch himself on his hands.

Shiori bolstered him with her body, with her kisses on his parched throat, with her words of praise. Words that burrowed into his heart and soul, leaving him emotionally and physically wrung out. She gently disconnected their bodies, laughing at his protest that he wasn't finished with her yet, and rolled him onto his back. She destroyed any brain cells he might've had left with her loving caresses as she removed the plug from his ass. A quick pinch on his cock and she got rid of the condom too.

This was what humbled him. The care she took with him in the aftermath.

When he could function somewhat normally, he pulled her into his arms.

She snuggled in, such contentment flowing from her that he swore he could hear her purring.

"I have no words for that, Nushi. Thank you."

"You're welcome. I missed you. Stay with me tonight."

Knox smiled against the top of her head because he knew how much she hated to ask. "I'd love to."

She drew her fingers up and down his stomach. "How was everything at Black Arts the past few days?"

"Same as usual. I put the guys to work in the training room getting it cleaned up."

"You nervous about meeting with Maddox?"

"Yeah." Not because of the money she'd fronted, or even how Ronin would react. Knox worried about his future with the MMA program. He didn't bring anything worthwhile to the table as far as a unique skill set. Ito had mad judo skills. Fisher knew boxing inside and out. Deacon could work with the other fighters and had a background in Muay Thai. Ronin worked with grappling. His only contribution was as Ivan's fighting partner, because they were the same size. So of all the instructors, he was deadweight, and Maddox would see that right off the bat.

And the really stupid thing was he worried Shiori had already come to the same determination. Seeing pity on her face would do him in.

Then she was nose to nose with him. "Stop."

"Stop what?"

"Obsessing. Everything—"

"Don't you dare say everything will be fine."

Shiori head butted him. "I'm no Pollyanna, asshat, so that wasn't what I was going to say."

"Then what?"

"I'd started to say everything about the program doesn't have to be decided at once. One step at a time."

Knox brushed her hair back over her shoulder. "You're right."

She grinned. "Ooh, did it hurt to admit that?"

"Yes. Is my tongue bleeding?"

After smooching his lips twice, she sat up. "I have something for you."

"But, kitten, you already gave me a butt plug tonight that resulted in an orgasm that almost put me in a fucking coma, so I think we're good."

She rolled her eyes. "Stay here."

"Nowhere I'd rather be than in a bed waiting for you." His gaze stayed glued to her ass as she sauntered across the room to her dresser drawer. Too bad she hadn't stashed whatever it was in the bottom drawer, because he'd love to see her bend over.

When she turned around, he manufactured an innocent expression that she didn't buy for a single second.

Shiori cocked her head and snapped her fingers.

Fuck. Maybe he should be worried about this gift. He rolled off the bed and walked to where she waited. Then he dropped to his knees. And the really fucking weird thing about it was it didn't feel weird.

"Give me your left hand."

He did as instructed but kept his head bowed.

Cool metal circled his wrist. "Now you can look."

The bracelet had thick chains on either side of a flat metal plate. It reminded him of cheap ID bracelets from junior high, but the weight and the color indicated it wasn't cheap by a long shot. His belly fluttered when he considered what this might be—what it might mean.

"I know we haven't talked about anything long-term between us. But I wanted you to have this."

Stunned by the gift and the emotions racing through him, Knox squinted at the kanji on the flat metal plate. "What does it say?"

"Watashi no."

"What does it mean?" His gaze met hers.

"Mine."

Holy fuck. Holy, holy fuck.

She traced the metal links with the tip of her finger, and all the hairs on his arm stood up. "It's up to you whether or not you wear it. It's not a collar, just a reminder."

"Of what?"

Those serious golden eyes hooked his. "Of me. Of what we are to each other."

"Mistress. I'm . . . humbled and flattered."

"As am I every time you drop to your knees for me." Her thumb rubbed the kanji, almost like she were polishing it. "Be aware that since I bought this in a BDSM shop, people in the life will know what it means."

"That I'm submissive?"

"Not only that, but you are taken."

"That I am, Nushi. I'm very taken with you." Knox took her hand and kissed her fingertips, then her palm, then the inside of her wrist up to the bend in her elbow. "I will wear this with pride. Thank you."

CHAPTER TWENTY

KNOX tried not to pace, but sitting in the conference room with his leg bouncing up and down must have been just as annoying because Shiori put her hand on his knee to stop it.

"It'll be fine."

"I'm not so sure. Especially when we tell him that Ronin wasn't involved."

"Let's see that as a plus at this point, okay? Maddox's salary is guaranteed for a year. If Ronin pitches a fit, then he can buy out the contract. Maddox takes the money and moves on."

"And Ronin fires me."

Shiori straddled his lap. "Wasn't your money or your name as the signer for Black Arts."

"Jesus. I hope you're right and this doesn't blow up in our faces."

"Maybe this will help." She curled her hand around his throat and leaned in to kiss him.

Her willingness to indulge in public displays of affection still surprised him—and delighted him. He spread his hands across her back, urging her closer yet.

"God, seriously? I have to watch you two make out again?

Christ. I'm shocked y'all don't have blisters on your lips," Deacon complained.

She broke the kiss with a smile. Then she stood. "Deacon. Glad you could make it."

"What am I doin' here besides interrupting your game of grab ass?"

"Supporting Black Arts, Yondan," Knox said.

"So do I have to kiss his ass, or can I act normal?"

"Normal meaning . . . a surly asshole? I don't think any of us would know how to act if you had a change of heart. Or showed that you actually *have* a heart."

Deacon rolled his eyes. "That ain't ever happening. And I liked it better when you two were at each other's throats instead of tryin' to get into each other's pants."

"You're more prickly than usual," Knox said. "Did your favorite stripper get fired or something?"

"No, she went to jail."

"Knock it off. Both of you." Shiori slid off his lap. When she walked past Deacon, she kissed the top of his bald head. "Don't worry. Maddox will want to work with you. You're an untapped talent waiting to explode."

Knox watched in amazement as Deacon squeezed Shiori's hand and mouthed, "Thank you."

Seemed his little She-Cat could calm the raging beast in Deacon too.

Shiori took her phone out of her pocket. "Maddox is at the front door. I'll get him and bring him up."

After she left, Deacon muttered, "Wish I had a shot of Jäeger right about now."

"Me too." Knox dropped his arm below the table and fiddled with his bracelet. It was still new enough he wasn't used to it, but it'd become his touchstone in such a short amount of time.

"I thought Gil was gonna be here?" Deacon asked.

"Guess he's coming later."

Silence settled between them so completely they heard the ping of the elevator.

They exchanged a look that said, *Here we go.*

Shiori entered the room first and Maddox followed.

Although Knox had seen Maddox on TV, in MMA magazines, and they'd had a Skype conversation, the man's size surprised him. He was an inch shorter than Knox, and he had the build of a boxer, not the doughy physique of a trainer who'd let himself go—which was the norm in the world of sports training. It was hard to tell whether his ancestry was Latin, Italian, or Native American. Dark hair in a buzz cut, a goatee, no visible tattoos. As Knox assessed him, Maddox's dark gray eyes met his, and he realized Maddox had been assessing him also.

Then he stepped forward and offered his hand. "Knox? Maddox Byerly."

Knox shook his hand. "Great to finally meet you in person." Then he hung back when Deacon moved in.

"Deacon McConnell. It's an honor to have you here, sir."

"I'm glad to be here. And no need for formality . . ." He looked between the three of them. "Unless that's a requirement since this is a martial-arts studio?"

"We use formal titles during class hours. Makes it easier for the students to show respect to us if we show respect to one another."

"Understood."

"What would you like to do first?"

"Since I've been sitting in the car the better part of the last two days, I'd like to stretch my legs and see the training areas."

So Knox took him through the dojo from the first floor up to the third floor. Deacon and Shiori tagged along, but neither had jumped into the conversation, which left Knox feeling like he'd been droning on for forty-five minutes by the time they returned to the conference room.

Shiori passed out bottles of water and they settled in.

"This is a great facility. I know the jujitsu program here is top-notch."

That was a nice . . . platitude. Some awkwardness was to be expected, but this meeting needed to set the tone for their working relationship, so Knox barreled ahead.

"Look, Maddox, we are thrilled that you chose to join us. With your reputation I imagine you had dozens of other offers, so we figured we'd better jump while we had the chance. Since Ronin is training in Japan with his longtime sensei and out of contact, we—Shiori and I—brought you on board without discussing it with him because we feel that you are the best person to reinvent our MMA training program."

His face remained blank. "Why are you telling me this now?"

"I wanted full disclosure. You're contracted for a year, so even if Ronin comes back and disagrees with our decision, you'll retain the full salary you were guaranteed. But I'd like to think Ronin would be more pissed off that we had a chance to hire you and didn't than that we've secured you for Black Arts."

Maddox crossed his arms over his chest. "I don't go into any situation with blinders on. I quizzed Gil about this situation and he admitted Ronin Black wasn't in the picture. I could've taken that two ways—that Ronin's second-in-command and his sister were trying to overthrow his leadership and take over his business. Or Ronin's second-in-command and sister were trying to expand the business for the benefit of all. Obviously, I banked on option number two."

Knox nodded.

"I'll be honest. Taking the owner out of the decision-making process has made it easier all around. It'll allow me do my job rebuilding the training program while Ronin does his job running a respected dojo."

"Gil is shit for keeping secrets. But I'm relieved he clued you in. We didn't want you to think we got you here under false pretenses."

"Leaving the familiar for the unknown is always a crapshoot. You leveled with me, so I'll level with you." Maddox sighed and laced his hands behind his neck. "This last year has been utter shit. I finally got the psycho woman I was married to, to agree to a divorce. It only cost me everything I had, and that seems like a damn bargain. I couldn't leave my former employer until the divorce was finalized because she would've demanded a chunk of my future earnings too."

"And you were married to Gil's sister?" Shiori said.

"To say they're nothing alike is putting it mildly." Then Maddox went on to explain his dissatisfaction with the company he worked for. The change in philosophy that affected the attitudes of the fighters. MMA had become big business, but at the same time he was training less because even the biggest fighters were lucky to get one bout in a year. "So the bottom line is, they wanted me to train a fighter at a time. They didn't believe that a strong training program with diversity builds strong fighters."

"You'll essentially be starting from scratch here. We've retained two fighters for you to gauge."

Maddox's gaze zoomed to Deacon. "You one of the two?"

"Yes, sir."

"Tell me your weak spot."

"Takedowns. Being a former wrestler and a third-degree black belt in jujitsu hasn't benefited my fighting style, and it's frustrating. That weak spot is keeping me from advancing like I should."

Knox withheld his surprise that Deacon had analyzed the situation with such precision.

Maddox looked at Knox. "I'm keeping him on the roster."

"Without testing him?" Shiori said.

"I just did. A fighter who's honest about his weak points is a better bet than a fighter who doesn't think he has any weak points or makes excuses for them."

Deacon grinned. "Now I could really use that shot of Jäeger."

Knox said, "We weren't sure if you had dinner plans. We could order food in and just relax here."

"I appreciate the invite and I'll take a rain check, if you don't mind. It's been a long haul, and I'm ready to call it a day."

"Not a problem."

They all stood.

Shiori asked, "Where are you staying?"

"With Gil just for tonight. I'll need tomorrow to get my bearings, so I'll keep in touch about when we can get things going this week. Will that work?"

"Sounds like a plan."

Deacon said, "I'll walk you out since I'm headed home."

Knox didn't breathe again until he heard the elevator doors close.

Shiori wrapped her arms around him.

He loved that she was so attuned to what he needed without him even having to ask.

After a bit he said, "That went better than I expected."

"I was glad to see he wasn't an asshole prima donna. Guys like him with that much raw masculine energy can have serious ego problems."

"Raw masculine energy?" he repeated. "Should I be jealous?"

"No, because you have it too. Maybe it just comes with the territory with big, good-looking guys."

Knox had a momentary flare of jealousy. "Now you're saying he's good-looking too?"

"Yes. He'd be at the top of my list of if I were attracted to tall, dark, and handsome. But tall, blond, and gorgeous is my type."

He snorted.

"What?"

"I thought you'd say tall, blond, and submissive."

"Well, that goes without saying." Shiori pulled him in closer to her. "So now that we're alone . . ."

"Got some plans for me, Mistress?"

"Let's grapple. Or spar. Or break out the katanas."

"Seriously? Why?"

"I'm feeling out of sorts. I can't put my finger on why."

Knox brushed his mouth over hers. "Have you talked to your mother?"

She shook her head.

He had a feeling that was part of it. Shiori missed her mom. He suspected she also missed her grandfather. Maybe even Ronin. Since he couldn't commandeer the Okada jet to whisk them off to Tokyo so she could visit her family, he'd do the next best thing. "How about we work out for an hour, and then we'll clean up and drive to Golden. You can meet my mom and her husband, Rick. We'll see what the wonder brats are up to on a Sunday night. I'll even spring for sushi since I know Vivie and Zara love it as much as you do."

The smile she beamed at him made him feel like a fucking king.

"I'd love that. Really love that." She stood on her tiptoes to kiss him. "You're so good to me. Thank you."

THE closer they got to Golden, the more nervous Shiori acted. Unlike her brother, she didn't fidget from nerves. She became unnaturally still.

Knox picked up her hand and kissed her palm. "Relax. My mom is gonna love you. Vivie and Zara have been singing your praises to her for weeks."

A small smile curled her lips. "That's sweet. Can you tell me about your mother before we get there so I don't say something stupid?"

"Don't ask her about my biological father, because she doesn't know who he is."

Shiori turned and looked at him. "Can I ask you how that's possible?"

Few people knew the truth about his parentage. It wasn't something he was ashamed of; he just figured it wasn't anyone's business. "Freshman year in college my mom went to a Halloween party. Alcohol was involved and she slept with a guy dressed up like Mr. Universe. Free love and all that crap in the seventies meant she didn't get his name. Hell, she had no idea what he looked like without a costume and the party hadn't been on her campus. Anyway, she wound up pregnant. Her family cut her off, and she moved away from Washington and raised me alone. We lived in government housing and we were on public assistance until she earned her teaching degree when I was eight. But I never felt like I went without because I had her. She might've been young, but she was always a great mom."

She squeezed his hand. "She sounds wonderful."

"She is. She married Rick Christensen when I was sixteen. The year I graduated from high school they had Vivie. Then Zara a year and a half later. It would've been easy for them to be their own little family since I'd joined the army, but Mom and Rick have made sure I'm part of their lives."

"Vivie and Zara are lucky to have you."

Knox parked in front of the two-story Colonial that'd been the only home his sisters had ever known. He climbed out of his truck and came around to help Shiori out just as the two wild girls barreled out of the house.

Vivie threw herself at him, nearly knocking him down. "God, how slow did you drive? We thought you'd never get here."

He pecked her on the forehead. "Nice to see you too." He watched as his sisters tried to maintain decorum with Shiori rather than bowling her over.

That lasted like fifteen seconds.

Then Zara gave him a one-armed hug. "We're starving, so get the introductions over with so we can go eat."

His mom and Rick came down the sidewalk. He kept his hand in the small of Shiori's back, hoping to relax her tense posture, even as he leaned forward and kissed his mom's cheek. "Mom, this is Shiori."

Shiori offered her hand. "Nice to finally meet you, Mrs. Christensen."

"Please call me Lisa. The girls have been talking nonstop about you."

Rick set his hands on his wife's shoulders. "I'm Rick, Lisa's husband. It's nice to meet you."

"Same here."

Zara moved in and addressed Shiori. "I know what you're thinking."

Shiori lifted a brow. "Really? What?"

"That when we're all together we look like a band of Vikings. I heard you say something like that to Knox. We can't help it that we're all tall, blond haired, and blue eyed."

She laughed. "I'd never complain about that." She looked up at Knox. "I'm rather fond of my Viking."

Knox couldn't help but kiss her. When he raised his head, he saw his mom smiling at him. And why were there tears in her eyes?

Rick squeezed Lisa's shoulders. Then he said, "Girls, didn't you have something to show Shiori before we head to the restaurant?"

Vivie tugged on Shiori's free hand. "Remember that dress I tried on? Knox bought it for me! Isn't that the sweetest thing ever?"

"The absolute sweetest," Shiori agreed.

He fidgeted under Vivie's look of adoration.

"Anyway, Mom found the perfect shoes for it. They're like glass slippers! You've gotta check them out. I totally look like a princess."

His sisters led her away, chattering a mile a minute.

Rick grinned at him. "Way to go, Knox. She is a beautiful woman."

"That she is."

"I'll make sure the girls don't get sidetracked. They'll riot if we don't feed them soon." Rick kissed his wife on the back of the head before he walked away.

While Knox appreciated Rick giving him time alone with his mother, he wasn't sure he wanted it. He studied her as thoroughly as she'd studied Shiori.

Tall and thin, Lisa Lofgren Christensen was a striking woman. Her shoulder-length blond hair framed her angular face. He'd inherited her big blue eyes, and if anyone's eyes could smile, it would be hers. Happiness radiated from her, and he could hardly remember her as the overworked single parent she'd been to him. She'd aged well, looking more like forty-four than her current age of fifty-four. "Am I in trouble?"

"Can't a mother be happy that her boy has finally found the one woman meant for him?"

"Mom."

She moved forward. The metallic lettering PROUD ARMY MOM on her T-shirt glittered in the fading sunlight. "Thank you for bringing her here. It eases my mind."

"Why would you have doubts about her?"

"Any doubts I had are gone after seeing you two together."

He sighed. "You know you're not making any sense, right?"

She laughed and hugged him. "Or I'm making perfect sense and you're playing it cool."

How did his mother always know?

"Talk to me, son."

"I'm so crazy about her it's kind of scary," he admitted.

"I imagine it is."

"So you got any motherly advice for me?"

"Yeah. Don't be a jackass and screw this up."

"That's it?"

"Yep." Then she stepped back. "Let's round up the troops and head out. I'm starved."

"Like mother, like daughters," he joked.

She poked him in the chest. "Just for that, I'm sitting by Shiori at dinner and telling her embarrassing stories from your childhood."

The front door opened and his sisters raced down the steps with Shiori strolling behind them.

"I thought by now they would've outgrown their need to run everywhere," Knox said to his mom.

"You didn't outgrow that until you left the service, smarty."

Zara elbowed Vivie aside to speak first. "Can Shiori show us how she got you to submit to her?"

His gaze narrowed on his girlfriend. What had she been talking about with his sisters?

When Shiori reached him, she slipped her arm around his waist. "I tried to tell them the techniques I used on you that first day we met at the dojo are jujitsu black belt secrets, but they didn't believe me."

He pushed her hair behind her ear. "Well, I can't have you giving away our secrets, now, can I?"

Her golden eyes turned solemn. "I'd never do that, Knox."

"I know." Just as he lowered his mouth to hers, Rick blasted an air horn, startling them away from each other.

His sisters laughed hysterically.

Rick grinned. "I knew this would come in handy one day, but I never thought I'd have to use it on you, Knox."

"Bring it along to dinner, Dad," Vivie suggested. "These two play kissy-face all the time."

Knox lightly whopped his sister on the butt. "Get in the truck, brat. And no, you don't get to pick the music we listen to."

"Then I'm riding with Mom."

Shiori shook her head. "Sneaky move, Shihan."

He smiled. "It works every time."

LATER, after they'd returned to his house and were curled up in his bed, Shiori said, "Thanks for today. I had a great time with your family."

"I told you there was nothing to worry about."

"Your mom is sweet. Now I know where you get it from."

He snorted. Sweet. Right.

Just when he thought she might've drifted off, she said, "Why don't you talk about your time in the army?"

That'd come from out of left field. Knox shifted his arm and trailed his fingers up and down her spine. "Some of it I can't talk about because I dealt with classified information."

"Ooh, international intrigue."

"Which is code for lots of paperwork," he said dryly.

"Where was your home base?"

Sometimes he forgot her father had served in the armed forces and she'd lived on military bases. "Fort Benning, Georgia. Then my . . . unit, for lack of a better term, which was part of the thirteenth CSSB, was transferred to Fort Lewis/McChord in Washington just as I was getting out of the service."

"Were you ever in war zones?"

"I got stationed in support outposts in combat zones, but never saw any combat. The luck of the draw, I guess. A couple of my buddies were deployed to those shitholes every other year."

"You sound like you're sorry you didn't see action."

"Not really. I mean, it is war. It's ugly and brutal. There's a dynamic of almost dying together, or seeing others die, that binds those guys in a way I can't comprehend. So yeah, I took my share of crap about not being a 'real' soldier."

"Did it bother you?"

Knox had to think about that for a minute. "Maybe at first. But the guys who lived through the horrors of war dealt with the after-effects for years. After I out-processed, I moved on from being a grunt and haven't looked back. It put things in perspective for me."

She made a purring sound when his fingertips brushed the curve of her ass. "Are you in contact with any of your fellow soldiers?"

"I keep in touch with the two guys I worked most closely with during my last enlistment. They're both working for telecommunications companies."

"And you're Shihan at Black Arts."

"No doubt I have the better job."

"Were they surprised when you didn't find a job like theirs?"

"After I got out, I'd decided to live in Denver to be close to my family, but I couldn't find a job. I ended up working as a security guard and moonlighted at Twisted part-time. That's where I met Ronin. He offered me a temp position at the dojo as he tested my skills." Then all that crap happened with Naomi and he moved up to a full-time position at Black Arts.

"How did you keep up with jujitsu training when you were in the army?"

"I was mostly stationed stateside, so I trained at the martial-arts studio in Fort Benning."

Shiori rolled onto her stomach and looked at him. "Your mom is really proud of your service."

Knox blushed. "If not for her putting me in jujitsu when I was a surly fifteen-year-old, I probably would've gone to jail."

"I doubt it. You're too honorable for that." She leaned over and rubbed her mouth across his nipple. "Let's play a game, soldier."

"I guess we're done talking."

"I've got a better idea on how to use my mouth."

He groaned. "Is this another one of your *rewards*?"

"Yes." An evil laugh drifted up as she scooted her body down the mattress. "Let's see how long you can stand at attention as I polish your pole." She settled between his thighs and licked his cock from root to tip. "You up for that?"

"Yes, ma'am."

When she finally let him come, a full hour later, she'd wrung him out so completely he couldn't even salute.

CHAPTER TWENTY-ONE

ENERGY in the entire dojo had been running high in the two weeks since Maddox had officially rebooted the Black Arts MMA program. Inside the training room "Mad" Maddox would give Sensei Black a run for his money with his intimidating persona. Except where Ronin was icy-eyed and expressed his disapproval with cool detachment, Maddox was hot-tempered and yelled at the top of his lungs if something met with his disapproval. On the second day of training, Knox feared Deacon and Maddox might actually kill each other. But they'd figured out a way to work together.

Fisher and Ito fit right in, and they couldn't say enough good things about the new trainer. While Knox was relieved things were off to a great start, his fear that his skills weren't needed in the MMA program had proven true. Maddox asked his opinions on everything—except training. So Knox devoted his time to running Black Arts and working with Blue and Katie on the rescheduled smoker in two weeks.

They'd secured a new sponsor, and that asswipe Steve Atwood had agreed to provide two fighters for the bout. Knox wished Ronin were here so they could both see the look on Steve's face when the Black Arts fighters made a clean sweep of the fight card on fight night.

But Knox's great mood vanished the instant he walked into the Black Arts office and saw the man sitting on the edge of Shiori's desk. Sitting way, way too close to Knox's woman for his comfort.

He affixed his "fight face" in place before he moved in behind Shiori. That's when he noticed who the asshole was.

Max Stanislovsky.

One of the richest men in Denver. Ronin's sometime pal, sometime nemesis. A man with ties to gambling, prostitution, nightclubs, sex clubs, real estate, and construction crews.

Knox didn't doubt the rumors about Max being a key player in the Russian mob. All the Cold War had done was expunge some of the undesirables from Russia, and they had set up shop in the United States. And unlucky for Coloradans, the population and the climate was reminiscent of Russia, so many of them flocked to the Centennial State.

Ivan had some kind of love-hate relationship going on with his father, but in this case the apple had fallen far from the tree. Ivan was a good guy, a hard worker, and had the potential to do well as a pro MMA fighter, especially now that Maddox Byerly had signed on to train him.

Knox realized he'd been glaring at Stanislovsky and attempted to play it cool. "Max. What brings you to Black Arts? I'm sure you know Ronin is out of the country."

Max's eyes narrowed at Knox's use of his first name. Before when he'd dealt with Max, he'd called him Mr. Stanislovsky. But that was before Ronin had left him in charge.

"Yes, I was telling Ronin's lovely sister about my visits to Japan. It's been a few years, but I've always found Japanese women so very . . . intriguing."

"We're like women everywhere else, Max. We're overloaded with work and family."

Max leaned closer. "Your grandfather should not have put you in such a position. Working so much . . . not good for anyone.

Especially not a beautiful woman like you. You should be pampered. Put on the pedestal you so clearly deserve."

Knox snorted. "That lifestyle would set Shiori on a murderous path. Her contributions to Okada have been enormous over the years. So I'd say her grandfather knew exactly what he was doing by putting her in a position of authority and not on a pedestal."

Shiori's shoulders stiffened.

What? He wasn't allowed to brag on her? Bullshit.

"Is the penthouse to your liking?" Max asked, ignoring Knox completely.

"Yes. The view is incredible and it's a quiet building."

Max Stanislovsky had helped Shiori choose a place to live? Why was this the first he'd heard of it?

Max sighed dramatically. "I'll admit sadness that Ronin did not approach me about fulfilling your needs. But Ivan proved himself capable, so all is not lost."

"Speaking of Ivan . . . is that why you're here?"

Max's gaze flicked over to him. "I heard about impressive new trainer. I wanted to meet man who will be spending time with my son."

"Where are your leg-breakers, Max? I never see you without your bodyguards."

That's when Knox figured out why Max had shown up. He knew Ronin was out of the picture, so it was a free pass to schmooze Shiori in the office while one of his associates cornered Maddox in the training room and offered Maddox an obscene amount of money to become Ivan's personal trainer.

Max shrugged. "They are around."

Shiori turned her head and looked at Knox at the same time that Maddox stormed into the office with a sheaf of papers in his hand. "What the fuck is this?"

Bingo. He'd called it.

Knox pointed to Max. "Ask him. This is Ivan's father, Max Stanislovsky."

Maddox got right in Max's face. "Let's get one thing straight. I am not for sale. For any amount of money. And this?"—he shook the papers in the air—"is ridiculous. Obviously you have more fucking money than you have sense."

"I only want best for my boy."

"Your boy is a twenty-three-year-old man."

"He good fighter, no?"

"Yes. He's got a lot of potential. I will work him to get to the next level because he has the drive to succeed. He listens. He works hard. And that has nothing to do with you." Maddox ripped the contract in half. "So if I ever see you or any of your goons in my training room again? I'll cut Ivan loose. Understood?"

"Yes. I apologize for offending you," Max said smoothly.

"Does Ivan know you're here?"

Max sighed again. "No. He will make me pay for this little visit. He stubborn, independent man. Makes me proud, but makes me crazy too."

Maddox walked back to the door. "I mean it. I even get a whiff of that smelly-ass cologne you're wearing around here, and your son is done. Done."

Silence echoed in the room like the aftermath of a shotgun blast.

Max grinned. "I like that one. You did good."

Un-fucking-real.

Then Max took Shiori's hand. "When your brother returns and you have free time, I have villa in Italy. It is beautiful this time of year."

Knox rolled Shiori's chair away from Max, forcing him to release her. "That is thoughtful of you, Max. Shiori and I have been talking about getting away somewhere just the two of us. Offering us your villa is appreciated."

Max cocked his head. He looked from Shiori to Knox and back to Shiori. "You and big Viking guy are together?"

"Yes."

"Such a pity, *milaya moya*."

When it looked like Max was reaching for Shiori after calling her some Russian endearment, Knox warned, "Don't touch her again."

Max lifted a brow. "Not wise to threaten me."

"Not wise to put your hand on a woman who is spoken for. If the situation were reversed, how would you react?"

"I start breaking legs."

"I'm less civilized." He flashed his teeth. "I'd break your face."

Max shook his head. "So much violence in building. Might be contagious. Time for me to go."

And he left the room with a flourish, his long jacket flapping like bat wings.

Shiori spoke first. "This might sound weird, but did that remind you of—"

"Dracula? Yeah."

"Poor Ivan."

"I'm sure Daddy's millions take the sting out of humiliation." As soon as he'd said it, he wished he hadn't.

His beloved gave him a cool once-over. "If you're done swinging your big dick around, we actually have some work to do."

Knox boxed her in. "Let. Me. Make. This. Clear. He had his fucking hand on you. He's goddamn lucky I didn't break it off and shove it up his ass."

"Knox—"

"Don't." He moved in until they were almost nose to nose. "No man gets to touch you. Especially not a rich asshole who acts like it's his fucking right. The only man who has that right is me. And I will fuck up any man—I don't give a shit who he is—for even thinking he can freely touch what's mine."

"You done?" she asked coolly.

"I don't know. Is there anything else I need to clarify for you, Mistress, before I take my big swinging dick out of here and punch the fuck outta the heavy bag?"

Shiori framed his face in her hands. "You've made your point."

"Good."

"Can we kiss and make up now?"

He crushed her lips beneath his, intending to prove his ownership of her with a brutal kiss. But she wouldn't allow it. She gave him tenderness instead. Letting her fingers stroke his cheeks and the line between his eyebrows. There was plenty of passion between them, but her forcing him to keep it contained had a staggering effect. It showed her deep understanding of him. Her acceptance of this side of him. And he understood that he'd needed her to take control because he had none.

She eased back on the kiss, but her hands remained on his face. "Better?"

He could only nod. Because he had the overwhelming urge to shout out his love for her.

"Now go punch something. I'll put that big swinging dick of yours to good use later."

THE following Friday night Knox draped his arm across the back of Shiori's chair and surveyed the group that'd overtaken the corner booth at Diesel. It'd been a hellish week at Black Arts. As they counted down the days to the smoker, he decided everyone deserved to cut loose, if only for a few hours.

Even Maddox had accepted the drink invite. Deacon and Gil were on the far end of the booth, with Maddox in the middle, Fee sitting between him and Katie. Blue and Terrel were providing security for some teen concert, so they'd skipped out, as had Fisher, who had to be on the job early. Knox preferred to keep things informal, so he wondered how the dynamic would change when Ronin returned.

"I wish we could convince these guys to go someplace other

than Diesel for a beer," Fee said to Shiori. "Before you and Knox started sneaking around, we had a great time at Jackson's."

"We weren't sneaking around that long before we let everyone know we were involved," Knox said, leaning in to swipe one of Shiori's fries.

"And some of us figured it out," Katie said smugly.

"How did you think you knew something was going on?" Shiori asked.

"I saw you two the night of Ivan's party at Fresh. When you went to 'look around.'" She made air quotes.

"Jesus, Katie, way to be a creeper. Did you follow them?" Fee asked.

"No. I'd had too many shots and went to barf in the bathroom." Katie also swiped one of Shiori's fries. "I got lost on my way back. And I saw these two together at the rope demo station. Knox was tying her up in some fancy rope pattern. Like he'd done it a hundred times before, which kinda freaked me out. So anyway, I figured something had to be going on."

Shiori patted Katie's hand. "Can't pull anything over on you."

Fee choked on her drink, and Katie smacked her hand into the table. "That's what I try to tell everyone, but no one believes me."

"I believe you, sweetheart," Deacon said to her chest.

The empty chair next to Knox was yanked back and spun around. "Well, if it isn't Black Farts and Blue's Clues. God. Is it like a Sensei Ronin Black mandate that you guys train together and hang out together? Do you wash each other's dicks too? That might be kinda hot to see."

Knox turned around and faced Mia, a scrappy redhead who trained with Steve Atwood.

Before Knox could say anything, Deacon jumped in. "I don't remember anyone inviting you to sit with us. So beat it, skank."

"Make me, Scarface."

"I'm surprised your pimp let you out of his sight. Unless you're here drumming up business? It's a waste of your bad breath, because you'd have to pay us to fuck you."

Shiori silently watched the exchange between Mia and Deacon.

Mia looked at Knox. "Yep, still hate this ass-licker as much as I thought I did."

"What are you doing here?" Knox said.

"Saw the sad-sack table and thought I'd swing by and say hey." Mia's gaze roamed over Knox's face and chest, then dropped to his crotch. "You're looking good, big man. Very good. It's been a while."

Not long enough.

"Excuse me, but who are you and why are you at our table?" Katie asked.

Mia laughed. "Please, please, please make my day and tell me Barbie Perky Tits is one of your new fighters?"

Jesus. "Mia. Stop stirring shit and go."

"But it's so fun. I can admit Sensei Atwood sent me over here to check out the competition." Her gaze swept the people at the table and she sneered. "And this is it? Pathetic. Oh, how the mighty have fallen."

"Sensei Atwood? That's what he's calling himself now? What a fuckin' pompous prick. Tell your no-balls boss he's welcome to come over and size me up himself," Deacon said.

"I don't think her pimp is here," Fee said. "Didn't Atwood end up banned from this bar a few months back because he'd gone into a 'roid rage?"

"Shut your fucking mouth," Mia snapped.

"Ooh. Hit a nerve, did I, *puta*?" Fee said.

"I'll hit a nerve. In fact, I'm gonna hit all of your nerves," Mia said, adding a nasty smile. "Gonna be a long match for you, with me doing a ground and pound on your face. Or will you show your true pussy self and tap out? Like my last ten opponents."

"But you're still fighting in the minor leagues, aren't you? Why is that? Oh, right, because you suck—and I'm not just talking about all the guy's dicks in the whorehouse where you train," Deacon said.

Mia laughed. "No wonder Knox is the only one of you Black Farts assholes I ever fucked. He's got the smarts to know when to keep his mouth shut."

Christ. Thanks for that, Mia.

Then Mia rested her head on Knox's arm. "I miss those days. How about if we ditch these losers—"

Mia was there one second and gone the next.

Shiori had fisted her hand in Mia's hair and pushed Mia's face into the table, chicken-winging her left arm. "Don't you fucking touch him again. And get out of here before I break your fucking arm in such a way your fighting days are over for good. Understand?"

"Your newest cunt girlfriend is messing with the wrong person, Knox. Call her off."

"Don't you dare," Deacon said to Knox. "For once Mia is entertaining me, seeing her pinned to the table like a bug to a board."

"Let her go," Maddox said to Shiori. "We wouldn't want her to claim she was injured prior to the fight as an excuse on why she gets her ass handed to her."

Shiori released her and immediately backed up into defensive position.

Mia rubbed her neck and glared at Shiori. "I don't know who the hell you think you are, bitch—"

"I'm Ronin Black's sister, *bitch*, and I know a little bit about fighting dirty. So watch your back."

After Mia stormed away, Knox tried to talk to Shiori, but she held up her hands and said, "Not now," and walked over to the bar.

"Guess that ends our night out," Katie said.

Knox put his hand on Katie's arm and looked at Fee. "Give it about ten minutes before you leave to make sure she's gone."

"Good idea."

"Fee, do you have any fight tapes from the smokers you've done?"

"We have some; Black Arts has some. Why?"

"I want to see how Mia fights. I want you to be prepared for anything. Guaranteed she'll be gunning for you now."

Deacon clapped Knox on the shoulder. "Hope you've got a way to deal with Shiori, because She-Cat has turned into a tiger and she's out for blood."

Like I didn't already know that.

Shiori had her back to the table and was scanning the crowd.

To Maddox, Knox said, "You want me to stick around?"

"No. Go ahead and take off. I'll make sure Fee and Katie get out of here okay."

"Thanks, man. See you tomorrow." When Knox set his hand on Shiori's shoulder, she flinched, which pissed him off. "Let's go."

"Where?"

"The fuck if I know, but we're not staying here." He moved his hand to the small of her back and steered her around the side of the booth. He caught the owner's eye and indicated they were going out the back door.

Knox took her hand and led her through the kitchen and into the alley. He nodded to the cooks having a smoke break as he headed toward the lot where he'd parked his truck.

But Shiori was having none of it. As soon as they cleared the alley, she wrenched her hand free from his and leaned against the side of the building.

"What?"

"I'm just supposed to ignore the fact that you slept with that horrible woman?"

Fuck. "Ancient history."

"How ancient?"

"Two years ago."

"Were you in a relationship with her?"

"No. We ended up at the same events. We ended up fucking. That's it."

She came chest-to-chest with him. "That's not it. What kind of events?"

"Fights. She was fighting. I was doing whatever the fuck Ronin wanted me to do. After a fight, she got horny. I was convenient."

Shiori shrank back.

"What? You think you're the only woman who has that primal urge to fuck a man stupid after you've beaten the crap out of someone? Jesus, Shiori, that's human nature. We're all like that."

"I'm nothing like her."

"No shit." He counted to ten. "Can we go now?"

"Fine. Take me home."

They didn't talk on the way to her place, but the air in his truck was heavy with tension.

Neither did Shiori speak in the elevator on the way to her penthouse. But once they were inside? She unloaded like he'd never seen.

He let her pace and yell in Japanese until he worried she'd have an aneurysm from the way the vein in her neck visibly throbbed.

"Shiori," he said sharply. "Calm down. And for fuck's sake, switch to English so I know you're not yelling at me."

"I'm tired of yelling. I want to track her down and I want to make her fucking cry."

Knox took the hand she'd balled into a fist. "Why? Because she banged me a couple of times? Big deal."

"That's my question. Did she bang you? Or did you bang her?"

"I don't fucking remember, okay?" he shouted, and then felt like a total dick. "Look, I can't change the past. But you weren't there, so you don't get to go attributing meaning to a meaningless fuck."

She stared at him, the picture of confusion.

"What?"

"I've never felt this angry before. I've had moments of jealousy when I saw you flirting with Katie or any of the other students who drool, giggle, and make lewd gestures when you walk by. But it was different tonight. I wanted to crush her. Then I wanted to fuck you in front of her."

"And at any point during this violent fantasy of yours was I wearing a collar or on my knees?"

"What? No. Why would you even ask that?"

He crowded her against the wall. "Because that's who you are. You saw Mia as balls-to-the-wall Dominant. I had sex with her, which means she probably dominated me. And since you're my Mistress, you want to prove to her—and to me—that only *you* dominate me now. No one else."

"Yes, goddammit. That's what I want her to understand." Her gaze met his in challenge. "That's what I want *you* to understand."

Knox pressed his lips to her forehead. To the corners of her eyes. To her cheeks. To the curve of her smile. "I do understand, Nushi."

When Shiori initiated a kiss, any gentleness he'd used to calm her down was gone. It was replaced with passion, heat, and ownership. "I need to fuck you," she panted against his mouth. "But I'm feeling vicious," she warned. "Think you can take it?"

Knox stepped back and pulled off his shirt. Kicked off his shoes. Shucked his jeans. Naked, he stood in front of her and taunted her. "You think you can break me? You think I can't take what you want to dish out?" He gave her body a slow perusal before he met her eyes again. "Bring it." Then he walked away.

She let him get to the bedroom before she took him down with a full frontal sweep.

And she tried her damnedest to break him. They didn't speak beyond grunts and moans and the occasional scream. She didn't need to direct him, because somehow he knew what she needed.

They fucked on the floor.

They fucked against the wall.

They fucked on the bed. Twice.

They fucked against the windows.

When she came the last time, her body shuddering violently as he plowed into her, she whispered, "Mine. You are mine. I'm never going to let you go."

He closed his eyes, his muscles aching, his body absolutely fucking spent. He had scratches and bite marks and hickeys from his neck to the tops of his feet. He'd never felt so used. So owned.

And nothing in his life had ever felt so right.

CHAPTER TWENTY-TWO

FIGHT night had finally arrived.

Spirits were high when they set up camp at the event center.

Knox and Blue were handling the promotional duties. The referee was present in the locker rooms for the weigh-in. Luckily, none of the fights would have to be scrapped.

Maddox remained low-key but involved. Deacon, Ivan, Terrel, and Fee were on the roster, along with three other fights. He'd drilled his fighters relentlessly. So Knox had ended up on his ass plenty of times, since he was the only one big enough to go head-to-head with Ivan. Shiori had been called on to spar with Fee. Blue had partnered with Deacon. But all the prefight prep did was cement the other problem with their training program—not enough practice partners.

The promotion side was much more hectic than getting the fighters pumped up in the locker room. The payouts were nominal for this type of event; the experience for the fighters was worth way more. But each winner would get a payout, so Knox would have to stick around and wrap that up afterward. Ticket sales had improved, so maybe they'd recoup some of the up-front costs.

Two other MMA programs provided fighters besides Steve Atwood. Apparently, as acting head of Black and Blue Promotions, it

was Knox's job to make everyone feel welcome and foster camara-
derie among Colorado dojos. Which was fine. He wasn't bad at
glad-handing. But Ronin was. So how had he made it through
these things? Because Amery had been with him?

Was that why Knox wanted Shiori by his side?

She'd stayed in their fighter's room as support for Fee.

Katie walked by in her ring-girl outfit, and Blue's eyes about
bugged out of his head.

"Man, why do you still go all slack-jawed and stupid when you
see her?" Knox suspected Katie went out of her way to sashay past
Blue as many times as possible. Plus, she stayed in her getup after
the event ended while she did final reports and tallied up payouts.

"Because every fucking time I see her dressed like that, I'm
reminded there is a god and he has a nasty sense of humor to place
an apple like her in front of a snake like me."

"What?"

"Never mind." Blue walked away.

"Where are you going?"

"Bathroom to rub one out."

Like he needed to know that shit.

Knox did the final run-through with the announcer and the
sponsors. He made sure the judges had everything they needed. He
even managed to keep a civilized tone with that smarmy prick
Steve Atwood.

Fifteen minutes from fight time, Knox and Blue walked into
the fighters' room and saw complete chaos.

Fee was lying on a bench. "What the hell happened?" Blue
demanded.

Ivan pointed to the portable lockers the event center had brought
in. "She went to put her bag in her locker. The handle stuck, so she
pulled on it and the whole thing came down on top of her."

Blue murmured to her in Portuguese.

Tears rolled down her face and she shook her head.

He stood and walked over to Knox.

"Is she okay?"

"She's in no shape to fight now. We can have medical check her out, but she's confused and in pain."

Fuck. "Get her seen. That's what's important."

Blue motioned to Gil, and he crouched down by Fee. Then he returned to Knox's side. "What now?"

"We cancel. We've had to cancel fights before, so it's not a big deal."

"I'll go tell the announcer and the judges," Blue said, and turned to walk out.

"Wait!" Shiori shouted.

Everyone looked at her.

"We don't have to cancel the women's bout. I'll fight in Fee's place."

The fuck that was happening. "I appreciate the offer, but this schedule tonight is good enough—"

"I want to fight her, Knox."

"Not an option."

"Why not?"

He lowered his voice. "Getting in the ring with her will be personal for you, and that is too goddamn dangerous at any time, say nothing of an hour before a fight. So the answer is no."

"If I'd been scheduled to fight and got injured, would you put Fee in, in my place?"

"Yes, but it's not the same thing."

"Because we're involved?"

Knox couldn't say, *No, because Fee is a more capable fighter than you,* so he tried to be diplomatic. "That has nothing to do with it. You don't know what Mia is capable of. There's no fucking way I'm going to stand by and watch you get in the ring with her."

Her eyes went flat and cold, and in that moment she looked just like her brother. "You don't think I can win?"

"It's not about winning. It's about your safety."

"The fuck it is, Knox. You're the one who's making it personal, not me. And that has no place in this discussion. We need a qualified fighter. I'm here. So I am fighting."

"Like hell you are. Don't forget that I'm Shihan. I said no, and that's that. Do you understand?"

Maddox cleared his throat.

At some point they'd both forgotten they were in a roomful of people.

Fucking awesome.

"Actually, Knox, to be fair, that isn't your decision to make," Maddox said. "I'm the trainer. I've been working with Fee and Shiori as her fight partner. From what I can see, there's no reason that Shiori can't step in. She's watched all of Mia's fight tapes. There's nobody better qualified. And Black Arts could use a win."

"See? The voice of real reason, not personal reasons," Shiori said. "I'm fighting, Godan, and that's that. And there's not a damn thing you can do about it."

Godan. Not *Shihan.*

His face burned. She'd openly defied him in front of everyone, calling his leadership into question.

Shiori had sworn she wouldn't humiliate him, and she'd done just that with absolute defiance, daring him with her Domme voice to contradict him.

Knox dropped his gaze to the floor. It took every bit of his resolve to keep his expression neutral when he looked up. Everyone in the room still stared at him, some with fucking pity.

"As the fight promoter, it's within my purview to move the bout to the last fight of the night, to give the replacement fighter time to prepare."

Maddox said, "Thanks."

He didn't—couldn't—look at Shiori. "Good luck, everyone. I'll be seeing to the front-of-the-house duties tonight, so if you need anything, peg Maddox." He turned and left the room.

A familiar hand clapped him on the shoulder after he'd made it halfway down the hall. "What?"

"You okay?" Deacon asked.

"I'm fine."

Deacon stepped in front of him. "I suck at this kinda stuff, but I don't blame you for sayin' no and bein' pissed that Shiori jumped in like that. You and I both know those fight tapes don't tell the real story of what Mia is capable of. When she sees it's Shiori in the ring . . ."

"Yeah, I fucking know, all right?"

"Do you want me to talk to her?"

"No. What's done is done." Knox looked Deacon in the eyes. "I can't watch."

"No one expects you to."

"And by that . . . I mean I can't be anywhere in here. I'll take off right after your fight."

"Blue will be okay with that?" Deacon asked.

"He'll have to be. After all this, I'll need a couple of days to get my head on straight."

"You deserve the break. And yeah, I figured that this would fuck up things between you two."

"Thanks, man. Good luck tonight."

"Don't need it when I've got these." Deacon did some shadow-boxing moves as he backed up down the hallway.

Knox looked at the clock. Two hours. Then he was gone.

KNOX was pissed off at her.

But she was pissed at him too, so in the long run it probably evened things out.

They'd talk about this later. Yell at each other most likely.

Whatever happened, it had to wait until after the fight. And she couldn't fucking wait to get in the ring. Every bit of anger she'd felt that night at the bar with Mia resurfaced. She'd use that rage as rocket fuel.

She stayed in her corner of the room, away from the lockers. Gil had taken Fee home after the on-site medical staff had called it a mild concussion.

Maddox was in and out, shifting his duties between being ringside with his fighters during the match and making sure the upcoming fighters were ready.

Ivan wore headphones and blocked out the world as he got set to fight. Deacon hadn't come back after he followed Knox out of the room.

If looks could kill, she would've been dead.

She paced in her corner, running through drills in her head. She hadn't stepped in the ring in months, since she'd filled in at another smoker and fought Fee. Since Fee was the lone female fighter at Black Arts, they'd fought another half a dozen times. After sparring with her, Shiori wasn't sure she'd win if she was put in the ring with Fee again for real.

But she sure as fuck would win against Mia.

Maddox bounded in and grabbed Ivan. He gave her the thumbs-up and then she was alone.

Clear your mind. Visualize yourself winning. Visualize Mia bleeding as Knox gives you the victory kiss.

She couldn't allow her thoughts to keep bouncing back to Knox. She needed to focus. In times like this the only thing that quieted her mind was recitation. Poems, plays, prayers, business philosophies, multiplication tables. She turned her mind inward and time lost any meaning.

The door to the room slammed. Footsteps came closer. A hand pressed into her knee.

Shiori opened her eyes and felt a quick pang of disappointment that Maddox crouched in front of her, not Knox.

"You ready?" he asked.

"Yes."

"Good. Let's head out."

She waited outside the entrance to the arena. She tuned out the music and the crowd, focusing on her anger. Maddox nudged her and they started the trek to the ring.

Ringside the ref checked her over. Gloves, clothing, mouth guard. Everything was in place.

Then she climbed up the stairs, bowing before she entered the ring. She bounced on the balls of her feet as a warm-up and swung her arms, giving Mia her back.

Maddox set up ringside. "All right. You know what to do. Watch her hip throws. She's got a vicious uppercut. She'll switch it up and try to get you to look at how she shuffles her feet, and then she'll clock you. Don't fall for it."

Shiori nodded.

"All right, ladies and gentlemen, this is the last bout of the evening. In the women's featherweight division, in the black corner, is our replacement fighter, with an amateur record of one win, zero losses, hailing all the way from Tokyo, Japan, weighing in at one hundred and twenty-two pounds, representing Black Arts dojo, Shiori 'She-Cat' Hirano.

"And in the silver corner, with an amateur record of eighteen wins and four losses, and a professional record of six wins and zero losses, from Denver, Colorado, weighing in at one hundred and thirty-two pounds, representing Steve Atwood dojo, Mia 'the Meat Grinder' Sedladcheck."

Wait. What? Mia had a professional record and an amateur record? How was that possible at a smoker?

"Ladies, here are the rules."

As the ref read the rules Shiori reconnected with that burning hatred as she looked at Mia, who seemed a lot bulkier than she remembered.

"Touch gloves."

Neither did. They returned to their corners.

The bell dinged and it was on.

Mia came at her hard and fast from the start. She did a dive roll that knocked Shiori off her feet, but Shiori recovered fast and narrowly missed a takedown.

Then Mia started to kick. She'd pull in close and try to land some punches, and when she backed off, she'd level a slapping front kick to the inside of Shiori's right leg. Mia connected with that move six times before Shiori switched her fighting stance.

But as soon as she did that, Mia abandoned the kicks and charged her for a takedown. She got ahold of Shiori's waist, performing a judo hip throw that put Shiori on her side.

Ow. Fuck. At least she hadn't knocked the wind out of her.

Shiori arched and spun on her back, but that just put Mia in guard position. And Shiori couldn't get a reversal when she was busy dodging Mia's blows. Mia nailed her in the jaw, and she could taste blood from her lip. She was completely in a defensive position.

The clicker counted down the last ten seconds, but Mia managed to work in another blow to the head.

Bleeding, breathing hard, she walked back to her corner, and Maddox was right there with the stool, water, and Vaseline for her cut lip.

"Okay, you've got to try to keep her on her feet. I know you've been working on Muay Thai with Deacon, so use some of those drills to knock her off balance. Any spinning moves you do, do them fast before she grabs any part of you, understand?"

Shiori nodded. Rinsed her mouth and spit into the bucket. "Why does she have a professional record? Isn't this amateurs only?"

"In a smoker like this, anything goes. As long as her amateur record has more fights than her pro record, she can enter these things."

"She's not fighting like the tapes."

Maddox looked into her eyes. "No, she's not. But you can adapt, Shiori. You have to. She won that round. Get her this time."

At the start of the second round, Mia started in again with those snap kicks that landed on the inside of Shiori's knee. She blocked a couple, but she hadn't landed any kicks because she was too focused on dodging Mia's kicks.

She tried a spinning back fist, hoping to knock Mia the fuck out with one blow, but it landed low. The attempt made Mia mad enough that she charged.

Unprepared for that move, Shiori hit the mat on her back. She did land a knee to Mia's head before Mia got into guard position again. Then Shiori was getting whaled on.

Things were starting to get a little fuzzy, and she lowered her hands for just a second and Mia punched her in the eye.

That motherfucking hurt.

And she was bleeding again.

Enraged, she bucked hard and threw Mia off, which allowed her to get a reversal. She knew she didn't have a chance of getting her arm for an arm bar, so she settled for delivering blows to the side of Mia's head. As the last ten seconds clicked down, Mia twisted her arm around and punched the inside of Shiori's right knee—the knee that'd been kicked a hundred times.

Somehow Shiori walked a straight line to her corner. She sat on the stool and closed her eyes against the blood seeping down the side of her face.

"Jesus. She got you there."

"She. Got. Me. Every. Where," she wheezed.

"You did better this round. You earned a few offensive points, which helps, because that tells you she has weak spots."

"Where?" She rinsed and spit.

"When she does the punch, punch, fake-out, kick combo? Sweep her standing leg out from underneath her. Then make sure you get into guard position." He smeared more Vaseline on her split lip. "Three more minutes. You've got it in you."

Mia mixed it up at the start of every round. She attempted a spinning back kick, but Shiori saw she'd compromised her balance point and she swept her leg out. This time she did land in guard position, but she couldn't sustain it against Mia's monkey feet, which worked their way to Shiori's hips.

Then a real bell-ringing blow caught her on the cheek, and she loosened her hold. Mia forced a reversal, and Shiori found herself facedown on the mat, bleeding again, not able to make any offensive moves against this beast.

Tap out.

She ignored the voice and struggled to keep her arms away from Mia.

No shame in tapping out.

Yes, there is! Ronin's voice. *What happened to your rage? Find it. Use it.*

Her rage had fled the building, along with her sanity, because she should not have gotten in the ring with this woman.

Then coherent thought disappeared completely when Mia got her into a rear naked choke. But she knew a trick to get out of this one and it worked. She rolled upright, determined to end this round on her feet.

Mia was bouncing from side to side, trying to distract her with her footwork. So when the wheel kick came, Shiori was ready. She used the last of her energy to do a jumping knee, and it caught Mia under the chin.

The ten-second clicker ticked down and Shiori kept her hands up, protecting herself, but Mia didn't strike.

The final bell rang.

Would anyone object if she crawled to her corner?

Her butt hit the stool, and she spit out her mouth guard. She looked at Maddox as he did more patch-up jobs on her face. "How bad did I lose?"

He shrugged. "I've seen worse."

The ref brought them both into the center of the ring and held their hands. "After three rounds, the judges have scored this decision unanimously. Your winner tonight." He lifted Mia's arm. "Mia 'the Meat Grinder' Sedladcheck."

Shiori shuffled back to her corner.

Maddox held out her robe. "That cut above your eye might need stitches."

Knox was going to lose his shit when he saw her face up close. She felt it swelling. Stitches could wait until after she'd cleared the air with Knox. Still, it was all she could do not to shamble out of the arena like a little old woman.

Once they'd reached the private room, she sat on the bench against the wall to wait for Knox to get done with his payouts.

Shiori had started to doze off when she heard arguing in the hallway. "Tough titties, Deacon. Shi is my friend and I wanna see her."

She opened her eyes as Molly barreled in.

"Omigod. Look at you."

"Or don't," she joked.

Then Presley, Molly's coworker, leaned in really close. "Better get some ice on your face. I had a cut like that once too. See?" She turned her head and pointed to her eyebrow. "My coach forced me to get it sewn up. It needed, like, ten stitches, but as soon as those stitches came out, I pierced it."

Molly pulled Presley back by her suspenders. "God, Presley, she doesn't need ten stitches."

"How'd you get your badass scar?" Shiori asked.

"Got clipped in the head with a roller skate. It bled a fuck ton. They had to stop the match to mop up the blood, which was sort of cool."

Molly nudged Presley aside. "I swear if you get her started on roller-derby-injury stories, we'll be here all damn night." She took Shiori's hand. "Is there anything I can do for you?"

"No. Thanks, though. And thanks for coming to the fights."

"Amery would be horrified by what happened to you."

"I know. I'm glad she's not here. And if you talk to her . . ."

"Don't worry. I won't say anything. Take care, okay? Katie said something about us celebrating next week. I guess we'll see how you and Fee are faring first."

"Good plan."

They left and the room became quiet again. She shifted on the hard bench and felt a sharp pain in her hip.

But in the quiet void Deacon's and Maddox's voices drifted to her.

"We had no way of knowing that," Maddox argued.

"Yes, you did. Knox tried to tell her, and she basically called him a dumb shit in front of a roomful of people."

Her stomach knotted—and not from her fight injuries.

"How was I supposed to know that he wasn't just being the paranoid boyfriend? Because that's what it came across like. And I'm not the only one who saw it that way."

"Shiori doesn't fucking count," Deacon snapped. "If you'd seen those two before they started dating, you never would've believed they'd end up together. Knox would say white, and even if it was obviously white, Shiori would say black—if only to get a rise out of him."

"So you're saying that she stepped in to fight just to piss Knox off?"

"No. I won't pretend that Knox's feelings for Shiori didn't play a part in his decision. But the thing neither of you understood is it wasn't his *only* reason for wanting to cancel that bout. *Shiori* made it personal. She stepped in to fight because Mia and Knox hooked up a couple of times. You were there at the bar last week. You saw what kind of a woman Mia is. She's vindictive as hell. How Knox got away from her unscathed is a miracle."

"Shiori sure as fuck didn't get away unscathed." Maddox sighed. "Mia whipped up on her, and I never expected that. We watched the fight tapes. The woman in the ring tonight was not the woman on those tapes."

"That brings me back to my point. Knox has seen Mia fight. He knows what Mia's capable of. He tried to keep Shiori from doing something stupid and getting herself hurt because of her pride. But she didn't listen to reason. She just jumped in and assumed Knox said no for personal reasons only. She made him look like a fool, and you were the hammer that drove that nail home."

"Fucking great. I put Ronin Black's sister in that ring with psycho chick who downplays her fighting abilities so she can destroy unsuspecting challengers. I backed Shiori because I wanted a win. So as far as my debut as the head of Black Arts MMA program, not only is the head of Black Arts questioning my judgment, but I threw in with his girlfriend and disrespected him in the most public way possible."

Good thing she was sitting down. The reality of what she'd done knocked all the air from her lungs. Every bit of her earlier indignation taunted her, playing on a loop that highlighted her verbal idiocy. Her treatment of Knox was beyond reprehensible. Talk about turning into a self-important blowhard. The ache in her head increased exponentially, but it didn't hold a candle to the ache in her soul. Because she'd done the one thing she'd sworn never to do. She'd humiliated him. Their conversation about the consequence of boundaries being crossed slammed into the forefront of her thoughts as hard and as fast as a Japanese bullet train.

"Any type of humiliation in any setting is my hard limit."

"I'd never do that to you," she said softly.

"Promise?"

"I promise."

"Be warned—if it ever happens, I will walk away."

And he had done exactly that.

At least he'd kept his word, because she had blatantly broken hers. Fuck.

Numb, yet in the worst pain of her life, Shiori pushed to her feet and gathered the rest of her stuff, blindly shoving it in Fee's duffel bag.

By the time she reached Maddox and Deacon in the hallway, she'd erected a brave front.

Deacon frowned at her. "I was coming to see if you've got a ride home."

She waggled her phone. "Car service is on its way."

"Oh. Okay."

"Night, guys. See you tomorrow."

"Shiori, given how shitty you look, maybe it'd be best if you didn't come in tomorrow. You'll definitely scare the little kids' classes."

"I'll ice up, take something for the pain, and sleep for fourteen hours. Then I'll be good to go."

"Whatever. You'll do what you want anyway." Deacon turned toward Maddox, effectively dismissing her.

She hobbled to the front entrance. She'd never felt more stupid or alone in her life.

CHAPTER TWENTY-THREE

KNOX hadn't known what to do with himself after he'd left the fight. He'd been grateful for Blue's understanding on why he couldn't stay. At a loss for better ideas, he drove straight home, parking his truck in his garage just in case Shiori showed up. Then he'd realized how ridiculous that was, because he had no intention of sitting in the dark the rest of the night.

He settled on the couch with a soda and flipped through channels, needing something to hold his attention and distract him. Some station was running a marathon of *Supernatural*. Nothing in that series would remind him of Shiori. Or tonight.

But once the fighting sequences started, he had to change to something else.

Maybe he oughta grab a bottle and drink until he passed out. But he'd never used booze as a coping mechanism, and he wasn't about to start now.

Two hours after he'd sat down, he got back up and wandered through his house. He'd turned his phone off, and he turned it back on to see if he had any messages.

One, from Deacon.

The fight went like we expected. Thought
u should know. Call if u need something.

His stomach twisted. So Shiori had gotten the fuck beat out of
her. How was he supposed to deal with that?

Get in your truck and go to her.

No. It was her choice; she needed to deal with the consequences of her rash decision.

He went around and around with himself, but he finally shut
the lights off and crawled into bed.

All night his dreams were filled with her. She wore one of her
business suits—a short, trim jacket that outlined the power in her
back and arms with a skintight skirt that showcased her ass—and
four-inch stilettos that did amazing things for her calves.

When Knox tried to get her attention, she ignored him. So he
moved in closer and tapped her on the shoulder. When she turned
around, blood flowed down her chin and neck. Her teeth were
broken. So was her nose. Her eyes were swollen shut. He started to
back away from her, but two strong arms held him in place. Then
Ronin's voice exploded in his ear. "This is your fault. You should've
tried harder to stop her."

That was the first time he woke up.

The next dream had them playing bedroom games. She'd tied
him to a bench with his knees spread wide, giving her free access
to his cock and balls. Then, after he was blindfolded, she'd put
nipple clamps on him. And she'd lubed up something and shoved it
up his ass. Something soft floated over his skin from his face to his
toes. Shiori excelled at tactile sensations, and he was about to climb
out of his damn skin. "Nushi, let me touch you."

"Tell me who I am to you."

"My Mistress."

"And what does that mean?"

"I'm yours. I follow your desires and fulfill them and turn over all free will to you."

"Very good, pet."

Pet?

"Are you proud that I'm your Mistress?"

"Yes."

"Would you wear my collar so everyone can see who you belong to?"

That caused him to struggle against his bonds. "I—"

"Sounded like a yes to me." Something cold and tight clamped around his throat. Before he could tell her it was too tight, his hands were freed. Then he was jerked upright. Chains weighted his hands when he tried to claw at his throat to find some air.

She yanked off the blindfold and the lights blinded him. His eyes watered, but he forced them open. That's when he noticed they were in the ring. In the middle of a big arena filled with people. All pointing and laughing at him.

Her voice teased his ear. "Remember when I said I wouldn't humiliate you?" She paused. "I lied. Humiliation is how you get your dog to heel. Because you are a pet I play with when it suits me. Now show these people how well you obey your Mistress." She yanked on his leash hard, not caring that he couldn't breathe or that he didn't have the use of his hands. He fell forward, right onto her pointy boot. "Lick it," she hissed. "Show these people what a pathetic little boot licker you are."

After that nightmare, he didn't bother to try to go back to sleep. He lay restless in his dark bedroom until the hours passed.

Friday morning Knox wandered around his backyard with a mug of coffee, feeling wrung out. Mindless physical activity numbed his brain, and he wished he had a pile of wood to chop. Or paint to scrape. But he'd caught up on his house maintenance last fall.

He debated on heading to Golden to see his mom and sisters,

but they'd ask about Shiori. He needed to do something, though, because the thought of staying here . . . That's when he saw his fishing gear still out on the back deck.

Driving up into the mountains, finding a stream, and throwing a line would eat up his day. He'd decide how to fill his night later.

ALTHOUGH Deacon had told Shiori to take the day off, she needed to talk to Knox.

She stayed in her shower until her skin turned pruny. That helped with some of the aches and pains. Good thing she'd stopped at the drugstore last night, because she'd had nothing in the penthouse to deal with her injuries.

Jesus. She looked like Ronin the last time he'd fought. The reflection in the mirror showed busted blood vessels in one eye, and the skin surrounding the other one was purple. The bruise on her cheekbone had benefited from an ice pack; the swelling had gone down considerably in the past twelve hours. More bruises dotted her jaw. Her bottom lip was puffy, and she had to keep Vaseline on the cut or it'd rip open and bleed. The gash above her eyebrow was nasty. She'd cleaned it with antiseptic the best she could and applied a small butterfly bandage to hold the skin together. Those things were hard to put on by yourself. It'd taken her three tries before she'd affixed one properly.

But none of her teeth were loose. Not a scratch or bump on her nose. No blows to her ears.

Her gaze moved down. No marks on her chest. She had bruises on her ribs but none on her stomach. However, the outside of her hip had sustained damage from Mia's powerful kicks. She ran her hand along the red welts on the inside of her knee where Mia had connected repeatedly through all three rounds. The skin was swollen, hot to the touch, and ached down to her muscle. That one might not bruise, but it definitely hurt.

She probably had marks on her back, but she didn't bother to look. Too damn depressing.

After downing over-the-counter pain relievers, she brewed a pot of tea and wandered around her place. As she paced, it occurred to her that she'd never once considered the penthouse home.

Why not?

Because it didn't feel like home. Home was Tokyo. Home was her apartment filled with the quirky things that made her happy. She'd left everything behind when she'd fled to America. Partially because after making a decision about her future at Okada, she'd needed to follow through and just . . . go.

As much as she'd adored living at the Ritz, it wasn't practical. Not knowing how long she'd be in the States, she'd opted to lease a penthouse while the owners lived abroad. The security was top-notch, and she'd fallen in love with the view. For someone who had a hard time sitting still the past fifteen years, she spent an inordinate amount of time just gazing out the windows.

The space did have an austere feel. Modern architecture, sleek furnishings in neutral colors. The owners' personal belongings were locked in one of the bedrooms, and she hadn't seen the point in making this place more personal.

Shiori wandered into the closet, looking at her clothing options. As much as she liked the extra confidence a power suit gave her, she needed comfort today.

After dressing in gray silk pants and a black and silver Japanese-styled peasant blouse, she returned to the bathroom. She debated on whether to wear makeup. But there was no sense trying to hide the bruises. Everyone at Black Arts knew what'd happened last night.

She called for a car. And it was a little depressing that not only hadn't Knox called her, but none of her friends had either.

After a quick stop at the Taco Cabana drive-thru for an early lunch, she arrived at Black Arts.

She took the stairs to the second floor. Her heart raced as she walked down the corridor to the office. The lights were off. She couldn't tell if anyone was in the conference room, but the place felt empty.

Everything in the office was exactly how she'd left it Thursday—yesterday afternoon before she'd headed to the event center. Which meant Knox hadn't been in today.

As she looked around, she wondered what she'd do now that she was here. The schedules were set. Payroll had been submitted to the accountant. Finalizing the paperwork for last night's event would be Katie's responsibility.

Maybe she'd go up to the third floor.

She was standing in the middle of the dark room, her keys in her hand, when Deacon walked in.

Startled, he said, "What are you doing here?"

"I needed to check on some things."

He gave her a slow once-over. "You look like dog shit. Go home."

"Thanks." She let her gaze wander over him. "You don't look any worse for the wear."

"Got a bruised hip and a helluva headache."

"I assume Maddox is happy with your win."

Deacon shrugged. "It's a win. More than anything, the fight showed him the areas where I need to improve."

"Maddox didn't have much time to gauge Ivan's fighting skills since he knocked the guy out in the first round."

"The kid's got a fist like a sledgehammer."

Shiori spun her key ring on her finger, nervous to ask Deacon what she wanted to know because he looked mighty unhappy with her. Then again, Deacon had two expressions: blank and mad. "Where is Knox?"

"No idea. He's taking some time off."

Everything inside her seized up.

"You're surprised by that?"

"Of course I am. He's supposed to be running Black Arts."

Deacon crossed his tattooed arms over his massive chest. "Maybe he questions who's really in charge after that bullshit stunt you pulled last night."

"I didn't—"

"The fuck you didn't, Shiori. Ronin put him in charge. You're assisting him. So last night you made it perfectly clear what you think of his leadership when you basically said, *Fuck off, Godan. I don't have to listen to you . . .* in front of a roomful of people."

She felt the blood drain from her face.

But Deacon was on a roll. "You and Knox are involved. His reasons for wanting to cancel that fight weren't personal, but instead of letting him explain that, you went on the offensive and accused him of using your relationship as an excuse to cancel the fight. You questioned his decision-making process and his motive. On the personal side, I can see why you'd act like such a fucking ballbuster. God forbid you'd want Knox protecting you, looking out for you, caring about putting you in the ring with an unpredictable psycho who had it in for you."

"I didn't know any of that."

"And you didn't listen to him, either, because he *did* know that. You humiliated him. Maddox had a small part in it, but you telling Knox that he couldn't make decisions for you was dead-ass wrong, because actually, as Shihan, he *can* decide to pull anyone at any time."

She felt so sick she had to sit down. Deacon was absolutely right in his accusations.

"And the worst part of this? I've watched Knox grow more confident since Ronin left him in charge. He's been Ronin's second-in-command for so long, waiting for Sensei to make a decision, that he became Ronin's mouthpiece. Ronin's way of dealing with things is to make Knox do it—but that doesn't mean Knox has a voice. So with Ronin being away, Knox has had a chance to show he's a good, strong, fair leader. And he'd counted on your support—if not in private, definitely in public."

"Until last night."

"If you cared about him, you wouldn't have acted just like your fucking brother."

When Shiori's expression must have looked blank, Deacon clarified. "Knox has had to watch Ronin fight and listen to Ronin's 'I don't give a fuck what you think' attitude for several years. Knox had been helpless to stop it. And now you did the same thing to him? You think he wanted to watch the woman he cares about get a public beating? No."

Her tears fell when the magnitude of what she'd done finally hit her.

"I'm not a touchy-feely guy. I'm an asshole. But Knox is a good man. And to be totally fucking honest, he doesn't deserve the shit you've brought into his life. What the fuck do you think will happen when Ronin finds out you two are involved? He'll be a dick. But it's doubtful he'll be a dick to *you*, because even though you are a haughty bitch, you're his family. Ronin will take every single bit of his frustration out on Knox. Know why? Because he always does. But this time it'll be worse, because it is personal. And when Ronin finds out you were beaten to a pulp in the ring, who's he gonna blame? You? Fuck no. He'll blame Knox because he's Shihan. Ronin knows who is supposed to make that final decision— and it's not the goddamn fighter. The reason for that is exactly what went down in the ring between you and Mia last night."

"I didn't mean for any of this to happen."

"It happened all the same."

"What do I do now?"

"Why're you asking me? I saw one of the best guys I've ever known embarrassed and forced to leave a fight he'd helped set up because he couldn't stand to see you get hurt. And knowing you, you expected him to be waiting around, ready to pick up the pieces."

She had.

"I'm proud of him for walking away. I'd be even happier yet if you went back to Japan." He paused. "Because we all know that's what'll eventually happen. You're leaving. You've got Knox all wound up and caring for you when you've never had any intention of staying here."

She wanted to scream that he couldn't make assumptions when she hadn't made any decisions about that. Instead she snapped, "My personal relationship with Knox isn't your business, Deacon."

"Yes, it is. Who do you think he'll lean on after you're gone? Won't be Ronin, because he's firmly on Team Shiori."

"Where is Knox right now?"

"Like I said, I don't know. But even if I did? I wouldn't tell you."

Last night Shiori had thought she couldn't feel worse or more alone.

Turned out she was wrong.

CHAPTER TWENTY-FOUR

SATURDAY night Knox went to Twisted.

Security was on the slim side, so Merrick had been glad to see him and put him to work.

For the first two hours Knox tended bar. He kept his eyes on the new submissives who seemed determined to cause a scene—and not the good kind of scene.

The bar stayed busy. When it slowed down, he got to catch up with the regulars, who asked why they hadn't seen him in the past few weeks.

Because I have a Mistress. And it's a little fucked-up with my refusal to let her claim me in public even when she's one of the best things that's ever happened to me.

That's why Knox hadn't removed his bracelet before coming to the club. But none of the regulars had commented on it, which he found odd.

Since the club members exchanged first names only, Knox had deemed the conversations here superficial. But Merrick claimed money and job prestige automatically segregated people. By having their baser desires out in the open, it brought like minds together, not like bank accounts.

That was another wrinkle in the Shiori situation.

But he didn't want to think about that right now. He tried to refocus his attention on the clubgoers around him. He should talk to Bobby Sue about why she chooses men who are old enough to be her father. Talk to Ridge about the appeal of violet wands. Talk to Merrick about—

"Knox?"

He spun around and smiled when he saw the redhead at the bar. "Vanessa. I haven't seen you in ages. How've you been? You're looking good."

Vanessa blushed. "Thanks. I've been working out of town. But to be honest, I considered giving up my membership."

"Why?"

"I'm just not getting what I need out of it anymore."

"Weren't you hooked up with Master Jack?"

"For a short time. But he's not a one-sub guy, and I've no interest in being part of a harem."

He rested his elbows on the bar. "What are you looking for tonight? I can give you the rundown of what's happening. It's probably not too late to get in on the disco orgy at the main stage."

She wrinkled her nose. "Might be fun to watch, but too many players. Once, at an orgy I turned my head and this guy was about to stick his dick in my ear."

"No shit?"

"I'm thinking . . . of all the holes in this room you can put it in, you're eyeing my ear?"

He laughed for the first time in forty-eight hours.

"You have a great laugh, Knox." Her gaze lingered on his chest. "You have a great everything. So what are you doing here?"

"Helping out. I needed a distraction from my real life."

"I could be that distraction, if you're interested."

Knox picked up her hand and kissed her knuckles. "I'm flattered. And if I weren't spoken for, I'd take you up on it."

"That sounds like a permanent spoken for, not just tonight."
She curled her hand around her glass and studied the bracelet dangling from his wrist. "Am I right?"

"Yeah. It's a little fucked-up. Actually, it's a lot fucked-up." He
sighed. "Sounds like paradise, huh?"

"Rough times are what makes the good times so sweet."

Before his bar shift ended, Master Dan approached him. "Hey,
Knox, you have free time tonight?"

"As of right now, I'm on security for two hours and then I'll get
a break."

"Can I schedule you?"

"Sure. Just have someone tell me what room you book." But
chances were high it'd be the green room, since he preferred it.

"Great. Thanks."

Master Dan was a pain slut. Normally he had Master V the
sadist work him over, so Master V must not be here.

Soon thereafter Greg relieved him from bar duty and sent him
to monitor the orgy. Not his favorite assignment only because
watching orgies was too damn distracting.

"Knox?"

He half turned toward the male sub Vic. "Yeah?"

"Are you booked for tonight?"

"I've got a couple of things going on. Why?"

"I'd like to book you for half an hour. Just me."

"What've you worked up to now?"

"Canes. It'll be my first time."

"Okay. I've got one that'll work. Look for me in the green room."

After the orgy group took a break, he did too. He prowled the
halls, telling himself he wasn't looking for an exotic woman wearing a mask.

But he didn't know what he'd do or say if he ran into her.

Any doubts he'd shoved aside about letting her define his orientation had come back stronger than ever.

If he was truly submissive, he wouldn't have a problem telling people in the club. People outside the club didn't matter; he didn't ask for the gritty details on their sex lives, so offering up his own preferences wasn't an issue.

The other thing that'd been niggling in the back of his mind? Most of the time Shiori didn't feel like a Domme.

What if when she came to America she'd created this whole new persona for herself? Even her background in the Tokyo clubs could've been fabricated if she'd paid the right person enough money. God knew she had plenty of the green stuff.

But his angry mental accusations didn't ring true either.

Shiori *was* a Domme. He suspected she'd been an unsatisfied Domme as she tried to find her own way. She was such a sexual woman; how could she take on subs who weren't fulfilling that need in her? He might still have reservations about how far he'd be willing to follow submissive behavior, but he couldn't imagine anything he'd rather do than spend time naked with Shiori, catering to her every sexual need.

Yes, sexual incompatibility hadn't ever been a problem for them.

It wasn't doing him any good dwelling on this shit, so he cut down the hallway and knocked on the door to the green room.

Master Dan waited completely naked. He wore a different expression from his usual—normally anticipation was etched on every line in his face. Tonight he looked like he'd already been beaten.

That set him on edge. As far as Knox had seen, Master Dan didn't have any limits for pain play. They'd discussed a safe word one time, and the man had never uttered it—not even the one time Knox had accidentally made him bleed. "So, Master Dan, you know I'm gonna ask what's up."

"What do you mean?"

"First, why aren't you having Master V give you what you need? And second, why have you got more dread going on than excitement? Sets off my warning bells, man."

Master Dan slumped in the only chair in the room. "You noticed that, huh?" He sighed. "Of course you noticed because you're
damn good at what you do."

"Thanks . . . I think?"

"You don't take that as a compliment?"

Knox scratched his head. "I don't know how to take it. As it's
something I can't put on a résumé. 'I excel at beating the fuck out
of men with whips, canes, and floggers. I've been given excellent
recommendations from the masochists on being able to deliver extreme pain without breaking the skin. Sorry. No references are
available because of privacy restrictions.'"

Master Dan looked at him sharply. "Having a crisis of faith, son?"

Knox didn't mind that Master Dan called him *son*, since he
was Knox's elder by twenty years. "Yeah, I am."

"Can I help?"

Here was a chance for an unbiased opinion. "How would you
categorize me?"

Master Dan scrutinized him to the point where Knox felt fid-
gety. "Gut reaction?"

"Yeah."

"A switch." Master Dan grinned. "Surprised?"

"A little. So you must know I'll ask you why."

"Because you couldn't do this"—he gestured to the wall with
the instruments of pain—"if you weren't somewhat Dominant. No
offense, but no one would trust a submissive to get the job done.
And you have earned the trust of the most experienced Masters
here."

"But?"

"But being a pain expert isn't sexual for you. You don't get off
on it like sadists do. And you have a hard line against using your
skills on a woman. Which to me says you hold women in a higher
regard than men. You're in security, and that proves you have a protective nature. So when it comes to sex, I'd say you were submissive.

But not to just any Domme. And yes, it has to be a real Domme you'll submit to, not just a bossy bitch in the real world."

"How the fuck did you know all that?" But what Knox wanted to ask was how long Master Dan had suspected that about him.

"Being a Master or a Mistress—a good one at least—involves more than agreeing to a temporary power exchange for a mutually beneficial sexual encounter. I've learned to read people. Am I always right? Nine times out of ten. But that's only because I've had years of practice."

"So I've been in self-denial? Because until I met her, it never even crossed my radar that I'm submissive."

Master Dan shook his head. "No. I suspect you didn't know because you'd never met a Domme who made you curious enough to explore those tendencies. And since you're a big, macho guy, I can only guess how much that freaked you out."

"It did."

"Past tense?"

"I've accepted it—more or less."

"That isn't convincing me, Knox."

"It's complicated. My Mistress . . . She and I work together. For lack of a better way to explain it, I'm her boss. So we do have real-world power exchanges and adjustments. I thought I was the one having a harder time making the transition, but then she completely fucking blindsided me in a work situation."

"That does make it more difficult. This happened recently?"

"Two days ago. I've been avoiding her ever since because I don't know what comes next." He sent Master Dan a sheepish look. "I figured putting my skill set to use on someone here would help me forget. Not good to be here and be unfocused. So I'm sorry I won't be able to help you tonight."

"You've helped me more than you realize. More than whipping the shit out of me would have."

"Really? Why?"

"As you could tell when you walked in this room tonight, I came here for the wrong reasons. So talking to you has brought me out of the dark place I sometimes drift into."

"Are you involved with a sub right now?"

He smiled sadly and pulled on his clothes. "No. Hence the dark place."

"Are you looking for a distraction?"

"Maybe. Why? You playing matchmaker now?"

"That comment might've earned you extra-hard lashes next time." He grinned. "Do you know Vanessa the sub? She's somewhere between my age and yours?"

Master Dan's interest perked up. "Very curvy redhead?"

"That's her. I was talking to her earlier at the bar. She's having some of those same thoughts you are, so maybe you two could commiserate together."

"I'll see if she's still around. Thanks for the tip."

Knox remained in the room for ten minutes, waiting for Vic, who only showed up about half of the time, until he gave up and returned to the main bar area.

The place had filled up.

Just as he headed to the bar to tell Greg he was done for the night, he heard a familiar voice saying his name. It was like music coming from her lips. He turned around slowly, wondering if he'd just imagined her voice because he needed to hear it so badly.

It was Shiori, acting every inch the Domme in tight black leather pants, a crop top emblazoned with watercolor images of peacock feathers, and a vivid blue eye mask.

Dammit. She looked good enough to eat. One tiny bite at a time.

He bowed to her. "Mistress B." Then he started to retreat.

She grabbed on to his forearm. "Knox, wait. I came tonight to talk to you."

"How'd you know I'd be here?"

"I didn't. I just hoped you would be after trying to get in touch with you since Friday morning."

"This is not the place for the discussion we need to have. You know that. And I don't appreciate you showing up at Twisted expecting me to fall in line to deal with a problem that has nothing to do with our intimate relationship."

"You really think I'd do that? Try to enforce the Domme-sub rules here between us now?"

"Why else would you be here and not sitting on my front porch?"

"Because I tried that for a few hours and you didn't come home."

Knox could see the bruises on her face even beneath the mask, and his mind's eye quickly imagined how the rest of her body was ravaged—and that pissed him the fuck off.

"How bad?" he gritted out.

Shiori didn't play coy. "Bad. No TKO. But after the first round, I knew I didn't stand a chance against her." Her haunted eyes searched his. "I knew you were right."

"Jesus, Shiori." Then he remembered where they were. "What am I supposed to do with that admission now? It fucking kills me that you got into the ring with her."

Her words tumbled out in a rush of emotion. "I'm cocky, and it bit me in the ass. I proved what a know-it-all bitch I can be. I accused you of using our personal relationship to keep me from stepping in the ring with her even when you tried to convince me it wasn't personal. I'm stubborn. And it didn't help matters that I was jealous and I took the chance to beat the piss out of a woman you used to fuck. So I was the one who used our relationship as a reason to defy you. And in doing so I realized—too late—that I'd undermined you in the worst way possible." She took a second to breathe. "I'm sorry. It's not enough, and it's probably too late, but you need to know that I didn't walk away Thursday night unscathed. And my hurt had nothing to do with the pain Mia inflicted on me."

They stared at each other.

"Where do we go from here?" she asked.

There was the opening to ask the question that'd been weighing on him. "What's your favorite part of being a Domme?"

She blinked at him, startled at the change in subject. "What?"

"Answer the question. What's your favorite part of being a Domme?"

"Not my favorite part of being *your* Domme?"

He shook his head.

As she struggled to answer, Knox felt compelled to point out, "It's not sex, since you haven't fucked all the subs you've been with."

"*All the subs* makes it sound like I've had a cast of thousands," she murmured. "I could answer this better if you gave me some options, because I'm drawing a blank."

"You need power in the bedroom. Why? At Okada you were one of the top ten executives. It wasn't like you were a whipping boy who needed another outlet to reclaim power. You already had it."

She looked down at her hands. "I was the whipping boy in my marriage. I had to settle for the little he gave me. So my favorite part of being a Domme is getting what *I* want for a change."

"What do you want?"

When her gaze met his, the raw emotion in her eyes robbed him of air. "Affection."

He couldn't speak.

"Do you know what it's like to be starved for a lover's touch? I do. I craved the caress of a man's hand on my skin. I wanted kisses, touches, a connection of the intimate kind because every guy I'd been with had denied me that basic pleasure." She closed her eyes. "Why do you think I didn't have sex with my previous submissives? Because when I was in charge, I could demand they give me what I'd been deprived of. I wanted that affection even if I had to force it. I needed it so much more than another emotionless fuck."

Sweet baby Jesus. How had he not seen this? From the very first time they'd become intimate, Shiori had insisted some part of his body stay in constant contact with hers. He'd considered it a cute quirk, not a deep-seated need. To realize she'd been denied that made him ache for her.

"I've never told anyone that." Her voice broke. "The poor little rich girl who has to command a man into giving her simple human affection." She glanced up. Her voice was barely above a whisper. "Please tell me what I can do to fix this between us."

How about you humiliate yourself like you humiliated me?

He'd never demand that of her, but that's what his male ego wanted, because that's how she'd handle it. Like when she used the switch on him for acting like one.

"Should I apologize to everyone at Black Arts for questioning your authority? I will. But after I got the beat-down in the ring, I'm the one who looks like the fool and the tool. Not you."

When he loomed over her, the scent of her skin drifted into his lungs as a potent lure. Lust grabbed him by the balls and distracted him.

Before he crafted a response, Shiori dropped to her knees into the submissive pose. She tore off her mask and let it fall to the floor.

Shocked, he just stared at her as she lowered her body even more, in a traditional *dogeza* bow, her forehead and arms to the floor, the Japanese way of showing the highest level of respect from the most humble position.

He'd sensed their intense conversation had drawn interest from the club members. But after Mistress B genuflected at his feet, the room had gone quiet.

Knox's heart raced. Sweat broke out on his brow. His eyes burned. And everything that had been tight and angry inside him . . . loosened.

Shiori sat up and snaked her hand around his calf, pressing her face against his knee. Her whispered, "Please forgive me," was reverent and quiet enough that he doubted anyone else heard her.

But he'd heard her, and that was all that mattered.

In that moment Knox finally understood what he meant to her. And he couldn't deny what she meant to him. He lowered into a crouch and cradled her face in his hands, wiping away her tears. "My Mistress should never sit at my feet. I should always sit at yours." He kissed her softly, chastely, showing them both the power in their connection. "You're forgiven," he murmured against her lips.

With innate grace, she returned to a standing position. Keeping one hand on his shoulder, she helped him up.

Once he was upright, she slid her hands around his neck. The rush of emotion arcing between them had him swaying into her. "Can we please get out of here now?"

"Yes."

Applause broke out around them, and he felt his face flame—not from embarrassment that he'd been caught on his knees, but because too many people had witnessed their intimate moment.

Knox held his head high when his Mistress led him out of the club.

CHAPTER TWENTY-FIVE

SHIORI didn't speak on the drive to Knox's house. But she did clasp his right hand in both of hers and run her fingers up and down his forearm until he said, "Baby, I need that hand to drive for a minute."

"Okay."

He kissed her knuckles. "But then you can have it back. I promise."

Rain started to pour down. After Knox parked in front of the garage, he came around and helped her out of his truck. He didn't let go of her hand until they were in the house.

Before he turned on any lights, he pulled her into his arms, holding her so tightly her face was smashed against his chest.

She didn't mind. During the long night she'd spent pacing alone, she worried she'd never feel these strong arms around her again.

He brushed the hair from her damp face—when had she started crying?—and rested his hands on her cheeks. Knox stared into her eyes for so long she wondered what he was looking for. Then he pressed his mouth to hers just once.

She had an overwhelming sense of panic. Was this how he'd punish her? Withhold his affection? Because that would kill her.

"Shiori. Breathe."

"Don't . . ." She couldn't get the words out; she didn't have enough air.

Knox bent down until they were eye to eye. "I'm here. Right here. Breathe with me."

She inhaled and started to cough.

He gathered her in his arms again. "Breathe in. Slow and steady. You tell me that my scent calms you. Bury your nose in my armpit if it'll help—but, kitten, I wouldn't recommend that."

She managed a laugh, but it came out sounding like a sob.

That's when he enveloped her in his affection. Kisses on the top of her head. Hands caressing and rubbing her back and her arms.

Shiori did use the scent of his skin as a calming form of aroma-therapy.

He tipped her face back and peered into her eyes again. "Better?"

"A little."

"I know we need to talk. But it's late and I am whupped. And I see dark circles under your eyes too, so I suspect you haven't been sleeping either."

"Part of the dark circle on this side is actually a bruise." Immediately after she said it she wished she hadn't.

"I know. But we can talk about that when we both have clear heads."

"All right."

Knox placed a lingering kiss on her forehead. Then he clasped her hand in his and led her to his bedroom. The lamp he turned on in the corner cut the total darkness. After she kicked her shoes off, she stood at the end of the bed with her arms curled around herself, wondering why she couldn't just whip off her clothes and crawl between the sheets. That's when she started to shake. From her wet clothes, from her relief, from her fear.

Instantly Knox's warm arms seemed to cover every inch of her upper torso. "Shiori, you're scaring me. What's going on?"

"I don't know."

"Let's get you undressed." He turned her around and pulled her shirt over her head. Then he unhooked her bra and unzipped her pants, tugging the leather down her legs, leaving her in just her panties. Part of her wanted to protest that he didn't need to treat her like a child, but it was a small part. He slipped a T-shirt over her head and softly kissed her lips. "Crawl in. I'll be right there."

The sheets were cool on her bare legs. Strange that she felt warmer now in just a T-shirt than she had fully clothed. She watched Knox open the windows before he turned the light off. Then the mattress dipped and a warm body moved in behind her. He draped his arm over her side, tucking her more firmly against him. Then his other arm slipped beneath her pillow.

A damp breeze wafted over her and she closed her eyes.

But she couldn't sleep.

"It'll keep until morning," Knox mumbled.

"What?"

"Whatever it is that's keeping you awake."

"Maybe I'm just lying here enjoying the fresh air on my face. I never open my windows."

"Never? Why not?"

"Too smoggy in Tokyo."

"What about in your penthouse?"

"Guess I didn't think about it."

"So you haven't ever lain in bed and listened to the rain?"

"No. It smells good. I never noticed that before."

"I could say something corny like it's past time you stopped to smell the rain, but I'll just say the scent and sound of rain falling is one of the most relaxing things in the world." He rubbed his mouth across the shell of her ear. "Let it lull you to sleep."

Shiori listened to the *ping-ping* of raindrops connecting with metal. And the soft patter of water on the concrete. The breeze brought the scents of dirt and growing things.

Her eyelids grew heavier. Before sleep overtook her, she believed she'd found heaven, being cocooned in bed with Knox as rain fell.

THE next morning when Shiori awoke she curbed her wave of disappointment that the windows were closed. She had another pang when she realized Knox wasn't in bed with her. Pushing up, she glanced at the clock. Nine a.m.

No sound of him banging pots and pans in the kitchen. No sound of the TV blasting some sports channel. No sound of the shower running.

She got out of bed to track him down.

Her feet made no noise as she ventured to the main part of the house. She froze when she saw him standing in front of the picture window, shirtless, in just his boxers.

"You aren't nearly as stealthy as Ronin," Knox said without turning around.

"Ronin has trained with a master who is a seventh-line descendant of ninja warriors. So he's got the rolling-in-and-out-like-fog thing down." She edged closer. "Are you okay?"

"I don't know. Lately, I'm just . . . out of my element."

"With what?"

"With the dojo. With the MMA program. With you." He paused. "And the one person I always talk to about this stuff isn't here. And even if he were, I couldn't talk to him."

"So talk to me."

"I can't."

"Why not?"

"Because it's guy stuff."

"Does some of it have to do with the way I disrespected you Thursday night?"

His shoulders stiffened. "Some."

"I want to make this right between us. I'd planned to make an apology at the next staff meeting about—"

"Jesus, don't do that." Knox whirled around. "Don't you understand that'll just make it worse? Make me look even more like a chump."

She stared at him, wondering if her pride had cost her the best thing that had happened to her.

"You apologized to me. No one else needs to know the particulars. And I'd be surprised if you openly defied me in public again." He offered her a brittle smile. "But in private? That's a whole other story."

"Knox, I feel like you say you've forgiven me, but you haven't. I don't want you holding back because you're waiting for that defiant bitch to show up again."

"Maybe part of me is."

That blow from him hurt worse than Mia's elbow to the head.

Knox stepped closer. "But another part of me wants to rewind. Return to Thursday at noon when we were locked body to body, mouth to mouth, in the Crow's Nest."

Shiori touched his face. "At that point in time we knew what we both needed. I have no idea what you need now."

"I need you."

"How?"

"With no pressure. Can we just be in the same space today without any of this hanging over us? If we end up wanting to bang each other's brains out, I'll hand you the reins. But for everything else? I get to choose what we do on this rainy day."

"Okay." She looked down at her feet.

Knox tipped her face up, forcing her attention. "First thing I want today?"

"What?"

"To see your fight injuries." She tried to jerk out of his hold, but he held firm. "Not kidding. Strip off the T-shirt."

Ten arguments danced on the tip of her tongue, but she bit them all back. Then she lifted her arms above her head and looked at Knox. If he wanted her shirt off so bad, he could take it off.

He eased the fabric over her head.

So she stood in front of him naked, except for her panties. She kept her eyes closed as his rough-tipped fingers mapped every bruise, welt, and cut. Front and back. When he finally finished, he wrapped a blanket around her nakedness and pulled her into a hug. He didn't say *I tried to tell you*, or *I'm sorry*. He just held her like a precious, fragile thing.

That's when she finally admitted to herself that she loved him.

RONIN and Amery were expected to return home soon—not that her brother had called anyone to share his exact plans. The e-mail he'd sent Knox that said they were staying in Hawaii before they returned to Denver had no specific dates.

The week after her extreme fuckup with Knox had been wrought with challenges. Not for Knox—her screwup had put more people on Team Knox.

Fee had been so pissed off that Shiori worried she'd take a swing at her.

Blue looked at her suspiciously.

Maddox steered clear of her.

Deacon growled and snarled, which she hoped meant he was coming around.

Katie . . . well, she'd been a welcome surprise. She'd gotten teary-eyed when she'd talked about watching the fight. But she said she understood why Shiori had gotten in the ring. Katie didn't like men telling her that she couldn't—or shouldn't—do something either. Then she'd gone off on a tangent about her childhood dog, Pixie, that had nothing to do with anything they'd been discussing, but the story had made Shiori laugh so hard she'd cried. And when the tears became real tears, Katie had just handed her tissue after issue and told her to get it all out.

But things had gotten back to normal for her and Knox. It'd taken a few days. It'd taken a small whipping after Knox kept testing her boundaries. But she would've been disappointed if he hadn't tried to use her fuckup to his advantage. Holding firm with him had proved she could, and after that his trust issues weren't an issue.

So today was a good day. Clear blue skies. Temperate breeze. Sun shining. No wonder Colorado had so many outdoor enthusiasts— the weather was gorgeous.

She had to run a few errands before heading to the dojo. She waited outside her apartment high-rise, going over her to-do list on her phone, when a black Town Car pulled up. When Tom exited the driver's side, she smiled with relief. She liked him, despite Knox's claim that Tom eyed her like a juicy slab of steak.

Tom grinned at her and opened the rear door. "Morning. Lovely day, isn't it?"

"Yes, I was just thinking the same thing. Made me wish I could just walk where I needed to go today."

His gaze dropped to her feet. "I wouldn't recommend it in those shoes."

The shoes were impractical—Dolce & Gabbana black lace pumps with rhinestone flowers on the toes and four-inch heels— but she had a ridiculous love for them. Right before she climbed into the back, she noticed a dark stain in the middle of the seat.

"Problem?" Tom asked.

"Looks like someone spilled coffee or something else in here."

Tom leaned inside for a better look. When he straightened up, fury blazed in his eyes. "I apologize. Evidently this car didn't get cleaned last night. I can call for them to bring us a different car—"

"Not necessary. I'll just sit on the other side."

"Are you sure?"

"Positive."

"I'll at least cover it up so you don't have to look at it."

Shiori skirted the back end of the car and climbed in, happy that she'd seen the stain before she sat on it in her white linen pants.

After Tom draped a blanket over the stain, he slid into the

driver's seat and met her eyes in the rearview mirror. "Are we still on the same itinerary you e-mailed us this morning?"

"Yes. With one addition. There's an art-supply store I want to stop at." She rattled off the address and he poked the info into the GPS.

"That's a ways out. We can either make it our first stop or our last."

"Last works for me."

Shiori stared out the window as they zipped down the freeway. Since she'd started teaching nights at Black Arts, she hadn't attended any events at the Japanese Social Club where she had been a frequent patron upon her arrival in the United States. But she'd always had mixed feelings about the place where she'd introduced Ronin to his now-ex, Naomi, a few years back, which had ended in disaster. After she'd first come to Denver, she'd hung out a fair amount at the club since she hadn't known anyone in the city besides her brother. She'd met some nice people, but no one indicated they'd like to see her socially outside of the club. Hearing her native language had eased her homesickness. But being there also reminded her Americans were friendlier than her countrymen.

A couple of months ago she'd promised to donate to their fund-raiser for a children's art center, and since she'd pledged such a large amount, she had to sign the contract in person.

After they pulled up to the clubhouse and Tom opened the door, she said, "This meeting will take fifteen minutes at the most."

The club director decided to hard sell her on becoming more active in the club—meaning giving more money. She forced a smile and wondered what the guy would say if she admitted she'd traded their culture club for a sex club. By the time she'd extricated herself from his clutches, thirty minutes had passed.

The next two stops were recon for businesses that had applied to be sponsors for Black and Blue Promotions's next event. After each visit, she jotted down her observations so Katie could follow up.

With the traffic and the distance between her stops, two hours had passed since she'd left the penthouse. But this art store had a different kind of paint she wanted to try. And since her new project would be on much larger canvases, with a vivid red backdrop, she needed several large cans of the base paint.

She managed to keep her art store visit to thirty minutes.

Tom helped her carry the bags out. When he tried to store them in the trunk, she asked him to put them in the backseat so she could look through the books she'd bought.

"Back to your apartment?" Tom asked.

"No. Take me to Black Arts."

"Not a problem. I apologize about the seat. I'll make sure you're not charged for today's service."

"Thank you."

The drive proceeded without incident. Until on the freeway a semi lost control and T-boned the car.

The last thing Shiori remembered was a jarring impact like nothing she'd ever experienced, the sickening crunch of metal, and flashes of red as glass rained down on her.

CHAPTER TWENTY-SIX

WHERE the hell was Shiori?

Knox knew she ran on her own time frame, but she was more than two hours late. Ronin and Amery were supposed to be back in the next couple of days, and they needed to make sure they had every detail of what'd happened in the past few months nailed down.

Deacon popped into the office and frowned. "I thought Shi-Shi was coming in today."

"I expected her a while ago. She's not answering her cell. I'd say that's not like her, but it's exactly like her." She'd mentioned working on a new painting. And after seeing the level of concentrated joy whenever she held a paintbrush in her hand, he suspected she'd lost track of time.

His cell phone rang. Shiori's name flashed on the screen. "About fucking time." He answered with, "I hope you're bringing me something good to eat since you missed our lunch date."

"Ah, is this Knox?"

He pulled his phone away from his ear and scowled at it. "Who the fuck is this, and why are you on Shiori's phone?"

"This is Tom. Her driver."

Why would her driver be calling?

"There's been an accident."

His heart stopped. "When?"

"A couple of hours ago. We were on the freeway and a semi hit us."

Bile churning in his stomach crawled up his throat and threatened to choke him. He couldn't speak.

Deacon stood across from him. "What's happened?"

Tom said, "She's in the hospital. Denver Memorial General."

"Is she okay?" Knox asked.

"I don't know. They won't release any information to me," Tom said. "I managed to get her cell phone after they brought her purse in so they could ID her."

Jesus fucking Christ. ID her? Like she was . . .

No. No fucking way.

"I figured she'd want you to know," Tom continued. "Or is there someone else who should be called?"

"No." He cleared his throat. "Thank you for calling me. I'm on my way now."

Knox ended the call. Feeling nauseous, he set his forehead on the desk, trying to control his need to roar with rage, punch something, or throw up.

"What the fuck is going on, Knox?"

He slowly raised his head. "Shiori's been in a car accident."

Every bit of blood drained from Deacon's face.

"That was her driver who called. I need to get to the hospital." He stood. Where were his keys? He panicked. What if he'd left his keys in his truck? He didn't remember where the hell he'd parked.

Then Deacon was in his face. "Which hospital?"

"Denver Memorial General."

"Get your coat. I'm driving."

Knox stared at Deacon. The mean man looked pasty-faced and wide-eyed. Was Deacon's face just reflecting back what he saw in his?

"Come on. We'll fill Blue and Maddox in before we go."

He paid little attention when Deacon spoke to the guys in the training room. His brain started the mantra—*I love you. Please be all right. I love you. Please be all right*—and he couldn't get it to stop.

Deacon drove his Mercedes like a madman, but Knox didn't complain since he needed to get to the damn hospital now.

But Deacon didn't pull up to the emergency doors and let Knox out. "What the fuck—"

"You are not goin' in there alone. First off, because you can be a prick when you're agitated. Second, I can't sit in the waiting room without goin' fuckin' crazy if they take you to her right away. That's too much to ask of me, man."

Knox hadn't ever seen Deacon this freaked-out. "That's fine. I'm just losing my shit, D."

"I know. Just keep it together for her."

Inside the hospital Knox had to wait in line to speak to a receptionist. When he finally made it up to the window, he had to repeat himself because he'd spewed everything so fast. "Shiori Hirano was in a car accident a couple of hours ago. I was told they brought her here."

"Who are you?"

"Knox Lofgren. Her fiancé."

She frowned. "It lists Ronin Black as her next of kin."

"That's her brother, and he's been out of the country for months. Shiori probably hasn't updated her information since we just got engaged two weeks ago."

It appeared the middle-aged woman was going to brush him off. Then she noticed his bracelet. To most people it looked like a nice chain-link bracelet. But to anyone in the BDSM life, it was a symbol of ownership. Her gaze sharpened. "Did she give you that?"

Knox said, "Yes, ma'am. Two weeks ago."

She patted his hand. "Have a seat, son, and I'll tell the staff you're here. They'll come out and talk to you as soon as they can."

"Thank you."

After they took seats closest to the doors leading to the medical rooms, Deacon said, "What was that about?"

"Shiori gave me the bracelet."

"Why is that a big deal?"

What did it matter if Deacon knew the truth? "Shiori is a Domme."

"No shit?" A pause, then, "Don't know why I'm surprised. She has that whole power thing going on even when she's not on the mat."

Knox ran his thumb over the bracelet's band. "That she does. And that's what drew me to her."

"Wait. I know you guys are seeing each other, but that's part of it too?"

"Yeah. She . . ." *Just fucking spit it out.* "She's my Domme. She gave me the bracelet as a reminder of the importance of our relationship."

Deacon didn't respond right away. He rubbed his hand over his shaved head. "Like a collar?"

"Sort of."

"Not sure what to say to that besides it's none of my damn business. Except I'm shocked that you're submissive."

"It shocked me too. I didn't know that's what I was until I was with her."

"As long as we're sitting here, killing time, tell me how that works."

So much for his "it's none of my damn business" comment. "She belongs to me as much as I belong to her. It's the most powerfully intimate thing I've ever experienced."

"Does she make you wear a bow tie and a Speedo when you're alone? Oh, wow. Does she make you hand-feed her grapes and fan her with palm fronds too?"

His head whipped up, and he saw the humor dancing in Deacon's eyes. "Fuck you."

Deacon bumped him with his shoulder. "I couldn't resist."

They didn't say anything for a while. But neither of them were watching people either.

"Excuse me . . . Knox?"

He looked up and saw Tom the driver standing there. His face had bumps, bruises, and cuts. His arm was in a sling. His clothes looked like he'd rolled in the dirt. He was walking hunched over. "Jesus, Tom. Are you okay?"

Deacon pulled a chair over for him.

"Thanks. I'm . . . still a little in shock, to tell you the truth. Any word on Ms. Hirano?"

"Not yet."

Tom sighed and slumped back in the chair with a wince. "Before you ask, I didn't see her at all after the accident. I got knocked out because the air bag didn't deploy."

Knox saw Deacon clenching and unclenching his fists. He swore he could hear the man grinding his teeth. He returned his attention to Tom. "Do you remember how the accident happened?"

"We were in a construction zone, so I wasn't driving more than forty-five. The truck was coming down the ramp and he swerved to avoid something. He overcorrected and the truck skidded off the ramp into traffic. We were the unlucky car in its direct path."

He couldn't suppress a shudder.

"The truck T-boned us, but the other cars around us managed to avoid hitting us. Or so I've heard." He squeezed his eyes shut and muttered, "Thank god for that damn stain."

"Excuse me?"

Tom looked at Knox with anguished eyes. "When I picked Ms. Hirano up this morning, she noticed a stain on the right rear passenger seat—where she prefers to sit. Rather than having another car sent, she sat on the opposite side. If she'd been sitting there . . . that entire side of the car was caved in and demolished. She would've been crushed."

All the breath left his lungs. His heart dropped into his stomach, and every hair in his body stood on end.

Deacon abruptly got up.

"So that stain I was so pissed about probably saved her life," Tom said.

This was a brutal reminder that everything could be gone in the blink of an eye. Shiori had to be okay. *Had* to. He had this miracle, this chance to tell her how he felt about her.

"I've been discharged even though I've got a screaming headache. My boyfriend is on his way from Colorado Springs to take me home," Tom said.

Knox glanced up and frowned at the other man. Tom was gay? Not that it mattered. But that disclosure did indicate that Shiori had been right about how quickly Knox overreacted to any man's attention to her. "Headache? Did they diagnose you with a concussion?"

"No. The EMTs were concerned about my dislocated shoulder and whether the impact with the steering wheel broke any ribs. They gave me some painkillers, but I haven't taken any yet."

"Then you should go home. Be on the lookout for late-appearing concussion symptoms. They're nothing to mess around with."

"Thanks, Doc." He slowly stood.

Knox snorted. "I've spent my adult life in martial arts, and head injuries are our number-one concern. Get yourself checked out again next week, just to be safe."

"My number is on here"—he passed Shiori's phone over—"so if you'd leave a message letting me know how she's doing, I'd appreciate it."

"Will do."

Tom shuffled away.

Deacon hadn't returned. Knox saw him standing by the windows. More tension vibrated off him than he usually saw before Deacon stepped into the ring. He moved to stand beside him, wishing the man would ramble about some random shit to take Knox's mind off this gut-wrenching waiting.

After several long moments Deacon said, "I fucking hate hospitals." Then he released a sharp bark of laughter. "Stupid statement. I highly doubt anyone loves them."

The doctors and nurses here saved lives. Knox was damn glad someone was saving Shiori.

More silence followed. Then Deacon said, "I really fucking hate car accidents. One second everything is fine and the next . . ."

Knox couldn't let that one go, especially since he'd had that same flash of fear about the fragility of life. "Someone close to you die in a car accident?"

"My brother."

"I'm sorry." He paused for a moment. "Older brother? Younger?"

"My twin brother."

"Fuck, Deacon. That's awful. How long ago?"

"We were fifteen."

Now Deacon's deflection when anyone asked him about his family made sense.

"So being in the hospital is a special kind of torture for me. And I don't mind telling you, man, I'm about to run the fuck outta here now before I run the fuck outta here *screaming*."

"Then go," Knox urged. "I'm grateful you drove me here. You can't go back to the medical rooms with me, and after hearing that, I won't make you sit out here in misery and wait."

"Thanks. I just . . ." He laced his fingers together and set them on his head. "Fuck." Then he dropped his arms by his sides again.

"Go. I'll text you or call you when I've got news."

Deacon nodded.

Before Knox returned to his seat, he said, "I've known you for what? Four years? What made you tell me this today?"

Deacon finally looked at him. "You trusted me with your secret; I'm trusting you with mine." Then he walked out.

Twenty thousand fucking years passed after Deacon left, in which Knox stared at the floor.

Every time the door opened he'd turn and look, hoping they'd call for him. At last when the door opened he turned and heard what he'd been waiting for.

"Hirano family?"

Knox nearly leaped to his feet. "Yes, I'm here."

The nurse said, "Come with me."

He followed her through the maze of curtained-off areas and down a hallway. The nurse stopped in front of a door. "Sorry for the delay. When the EMTs first brought her in, she was speaking Japanese and we didn't have anyone to translate. Then she became agitated, so we sedated her. We couldn't examine her until she calmed down."

"She's all right?"

"She sustained a concussion, as well as contusions and cuts on her face. No broken bones. Nothing sprained or dislocated. There is some concern about her tongue. She bit it during impact, and it's swollen."

"Can I see her?"

"Of course. Be warned; we're suggesting she doesn't talk."

Knox opened the door to the most beautiful sight. Shiori, conscious, although with a slightly vacant look in her eyes, her mouth set in a stubborn line. He barely noticed the marks on her face because his gaze caught on her white pants splattered with blood.

Jesus. What hadn't the nurse told him about her injuries? Because from where he stood, she had to have major damage somewhere.

"Sir?"

He looked up to see Shiori trying to talk and the nurse shushing her. Shiori grabbed a pad of paper and a pen and wrote something. She turned it around and underlined it twice.

But she'd written it in Japanese.

The accident had scrambled her brain.

Knox took a step closer to her. "I don't read Japanese. English, please."

She spun the pad around, frowned, and wrote something else and turned it.

IT'S RED PAINT. THE CANS I BOUGHT AT
THE ART STORE EXPLODED UPON IMPACT.

"Thank god." Then Knox was by her side, cupping her precious, precious face in his hands, pressing soft kisses everywhere he could reach. On her forehead, her hairline, the corners of her eyes, her cheeks, the tip of her nose and chin, along every inch of her jaw. And then finally, with infinite tenderness, he kissed her mouth. When she parted her lips to speak, he shook his head. "For the first time since I've known you, I can say keep your mouth shut and pass it off as a doctor's order."

Those beautiful golden eyes filled with tears.

"Nushi," he whispered, "don't. I died a thousand deaths today, not knowing if you were all right."

She reached up, her hands mirroring his as she held his face.

They stayed like that for several long moments.

Then Knox remembered the nurse. When he turned around, he realized she'd snuck out. He looked at Shiori again. "I need to find out what they're doing with you. I'll be right back."

Luckily, the nurse hadn't gone far.

He smiled sheepishly at her. "Thanks for giving us a moment."

"No problem."

"What happens now? Can I take her home?"

"I don't see why she'd need to stay here, but I'm not the doctor. I'll see if I can get a doc to sign off on her. It might take me a bit, so be patient."

"I will. Thank you."

Shiori had slumped back into the pillow.

He scooted the lone chair closer and took her hand, bringing her knuckles to his mouth for a kiss. "I'm hoping to get you out of here soon."

She nodded, then winced.

"Rest. I'll be here when you wake up." Knox watched her until her breathing slowed. Keeping hold of her hand, he rested his forehead on the edge of her bed. Relief like he'd never known finally swept through him. She was all right. Banged up and battered but here, *right here*, with him where she belonged.

Knox fished out both phones and started sending text messages. First to Deacon, then a brief explanation to the Black Arts crew. He used Shiori's phone to text Tom, Fee, Katie and Molly. It was a damn good thing she used pictures to identify who was who, because all her contact names were in Japanese. His finger hovered over her mother's picture. She had a right to know her daughter had been in an accident, but was it his place to tell her?

No.

He had the same hesitation over Ronin's number. Sensei Black had been gone three months. In that time they'd heard from him once, when he'd sent an e-mail indicating he and Amery were spending time in Hawaii before they returned home. So yeah, he'd skip contacting Ronin too.

Half an hour later a hacking cough woke him. He'd dozed off with his head on Shiori's bed. He handed her a glass of water. "Here."

Shiori drank it down, and Knox could tell she had trouble swallowing.

"Do you need a straw?"

She shook her head.

"Can I see your tongue?"

She shook her head vehemently.

"Come on, She-Cat. You always want to stick your tongue out at me. Here's your chance."

She turned her head away from him and a tear rolled down her cheek.

That hurt him worse than the time she'd accidentally stomped on his kidney. He leaned over her and swiped it away with his thumb. "It's not morbid curiosity making me ask, kitten. I'll be taking care of you while you recover, and I want to see the injury at its worst so I know when it's healing."

Shiori faced him and closed her eyes before she opened her mouth and stuck out her tongue.

His gut clenched. Her tongue had swelled so much he wondered how she kept it in her mouth. Not only had she bitten it a few inches down from the tip with enough force that she had left deeply indented bloody teeth marks, but she'd also bitten the sides of her tongue with her back teeth, so that was swollen and bruised. When he noticed the blood underneath her chin and streaks on her neck, he imagined it'd bled like a son of a bitch.

She made a noise, and he looked up at her. Such mortification on her face.

Keeping his eyes connected to hers, he bent down and kissed her poor abused tongue. When he pulled back, he shrugged and said, "I expected worse."

The door opened and a harried-looking woman in blue scrubs walked in with a clipboard. "I'm Dr. Ballard. I see you've requested to be discharged."

Shiori nodded.

The doctor looked at Knox. "You'll be taking care of her?"

"Yes, ma'am."

"You know what signs to look for if she has complications from the concussion?"

Knox rattled them off with ease.

"Now, you know I'm going to ask how you're so familiar with them," Dr. Ballard said.

"Shiori and I are both jujitsu instructors, and we've seen more than our share of concussions over the years. She's in good hands with me."

"Sounds like it. As for the tongue injury, it didn't require stitches, but if it doesn't show healing even in the next twenty-four hours you'll need to call an oral surgeon. She needs to keep an ice pack on her tongue at least fifteen minutes every hour. The less she talks, the less trauma to the tongue and the faster it heals. But between that and the concussion, I can prescribe painkillers—"

Shiori shook her head.

The doctor looked at Knox and he shrugged. "It's a family thing. Her brother, our Sensei, has the same mind-set."

"Over-the-counter meds?" the doctor asked Shiori.

She nodded.

"Motrin or Tylenol. No OTC with aspirin in it." She took out a prescription pad and scrawled across it. "A cycle of antibiotics is nonnegotiable." She handed it to Knox but spoke to Shiori. "You'll be sore for a few days—nature of the beast with car accidents. Although if you practice martial arts you have a higher pain tolerance than most people. Biggest thing? You need to rest your body because you have been through a trauma." She pointed at Knox. "Lucky you, having this handsome man at your beck and call. But I wouldn't get used to it."

Shiori choked, and Knox immediately handed her a glass of water.

Dr. Ballard smiled. "You're officially discharged. I'll send an orderly in with a wheelchair." She eyed Shiori's pants. "And something else to wear out of the hospital. I can tell that's not blood, but the folks in the waiting room can't." She swept out of the room.

That's when he realized he didn't have a vehicle here to take her home. Classes had started at Black Arts, so none of them were available. He used Shiori's phone and found the contact he wanted. The person who answered started the conversation by apologizing profusely. "Yes, I'll relay your apologies and recovery wishes to Ms. Hirano. But right now we're stranded at Denver Memorial General since she rode here in an ambulance." He listened. "That would be great. Emergency exit in fifteen minutes. Thank you." He hung up.

Shiori narrowed her eyes.

"What? They at least owe you a ride from here."

She grabbed the notepad.

YOU ARE TAKING ME TO MY PLACE?

Knox shook his head. "You'll stay with me."

NO.

"Yes." He got right in her stubborn face. "As your submissive, it is my right, my duty, and my honor to take care of my Mistress. My house is a better option."

WHY?

"Because your penthouse is a damn fortress. Everyone from Black Arts will want to see if you're okay. The security checks at your building would be exhausting. There are no grocery stores within five miles of your place."

She sighed.

FINE.

Knox kissed her forehead. "Thank you."

CHAPTER TWENTY-SEVEN

THE first night Shiori spent under Knox's care had been a bit of a blur. She'd slept a lot. In Knox's arms on the couch and then in his big bed.

When she woke the morning of the second day, she'd hobbled into his shower, surprised by how sore she felt—every bone in her body ached. Standing under the hot spray did wonders, though, and she felt a million times better. She wrapped a big bath sheet around her body and stopped in front of the sink.

Shiori hadn't actually looked in a mirror since the accident. She opened her mouth and stuck out her tongue. Her stomach roiled, and she made it to the toilet before she threw up. Twice. Once she was reasonably certain she was done hurling, she flushed and faced the mirror again.

Tentatively, she stuck her tongue out again and studied it with a critical eye. Damn lucky she hadn't bitten it off, so she should be grateful. But it sucked not to talk. She couldn't eat anything, and she had to ice it once an hour. She dumped a capful of mouthwash in her mouth and swished it around, squeezing her eyes shut against the zing of pain when the alcohol soaked the injuries. After a minute or so she spit it out, then put a dot of toothpaste on her toothbrush and gently cleaned her teeth.

Without any of her own clothes here, she raided Knox's T-shirt and sweatpants drawer. She combed out her hair and ventured out of the bedroom to find Knox.

But the kitchen and the living room were eerily empty. She glanced out the front window but didn't see his pickup.

Daytime TV held no appeal. She really hated being stranded in a strange place with nothing to do.

Sleep. You're supposed to be resting.

Next she meandered through Knox's living room, looking at the objects he'd chosen to display. A warm, sweet feeling bloomed in her chest when she saw the picture she'd painted for him front and center on the mantel. He had a bunch of military history books and several piles of martial-arts magazines. She grabbed a stack of those and curled up on the coach.

Some of the magazines were older—as much as five years. Tucked in the middle of the stack was an issue of *American Jujitsu Association*. The front cover included a headline that the ten best dojos in the United States were listed inside. She flipped to the article and her heart leaped at seeing Black Arts in Denver, Colorado, listed as number three. There was a breakdown of why each dojo had been chosen, the owner and the instructing staff. Her stomach dropped when she saw the list:

Sensei Ronin Black, seventh-degree black belt

Beck Leeds, fifth-degree black belt

Gunnar Whatley, fifth-degree black belt

Brody Pearson, fifth-degree black belt

Knox Lofgren, fourth-degree black belt

Ito Tohora, third-degree black belt

Langston Reed, third-degree black belt

Shiori closed her eyes. The reason those men were no longer employed at Black Arts was her fault. Because of Naomi. When it came out that Naomi had been paid to be with Ronin, he immediately suspected that Beck, Gunnar, and Langston were also spies planted by their grandfather. He'd fired them without giving them a chance to defend themselves. In the aftermath, she'd questioned Ojisan and he'd sworn he'd never meddled in Ronin's professional life.

She wondered now if these guys held a grudge against Ronin and Black Arts.

Ronin still hadn't recovered from losing his highest-ranking belts. Brody Pearson had left in protest of Ronin shitcanning the other instructors. Most of the new staff were first- and second-degree black belts—Knox had passed his fifth level right after he'd been hired full-time. She knew from talking to Deacon that testing for the fourth-level black belt was at least a couple of years away since he'd focused on MMA instead.

The key rattled in the front door, and she hastily shoved the magazine back in the stack.

Knox strolled in, plastic grocery bags clutched in his hands. He didn't notice her as he headed to the kitchen. After dumping the bags on the counter, he cut down the hallway to the bedroom. Half a minute later he returned, relief lighting up his face when he saw her.

"Hey." He dropped to his knees in front of her—without conscious thought, it seemed, which thrilled her. His gaze took her in from head to toe. "Happy to see you up and around. How're you feeling?"

She made the so-so motion.

"Take any Motrin?"

She shook her head.

"Probably not a good idea on any empty stomach anyway. I'll fix you lunch. I bought chicken and beef broth."

Oh joy. A clear, salty wannabe soup.

"I also picked up a bunch of Popsicles." His eyes glommed on to her lips. "And I know it sounds damn perverted, given the mouth injury you're sporting, but watching you eat them will give me all sorts of dirty, bad, wrong ideas."

Shiori reached out and touched this face she knew so well. This face she loved so much. And how ironic was it that the day she'd decided to tell him she loved him . . . her tongue had been severely injured? Should she consider that a sign?

Only that you should've told him sooner.

"I need to put the food away before some of it melts." He kissed her fingertips and returned to the kitchen.

She'd lost interest in the magazines and replaced the stack where she'd found it. Then she sat at the breakfast bar and wrote on her notepad.

I NEED CLOTHES.

Knox leaned over and read it. "Yes, kitten, I know you need clothes." When he lifted his head and grinned, her belly rolled again. "Which is why I picked up a few things for you today."

YOU WENT SHOPPING?

"Yep. And the salesgirls were very helpful."

I'll just bet they were happy to see a strapping Viking striding into their store.

He smoothed her lips with such tenderness she ached. Because he had no choice but to be tender. Knox preferred the kind of kisses where they tried to eat each other alive.

"I'll be right back."

He jogged out of the house, but his eyes held wariness when he walked back in carrying two bags. The black logo of the Victoria's Secret bag caught her attention first.

No doubt those saleswomen imagined what it'd be like for Knox's hands to be cupping their breasts as he picked out bras. Or they imagined Knox latching on to the tiny string by the hip as he pulled the panties down with his teeth.

"Kitten, you okay?"

FINE. WHY?

"Sounded like you growled."

THAT'S YOUR JOB.

He laughed. "True."

SO DID YOU BUY KINKY STUFF?

"No. But I did buy what I'd like to see you in, Mistress, so please cut me some slack."

SHOW ME!

"All right." Knox reached into the bag and came out with black panties. Sheer, with pink rosebuds on the string that sat on the hips. Next he pulled out a pair of mint-green lace panties, followed by a pair of boy shorts, the deep purple of a ripe plum, and finally an ivory-colored thong with a peach on the front as well as the words BITE ME.

VERY FUNNY.

"So I did okay?"
She nodded.
"Good. There's matching bras in there too for each pair of underwear."

Why hadn't he shown her those? She plucked the bag from his hold and dumped the remainder on the counter to see what screamed sexy to him. If any of these bras were padded, she'd use one to gag him.

Fortunately for him, he'd paid attention to the types of bras she wore and his selections were all very lovely.

THANK YOU.

"No problem. But I'm such a pig I'll admit I like seeing you in no bra best."

She smiled.

The next bag was from Saks. Two pairs of Juicy Couture lounge pants, with matching camisoles. And two pairs of black yoga pants with two long-sleeved shirts, one gray, one a pale pink.

AWESOME.

"And lastly . . . shoes." He dropped a box containing the same Asics athletic shoes she already had—in the right size—plus a pair of rhinestone FitFlops in black, and a pair of sheepskin slippers.

Shiori studied this man who knew her better than she'd imagined.

HOW DID YOU KNOW MY SIZES?

Knox pulled her into his arms. "Not only have I had my hands and my mouth all over you for almost three months, but I pay attention when it comes to you. Not because I have to as some sub requirement, but as a man who wants to know everything about you, including your offbeat color choices in underwear. I'll admit I had to call Katie and ask your shoe size."

She managed a thick-tongued, "Thank you, Knox."

He tipped her chin up. "No talking."

She disentangled from his embrace.

NO KISSING EITHER.

"Afraid not."

*BUT YOU CAN KISS ME IN PLACES BESIDES
MY MOUTH.*

"You were in an accident. Your body has been through a lot."

*MY BODY NEEDS YOU. I NEED YOU. TAKE
ME TO BED. AND I DON'T MEAN TO SLEEP.*

"Is that an order, Nushi?" he asked softly.

She nodded.

"Hang on." He carefully picked her up and carried her to his
bedroom. The first thing he did after depositing her on his bed was
take off his shirt.

"I know you don't think you're fragile, but you are. I don't
want to hurt you."

She mouthed, "You won't."

He ditched the pants. Then he kneeled on the bed and lifted
the baggy T-shirt over her head. He tapped her hip for her to lift
up and the sweatpants were off. Gently pushing her thighs apart, he
made a place for himself there. His hands slid under her butt cheeks,
being careful not to squeeze too hard.

Teasing kisses skimmed the inside of her thigh. Left, then
right. Knox pressed his mouth against her core, licking her softly
up one side and down the other. Swirling that tongue around her

clit and then back down to her opening. That's when his hands tightened—when he had his tongue buried so deep inside her she wondered how he could breathe.

Shiori touched his forehead, then let her hands stroke his hair.

He looked up at her with his tongue still licking her pussy from the inside out. He eased back, gifting her with more soft, sucking kisses. "Sometimes when I'm kissing your mouth, I imagine kissing your pussy that way. But today, when I'm tonguing this hot cunt, I'm imagining kissing your mouth."

That sweet confession had her lying back on the bed, giving herself over to his care completely.

Knox ate at her delicately. Languidly. But with the same passion that flared between them at the first touch. And she'd focused on letting the sensations roll over her. No hurry, no need to guide him. Hearing his sucking sounds, the occasional grunt, and her quick intake of breath that meant her orgasm had crept up on her. Starting with a tiny pulse in her clit, followed by stronger contractions until that moment when every sensation coalesced and she went soaring.

He peppered kisses across the top of her mound as he slid his hands free.

As the fog cleared, she tried to rise up and bring him where she wanted him—on her, in her.

But Knox had other plans. He pushed up to his knees, his eyes roaming over every naked inch. "I want to roll you in Bubble Wrap so I don't ever have to live through another day like yesterday." His hands spanned her waist and then drifted up to cup her breasts. "But that's the kicker, kitten. You are alive and here with me, and there's no way I'll ever be able to let you go. Not because you're my Mistress, but because you're the woman I love. The woman I've waited for my entire life."

Before she could find any way to respond, she realized that she was crying. His sweet confession had brought her to tears, yet she had never felt happier.

Knox petted and stroked her, every touch filled with the depths of his love and possession. He rolled the condom on one-handed so he never stopped touching her.

Shiori reached between them and held his cock as he eased in inch by inch.

He rested his forehead to hers. "I love you, Shiori."

If he hadn't been gently sucking on her neck as he moved inside her, he would've seen her mouth the words, *I love you, too.*

AFTER Knox so thoroughly wrecked her, she curled into a ball and fell asleep. When she came to, shadows fell across the windows. Voices drifted down the hallway from the living room. She stood and stretched, seeing that Knox had set clothes on the end of the bed for her. She dressed, used the bathroom, and went to see who'd shown up.

Deacon and Maddox were having a beer with Knox. As soon as Deacon saw her, he was off the couch heading toward her. He wrapped those muscled, tattooed arms around her in a gentle hug. A long hug too. It had nearly reached the uncomfortable stage when Deacon whispered, "Thank fuck you're all right, Shi-Shi."

He returned to his seat, and Knox held his hand out for her to sit on his lap. She curled into his solid warmth and sighed.

Maddox smiled at her. "Glad to see you're on the mend."

She smiled back.

A huge bouquet of flowers sat on the entryway table.

Knox noticed where her focus had gone and said, "Get well soon from everyone at Black Arts and ABC."

"Fee and Katie wanted to drop them off personally, but your guard dog here is denying everyone visitation," Deacon said.

"She needs to rest. And, come on, those women would poke and prod her and probably Instagram pictures of her tongue as well as convince her that shots of tequila are the best remedy."

Deacon nodded. "Shihan does have a point."

For the first time since the accident, Shiori wondered who'd taken over hers and Knox's classes. She grabbed her notebook.

WHO IS TEACHING?

"Fee is taking over your classes. Blue spared Terrel. Zach pulled the stick out of his ass finally and stepped up too."

ANY WORD FROM RONIN?

"No," Knox said. "We were just discussing how much fun it was gonna be having the conversation with Sensei about going off the grid for so long. It wasn't a big deal when he left for a month. But it's a big damn deal when he blows off all responsibilities for three months."

SO ARE YOU GUYS TRYING TO FIGURE OUT HIS MOTIVE FOR LACK OF COMMU- NICATION?

Deacon snorted. "It's his dojo, so he can do whatever he wants. Putting Knox in charge means his decisions stand during that time frame. Ronin has zero right to bitch. We stopped by to tell Knox he has full support of everyone at Black Arts."

Knox seemed embarrassed. "Thanks."

Maddox and Deacon got up and said hasty goodbyes before letting themselves out.

Neither of them spoke. Knox just set his chin on top of her head and absentmindedly stroked her arm. After a while he said, "Do you mind if I go for a run? I've got energy to burn."

She wrote on her pad: GO AHEAD.

"Thanks. You wanna watch TV until I get back?"

NO. I'LL JUST GO BACK TO BED.

"Want me to carry you?"

Shiori rolled her eyes.

He draped a towel around his neck and paused with his hand on the doorknob. "You sure you'll be okay?"

She gave him two thumbs-up and made a shooing motion.

By the time she reached the bedroom, she felt woozy. She was glad Knox wasn't here because he'd try to haul her to the hospital. Especially if he knew she'd thrown up and had the bouts of dizziness and nausea several times since yesterday.

But the doctor had warned her about the aftereffects of a car accident. This was all part of it. The more she slept, the faster she'd heal, so she hunkered beneath the covers, hoping to get her life back soon.

CHAPTER TWENTY-EIGHT

"LEMME see your tongue."

Shiori stuck it out at him quickly.

"I need to see if it's healing."

She closed her eyes and opened her mouth.

He noticed the swelling along the sides was nearly gone, even when red spots and bumps were visible. "Does it hurt?"

She shrugged.

The big bite mark looked fifty times better. He put his fingers under her jaw, closing it. "I think you'll be okay to talk tomorrow."

They were on day four after the accident, and Knox knew Shiori intended to return to her penthouse today. Although he wished she would've been here under different circumstances, having her living in his home had seemed right. But if he said that, he'd spook her, so he had to pretend it was cool she wouldn't be in his bed every night.

Three precise knocks sounded on the door.

Knox answered and was shocked to see Ronin on his doorstep. "Do my eyes deceive me, or is it the great jujitsu Master Black?"

"Are you gonna let me in?"

Before Ronin dodged him, Knox gave him the acceptable man half hug. "Come in. When did you get back?"

"Last night. Where is she?" Then Ronin brushed past him when he spied Shiori. But he stopped three feet away, keeping his hands at his sides as he catalogued her injuries. "Why did I have to hear from Katie that you were in a fucking car accident?"

No hug. No, "I'm glad you're all right." Just anger.

When Shiori looked at her brother with disappointment, Knox immediately went to her side. "She's damn lucky to be here. The semi that hit them T-boned the fucking car. She ended up with a mild concussion and nearly bit her tongue off, so she's under doctor's orders not to speak." Fuck this shit. "So I'll speak for her. 'Hey, bro. I'm glad you're back. I can't wait to hear the details of your trip. Even though I'm still a little banged up from the car accident, yes, you can hug me.'"

That did jolt Ronin out of whatever fugue state he'd been in. He opened his arms and Shiori met him halfway. After he'd wrapped her in a hug, he rested his cheek on the top of her head and spoke to her softly in Japanese.

Knox hated not knowing what Ronin had said.

Then Ronin let her go. He turned and jammed his hand through his hair. He didn't look at either of them when he said, "We need to talk. Sit. Both of you."

Sensei Black back to issuing orders. No surprise there.

Knox wanted to pull Shiori onto his lap. Instead they sat side by side on the couch.

Ronin spun around. "I don't even know where the fuck to start." His eyes narrowed on Knox, then Shiori. "So you two are what? Dating now?"

Dating was a trivial word to describe what'd happened between him and Shiori in the last three months. "Yes, we're involved."

"How long has this been going on?" he demanded. "Were you

two fucking around the entire time behind my back, pretending to hate each other?"

"No!"

"When did hate turn into . . . ?"

"After you left. Things between us . . . changed."

Shiori reached for Knox's hand and threaded her fingers through his.

Ronin's jaw tightened at that show of solidarity. "I don't fucking believe this."

"We've heard that a few times."

"Is *he* the reason you haven't kept in contact with Mom? You're too busy playing house with him?"

Was Ronin's intent to rile Knox up? Because it was working.

Shiori reached for her notebook and scribbled furiously.

"What's she doing?" Ronin asked.

"Answering you. She can't talk, remember?"

She flipped the notebook around.

I HAVE KEPT IN CONTACT WITH MOM. AND YOU ARE ONE TO TALK ABOUT NOT KEEPING IN TOUCH.

"That was six fucking years ago, so you can let that go at any point, Shiori."

She wrote fast.

I'M NOT TALKING ABOUT THAT. I'M TALKING ABOUT NO ONE HEARING FROM YOU IN THE LAST THREE MONTHS. THAT'S IRRESPONSIBLE. YOU GAVE US THE IMPRESSION YOU DIDN'T GIVE A DAMN WHAT WE DID AS LONG AS YOU DIDN'T HAVE TO HEAR ABOUT IT. SO YOU

DON'T GET TO LECTURE ME OR KNOX
ABOUT ANYTHING.

Ronin's gaze winged between them. "Seriously? I don't get to
question any of this? I come back and not only are my Shihan and
my sister hooking up, but they've joined forces to dismantle my
existing MMA training program and start fresh?"

"Like Shiori said, if you would've called in, we would've filled
you in."

"You know how I found out about the new MMA plan?
This morning after Amery left for work I went down to the office
and no one was around. So I checked out the first floor. Then I unlocked the door to the Crow's Nest. Forty-five minutes later I returned to the second floor and some man I'd never seen before was
running on the treadmill. I asked him who the hell he was and why
he was in my training room unattended. That's when he made the
craziest claim I'd ever heard." Ronin glared at them as he paced.

"He said he's running the Black Arts MMA program. I laughed
and asked if it was a 'welcome home' practical joke. He assured me
he'd been hired by you two. But I thought to myself, Knox and Shiori
would never pull that shit—hire someone without my approval. So I
went up to the third floor, looking for Blue to see what he knew about
it, and ended up talking to Katie, who was more than happy to gossip.
Yes, you two had brought Maddox Byerly on board and he'd signed a
one-year contract. Then Katie started getting misty-eyed when she
babbled on about how you two were such a cute couple. And I stupidly
asked, 'A couple of whats?' and I felt like an idiot because I didn't have
a fucking clue about . . ." He gestured between them. "This. And Katie added she wasn't sure if either of you would be in on account of
your car accident. So that was another fucking thing I found out thirdhand this morning. Then I tried to get in touch with Deacon because
I couldn't get ahold of either of you. But apparently he dropped Molly
off at work this morning and they had a shouting match in the middle

of the office. Which resulted in an angry phone call from my wife about why Deacon was such an asshole for making Molly cry."

"For fuck's sake, sit down," Knox said. "You're prowling like a caged animal."

"I feel like a caged animal, watching this soap opera unfold." Ronin dropped into the easy chair and closed his eyes. He breathed deeply for several long moments. When Shiori scooted to the edge of the couch and took his hand, he opened his eyes. "I'm sorry about your accident, Shi. You sure you're okay?"

She made the so-so sign.

"Anything you need?"

She shook her head and pointed at Knox.

"I'm glad he's taking care of you."

Was that Ronin's approval?

Nah. Temporary at best.

"Since you can't talk, I'll call Mom and let her know what happened." Ronin looked at Knox. "You'll fill me in?"

"Of course."

Ronin kept ahold of his sister's hand, and it seemed to ground him. "Look, I'm sorry for showing up unannounced and losing my shit. I just hadn't expected to come home to any of this. Normally when I get back . . . everything is normal." He sighed. "But you're both right. The way I handled these last three months, being totally out of touch, was shitty. I figured Amery and I would get only one honeymoon, and I didn't want to share a minute of our time with anyone. But I am sorry, and thank you for keeping everything together in my absence."

Knox said, "You're welcome. But don't do that next time, okay?"

"There won't be a next time."

"What the hell happened in Japan, Ronin?"

"Besides the most brutal training schedule I've ever faced? Basically, Master Daichi cut me loose. It was bizarre, and I still can't wrap my head around it."

That was a huge development. "Why'd he cut you loose?"

"According to Yasuji? I'd learned everything I could from Master Daichi. I ended up leaving training early. While Amery and I were in Tokyo, a few things that'd been hanging between us came to a head, so we stayed five more days than I'd planned. Then I thought, what the hell; why not extend the trip another week in Hawaii. The day before we left, Yasuji called me with the news Master Kenji agreed to meet with me about supervising my training."

Knox frowned. "Master Kenji? Where's he?"

"San Francisco. So I spent three days having Master Kenji assess me. He agreed to take me on, which I'm grateful for because there are only three other jujitsu masters I'd consider working with."

Shiori grabbed her notebook and started writing.

MASTER KENJI IS MASTER DAICHI'S PROTÉGÉ?

"Yes. He's Daichi's oldest student." Ronin smiled. "I believe Master Daichi found irony in having his youngest student being taught by his oldest living student. Anyway, we—Black Arts Jujitsu—will be listed under the House of Kenji."

Shiori wrote another message.

YOU WERE WORRIED BLACK ARTS WOULD FADE INTO OBLIVION AFTER HOUSE OF DAICHI RELEASED YOU?

"It had caused me a few sleepless nights. I'd hoped to find a new sensei, but I'd never imagined it'd happen that fast and that Master Kenji would come to me."

Ronin had a healthy ego—as he should. So the moments when he was surprised and humbled served as a reminder to Knox that no matter what skill level was reached, there would always be doubts and fear about being good enough.

"Granted, Master Kenji has a few requirements for the dojo that I'll implement as soon as possible." Ronin locked his gaze to Knox's. "We'll go over those in detail."

Knox gave him a fake smile. "Looking forward to it."

Shiori wrote something else.

THERE'S MORE TO IT. TELL US.

He loved how she used *us.*

"You're included in those conversations too, Shi."

THAT'S NOT WHAT I MEANT.

Ronin looked torn. His gaze moved between Knox and Shiori again before he sighed. "Remember Beck Leeds?"

"Wasn't he your second-in-command when . . . ?" Everything fell apart after the Naomi debacle. Why the fuck would Ronin bring up that situation now?

Because Shiori pushed him to.

Shiori held up her hand, and they waited while she jotted something down.

BECK WAS ONE OF THE THREE BLACK ARTS INSTRUCTORS YOU FIRED AFTER EVERYTHING WENT DOWN WITH NAOMI BECAUSE YOU THOUGHT OJISAN PLANTED THEM TO SPY ON YOU.

"Yeah. I realize I hadn't been thinking straight. But my whole life had just been turned completely upside down. I gave in to that paranoia—just another fun fucking piece of fallout from Naomi."

That statement took Knox back a step.

"Anyway, Beck is with the House of Kenji. At first I figured my fast dismissal of him would be a deal killer for Master Kenji. But I talked with Beck, and he isn't holding a grudge. He said he understood my reasoning for cutting ties immediately."

Knox made a time-out sign. "You never told me about Beck's connection to Okada, Ronin. All you did was shitcan him and move on. So how did that come about?"

"Another fucking stellar move on my part." Ronin looked at Shiori. "Maggie Arnold, who runs the Okada branch in Seattle, is Beck's mother."

"Jesus."

"She contacted me years ago and asked if I'd meet with him, and I hired him. That's why I thought he'd been spying on me from the beginning."

"Now I get why you lost it."

Shiori held up the notebook.

DID BECK KNOW WHERE YOUR OTHER IN-STRUCTORS ENDED UP?

Ronin closed his eyes briefly. "Beck does know because he's the one who recommended Gunnar and Lang to me, which is why I suspected them. Gunnar accepted a transfer to Brazil for his job and has been training with the Gracie program. Lang returned to New York. He hasn't heard from Brody."

Silence descended.

That'd been a hellish few months, even though Knox had benefited from Beck, Gunnar, Brody and Lang getting cut from the program since Knox had moved up to Shihan status.

Where would he be if Ronin had acted rationally? Being named Shihan had given Knox a full-time paid job in the dojo. He'd received a huge salary bump with the position.

"How'd we get so far off track?" Ronin asked.

Shiori turned her notebook around.

JUST TRYING TO FIGURE OUT WHERE
YOUR HEAD IS.

"My head has been one-tracking it until I saw you with my own eyes to ascertain that you were okay."

She mouthed, "I'm fine."

"You're better than I expected."

"She's still needs to take it easy," Knox pointed out.

"I know. So as far as I'm concerned, it's best you stay with her to make sure she'd doesn't overdo everything. I'm back. I can cover classes. Everything else can wait." He stood.

As soon as Shiori got up, Ronin hugged her again. "You know Amery will be over to fuss at you, right?"

Shiori nodded.

"Take care." He kissed her forehead. Then he looked at Knox. "Walk me out."

Not a request. Ironically, it was the same tone and inflection Shiori used in Mistress mode. "Sure." He squeezed Shiori's hand when he walked by.

Outside, Knox faced off against Ronin. Ronin braced his hand on the top of his Corvette; Knox leaned against the passenger door of his pickup.

"I don't know whether to be pissed off you're fucking my sister, or relieved."

Knox said nothing; he just waited to see how this would play out.

"I thought when she left Okada she'd left it for good. Not so. She's been working for the company the entire time she's been here. Did you know that?"

"Not until she told me a few months ago, but I assumed you knew."

Ronin mimicked Knox's pose, defensively crossing his arms over his chest. "That sounded accusatory."

"It was. She's your sister. She's been here for almost a year. How did you not know what's going on in her life? Yeah, I get that you're a newlywed and you've had health issues, but Shiori has stepped up at Black Arts. She's stepped up for Black and Blue Promotions. You've taken advantage of her. At least I get paid to handle that shit. She doesn't. So between doing all that, she's also at your mother's beck and call, flying all over for Okada business . . . and you knew nothing about it. She deserves better than that."

"You her champion now?"

"Yes, because she needs one."

"Look, Knox, I realize I fucked up monumentally where my sister is concerned. That seems to be a pattern with me. I ignore her, get pissed off at her, have a reconciliation with her, and then the whole cycle repeats." He looked away. "It sucks. I suck. I spent too goddamn much time thinking when I was in Japan about all the stuff in my life I wanted to change."

"And?"

"The changes are coming whether I want them to or not." Ronin's gaze flicked to the house and back to Knox. "What about you two? Are you just hooking up?"

Knox was used to Ronin's deflection. This time he handed it right back to him. "We're together."

When Ronin's hard-eyed stare didn't push Knox to babble like it did with everyone else, he sighed. "I deserved that."

"Yep."

"This is all so fucking surreal. It feels like I've been gone three years, not three months."

"Ronin, tell me what's really going on."

He shook his head. "I need to get every piece of information locked down before we talk about it. So by the time you're back next week, plan on having long meetings during the day." He flashed his teeth. "I know how much you love that shit."

"Fuck you. In your absence, I shaved our weekly staff meeting down to ten minutes." Knox also flashed his teeth. "Maybe you should give me your notes and I'll summarize."

"Funny. I won't have notes for another two days."

This secretive stuff didn't sit well with him. "So is that when you'll pass down judgment on us hiring Byerly?"

"I'll admit I was pissed. But I can't fault you and Shiori for doing it. I know Byerly gets results. He is the best of the best, and that's what the program needs to grow and thrive."

That's when Ronin's issue with the situation became clear to Knox. "You weren't sold on the idea of a full-blown MMA program at Black Arts, were you?"

"No."

"Why not?"

Ronin scrubbed his hand over his face. "For this reason. We didn't have the staff. We didn't have the talent. I've already started a promotion company that I feel I'm giving half-assed attention to. I don't know what my responsibilities will be after the dojo is under the umbrella of a new house. Amery understands I don't have a nine-to-five job, but I'm tired of spending only one whole day out of a weekend with her. So change is inevitable, and needed, and I'll be glad for it after it's all implemented."

"What can I do to help?"

"Just . . ." He sighed. "I don't know. Be aware it might be a rougher transition than I'd like."

Another vague response. "Okay."

Ronin's eyes met his. "I have a pile of shit to do today, so I'd better get on it. One last thing. Have you been to Twisted lately?"

"Define lately."

"You'd better not be fucking around on my sister, Knox, because that shit doesn't fly with me," he snapped.

Knox cocked his head. "Ease. Off. It's none of your business what I do or don't do at Twisted. It's none of your business what I do or don't do with your sister, so get to the fucking point."

"When was the last time you were there?"

"Two weeks ago. Why?"

"Does Shiori know about the place?"

"Yes."

"Does she know what kind of club it is?"

"Yep."

"Why the fuck are you being so goddamn vague?" Ronin demanded. Then he aimed a cool look at Knox. "Guess if I want answers I'll ask Merrick."

"You can ask him, but I doubt he'll tell you what you want to know. Maintaining member privacy is his one unbreakable rule." Knox pushed away from his vehicle. "I'm sorry you're having a hard time dealing with changes, Ronin, but don't take that shit out on me. I've got your back. I'll be by your side for as long as you need me. But there are some times when I have to draw the line between our working relationship and our personal lives. Not trying to be a dick, and for the first time I understand why you did it with Amery. I'm asking you to understand, not to push and punish—either me or Shiori."

Ronin squinted at him. "I swear I have no fucking idea what you're talking about. So I'll let that go." He opened his car door. "Remember this conversation, Knox, because it will come full circle."

No fucking clue what that meant, but he nodded anyway.

"See you at the dojo Monday morning. I'll make sure Amery texts you before she shows up this weekend."

"That'll work. Thanks for coming by. You have no idea what it means to her."

"Take care of her, and if you need anything, call."

Knox didn't watch Ronin drive away. He returned to the living room and saw Shiori sitting by the open window. Her knees were pressed against her chest and she'd wrapped her arms around her shins.

She'd buried her face beneath her hair, so he couldn't tell if she was crying.

He dropped to his knees in front of her. "Hey. You okay?"

Her head moved.

"I take that as a no." He gently pried her fingers loose and let his hands travel up her arms to her shoulders. "Can you look at me, please?"

When she slowly raised her head, he noticed her damp cheeks and his gut clenched. Shiori attempted to push her hair out of her face, but he stilled the movement.

"Let me." Knox brushed her hair from her beautiful face. "Were you listening?"

She nodded.

"Guess I forgot your ears work even if your mouth doesn't."

Shiori snatched up her notebook and wrote furiously before she showed him what she'd written.

YOU STOOD UP FOR ME.

"Always. Why are you surprised by that, Nushi?"

I'M NOT. BUT RONIN CLEARLY WAS. I WANT TO YELL AT HIM TO OPEN HIS EYES. I WANT TO KISS YOU UNTIL NEITHER OF US CAN BREATHE. CLEARLY I'M AN EMO-TIONAL BASKET CASE, AND I HATE THAT YOU'RE SEEING ME LIKE THIS.

"When I look at you, all I see is the beautiful woman I'm in love with."

Once again, Shiori didn't respond in kind. He'd told her

several times since her accident that he loved her. She'd smiled, gotten teary-eyed, but she hadn't repeated those words back to him.

She's suffering from a serious mouth injury and talking is the one thing she's not supposed to do. You bark at her every time she tries to speak, so what do you expect?

Knox kissed the tips of her fingers. "Kitten, it'll all work out. It always does."

But he had an unsettling feeling that might not be true this time.

CHAPTER TWENTY-NINE

IT'D been a week since the accident. Why did she still feel like she'd gotten hit by a truck?

Oh, right, because she actually had.

Shiori closed her eyes. She felt like dog shit. She'd finished her cycle of antibiotics three days ago, so that hadn't been the reason for her queasiness.

She attributed her tiredness to stress from Ronin being back. He'd thrown himself back into Black Arts business, questioning Knox on everything to the point Knox earned sympathy from everyone around him, even Deacon.

The number of students enrolled in jujitsu classes had remained the same the last three months. No growth, but no losses either. When Ronin asked why the numbers were static, citing ABC's increased enrollment numbers, Shiori kept mum. It wasn't her place to stick up for Knox—he hadn't asked for her backing.

Knox had answered honestly; Ronin's directive to him was to keep things going with the dojo as they were. That's what Knox had done. If Ronin had asked for them to try to increase enrollment numbers while he'd been gone for a quarter of the year, Knox told him he would've refused. When Sensei asked why, Knox said they didn't have enough instructors for the number of students they already had enrolled. And Ronin being gone had left them short-staffed. He worried they'd lose some of the instructors they had if things didn't change.

Of course Ronin hadn't wanted to hear that. Then, when he demanded to meet with the instructors, it wasn't meant to be taken as slap in the face to Knox, but that's how it'd come across to him—and to everyone else. It didn't matter that Ronin's meetings verified what Knox had told him, that the instructors couldn't work six days a week because everyone had other employment obligations; Ronin had become obsessed with fixing things.

When Ronin asked for her input, she demurred. He pressed her on why she didn't have an opinion since she'd been part of the staff for several months. Choose her brother over her lover? It was a lose-lose situation. That's why she'd refused to get dragged into it. But her bottom line was the same as Knox's; if Ronin wanted to grow the dojo, he needed to hire additional staff.

This morning Knox had left early at Ronin's behest. She yawned and forced herself out of Knox's comfy bed. She headed to the kitchen and saw he'd put out a mug and a tea bag for her. Such a sweet, thoughtful man. She loved that he did little things like that for her, not because she expected it as his Mistress, but just because he wanted to.

After setting the kettle on the stove, she tracked down her cell phone. Lucky thing Knox had plugged it in for her last night. It'd been completely dead. There were missed calls from a couple of clients through Okada. Her e-mail had exploded in the last day, so she tried to organize it.

The kettle whistled. She poured water into the mug, wrapping her hands around the ceramic, letting the heat warm them. Closing her eyes, she breathed in the scented steam. But the second the chamomile hit her nose, she gagged.

Before she could delve too deep into the question of whether tea could get rancid, her stomach cramped. She hastily set down her mug and stumbled to the sink, dry heaving for an eternity. When she could finally lift her head, her skin seemed clammy and she felt feverish.

Something wasn't right. She needed to see a doctor.

Knox would drop everything to take her, but she didn't want to put him in an uncomfortable position with Ronin. She thought about calling Amery, but she was swamped. That scratched Molly off the list as a potential driver too. Fee and Blue shared a car, and she usually took public transport everywhere.

Looked like she'd be calling the car service.

Shiori found a clean pair of yoga pants and one of Knox's old T-shirts. Normally she wouldn't be caught dead wearing this outfit in public, but right now she didn't care. She just wanted to feel better.

The car service sent a limo. Every twist and turn seemed magnified. Feeling completely green, she sent the limo driver away after he dropped her off at the emergency clinic.

It must've been the day for sick people. The clinic was packed. And now she was stuck until someone could see her. She found a corner away from the sniveling and crying kids and let her head fall back against the wall.

Names were called and people vanished into the abyss behind the clinic door.

She heard, "Shy-a-rye?"

Shiori looked around the waiting room, but nobody got up.

The nurse said, "Shy-a-rye . . . Hee-rhino?"

Jesus. She'd never had her named butchered that badly.

Luckily she didn't feel nauseous as she walked to the person holding the clipboard. "I'm Shiori Hirano."

"Oh, wow. Guess I got that one wrong. Pretty name. What is it? Chinese or something?"

"Japanese."

"Cool. Glad you speak English." She led her into a tiny waiting room. "Let's get height and weight and all that." She pointed
to the numbers on the wall. "Stand there." After Shiori had moved,
the woman squinted at her. "Five feet, four inches. Now, step on the
scale." The nurse adjusted the weights and said, "One hundred and
thirty pounds."

Pound measurements confused her. She said, "What is that in
kilograms?"

"I don't know. Never have to worry about that. Oh wait.
There's another set of numbers below." She leaned forward and
squinted. "Looks like about . . . fifty-nine kilograms?"

That had to be wrong. She had to be misreading it. Shiori had
weighed fifty-six kilos for years.

The nurse checked Shiori's blood pressure and rattled off two
numbers that didn't mean anything to her. Then she said, "Dr. Barr
will be in."

Left alone, Shiori turned on her side on the exam table and
closed her eyes.

She must've fallen asleep because a slamming door startled her
awake.

"You really are feeling punky, if you can sleep in this mad-
house," a woman's voice said.

"Sorry." Shiori rolled to her back.

The gray-haired woman wore neon-green eyeglasses and purple medical scrubs with one-eyed green aliens all over them. She
smiled softly and patted Shiori's shoulder when she tried to sit up.
"It's okay, honey. You just stay like that. I'm Dr. Barr. You want to
tell me why you came in today?"

Shiori explained about the car accident and how sick she'd
been in the week since. "I don't know if I'm still suffering effects or
what."

"It could be. I won't rule it out until I've ruled out everything
else. So we'll do some blood and urine tests as well as a throat

culture to see what's going on. Kirsten will take you to the lab and I'll be back after the results are available, which I'm warning you will be at least another hour."

"Guess I'll catch up on more sleep."

After what seemed like a full battery of tests, Kristen returned her to the room.

Shiori closed her eyes, sure she wouldn't be able to sleep, but she conked out again. She woke up when Dr. Barr returned.

"So I've got your test results. First stretch out on your back and lift your shirt up to your ribs."

Dr. Barr gently poked Shiori's lower abdomen.

"What's wrong with me?"

"You're pregnant."

Her mouth fell open in shock. "What?"

"Honey, you really didn't have any idea that you're pregnant?"

"No!"

"Feel this." She took Shiori's hand and placed it on a hard lump above her pubic bone. "That's your uterus."

"But . . . that isn't a contusion from my accident?"

Dr. Barr shook her head. Then she tugged Shiori's shirt back into place and helped her sit up. "All right. This is a surprise to you. So let's backtrack. What was your last period?"

Shiori scrolled back through the last month. No period. Did she have one the month before that? No. The last time she'd had her period had been . . . before Ronin and Amery had left for Japan. "Omigod. I haven't had one for months, but I've always been irregular."

"Any unprotected sex?"

"One time. Just one time . . . two and a half months ago." Her gaze flew to the doctor's. "But I took a morning-after pill."

"Was the intercourse consensual?"

"Yes! I'm still very much involved with him—the baby's father—omigod, how can I be pregnant?"

"How long after intercourse did you take the pill?"

Shiori thought back. "It happened Saturday night, and I took the pill around noon Monday."

"Pills you bought at a pharmacy here in Denver?"

"Yes." She looked at Dr. Barr, and she knew every bit of fear shone in her eyes. "Why didn't it work?"

"Well, honey, those pills aren't one hundred percent effective. The effectiveness drops after the first twenty-four hours, and it's about half as effective after forty-eight hours. That could've played a part in the failure." She patted Shiori's knee. "I can't give you a definitive answer beyond the pill failed and you are pregnant."

Shiori clapped her hand over her mouth.

"Feel sick?" Dr. Barr asked.

She shook her head.

"In shock?"

Shiori nodded. How could this be happening?

"Deep breaths. Don't pass out on me." She rubbed Shiori's back. "How old are you?"

"Thirty-five."

"Any other children?"

"No. I've never had a pregnancy scare. Never."

"You didn't want children?"

Shiori had to take a minute to slow her breathing. "I was in a bad marriage and it wasn't an option then. After that I devoted my time to work and I didn't have a steady relationship until recently."

Dr. Barr kept rubbing her back, trying to calm her down. "After hearing this, I'd guess you're about ten or eleven weeks along. Almost through the first trimester. I can do a pelvic exam, but I'm not sure I need to."

"Why not?"

The doctor moved in front of her. "Is terminating the pregnancy an option?"

She started to say, *I don't know.* But in that moment, Shiori did know. She was keeping this baby. "No." She cleared the emotion from her voice. "I'm in shock, and probably will be for a few days, and I have no idea how the father will react, but I'm having this baby."

Dr. Barr smiled. "It's your choice. For what it's worth, I think you're making the right choice."

"Why?"

"I was in your situation once. I'd ended up divorced because I'd focused solely on my medical career. I had a drunken one-night stand with an old friend from college and whoops . . . I got pregnant." She smiled again. "At thirty-five. That baby was the greatest thing that ever happened to me. She was the joy of my life. She still is thirty years later."

Shiori managed to keep her tears to just a few and not an outburst. "And the baby's father?"

"Oh, he was a deadbeat. Wanted nothing to do with either of us. Turned out we didn't need him. So since you are going through with the pregnancy, I'll do a pelvic exam and then . . . would you like to hear your baby's heartbeat?"

At that point Shiori did burst into tears.

SIX hours had passed by the time Shiori finished at the doctor's office. She had the car service take her to her place.

She showered. After she wrapped her hair in a towel, she stood in front of the mirror and turned sideways. Her belly didn't look like a baby was growing in there.

But one was. She had a couple of very grainy pictures and she'd heard the heartbeat. She wished Knox had been with her.

How did she break the news about her pregnancy? Buy a pair of baby booties and give him a *Congratulations on your impending fatherhood* card?

Buy a jar of pickles and a carton of ice cream, hinting that she'd be having cravings for it in the next seven months?

Just tell him. Straight out. Knox, the morning-after pill I took after the first time we had sex didn't work, and although we've used protection every other freakin' time, we're pregnant.

Shiori had to quit obsessing, and yet she still checked to see if she had any text messages from Knox. That's when she noticed a voice mail from a number she didn't recognize. She put it on speaker.

"Good morning, Miz Hirano. This is Jeff Jenkins of Executive Luxury Associates calling in regard to the penthouse lease. The owners of the property you're leasing have returned to the country two months earlier than planned due to health issues. The lease contract has a provision for medical emergencies, so you'll need to vacate the premises by one week from tomorrow."

What the fuck?

"Naturally, you will be refunded the entire deposit amount, the payment for the last month will be refunded, and we'll foot the cleaning charges. Please, Miz Hirano, call us as soon as you receive this message. Sorry for the inconvenience." The message ended.

"You're not one bit sorry for the inconvenience, you asswipes." Just what she didn't need to deal with on top of everything else.

After making sure she had her phone and the pictures from the doctor's office, she called for a car to take her to Knox's house.

His place was dark; only one dim light from the kitchen reflected in the front window. But Knox's pickup was parked out front, so she knew he was home.

She turned the handle, but the door was locked.

Hadn't he been expecting her?

Shiori dug out the key he'd given her, unlocked the door, and slipped inside. When she hit the living room lights, she saw Knox hunched over the breakfast bar.

He didn't acknowledge her. The half-empty bottle of booze clasped in his right hand could be the reason for that.

"Are you celebrating something?" she asked.

"Just the opposite." Knox didn't offer any further explanation. Instead he said, "What're you doing here?"

"You asked me to stay this morning, remember?"

"But you didn't stay. I figured you went home. Besides, when do you take into consideration what I want?"

"Since . . . always." Tired of talking to the side of his head, she moved into the kitchen to stand in front of him. "Where is all of this coming from?"

"Like you don't know."

"I don't. So tell me."

"Master Black. Sensei."

"What about him?"

"You missed a great fucking meeting today. The new rules for the House of Kenji were laid out."

"And?"

"And congratulations to you." Knox picked up the bottle in a mocking toast and swigged. "The rules are black-and-white." He snickered. "Black, get it? Ronin Black's rules? Funny, right?"

"Hilarious. Tell me what that means."

"It means Black Arts is under the House of Kenji, and since you outrank me, you officially get the title of Shihan."

That made no sense. Knox had to have misunderstood. "Ronin said this to you? This is not you extrapolating something you overheard?"

"You think I'm an idiot? I might be drunk now, but I sure wasn't drunk when Master Black informed me of the change. Effective immediately." He tipped the bottle and drank. "I never realized how short I fell of Sensei's expectations until you showed up here."

That wasn't true and he knew it when he wasn't full of booze and self-pity. "I'm not following."

"No, you're always leading, aren't you?" he shot back.

Shiori counted to ten, trying to keep her temper in check. "Do you want me to apologize for being a higher belt rank than you?

Guess what? I won't. I worked just as hard as you did to get where I am. Harder because I'm a woman."

"Which is why you're now Shihan. You should've been it the minute you walked into the dojo. I didn't question staying in the number two spot just because I was so damn glad to be there. I didn't know I'd retained the position only because Sensei felt sorry for me. I'm a fucking pity case. Or I was."

How was she supposed to respond?

"Do you have any idea what that feels like? Of course you don't. You're the anointed one."

"That's not something I—"

"Let me finish." His tone was curt. And a little raw.

"By all means, since this has been going so well so far."

Knox tilted his head back and gazed at the ceiling, looking anywhere besides at her. "You know why the Domme-sub thing worked between us? Because we balanced each other out. In the dojo I've been in charge. In the bedroom you've been in charge. I needed that separation or else I . . ."

"Couldn't have been submissive to me," she supplied.

"Yeah. I'da seen you as the ballbuster at the dojo and the whip cracker at Twisted." He snorted. "Like I needed another thing for you to lord over me."

She shrank back, but she didn't think he noticed.

"At least Master Black demoted me in the privacy of his office and not in front of the other instructors."

Why had her brother done this? In an attempt to break them up? A horrible thought occurred to her. Was this finally payback for her part in the Naomi debacle? Ronin could hurt her by taking away the one thing that mattered most to Knox—his position at Black Arts—and in the process turn him resentful and bitter toward her.

"Wanna know the really fun part of this whole thing? Now I have to find a paying job. Because the only position that pays full-time wages at Black Arts is yours, Shihan. So the billionaire heiress will get paid my salary, which is probably a joke amount to you anyway. But it's not a joke to me because it's all I fucking have." Another glug of scotch. "You even have another job—not that you need it. My other job at Twisted is a trade-out for yearly dues, so I don't even have that."

"Knox. You have to believe I didn't want this."

He shrugged. "Doesn't matter. Rules are rules. And Black Arts is definitely under new management."

"Why won't you look at me?"

"Because you read me too fucking well."

"Not a good enough answer." The Domme in her snapped, "Look. At. Me."

The submissive in him responded.

And she recoiled at the desolation and anger in his eyes.

"Happy now, Mistress?"

How could she ever be happy seeing him like that?

Shiori wanted to curl herself around him, but he'd closed himself off. "What can I do?"

His bark of laughter was near maniacal. "Not something you'll wanna hear."

"Try me."

Knox knocked back another mouthful of booze. "It's simple. Just follow through with your original plan. You were here temporarily, biding your time to return to Japan. So if you went now . . ."

He could retain his status as Shihan. That nauseous feeling surfaced again. "You want me to leave?"

His lips twisted into a cruel smile. "Wasn't that always your intent? Tokyo is your home. You've told me that several times."

Once again she took a mental step back.

Her leaving would solve the problem—Ronin couldn't force her to become Shihan if she wasn't part of the dojo.

But that wasn't the problem you came here to address.

Why hadn't Ronin discussed this with her? Especially the part where he planned to give her all of Knox's responsibilities? Her brother knew she had commitments to Okada—she'd heard Ronin and Knox discussing that just the other day.

When Knox tipped the bottle again, it was all she could do not to smack it out of his hand. Getting shitfaced wasn't helping.

"Just go. I'll get by on my own. I always do."

Shiori had the sensation of watching this unfold from behind a pane of glass. This wasn't her life crumbling before her—seeing the man she loved drunk and telling her to leave. Seeing the father of her child resentful of her.

God. How would Knox react when she told him about the baby?

She couldn't do it tonight.

Knox wasn't a hateful person, but he was drunk, and she had no idea what he'd say in that state. So it was best to let it go.

When the bottle hit the counter, she jumped.

Bleary-eyed, he pushed to his feet. He stumbled down the hallway toward the bathroom.

No use in sticking around.

Heartsick, she slipped out and called the car service as she walked along Knox's street.

While she waited for the car, she scrolled through her choices for a moving and packing company. "Your ad says twenty-four-hour service? Yes. I need to be packed up and out of the rental tonight. I understand it's premium pricing. Sir, money is not an object for me. Time is. If your movers can make my deadline, there will be bonuses all around." She rattled off the address. "Showing up within the hour would be great. Thank you."

Next she called Katie. She answered with, "Shi-Shi girl, you never call me. What's up?"

"I need a huge favor. Huge. But it needs to be kept quiet."

"Anything. Name it."

"My lease has been unexpectedly terminated, and I need a place to st—"

"Stay? Of course you can stay with me for as long as you need."

Katie really was very sweet. "While I appreciate that, I'm looking for a place to store my stuff."

"Oh, of course. You're probably staying with Knox."

Yeah, not so much with that. "There's not a lot, and I can pay you—"

"Don't be ridiculous. I have a huge house that's empty. You can store anything you want, for as long as you like."

"Thank you. The movers are coming tonight."

"Oh. Wow. Okay. That soon. Just text me and let me know exactly when. I'll have to give the security guy at the gate a heads-up you'll be coming through with a moving van. Those kinds of things set him on edge."

"Will do. And, Katie, thank you. I mean it. I owe you."

"This is what friends do for each other."

Lastly, Shiori called her mom. Before her mother said hello, or chewed her out for not keeping in touch, she said, "Shiori-san. What's wrong?"

"Everything."

"Be specific, sweetheart."

"I'm in trouble." That sounded ominous. "Don't worry. I'm not in jail."

"I would hope if you were in jail you'd call your brother first for bail money since he's closest."

Shiori burst into tears.

"I'm sorry. Badly timed joke. Tell me . . . What's everything?"

And it spewed out—probably way more than her mother needed to know. After Shiori finished talking, she tried to get control of her emotions, if only to stop crying.

Although the other end of the line was silent, she knew her mother hadn't hung up. "Where are you now?"

She wiped her face and peered out the window. How long had they been parked here? "In front of my apartment complex."

"The movers will be there tonight?"

"Yes. I don't have much to pack, and I lined up a temporary place to store it. Why?"

"As soon as you're squared away, I want you on the next flight to Tokyo."

Shiori closed her eyes. "That feels like running away, Mom."

"It is. But it's for a good reason. You're confused and scared and pregnant. Being home will give you a perspective you've been lacking." She paused. "You're an adult, Shiori-san, but that doesn't mean I don't worry about you. After the car accident and now this . . . I need you here for my peace of mind. If only for a little while."

"Okay." Relief filled her. Going home seemed like the first sound decision she'd made in a long time. Not that she'd really made it herself.

"Text me the flight information, or e-mail it to me. And yes, I wish you had the Gulfstream Five there."

"Me too. I'll stay in touch, Mom. I promise. And please don't say anything to Ronin, Amery, or Ojisan about this."

"I won't, sweetheart."

"Thank you. I'm sorry—" She started crying again.

"Nothing to be sorry about. One last thing. Make sure you have plenty of barf bags. Flying internationally always made me sick when I was pregnant. See you soon."

How weird would it be talking with her mother about what to expect during her pregnancy? She hadn't wrapped her head around the concept of a baby yet.

Another pang hit her. Knox should've been the first person she'd told.

You held back for a reason. Stop second-guessing yourself with every-thing.

She took a deep breath. Then she lowered the privacy partition in the car. "Hi. Are you on shift until midnight?"

"Yes, ma'am."

"I'll need to book you through then. I have some errands to run all over town, and I'm not sure when I'll finish."

"Not a problem. I'll find out from building security where to park while I'm waiting. Do you have the addresses of where we'll be going so I can get them plugged in to the GPS?"

"One address I don't have. But then we'll be going to Black Arts dojo before you drop me off at the airport."

Just as Shiori exited the car, the moving van pulled up.

Perfect timing.

Had to be a sign she was doing the right thing.

Wasn't it?

For once her subconscious was quiet.

CHAPTER THIRTY

KNOX woke up with a killer fucking hangover the next morning.

Jesus. Fuck. He couldn't remember the last time he'd downed a fifth of scotch. A guy his size could hold his liquor and then some.

But he hadn't held it very well last night. He'd blown chunks. Twice.

Took a ton of effort to slide to the side of the bed and sit up. His head and his stomach both protested. It even fucking hurt to scrub his hands over his face.

You're in bad shape.

No shit.

He had no clue how long he sat there with his head in his hands. Thinking about what'd gone down yesterday added to his screaming-ass headache.

Demoted.

He'd been in a state of agitation since Ronin had returned. He could deal with Sensei's questions about the dojo because it wasn't like he hadn't run through every damn scenario prior to the king reclaiming his kingdom. While he'd been grateful for the commiserating looks from his fellow instructors, Knox was a big boy. He could take the heat.

He just hadn't expected to get fucking burned.

First thing yesterday morning Ronin admitted hiring Maddox to head up the MMA program had been a great decision, so Knox had gotten props for that.

Then Maddox addressed the issue of space. He required a dedicated training area, not a corner of the workout room. The one good thing about the last facility he'd worked in was the private training area. No one could just walk in and watch or interrupt. He also found having the business offices and the conference room on the same floor as the training room distracting.

Ronin hadn't disagreed. So he'd brought Knox, Maddox, Blue, Deacon, and Gil into the discussion of how to reorganize the layouts of the rooms on all three floors to make the most use of them. When Maddox asked what businesses were on the other floors in the building, Ronin admitted he wasn't allowing the businesses on the fourth floor to renew their leases and the fifth and sixth levels were his personal space.

At that point Knox had a burst of pride in Black Arts because Ronin had achieved his years-long goal of having the entire building dedicated to his business.

For the time being, until the fourth floor had been cleared, MMA training would take place on the third floor, which belonged to ABC.

So Knox had been feeling good when Ronin asked him to his office. He expected they'd hash out the details of scheduling. Nothing had tripped his alarms. He made himself comfy in the chair across from Ronin's desk and tried like hell not to focus on the time he'd bent Shiori over said desk and fucked her with enough force to bruise her hips.

When he'd looked up to see Ronin fiddling with the stapler, his first suspicion all wasn't right had kicked in. Master Black wasn't a fiddler. Unless he was nervous.

Knox decided to break the ice first. "What's up?"

"As you know, we're aligned with the House of Kenji now. In addition to being tested, I had to send staff stats and all that bullshit paperwork that no one ever looks at." He paused. "Except they did."

"And?"

Ronin seemed torn, disgruntled, and nervous.

"Just tell me."

"Master Daichi never cared about dojo politics, which is why we got along so well. But House of Kenji has strict 'guidelines.' They're really ironclad rules. And since I'm new, I've been advised to adhere to them, even when it makes me fucking crazy."

Knox slumped in his chair. "I ain't gonna like this, am I?"

"No. You won't. Bottom line? Shiori outranks you . . . according to the Japanese belt system. In my opinion, that system has always placed students higher than their skill level indicates. For instance, eighth-degree black belt is a high rank for my age. I imagine if I'd continued in American jujitsu, I'd be ranked about seventh degree."

Breathe . . . Just listen.

"Shiori is Rokudan. Taking her belt system into account, I've always considered her Godan—on par with you. You've been here longer so you have the experience, which is why I never made the official title switch between you. I didn't bring it up with Master Daichi because he'd never put a woman as Shihan." Ronin looked away. "But the House of Kenji doesn't agree. Their third-highest-ranking belt—"

"Is a woman," Knox finished.

Ronin nodded. "So as of right now, I'm naming Shiori Shihan."

Everything went fuzzy at those words. He felt sick. Ronin's voice became distant. Unintelligible. Yet the voices in his head became considerably louder.

You should've expected this.

Now you'll have to find another day job.

So much for loyalty. No different from when you were in the army, where you had to suck up to the brass only to get a boot to the face.

How can you face the rest of the staff? How will they react to your demotion? Will they laugh? Whisper behind your back?

Why didn't she tell you this was coming?

Because she wants to rule you inside and outside the dojo.

Break it off with her. Then she'll return to Japan and things won't change. You'll retain your title and your job.

But I love her.

Does she love you? She hasn't admitted it.

Or are you just her plaything?

As your Mistress she's supposed to do what's best for you. Then shouldn't she leave the dojo to make you happy?

"Knox?"

Knox blinked and looked at Ronin leaning across the desk. "Yeah."

"Are you all right?"

"Surprised, but that's expected."

"Look—"

"No need to keep explaining." Knox stood. "In fact, I really wish you wouldn't."

"Fair enough." Ronin fell back in his chair. "But think about what I said."

I don't even know what the fuck you said because I was too goddamn deafened from hearing the pieces of my life crashing around me.

Knox walked out. He cut through the hallway and forced himself not to run down the stairs and out of the dojo.

He unlocked his truck and climbed in. His destination was the closest liquor store. Once inside, he went straight for the cheap stuff. Better get used to pinching pennies now that he was unemployed.

Fuck.

He'd parked at his house, locked the door behind him, and got his drink on. Hard-core.

So he deserved this motherfucking cocksucker of a hangover because he didn't remember anything after he hit the three-quarters-of-a-bottle mark.

Wait. He had a vague recollection of Shiori . . . standing in his kitchen glaring at him? Had she really been here? Or had it been another hallucination?

If he concentrated really hard—to the point it hurt his fucking brain—then he could sort of remember talking to her, congratulating her. Her pulling that Domme voice and attitude. Then . . . nothing. They could've had a fight. She could've tucked him in after he'd hugged the toilet.

No. He remembered crawling to his bed after the second time.

He shuffled to the bathroom and popped four Excedrin. Then he hauled his dragging ass into the shower and let the hot water beat down on him.

After Knox toweled off, he brushed his teeth and dressed himself, feeling somewhat better.

But still bitter. That wouldn't go away as quickly as his hangover.

When he couldn't find his phone in the house, he trekked outside and found it lodged in the passenger seat of his truck. Barely enough juice to check his messages.

None from Shiori. One from Ronin. About ten minutes ago. When he scrolled to his voice messages screen and pressed play, his phone went completely dead.

Fucking great.

Then again, he couldn't deal with Ronin today. The least the man could do was allow him some time to process this shit. The male pride part of him said he didn't have to jump when Master Black called anymore since he wasn't his second-in-command.

The last thing Knox needed today was face time in the dojo—with Sensei, the new Shihan, his fellow instructors, or even his students. He had to get the hell away. Clear his head, his lungs, his heart.

That forced him to stop. Was that really what he wanted? To shut Shiori out of his life?

No. The very thought of that made his stomach churn. No doubt they'd have to talk about how this dojo status change would affect the status quo in their personal relationship.

But that was another thing he couldn't deal with today. Especially after he had no clue how he'd acted toward her last night.

Fuck. He really, really had to get gone for a bit.

In the five years he'd been part of Black Arts, he'd never not shown up to teach his classes.

There was a first time for everything.

Knox packed his fishing and camping gear, figuring he'd stop for food on the way out of town. He wasn't running away; he was reevaluating.

Twenty-four hours later . . .

So maybe he was slightly stinky after being out in the wild, but he needed to see Shiori. He imagined she'd be pissed and demand to whip his ass for staying out of touch for a day and a half. But he felt calmer about the situation. Clearer.

In the hours he'd spent staring at the stars, he understood the last three months they'd been Domme and sub hadn't been a game, or a trial, or even a test. It'd been him falling in love with her. Completely, totally, never-want-to-let-her-go, sit-at-her-feet-forever kind of love. He believed he was a man strong enough to love her, knowing the challenges he faced in giving a woman like her his lifelong devotion.

No matter what happened with their roles in the dojo, he'd be by her side, at her feet, in her bed every night.

He pulled up to her apartment building and parked out front. It drove the security guy nuts, but after the time Knox had shown up in his gi, the guy hadn't said a word of complaint.

In a fit of pique Shiori might've scratched his name from her guest list, so he was forced to go make nice. He flashed a smile. "Hey. Knox Lofgren to see Shiori Hirano on the penthouse level."

The security guard typed on his computer. Then his lips formed a sneer. "Sorry. No one by that name resides in this building."

"Come on. Quit messing with me. Did she block me or something?"

"I have no idea what you're talking about, sir. The person whose name you gave me doesn't live in this building."

Now Knox was getting pissed. "Since when?"

Another smarmy sneer. "I'm not at liberty to disclose that information."

"Then what the fuck good are you, huh?" He slammed his hands down on the reception desk. "Two days ago she lived here. Now you're telling me she doesn't? That's bullshit."

"Sir. Your agitation is making me uncomfortable."

"I haven't even fucking *started* to make you feel uncomfortable, dickhead. Tell me where the hell she is."

The security guard's gaze moved to someone behind Knox and he whirled around.

The woman in front of him, although very pregnant, had the carriage of a former soldier. The hard eyes of one too. "Whatever the problem is, yelling at the security guard won't solve it," she said coolly.

Knox counted to ten. "This guy is telling me that the woman I've been involved with, who has lived here for almost a year, who lived here up until two days ago, is no longer a resident."

"I'm a resident here. Who are we talking about?"

"Shiori Hirano. She leased the penthouse."

"The exotic-looking woman about yay big?" She held her hand to her own shoulder level. "Ran around in a gi half the time like some ninja badass?"

"Yes. That's her. Have you seen her in the past day or so?"

She pushed a chunk of blue hair behind her ear and spoke to the security guard. "Thanks, Stevo. I'll handle this." Then she looked at Knox and gestured to a lounge area in the corner. "Let's sit over there."

Right. That was some kind of code for *wait here asshole; we're calling the cops.* Knox shook his head. "I'm fine standing."

"Well, I'm not," she snapped. "This baby weighs two hundred fucking pounds, and I need to sit. If you want to talk to me, park it."

And . . . Knox didn't argue. Maybe this chick was one of Shiori's Domme friends. She certainly had the air of command.

After they'd settled in, the woman gave him a shrewd once-over. "What branch?"

Yep, his former soldier impression had been dead-on. "Army. Twelve years. How about you?"

"Ironically . . . the same." She offered her hand. "Liberty Masterson."

"Knox Lofgren."

"So, Knox, have you been gone or something and didn't know your girlfriend moved out?"

"I've been gone twenty-four hours. Shiori and I also work together. We had some big changes at the dojo, and I needed time to get my head on straight."

"Dojo?" she repeated. "You mean she wasn't making a fashion statement with her clothing?"

"Hardly," Knox said dryly. "She is a sixth-degree black belt, and her fierceness compensates for her size. She's rubbed my face in the mat on plenty of occasions."

"Interesting. So you went to get your head on straight . . . ?"

"In the great outdoors, where there wasn't phone service. So I'm uneasy about the idea she might've just fucking moved in the forty-eight hours since I last saw her." He glanced at her distended stomach. "Shit. I'm not supposed to swear in front of kids."

Liberty rubbed her hand over her belly. "Junior gets an earful from me all the time, so no worries. Daddy and I will both clean up our language postbirth." She paused. "My husband, Devin, and I are on the floor right below the penthouse."

"Which unit?"

"Both of them. One is our residence; the other is for my husband's business. We knew the penthouse owners intended to rent out their place for a year. So I was surprised to see them back yesterday. I know a year hasn't passed since they left." She shot a look over her shoulder. "I asked the night security guard about it and he said that the renter had movers here packing her stuff up at ten o'clock, night before last."

His sinking feeling became more acute. That was the night he'd gotten drunk. Jesus. Had he said something so wrong and stupid that she packed up?

Liberty leaned as close as her belly allowed. "Level with me. You're a big guy; she's a little whip of a thing. Did you somehow hurt her and it scared her, so she bailed?"

He bit back a laugh. "No. I'll admit we had a fight that night. But I never imagined it'd result in this."

"You said you had problems at the dojo where you both worked? Where is that?"

Knox didn't blame this woman for her suspicions, but he couldn't give too much away. "We're both at Black Arts. I am—or I was—Sensei Ronin Black's second-in-command. And before you ask, no, I haven't contacted Ronin. I came here first."

"I'd try the next place on your list, then, because she doesn't live here anymore."

"Fuck." He pushed to his feet and waited until Liberty stood. "Thanks for your help."

"No problem." She eyed him with speculation.

"What? I swear I didn't hurt her." His voice dropped. "I could never hurt her."

"I believe you. I was just wondering about your comment regarding not being Ronin Black's second-in-command any longer. Does that mean you're looking for work?"

That'd come out of left field. "Maybe. Why?"

Liberty unhooked a small purse that Knox hadn't even noticed—he suspected she was carrying concealed too—and handed him a business card.

It read: GSC. SECURITY SPECIALISTS.

His eyes met hers in a silent question.

"We're diverse in our services. With your military background and your martial-arts abilities, we'd definitely be interested in talking to you. Not necessarily for security work in the field, but we have a very active training program for our existing security specialists."

"Thank you. After I get this mess straightened out, I'll look you up."

"Cool. Good luck."

Knox returned to his truck. His irritation surfaced again. He'd checked his phone as soon as he'd had service and he didn't have a single missed call or any angry texts. His calls to Shiori's cell had gone right to voice mail.

That's when he remembered he hadn't listened to Ronin's message from yesterday morning. He hit playback. Ronin's deadly quiet tone sent a shiver up his spine.

"I don't know what the fuck you've done or where the hell you are, but I came in to my office this morning and found a letter of resignation from my sister. Along with a note that indicated she'd returned to Japan."

Knox hit pause.

She'd really left. She'd left him.

Fury, fear, frustration filled him, choked him, grabbed him by the balls. He clutched his phone so tightly he popped the case off. Then he forced himself to set it down so he didn't crush it.

Breathe. Goddammit, breathe.

Once the roaring in his head quit and the white spots cleared from his eyes, he resumed listening to the call.

"What the fuck? You're MIA, Shiori is gone, and that's a clusterfuck of epic proportions. If I find out that you hurt her in any way, so help me god I will . . . No, Jesus, Amery! Let go. Give me back my goddamn phone." Knox stared at the screen, and a moment of silence passed before Amery's voice came on the recording. She spoke rapidly and quietly. "Knox. After you get this message, come see me at work—don't go to Black Arts. You did me a solid once, and I owe you."

The call ended.

Fuck.

At least he knew which direction he was going.

SO maybe he was a little wild-eyed when he stormed into Hardwick Designs half an hour later.

Molly was in his face first. "What the fuck did you do to her to make her go away?"

"Back off."

"I'm so mad at you right now, if I had my gloves on I'd pound on you."

Knox exhaled. "I'd let you do it. Maybe then I'd feel something besides being absolutely fucking numb."

Her eyes widened.

"You think I'm not dying inside right now?"

Amery stepped between them. "Molly, get back to work." Then she looked at Knox. "My office."

She scooted behind her desk and pointed to the chair opposite it.

But Knox ignored her and placed his palms on her desk. "Ronin wasn't bullshitting me through voice mail? She's gone to Japan?"

"Yes. And sit down."

He dragged the chair closer. "Talk."

"You first. What happened?"

"After Ronin made her Shihan? I needed time alone to think
things through. I came back into town today, ready to deal with
the demotion, ready to do whatever it took to keep her in my life.
And I discover she's moved out of her leased penthouse? None of
this was even on my radar, Amery."

"It wasn't on ours either." She tapped her fingers on the desk.
"I suspected the reason you two always fought is because you were
fighting your attraction for each other. I'm guessing you're good for
each other. I'm also guessing it's never been casual."

He shook his head.

"Ronin is being pulled in ten different directions. I told him
not to implement changes all at one time, so I'm just glad he's not
doing it all himself and he's passed some of the duties on to you."

"You mean that he demoted me?"

Now Amery looked confused. "He swapped titles, but your responsibilities as dojo GM didn't change. Ronin said you didn't give
him an answer about taking over more of the Black and Blue Promotions duties while you're studying for your next belt-level test."

"Whoa." He made the time-out sign. "What are you talking
about?"

Amery slammed her hands on the desk. "I fucking knew it! I
told Ronin not to lay all of this on you at once! I warned him after
he dropped the news about the Shihan thing first that you'd be in
shock and would zone out and not hear a goddamn word he said
about anything else."

"How'd you know?"

"It happens to everyone. Hell, it happened to him, and he's conveniently forgotten that."

"So getting shitfaced immediately after that because I believed my career with the dojo was over . . . was premature?"

"That's what happened?"

He sighed. "Yeah. I know Shiori came over. I don't know what the fuck I said."

"Knox. That sucks."

"Have you talked to her?"

She shook her head. "No one has. We've all tried to call her, and she hasn't responded. I did reach out to Tammy, their mother, and she said Shiori was in Tokyo."

"I stopped by her place. She moved out, sounds like the night she came to see me." Knox laced his hands on top of his head and closed his eyes. "So yeah, I'm thinking it was something I did or said. How the fuck do I fix this, Amery?"

"What are you willing to do to fix it?"

"Anything. Everything." Images of Shiori flashed behind his lids. "I want her for the long haul."

"That's not what I asked."

Knox opened his eyes and frowned at her. "I'm lost."

"Yes, you are. You don't know what you said that might've chased her away. Words can hurt, but words can heal too."

"You sure?"

Amery shrugged. "Relatively. Unless you told her something like she's a spoiled rich bitch you were only fucking because you were bored and you felt sorry for her since she's ugly, fat, uncoordinated, not to mention she's a failure in the sack, and you'd rather slit your own throat than spend another second with her."

His jaw dropped.

"Those kinds of words can't be taken back. But I doubt you said those to her, even under the influence, because you love her. And she loves you."

He let that statement lie. Amery didn't need to know Shiori hadn't told him that she loved him yet.

"The last big fight that Ronin and I had before we were married, I stormed out because he was acting like a selfish dick. Ronin's the man who swore he'd never chase after me, but he did. A few hours later he was at my door, apologizing, telling me right and wrong could be sorted out as long as we did it together. That's stuck with me. Sometimes it's not the words that carry the most weight but the action behind those words."

The image of Shiori dropping to her knees and kissing his feet in the club jumped into the forefront of his mind. She'd tracked him down and had shown humility in her apology. He needed to do the same.

But he'd up the stakes—because everything that mattered hung in the balance.

"I see the wheels turning," Amery said, snagging his attention back to the present.

"They are. I just need to figure a few things out before I go."

"Go where?"

"To Tokyo."

Amery grinned. "I was hoping you'd say that." She plopped her purse on her desk and rummaged around until she found what she needed. Then she handed it over to him.

Knox looked at the keycard. "What's this?"

"A key to Shiori's apartment in Tokyo. She asked me to check on her place while I was there. Lucky for you, with all that's happened since we got back, I haven't had a chance to return it."

"Very lucky for me." Symbols written in black Sharpie ran vertically down the back of the plastic card. "What's this stuff on the back?"

"The code to the elevator is in kanji. I had to write it down exactly so I didn't screw it up."

"Handy."

"Very. Do you have her address and apartment number?"

"No. If you'd give me that as well as her mother's phone number, I'd appreciate it."

"Good plan, letting Tammy know." Amery's eyes searched his. "Or are you worried she'll blow the surprise?"

Knox took a moment to breathe slowly and deeply. "This isn't a romantic surprise, Amery. This is me fighting for my chance to have a life with her. This is me proving to her she'll never find another man who gives her what she needs like I do."

Amery turned teary-eyed. "Good luck. I'll take care of things with Ronin."

"Thanks."

He walked out of Amery's office with a million things on his mind. So he wasn't paying attention until a solid wall stepped in front of him. He looked into Deacon's icy eyes. "What're you doing here?"

"I called him," Molly said. "You looked like you needed a friend."

Knox wasn't sure if the tension vibrating off Deacon was directed at Molly or at him.

Deacon moved the toothpick in his mouth from one side to the other. "What do you need?"

Just like that. No questions asked. "A ticket to Tokyo and a 'sorry I'm a fuckhead' gift."

"You got enough cash for both of those? If not, I could float you a loan."

Again his friend's generosity touched him. He glanced over Deacon's shoulder to see Molly watching them. He lowered his voice. "I think I can swing it. But thanks. It means a lot—"

"Don't mention it." Deacon held up his hand. "Seriously. Don't."

"Fine. Follow me to my place so I can get cleaned up and packed. Then on the way to Cherry Creek I'll fill you in on what went down."

"I'm never gonna get away from this touchy-feely friendship stuff with you, am I?"

"Probably not."

After a beat or two, he shrugged. "Fine. I'll listen until my ears bleed. But if you start crying, I'm punching you."

CHAPTER THIRTY-ONE

MORNING sickness sucked ass.

Shiori had spent a good amount of time on the plane ride to Tokyo with a barf bag in her hand.

After her mom had met her at the airport, she'd whisked Shiori off to her childhood home, tucked her in bed, and let her sleep for twelve blissfully dark, quiet, vomit-free hours.

She'd lost track of time in the mad dash to get here. How long had it been since she'd left Denver? A day and a half? Two days? It'd all blended together.

A shower and a change of clothes made her feel human. But the first whiff of tea had sent her scurrying back to the toilet to rid her stomach of the glass of water she'd managed to drink.

She brushed her teeth—for the third time—and detoured to the living room, stretching out on the long leather couch that'd been in their house since her childhood. It was one of the few things that'd belonged to her father, which was probably why her mother had kept it.

Her mother appeared carrying a glass. "Ginger ale might help. I'll set it over here."

"Thanks, Mom. You've gone above and beyond."

"Does it make me pathetic that I'm happy you need me for something?"

She fought another round of tears. "No. It makes me a crappy daughter that I've stayed so far out of touch you believed I didn't need you."

"It's been a strange situation the last year. Something caused you to reevaluate everything you'd worked so hard to achieve."

"Spending your birthday alone for the third year in a row will do it."

"That's what chased you away?"

"Partially. And that my personal life had become as cut-and-dried as my work relationships." It'd occurred to her that negotiating for time with a submissive at the sex club had become as routine as nailing down the terms for her business contracts.

Knox had changed that. He'd changed everything. He'd shown her that he could handle all sides of her—his respect and devotion meant more to her than anything in the world. So his drunken ramblings had caught her off guard. And rather than dealing with it . . . she'd left.

Real mature, Mistress.

Shiori's mom lovingly rubbed her forearm. "I knew you were struggling. After I stepped up at Okada officially—"

"You went from being my mom to being my boss," Shiori finished. "It scared me. You're the one person in our family I had a great relationship with, and I didn't want to lose that."

"So you backed off completely. Believe it or not, I understand." She sighed. "We're not so good at talking out personal issues like we are business issues, are we?"

"No. Finessing personal relationships is considered emotional manipulation. After dealing with Ojisan's manipulation on both levels . . . I worried you'd become just like him."

"I can't deny that in some respects I am my father's daughter.

Which is why I'm glad you took a break." Her mother leaned closer to hold Shiori's face in her hands. "This is what I wanted for you."

"Being pregnant and petrified about it at age thirty-five?"

She smiled. "No. I wanted you to experience life outside of the crushing job responsibilities you'd taken on at Okada. We both know if I would've told you to take some time off, you would've dug your heels in and worked even harder."

"Have I always been that difficult and contrary?"

"Yes. But you come by that honestly." Her mother dropped her hands but stayed in Shiori's personal space so she couldn't back away.

"If you wanted me to see what my life would be without Okada, then why did you send me to Mexico and Canada as Okada's spokesperson?"

She shrugged. "Those were family owned companies we wanted to acquire. Having Nureki Okada's granddaughter start the negotiations sent a message that we embraced the family-business philosophy."

"So I was a pawn?"

"No. You were more of a rook."

Great.

"Your presence also put our upper-level employees on notice that you were still crucial to the company. You always intended to return to Okada. Whether that meant you'd reclaim the position you left? I don't think you have that figured out. But I do know if you'd truly walked away, when I asked you to negotiate on Okada's behalf, you would've told me no."

Shiori's face heated. "That's what I mean. I couldn't say no to you. I was supposed to be figuring out my personal life, and instead I'm micromanaging my accounts from thousands of miles away because I don't believe anyone could ever do my job as well as I do." Her eyes smarted with tears. "This sabbatical to the States proved nothing. It changed nothing."

Her mom clasped Shiori's hands. "Wrong. It changed you. It's shown you that you're entitled to a life. Even in the midst of your nasty divorce, you carried on at work like you were invincible."

"How else was I supposed to act? Broken?" She closed her eyes. "You know how corporate life is. Don't show weakness. Don't show emotion. Be the first worker in and the last one to leave—even if you're the CEO's granddaughter, maybe *especially* if you're that. Take the minimum amount of personal time. Focus, focus, focus. Being a good employee is all that matters. If you show how hard you can work, you'll move up the ladder and get bogged down with even more work. But hey, you can almost see the Tokyo skyline from your corner office if you look over the mountain of paperwork on your desk.

"So I ran away. Had my fun. Lived in the States and worked for my brother. Made some friends. Fell in love." Needing to backtrack, she said, "I finally had some free time to pursue my love of art and learned that I don't have untapped talent as a painter."

Her mom laughed. "Same thing happened to me after you went off to school. I had it in my head I could create fancy tea cakes. Even when I devoted a fair amount of time to it . . . I didn't improve. And because I didn't improve, I didn't enjoy it." Her eyes searched Shiori's. "Did you enjoy the process of painting even if you didn't love the end product?"

"Sometimes."

"Then it wasn't wasted time." She smoothed Shiori's hair from her forehead. "None of your time away was squandered."

"So what happens now?"

"With your future with Okada? I'd love to dangle a huge promotion in front of you to keep you and my impending grandbaby close by." She smiled through her tears. "It really destroys my plans to spoil that child when you're in love with the baby's father and I doubt he'll be down with his child—and you—living in Japan."

Shiori managed a small smile. "Knox grew up in a single-parent home. He'll never agree to a periphery role in his child's life, and I'd never ask him to. I don't want him to have a secondary role in my life either."

"Then tell him, Shiori-san. While I'm glad you came to me, now you need to go to him and figure this out."

"I know."

"Has he called you?"

"Like twenty times."

"Call him back." Her mom clasped her hands and pulled her upright. "As much as I love having you here, I do have a social engagement tonight that I cannot break. Tell you what. Go to your apartment, change your clothes, figure out what you're going to say to him. Then look around and see if you can envision yourself living in that space with a baby."

Shiori envisioned herself living in Knox's house with him and their baby.

Soft lips brushed her forehead. "Have the life you were meant to. If that life means I'll be making a lot of trips to the States to see my grandchild, so be it."

"Thanks, Mom."

"It's what I'm here for." She stood. "I'll call for a car. I don't think you're feeling well enough to take the bus."

SHIORI arrived at the Okada building an hour later, feeling somewhat better. She'd needed the comfort of her mom, the comfort of home more than she realized.

She didn't recognize the security guard on the main level. Since this was a public building, security procedures were minimal until the fortieth floor, which was where private residences started. In the elevator she swiped her keycard and punched in a code.

Nothing had changed in the small waiting area on her floor, and she cut down the left hallway.

Home sweet home.

Shiori unlocked the door, dropped her duffel bag on the floor, and tossed her keycard on the catchall table like she always did. That's when she noticed her spare keycard was already there. Strange. Had Amery left it?

Awareness of something being not quite right set the hair on the back of her neck on end. She quietly removed her shoes and listened.

Nothing.

But wait. She closed her eyes and inhaled. The scent that hit her nearly buckled her knees. Warm skin with a hint of male musk and laundry soap.

Knox.

Don't be silly. He's not here. It's just wishful thinking.

As Shiori turned the corner from the foyer into the living room and stopped, a loud gasp escaped her lips.

Knox *was* here. Shirtless, stripped down to his boxers, on his knees, head bowed, facing away from her.

Holy fuck.

Knox.

Was.

Here.

On. His. Knees.

Waiting. For. Her.

Immediately she closed the distance between them. She fell to her knees behind him, stretching herself over his back, pressing her face between his shoulder blades. The familiar scent of him filled her lungs, quickened her heartbeat, and soothed her soul. "Tell me I'm not dreaming."

"You're not dreaming, Mistress."

Shiori held on to him for the longest time, letting her tears fall freely onto his back.

She gathered herself as she placed kisses up his spine to the nape of his neck. She moved to stand in front of him. "Look at me, please."

Knox lifted his head. Those blue eyes held such resolve.

"Why are you here?"

"Because I love you. It's been the worst three days of my life, not knowing what I'd done or said to make you leave."

She curled her hands around his face. "Say it again."

"I love you." He blew out a breath. "Have I fucked this up beyond repair, Nushi? That would kill me."

"Why?"

"It's been my greatest joy to belong to you. To love you."

Such simple, beautiful words.

"But if you don't want me here, don't want me as yours—"

She slammed her mouth down on his to shut him up. The kiss was electric from the start. A reunion, her affirmation, his repentance.

Knox recognized all the things this kiss was. His hands clutched her hips, and he gave himself over to her completely.

Shiori might've let the kiss go on forever until she got a crick in her neck and realized Knox had to be uncomfortable too. Still, she broke the kiss slowly, easing off in increments. Then her gaze hooked his. "You are mine. I love you, Knox. So much that it scares me."

"Say it again."

"I love you."

His eyes softened. "Don't be scared. We belong together. You know this. I will fight for you. Hell, I'll even fight you to have you."

The sound that exited her trembling lips was part laugh, part sob.

"You might outrank me, but I promise I won't follow the rules. I won't fight fair when I'm fighting for the best thing that's ever happened to me."

"You have that wrong. You're the best thing that's ever happened to me."

The joy that lit his handsome face cued the waterworks again.

"Since I'm already on my knees, although I'd rather not do this half damn naked . . ." Knox reached down and picked up a blue velvet box. His gaze locked on to hers. "I love you. Whether I call you Shiori, or She-Cat, or Mistress, or Nushi, or Shihan. You are all those to me, but there is one thing I want to spend the rest of my life calling you. My wife." He paused. "Will you marry me?"

Shiori gasped. She placed her hand on his chest to center herself, and she could feel his heart beating erratically. "Yes."

He briefly closed his eyes and exhaled. "Thank you."

"Did you really think I'd say no?"

"I wasn't sure. I didn't think you'd run off to Japan without telling me either, so this whole trip was a shot in the dark."

Silly man. She sniffled but let her tears fall without shame. "What's in the box?"

"A promise that I'll be everything you'll ever need. I wanted you to feel how I do every time I look at the bracelet you bestowed on me."

"Put it on me."

"Bossy." Knox kissed the base of her hand before he draped the delicate chain over her wrist. Then the two ends were attached to a heart-shaped lock. Once he snapped it on . . .

"It locks?"

"Yes, ma'am. I have the key. I'll always keep it safe."

Did he know what that meant to her?

Yes, of course he did.

She looked from the Tiffany box to the platinum bracelet to the way his eyes shone. "You one-upped me, didn't you, Ob-Knox-ious?"

"Yep." He grinned. "I'll get you a traditional engagement ring, if you want me to show my public claim on you, but this is a private commitment."

Shiori trapped his face in her hands and kissed him. "I didn't think I could love you more than I already do, but I was wrong." Another kiss. "Please get off your knees and hold me."

When he wrapped her in his arms, his skin held a chill.

"You're freezing. How long have you been waiting for me?"

"Your mother called after you left her place, so probably about an hour."

She tilted her head back and studied him. "She knew you were here?"

"I called her before I flew in. I needed to make sure you'd see me and Okada wouldn't toss me out on my ass for showing up at your apartment even when Amery gave me a key."

"Did my mom say anything to you?"

Knox's gaze narrowed. "Besides she was happy I'd chased after you? No. Why?"

"I have something to tell you. But let's get you warmed up first." She took his hand, intending to take him to her bed and crawl under the covers with him.

But the stubborn Viking wouldn't budge. "No. Tell me now."

She moved in close so they were body to body. "Remember that I still felt nauseous after my accident?"

He nodded.

"The day you had all those meetings at Black Arts, I got sick again and decided to call the car service to take me to a walk-in clinic."

"Why didn't you tell me you needed to go in? Baby, I would've dropped everything to take you."

"I know. But Ronin had already come down hard on you, so I wanted to spare you further chastising and went alone."

"What happened at the doctor's office?"

She pressed her palms against his pectorals. "The doctor ran a bunch of tests." The words stuck in her throat, bogged down by her guilt.

Then his big hands were cradling her face. "Tell me."

"I'm pregnant."

He blinked. Frowned. Knox shook his head as if he'd misheard her. "Say that again."

"I'm pregnant. That's why I continued to be sick even after the accident."

Shock distorted his features. His mouth opened and then snapped shut. "But we . . ."

"Used condoms every time. Except for that first time." Shiori closed her eyes. "I took the morning-after pill like I told you I would. But it didn't work for some reason."

He said nothing.

Finally she said, "I'm sorry."

"For?"

"Not telling you first. For making you chase me here."

"Is that what you came over to tell me the night I was a drunken asshole? That you were pregnant?"

She nodded.

"Look at me."

Shiori lifted her lashes despite the weight of tears on them.

"Are you sorry you're pregnant?"

"No."

Knox crushed her to his chest. "Thank god." His big body shuddered as he kissed the top of her head.

She felt like she was the only thing holding him up. "Let me go."

"Never gonna let go of you again."

She tried to squirm out of his hold, but he was having none of it. So she had to bring out the Domme voice. "Knox. Let go. If you faint, you'll take me down with you."

"I'm not gonna faint." Then he lowered to his knees again. This time his focus was entirely on her abdomen. "Show me."

"There's not much to see." She pulled her T-shirt over her head.

Immediately Knox tugged down her yoga pants. Gently holding her hips, he dragged his mouth all over her belly. "A baby. Jesus. Our baby is in here."

She hadn't been sure how he'd react, but she hadn't expected this. "You aren't upset?"

"Surprised? Yes. Upset? Not on your fucking life."

"Why not?"

"Because I love you." Soft kisses around her belly button. "Because this baby is meant to be." More soft kisses. "Think of what this sprout survived in the past eleven weeks." Knox looked up at her. His eyes were wet, heavy with emotion.

And her love for him grew even more. She shivered when his lips teased her stomach. "I'm relieved you asked me to marry you before you found out about the baby."

"I want you for you, Nushi. Little sprout is just sprinkles on the cupcake." He stroked the hard lump above her pubic bone with his thumbs. "You felt any movement?"

"No. But I do have pictures, and I got to hear the heartbeat." She ran her hand through his hair. "I wanted you there beside me so badly at that point I cried."

"I will be beside you for every damn thing from here on out. No matter what happens at Black Arts or Okada. No matter if we live in the States or in Japan."

"You'd move here for me?"

"Woman, I'd do anything for you."

His blue eyes held so much love and heat and respect it was hard to speak around the lump in her throat. "Promise?"

"Promise."

That roiling sensation started pushing past her sternum. "I'm about to test that theory. Oh god."

Even before she clapped a hand over her mouth, Knox was on his feet and leading her to the bathroom.

She had little in her stomach, so she mostly dry heaved.

Knox stayed beside her, rubbing her back.

After she flushed the toilet and stood, she rinsed her mouth. "Ack. I'm so tired of barfing."

He lifted her into his arms. "I'm putting you in bed." He slipped her between the sheets as though she were made of crystal, then covered her up. "Want some water?"

She nodded.

Knox stroked her cheek. "Be right back."

Everything that'd been spinning around and around in her head quieted.

He returned and held the bottle of water to her lips.

She swallowed two sips and hoped it didn't immediately come back up.

Knox crawled into bed beside her and wrapped himself around her as much as he could without moving her. He placed a soft kiss on her temple and one hand over hers on her belly. "Sleep. I'll be right here when you wake up."

THE room was completely dark when Shiori woke up. For a minute she was disoriented.

"Hey, how you feeling?"

"Better." She didn't move for several long minutes, hoping she hadn't spoken too soon. In the cocoon of Knox's body, she listened to the rhythm of their breathing.

Then the feeling stirring inside her wasn't from nausea but from desire. She loved the tease of Knox's breath across her skin, in her ear. The rise and fall of his chest against her back.

She wiggled her butt, as if trying to get comfortable, and felt his cock—hard and ready.

Until he tried to discreetly move it away.

She rocked her hips back into him again.

This time he said, "If you need more room, I can scoot over."

Shiori rolled to face him. "I need something." She pressed her mouth to the curve of muscle above his nipple.

"I'll give you whatever you need, Mistress."

She dragged her tongue across his nipple. "I need your hands on me. Your mouth on me. I need to feel you all over me."

He shifted and peeled her yoga pants and her panties down her legs. He made short work of her bra. Then his hands, his big, wonderful, callused hands were petting and stroking and teasing. His mouth zeroed in on all her hot spots and he was relentless in proving he knew exactly what would make her writhe and moan. He knew exactly how to drive her crazy with desire.

But Knox never ventured beyond their parameters. He wouldn't bury his face in her pussy until she gave him the go-ahead.

"Knox," she panted when she couldn't take it anymore.

"Yes, Mistress?"

"Put your mouth between my legs and make me come."

He threw the covers back and pushed her thighs wide apart. "I have one request."

Shiori looked down her torso to where he'd settled between her legs. "What's your request?"

"Pull the skin away from your clit with your fingers using the hand that has the bracelet." His eyes glittered in the darkness. "I want to look up and see my claim on you as you scream my name."

The sexy growl sent a delicious shiver through her. She slipped her hand down the flat—for now—plane of her stomach and hooked her first two fingers under the flesh and exposed her clit.

"Fucking beautiful." He blew a stream of air over the sensitive tissue, offering a wicked grin when she jumped. "Fast or slow?"

"Fast."

They had different definitions of fast. So by the time he'd thoroughly wound her up, all it took were a few concentrated sucks on her clit and she unraveled. A hair-pulling, gasping-his-name, hip-pumping orgasm that kept going with every sassy flick of his tongue. When Knox finally relented, she melted into the mattress.

Knox kissed her abdomen, and then he placed a kiss on the bracelet on her wrist.

When her brain unscrambled, she pushed up on her elbows to see him resting on his knees between her thighs. "Come here."

He ran his hand up the outside of her leg. "Would it be better if you were on top?"

"No. We'll have plenty of months where we'll have to get creative with positions as the baby grows. Tonight I want to look into your eyes when you're moving inside me and when you spill yourself into me without a condom. I want your ear close by so I can tell you how much I love you when you're making love to me."

"Yes, ma'am." He levered himself over her, keeping his eyes on hers as he slowly pushed inside. "Fuck, that feels good."

"Very good."

His eyes stayed intense on hers. He balanced on his arms, not putting his full weight on her.

Each long stroke drove her up, up, up that slow rise until she reached the crest.

Knox left her dangling there. "Let me come with you."

She pulled his mouth to hers in response, and they sailed into the abyss together.

CHAPTER THIRTY-TWO

Two weeks later . . .

KNOX sat on his back deck, enjoying the warm evening. He really enjoyed having his warm woman curled into him, her small body tucked against his. He ran his hand down the side of her body, stopping to palm her ass.

Shiori sighed against his neck, and he kissed the top of her head.

After they'd left Tokyo—on Okada's private jet, no less—they'd moved Shiori's stuff into his house. He'd found it funny that she'd left her clothes with Katie, since she wouldn't fit into them soon anyway. She hadn't seen the humor in that until he'd dropped to his knees and pressed his mouth against the tiny swell.

A baby. He couldn't quite wrap his head around it. His mother and sisters were as ecstatic about the pregnancy as Shiori's mother and grandfather were. Fee, Katie, Molly, and Amery were already planning a baby shower. Why they weren't planning a wedding shower stumped him, since he and Shiori were tying the knot in two weeks, after some snafu with Shiori's visa was settled.

Shiori nuzzled his throat. "What are you thinking about so hard?"

He placed another kiss on the top of her head. "How I can't wait until you're my wife, Mistress."

"I can't wait for that either. Shiori Lofgren has a nice ring to it."

"Yes, it does." He trailed his fingers up and down her thigh. "I love you. I'm so glad you're here with me."

"I love you too." She kissed the side of his throat.

The gate hinge squeaked.

"Were you expecting someone?" Shiori asked, pushing up to a sitting position.

Knox turned his head, and a dark shape materialized into Ronin Black. Stealthy bastard. He wouldn't have known the man was there if not for the squeaky gate. "Hey. Pull up a chair."

"Thanks. Hope I'm not interrupting anything."

"You're always welcome in our home, brother," Shiori said softly.

Our home. Damn but he loved the sound of that.

"Thanks, Shi. How are you feeling?"

"Like I'll get sick of that question in the next six months." She smiled. "Most days I feel great."

Ronin seemed at a loss as to how to respond.

Shiori set her feet on the ground and stood. "I'm hungry."

"Want me to fix you a plate?" Knox asked.

"I can do it. I know you guys have stuff to talk about."

"Nothing you can't be a part of," Ronin said. "I didn't mean to chase you off."

"You didn't."

Knox put his hand on her belly. "I'll be in to check on you in a bit."

"No rush." She bent down and kissed him with enough sweet heat to make his dick stir. Then she turned and ruffled Ronin's hair. "If your conversation turns to fisticuffs I'm calling Deacon, since I'm not allowed to fight or break fights up anymore."

"Like we can't take him," Knox scoffed.

"I don't know about taking him," Ronin said. "Maddox is turning him into a fighting machine."

"'Bout time he got his shot." Knox grabbed two Fat Tires, used the opener to pry off the tops, and handed one to Ronin.

"Thanks." Ronin took a couple of sips before he spoke. "I can't believe you knocked my sister up."

"You and me both."

"Jesus. You're gonna be a dad."

"I'll be a damn good one, if that's what you're worried about. Just because I didn't grow up with one—"

"Hold on. That wasn't what I was getting at. Not even remotely. Shiori and I essentially grew up without a dad, too. I just had an image of you carrying a diaper bag and baby talking."

"Fuck you. I ain't gonna baby talk. It's not good for their language development." He'd been reading everything he could on pregnancy and childbirth. It was already starting to drive Shiori crazy—which was half the fun.

Ronin laughed. "But there are diapers, strollers, stuffed animals in your future."

"Yep." Knox swigged his beer. "It's a good thing."

"I think so too."

Knox smiled. "Bet Amery's pregnant sooner rather than later."

"I'll admit after the shock wore off I was a little jealous." He gave Knox a sly look. "Ojisan offered Amery a million bucks if she got pregnant in the next few months."

"Seriously? Dammit. I knew we should've waited to tell him. I could've had a cool mil in the bank." He laughed. "But we're just so happy about this we couldn't keep it quiet."

"I'd be happy if we had a kid in the next year. But Amery's not ready." He shrugged. "So we'll wait until she is."

They sipped their beer and each got lost in their own thoughts.

After a bit, Ronin said, "That baby is one tough little thing. Surviving a car accident and an MMA fight."

"Strong, stubborn, and resilient. So I'm betting it's a girl."

Ronin laughed and clinked his bottle to Knox's. "Amen, brother."

Another bout of silence settled between them. A soft breeze stirred the leaves and carried the scent of freshly mown grass.

"Knox, I gotta ask."

"About my resignation as dojo GM?"

"Are you sure that's what you want?"

"Yes. It wasn't an easy decision to make. But you had to make some hard choices too." After the Shihan issue—misunderstanding, drama, whatever it was—Ronin opted to bring Beck Leeds back to Black Arts from House of Kenji. So Beck would become Shihan. Again. Knox had always liked the guy, and he'd be a great fit for Sensei Black and the dojo.

"How much will you be working for GSC Security?"

Knox had followed through and called the security company after returning from Tokyo. He'd passed both interviews. "Two to three days a week for a couple of hours, teaching hand-to-hand defensive tactics." He took another drink of beer. "Look, I hope you understand that I needed to do something for myself outside the dojo. After I quit wallowing, I realized I'd gotten complacent."

Ronin looked at him. "I never saw that in you. Just the opposite, in fact."

"It was a wake-up call when I realized I didn't have anything to offer the MMA program, but that didn't mean I didn't have skills others would find useful. I'll still be teaching at Black Arts, so it isn't like you're getting rid of me. Especially since we'll officially be family."

"That's fucking weird to think about."

"No doubt. Did you hire a replacement for Shiori?" Knox had nixed her teaching during her pregnancy, and she hadn't given him any grief about it. She had nagged her brother to hire a woman with at least a third-degree black belt to replace her.

Ronin sighed. "No. A few have expressed interest. I imagine now that Black Arts is paying an above-average salary for all instructors, we'll have more applicants for all the openings. I'm just damn glad it's summer and all these changes haven't affected the students."

"You still feeling guilty about using your inheritance to fund dojo expansion?"

"Honestly? Not as much as I thought I would. The money is just sitting there. Seems a waste not to use it." Ronin shot Knox a sly smile. "Does it bother you to be my sister's kept man?"

He laughed. Oh, if Ronin only knew how true that statement really was. In addition to meeting her scary-ass grandfather in Tokyo, he had gone with Shiori to her club where she'd become Mistress B. Afterward they'd decided they were done with any club scenes since they'd found what they'd been looking for in each other. "Not at all. It's not like I'm *not* working. Being part-time at GSC, teaching at Black Arts, and comanaging Black and Blue Promotions with Katie—all adds up to full-time work. After the baby is born and Shiori decides how invested she wants to be in a career at Okada, I'll need a job with fluidity that'll allow us to travel with her. I know my Mistress won't want to be away from me or baby Shox any longer than one night. Her inheritance allows us the luxury of focusing on our family so we both can be hands-on parents."

Ronin looked at him oddly.

Shit. He'd screwed up and called Shiori *Mistress*. "What?"

"Baby Shox?"

Whew. Lucky, Ronin had zeroed in on that. "We don't like calling the baby 'it' so she combined our first names; hence baby Shox."

"Jesus."

"That name is taken."

Ronin laughed. "Did you ever think a year ago our lives would be like this? Me married, you about to tie the knot and having a baby and the dojo not the most important thing in our lives?"

"Nope. But I'd always hoped for this."

"Me too."

Knox tapped his beer bottle against Ronin's bottle. "Change is good, brother."

"Change is very good."

EPILOGUE

Six months later . . .

SHIORI Lofgren wanted to beat the fuck out of someone.

And by "someone" she meant Knox Lofgren, her husband—the man responsible for putting her in such excruciating pain.

She grunted, and it might've turned into a frustrated scream.

"Nushi, come on. You're almost there."

"I don't . . . I can't . . ." she panted.

His soothing voice burrowed into her ear. "Yes, you can. You are the strongest woman I know. A couple more pushes and we can finally meet our girl."

She curled her hands more tightly around the metal bars and bore down when Dr. Barr told her to.

"Breathe, baby. That's good," Knox cooed, wiping the sweat from her brow.

Shiori waited for the next twisting squeeze of pain, unable to keep up with the breathing exercises. After another hard push, all the internal pressure vanished and she had such a feeling of relief.

"Your baby girl has arrived, Lofgrens!" Dr. Barr said.

Next thing she heard was a loud squawk. Then the nurses rushed her off to the medical equipment.

Shiori looked at Knox. "What's wrong with her?"

"I don't know."

"Go see. Please."

Just as Knox started to walk over, Dr. Barr turned, holding a wrapped bundle. "Sorry. Nothing to be concerned about. Just routine checks."

She reached out for her husband, and of course he was right there.

Dr. Barr set the baby on the pillow on Shiori's lap. "Congrats. I'll let you two coo and admire her for a few minutes while I finish up the medical end."

"I wanna see her." Knox pulled her hat off.

Beneath the hat was fuzzy blond hair.

Shiori laughed. "Of course I gave birth to a Viking child."

"We'll turn her into a ninja to even things out."

"Deal."

"Look at her. She's beautiful. Just like her mama." Knox brushed his lips over Shiori's. "I love you."

"I love you too."

They just stared at their red-faced little miracle. In awe.

"What are we naming her?"

Shiori stroked her baby's cheek, and immediately her head turned, looking for food. "How about Nuri?"

"After your grandfather?" he asked softly.

"Yes. Is that all right?"

Knox kissed her forehead and then his baby daughter's. "It's perfect." Then he touched Nuri's tiny hand with his pinky finger, and those itty-bitty fingers clamped down on his. "Whoa. She's got a strong grip."

"Our baby girl is already trying to wrap herself around Daddy's little finger."

"Something she'll learn from her mama, since I'm completely wrapped around your whole hand."

"Mmm. But I like it better when you're at my feet." Marriage and pregnancy hadn't changed her dominant nature, but it had made Knox even more protective of her. Every once in a while he'd take those instincts too far and she'd become the big bad Domme. But their dynamic worked beautifully.

"It's a shame with your medical restrictions that you'll have to wait six weeks until you can boss me around, Mistress."

She turned and looked at him. "*I* have restrictions. You don't. So nice try, but you're not getting a six-week sabbatical."

Knox smiled slyly. "Worth a shot."

"Having second thoughts about being my sub?"

"Nope." He smooched her mouth. "Since you finally put me in my place, you're stuck with me."

"For good?"

"Forever, kitten."

Shiori nuzzled her face into his neck. "Forever doesn't seem like long enough with you, but it's a good place to start."

Don't miss the next book
in the Mastered Series by Lorelei James,

CAGED

Available in May wherever books and e-books are sold!
Continue reading for a preview.

PRESLEY stopped in the middle of the hallway so abruptly that Molly ran into her.

When she glanced up to see what'd caught Presley's attention, she froze.

Deacon leaned against the wall, his muscled arms crossed over his chest, one knee bent with his cowboy boot pressed behind him. The pose seemed casual, but she wasn't fooled.

"Beat it," he said to Presley. "I need to talk to Molly."

Her stomach swooped.

"You have shitty manners," Presley said.

Deacon ignored Presley and continued to level his brooding stare at Molly.

Talk about unnerving.

Talk about hot.

Shut up, hormones.

Then Presley moved and blocked Molly from his view. "Tell me what to do."

"Go. I'll give him five minutes."

"Don't take his crap."

"I won't."

Presley's gaze darted between Molly and Deacon as she backed away. "I'll be right over there if you need anything."

"She won't," Deacon said.

"I wasn't talking to you, asshole."

"I know. Keep walking."

When they were alone, Molly kept the entire width of the hallway between them. "You were rude."

"So?"

"So you save your decent behavior for the strippers working the VIP section?"

His eyes flashed. "Sometimes. What are you doin' here?"

"Drinking with my friends and soaking up the naked entertainment."

"Doesn't seem like your scene."

"I hardly think *you* can chastise *me* for being here when it appears you're a frequent patron of this strip club, Mr. VIP."

In the blink of an eye, Deacon had caged her against the wall, his mouth next to her ear. "You trying to push my buttons?"

"Back. Off."

"Not on your life."

She shivered when his hot breath tickled her neck.

He muttered, "Goddamn flowers."

"What?"

"You always smell sweet. Even after sweating in class for an hour, you didn't reek like everyone else."

"There's a compliment." Molly put her hands on his chest and pushed him. "Move it."

A soft growl vibrated against her cheek. "You drive me crazy, woman."

"Hey!" a loud male voice shouted behind them. "Let her go."

Deacon retreated to face Black Bart. "I don't have my hands on your merchandise, so this isn't your concern."

Merchandise? Was that all the women who worked the club were to him?

Black Bart stopped a foot from Molly and set his hand on her shoulder. "Hey, pretty eyes, is this fucker harassing you?"

"No, I'm not harassing her, but I'll break your hand if you don't take it off of her," Deacon retorted.

"Deacon! What is wrong with you?" Molly asked.

"Got a case of *mine*, I'm thinking," Black Bart said. "You know this joker, sweet thang?"

What perfect payback to proclaim she'd never seen him before. But that'd set him off. And Deacon "Con Man" McConnell in a rage was dangerous for everyone. "Yes, I know him. He is—*was*—my kick-boxing instructor."

Black Bart grinned. "No kidding. You one of them *ka-rah-tay* chicks?"

"No. I've discovered I like beating the shit out of something a couple of times a week."

"I hear ya there." Despite Deacon's warning growl, Black Bart stepped between them. "Say the word and I toss him out on his tattooed ass. I don't cotton with any women being threatened in my club."

"Our conversation got a little intense, but we're done now."

Deacon's dark look said, *The hell we are*, but he kept his mouth shut.

"Okay. You need anything, come find me."

"I will. Thanks."

"I don't like the way he looks at you," Deacon said softly, the menace in his tone unmistakable.

"Like you'd know how he was looking at me," she said hotly. "You haven't stopped glaring at me since the moment you trapped me back here."

"Staring at you and glaring at you aren't the same thing, darlin', and you damn well know it."

"My mistake. But you're always glaring at someone. Is that MMA badass behavior? Daring someone to screw with you so you can beat the snot out of them?"

"'Beat the snot out of them'?" A smile curled his lips. "Babe. If I hit a guy in the nose, it ain't snot running out."

"Eww. Thanks for the visual."

Deacon inched closer. "No one here knows I'm a fighter."

"Why not?"

"It's my personal business."

"I don't imagine there's much talking going on during a lap dance anyway."

"Not usually, no."

"Whatever. I'm leaving."

He shook his head. "Not done talking to you."

"We have nothing to talk about. I ran into you at a strip club. Big deal. You're a single guy. It's your *personal business* if you pay some chick with fake boobs to grind her bony ass on your crotch." She paused. "Does that about cover it?"

"No, it doesn't begin to cover it." Deacon crowded her against the wall. "You still seeing that banker friend of Amery's?"

How did Deacon know that?

"What was it about the douche bag that caught your eye? The snappy suit? The nine-to-five work hours? The freakishly perfect groomed hair?"

"Maybe it's the fact he didn't stand me up for our first date." She gave his shiny head a blatant once-over. "Sounds like you're jealous of his hair, baldy."

His eyes hardened. "Shaving my head is a choice."

She shrugged. "How do I know you're not sporting a chrome dome because otherwise you'd have a bad comb-over?"

Omigod. I cannot believe I said that. To Deacon.

Molly braced herself for his reaction.

But nothing could've prepared her for his mouth coming down on hers in an explosion full of heat, need and possession.

Keep reading for a preview of

SCHOOLED

by Lorelei James.
Available now in e-book!

"WHAT did you have to promise Shiori to convince her to let us borrow her private jet?"

Amery felt Ronin staring at her beneath his sunglasses.

"Nothing. You realize she does not *own* this plane? It belongs to the company."

"Same difference. It's been here, in Denver, at her disposal, since her arrival. And it's not like Okada is missing it, right? How many personal aircraft does your grandfather own anyway?"

Now Amery suspected Ronin had narrowed his eyes beneath the dark lenses. "Five. Three airplanes and two helicopters. Do you have a problem with that?"

She wasn't quite sure how to answer that question. Although she and Ronin had been married for six months, she hadn't gotten used to the perks of having the heir to a corporation worth billions as her husband. Ronin didn't live ostentatiously—if she didn't count his penthouse suite atop the building he owned, or his SUV, or his sports car, or his custom motorcycle. But every once in a while the magnitude of his fortune hit her.

Like now.

Ronin stopped in front of her and pushed his sunglasses on top of his head. Then he curled his hand around her face. "Baby. Having access to a private jet just means we don't have to worry about airport security confiscating the bags of ropes I packed for us."

"Bags? Is that why you insisted I could pack as many suitcases as I wanted?"

"No." He feathered his thumb across her bottom lip. "We'll be gone for two and a half months. I want you to have anything you need from our home to help you to settle in."

She kissed the inside of his wrist. "All I need to feel at home is you, Master Black."

"You humble me, Mrs. Black."

"Mmm. You still love saying that."

"And I always will."

"Mr. Black?" a male voice spoke behind them.

Ronin's stern mask dropped into place before he turned around. "Yes?"

The blond pilot, a male somewhere in his fifties, offered his hand. "Mark Beauchamp. This is my copilot, Bernie Samuelson."

"Pleased to meet you both. This is my wife, Amery."

Another round of handshakes.

"We've done the preflight checks. We're scheduled to refuel in Hawaii. Then we're flying to Osaka. Do you have any questions?"

"Can I see your aviation orders from Okada?"

Amery's gaze moved between the two men. What were aviation orders?

Pilot Mark pulled out a manila envelope and handed it to Ronin.

Ronin removed three papers and read the first one; then he lifted the paper up to the light. After he read the second document, he scanned the third and handed the paperwork back to Pilot Mark. "Glad to see it's all in order."

"We're familiar with protocol with Ms. Hirano." He pointed to a burly man standing about twenty feet behind them. "Carver will handle your luggage. As soon as we've finished final checks, Nick, your flight steward, will bring you on board."

"Appreciated. Thank you."

"Our pleasure, Mr. Black." Pilot Mark smiled at Amery. "Mrs. Black."

Before she could ask Ronin a question, he strode toward Carver and handed him the luggage claim ticket. Then he returned to her. "You okay?"

"This is all really weird. What paperwork did he give you?"

"Authorization papers. In Japan, Okada has an aviation crew on standby. While this plane is here, it doesn't have a regular crew, so we hire a local aviation company. Due to kidnapping threats, my grandfather has a set of protocols in place for any crew who flies an Okada heir. Even on an Okada jet. It's up to me to verify this crew is the crew that Okada hired."

"So they passed?"

"Yes."

"Ever had a crew *not* pass?"

"Once. No nefarious plans, just a clerical error that resulted in them losing Okada's business." Ronin took her hand and led her to the big window overlooking the tarmac. "There it is. A Gulfstream Five."

She studied the airplane. It didn't have the Okada Foods corporate logo on it anywhere. "It's a lot bigger than I expected."

He chuckled in her ear. "A phrase a man loves to hear."

When she didn't tease him or call him a pervert, he turned her around to face him. "Are you nervous?"

"About flying? No. It's just surreal to think that we'll be living in Japan for ten weeks."

"For me too."

Amery gave him a skeptical look. "Why? You go to Japan at least twice a year for weeks at a time." She left the rest of it unsaid. *You were raised in Japan; you know the language and the customs—you're not a foreigner like I am.*

"But I always go by myself. While I'm there, I train. I sleep. I do that for two or three weeks. Then I spend a few days with my family in the craziness that is Tokyo and I return to Denver more worn down than when I left."

She brushed his hair off his face. "That makes me sad."

"But this time will be different. I'll get to spend three weeks with you. Just us, seeing the sights." Ronin squeezed her hand. "And after my daily training sessions, I get to return to you every night."

"But what if—"

Ronin slanted his mouth over hers and kissed her very softly. "You and me, Amery. Nothing else matters."

As much as she wanted to believe him, his claim wasn't entirely true. Master Black would spend six weeks training with his sensei, Daichi. He'd already warned her that the regimen was grueling. Fourteen-hour days, every day, for three weeks. Then they'd take a week and sightsee between session one and session two, but then they'd return to the remote village where Ronin would train for three more weeks—the last week of which he'd spend sequestered. That's when Ronin's mother would squire Amery off to visit the Okada Foods factories that were mass-producing her packaging designs.

"Mr. Black?" a voice inquired behind them.

They turned to face a good-looking Hispanic man she guessed was around her age. "Yes?"

"I'm Nick. Your steward. The cabin is ready if you are?"

"Of course. Thank you."

Ronin kept his hand on the small of her back as they crossed the tarmac. The wind blew like crazy, whipping her hair around her face.

Nick scaled the stairs and waited at the top. "It feels strange welcoming you aboard the plane you own, but welcome."

Amery waited for Ronin to correct Nick—that Okada owned the plane, not him, but Ronin didn't respond.

"May I take your coats?"

Ronin helped Amery with her long wool coat before shrugging out of his leather jacket. "I'll give my wife a tour. We can take off as soon as they're ready. I'll let you know if we need anything."

"Of course." Nick stepped back into a small galley kitchen.

Amery turned and felt her mouth hanging open as she stared at their surroundings. This was the inside of an *airplane?* The interior ceiling was white tufted leather. Silver-and-black zigzag-patterned wallpaper covered the walls. The plush chairs—four of them—were upholstered in a dark charcoal with red leather armrests. The carpeting was gray with flecks of red. Behind the chairs was a mini conference table. Directly behind that area were two more oversized recliners, which could swivel toward each other or face the red leather couch along the opposite side.

"Holy shit, Ronin. I don't know what I was expecting—okay, I had zero expectations because I've never been on a private plane before, but it certainly wasn't this."

"It gets better." He led her past the conference and lounging areas. He slid open a door, revealing a bathroom with a walk-in tiled shower.

"That is nothing like the tiny, cramped bathrooms on commercial airliners," she said with awe.

"This is Okada's transcontinental aircraft, so it was retrofitted for comfort on long flights." Ronin opened another door and brought her inside a bedroom.

A bedroom. On a plane.

Of course the decor screamed rich and classy. Plush black-and-cream-striped bedding with half a dozen fluffy pillows covered in solid black set against cream-colored sheets. The king-sized bed took up most of the space, but on each side of the headboard were built-in dressers in white and black lacquer. Heavy black curtains covered the walls. "The only thing missing is a big-screen TV."

"Got that too." Ronin punched a button on the wall, and a TV screen that she guessed to be about forty-eight inches lowered from the ceiling. She hadn't noticed it because the black panel had blended in with the black ceiling.

Amery gawked at the luxurious space and wondered if there'd ever come a time when she took things like this for granted.

Ronin kicked the door shut and pulled her into him so they tumbled onto the bed. Then he pinned her arms above her head and got right in her face. "Don't."

"Don't what?"

"Don't look at me like you don't know me."

Her eyes searched his. "But I don't know you in this context, Ronin. I'm sorry if that makes you uncomfortable."

"Do you want to get off this plane and fly commercial? Because I will."

"Are you kidding me? No. Way." She nuzzled his jaw. "I just don't want you to get short with me when I'm overwhelmed by who you are outside of our life in Denver."

He rested his forehead to hers. "You are my life, regardless of where we are. I know I'm selfish for demanding you come with me. I can't stand the thought of being away from you for two and a half months. But if that means you resent me—"

Amery lifted her head to gaze at him and then pressed her lips to his. The feel of his weight on her, the taste of him, his scent, those were familiar. Those things grounded her as much as they grounded him. That's why she was going. He needed her there with him. "No resentment. But you'll have to figure out a way to deal with my freak-out moments, because this is the first of many."

Ronin's lips curved into a wicked smile. "I've come up with a few ideas on how best to distract you, baby."

"Do those ideas involve rope?"

He rubbed his nose to hers. "Always."

The plane started to move. "Whoa."

"It appears they were as ready to take off as they claimed." Ronin kissed her quickly and pushed onto his knees.

"Do we have to go back to the main part of the cabin and buckle up?"

"Nope." He stretched out beside her, placing his feet on the pillows. "Do this."

"What?"

"Lie beside me like this."

She spun around. "Now what?"

He picked up her hand and kissed her knuckles. "Now have some patience."

It was weird, lying on the comfortable mattress, facing the wrong way, staring at the back of the TV screen as the plane rolled along.

After a couple of turns the plane stopped.

"Ronin—"

"Hang on. Wait for it."

The bumps were jarring when the plane started to accelerate. When it lifted off the runway, so fast, at such a sharp angle, she felt like she was standing up. And for just a moment . . . she felt weightless, as if she'd entered a zero-gravity chamber. Despite the stomach-churning sensation, she turned her head and looked at him with a smile.

He wore a boyish grin. "Pretty cool, huh?"

"How'd you figure it out?"

"I crawled in bed before the plane took off one night and damn near ended up ass over teakettle. It's a steeper climb for smaller jets to reach altitude. Now, whenever I'm on this aircraft, I act like a kid who thinks he's on a rocket ship during takeoff."

She laughed. "Crazy man-boy. I thought you dragged me to the bedroom because you wanted me to join the mile-high club."

Ronin rolled her on top of him and kissed her, mouth avid, keeping his hands clamped on her butt. Between his all-consuming kisses, he spoke against her lips. "Maybe we should take the edge off." He treated her lips to a few more teasing kisses. "You seem tense."

"You're up for a quickie?" She moaned when he nipped the side of her neck and then soothed the sting with hot, slow kisses.

"Who said anything about a quickie? It's a long flight."